THE MAN IN THE RED CAP

"I know you," Michael stuttered. "You attacked me the other night."

"Is that so?" said the man in the red cap. "And tell me then, from which eye do you see me?"

Michael realized that when he turned to the right and focused that eye, the man before him disappeared. But when he turned his head to the left and peered from his left eye, he saw him plainly standing before him.

"The left eye," Michael blurted out.

The man in the red cap gave a shrill whistle between his teeth.

Out of a dense gray mist came three ghostly warriors. They gave a cry of delight as they swooped like birds of prey over Michael, slamming him against the pavement. The man in the red cap was on him.

Michael remembered the iron spike in his overcoat pocket. He pulled it from his pocket and rammed the point of it into the man's calf.

The man let go of him, reared back his head, and howled. The ghostly warriors gave a cry of rage and suddenly vanished. The man in the red cap staggered away, and Michael saw the glint of his animal eyes before they winked out of sight.

Also by Midori Snyder

New Moon
Sadar's Keep
Beldan's Fire

The Flight of
Michael McBride

Midori Snyder

A TOM DOHERTY ASSOCIATES BOOK
NEW YORK

This is a work of fiction. All the characters and events portrayed in this novel are either fictitious or are used fictitiously.

THE FLIGHT OF MICHAEL McBRIDE

Copyright © 1994 by Midori Snyder

Cover art by Enric

A Tor Book
Published by Tom Doherty Associates, Inc.
175 Fifth Avenue
New York, N.Y. 10010

Tor® is a registered trademark of Tom Doherty Associates, Inc.

ISBN: 0-812-52271-0

Library of Congress Card Catalog Number: 94-30177

First edition: December 1994
First mass market edition: September 1995

Printed in the United States of America

0 9 8 7 6 5 4 3 2 1

With special thanks for my friends Ray Yeates, who gave out until I gave up and went, and for Cathy Kaiser, who was waiting for me when I got there.

One

Hearing footsteps just outside the door, Michael glanced up from the chessboard. He was a young man, just twenty years old, and a worried flush stained his nearly smooth cheeks as he waited for the door to open and admit the doctor.

"Concentrate on your game," his father ordered.

Reluctantly, Michael returned his attention to his father, suppressing his anger. James McBride was an imposing figure, not one to suffer disagreements lightly. In his early fifties, the man had grown stout, his waist expanding to the width of his squared shoulders. His face was roughly hewn, with a prominent forehead over a large nose. From beneath shaggy eyebrows, the dark eyes held the pattern of the chessboard with an intense stare. Graying side whiskers joined an impressive mustache that remained coal black through the aid of waxing. Thick fingers closed around the miter of a queen's bishop and he moved his piece with authority, capturing Michael's knight.

The door opened with a quiet click and Dr. Callahan entered, neatly tucking a pair of gold-rimmed spectacles into his vest pocket. He looked tired, his blue eyes watering with fatigue.

"She's asking after you, Michael," Dr. Callahan said.

Michael stood up quickly, his knee knocking the corner of the gaming table. The pieces on the chessboard wobbled. A rook toppled, followed by two pawns. A knight crashed into the white queen and she rolled to the edge of the gaming table and fell on the Persian carpet.

"Damn you, boy," James McBride swore. "You've ruined the game." He bent down to retrieve the queen, her serene face disappearing in the grip of his huge palm.

Michael beggared one guilty glance for the fallen pieces and then went to the parlor door. The doctor stopped him, a hand on his arm.

"Not too long now. She's weak enough as it is. And there's your father to think of. He'll be wanting his last words as well."

Michael nodded stiffly and shouldered out of the room. His father had no words to spare his mother, he thought angrily. He never had. In all the years Michael had watched them, James McBride had rarely spoken to his wife. They'd lived in the same house, taken their meals together, and at least once before had shared the same bed. But Michael had never heard them converse together. Even their eyes seemed to deny the other's presence, staring blankly or turning dispassionately away. As a child, Michael had decided it was his fault; that his presence angered them or, worse, caused them shame. The feeling of shame deepened as he grew older. As an adolescent he had asked his father the reason for his animosity, but the man refused any knowledge of it. His mother became distant when asked, and it seemed as if her mouth snagged on unspoken words. Michael didn't press further for an answer but determined by their silence that he was the wedge between them.

And yet his parents were not entirely without small measures of warmth and kindness. In James McBride the game of chess evoked an expression of intimacy. In the thick of the battle, his face glowed, his skin grew ruddy, and his eyes sparkled. He spoke to Michael then, his voice direct even though his eyes were trained on the complicated patterns of the chessboard. He had taught Michael to play when the boy was barely old enough to hold and remember the function of each piece. Michael had endured long afternoons of chess in the hope that it would soften the man's temperament. After fifteen years of play, Michael had acquired considerable skill in the game but was no closer to knowing his father.

Michael walked up the carpeted stairs, glancing as he always did at the hanging portrait of his mother, Eileen McBride. His heart beat anxiously and he felt a heavy weight press against his ribs. The painting showed her sitting on a parlor chair, her back erect, a gown of pale green silk elegantly draping the rounded shoulders. Her ash-blond hair was coiled high on her head, accentuating the graceful arch of her neck. Her hands rested on her lap, and in her long tapered fingers she held an embroidered fan. Intelligent green eyes stared back at the viewer; the lift of one golden eyebrow and the subtle crook of the rose-colored mouth made her seem amused by what she saw. The painter had accurately caught the translucent quality of her skin that absorbed light with the soft sheen of a pearl.

But that was in 1858, when she was a young woman newly arrived in New York. A scant twenty years later, she was dying. They all knew it, though until recently the doctor had refused to admit it. He had come often in the last three months since she'd taken to her bed at the New Year. He had given her tonics, tinctures, and mercury pills, steamed her with pungent vapors and swaddled her chest with mustard plasters. But despite his best medical efforts she had failed to thrive. She refused to eat, and what they did manage to coax down she vomited later. She drank only herbal tea, sweetened with a spoonful of wildflower honey.

Michael hesitated at the top of the stairs, afraid to see her. In the cold hollow that was his childhood, she had provided him with one escape. Eileen McBride never spoke of herself, nor her past, and had never once told Michael that she loved him. But she had filled his young ears with stories from home. In the absence of a loving touch, her voice had seduced him with its lilting music. With an immigrant's nostalgia she spoke longingly of Ireland, of its soft green valleys, the warm moist breezes, and the long summer days when couples danced beneath a pale moon at the crossroads. A blue-green sea, brighter than sapphire, lapped at a rocky shore, and narrow strands of white sand speared the water. The linnets and the thrush sang in the hedges, and horned stags belled in the few remaining forests.

As she spoke, weaving a glittering net of images, the crowded and dirty streets of New York faded. The city's harsh noises were replaced by the clash of swords in the great battles of Maeve and Cuchulain. The cobblestones became the steps of Finn Mac Coul's giant causeway; the bridal paths of Central Park where they went riding became the forests of the Sídhe, and he and his mother a part of the fairy rade. When Eileen McBride leaned her mouth toward Michael's ear and told him stories of the fairy world, all else around him ceased to exist in the lulling beauty of her voice.

Michael ran his fingers through his black wavy hair. He loved her desperately and he feared her death, feared his loneliness that only her voice kept at bay.

Mary, his mother's personal maid, stepped through the bedroom door carrying a tea tray. She was an older woman, heavyset, with a rounded face and a rosy complexion on her finely wrinkled cheeks. On the tray rested Eileen's favorite teacup made of a cream-colored porcelain with a pattern of ivy leaves vining around the rim and the plate. The cup was full, the amber tea unsipped, the cutwork napkin lying folded beside it. Mary caught sight of him and clucked her tongue.

"I know, I know," she said softly, shaking her head at Michael's distraught face. "Go in then. She'll not last the night, I'm thinking, and then her suffering will be over, thanks be to God." She heaved a sigh, the starched linen of her blouse crinkling over her large bosom. "I'll bring the master a tray with some food to the parlor. Come yourself after and take a bite to eat," she finished. Her petticoats shushed beneath her long skirt as she passed him, leaving him alone on the landing.

Michael gathered his courage and opened the door to his mother's sickroom.

Though the early spring weather had been mild, a fire had been lit in the grate. The room was hot and stuffy, and sweat prickled Michael's forehead. It was a small, charming room, with high ceilings and ornate moldings. The wallpaper was a dove gray, with twisting vines covered with tiny leaves. The patterned leaves trailed over two huge bay windows that looked down into the street and Gramercy Park below. It had been his mother's study, and along the fireplace two bookcases held the leatherbound books that had been her pleasure to read. A desk with turned legs and inlaid drawers sat in front of the windows, the chair neatly tucked in, hiding its needlepointed seatcover. Unanswered letters lay stacked, weighted down by a silver letter opener. Near the inkwells sat a vase with bright yellow daffodils, their lifted throats like trumpets. At her request, the servants had moved a bed into the room when she first became ill. She said the view was more pleasing, though from her bed, even propped up with bolsters, she could only see the tops of the trees in the park. The rest was sky. The drapes had been pulled at dusk, and their deep folds closed out the chill of the night.

Near the bed was a little table covered with a linen cloth edged in Limerick lace. On the table sat a small lamp, the wick trimmed low to give off a gentle light. There were gas fixtures on the wall, but his mother had never liked them, saying she didn't trust the hissing blue-green flame. Michael's feet tread noiselessly over the Liberty carpet as he approached the bed. His heart was rattling, and his mouth tasted sour.

He sat in the chair beside her bed and gazed at her sleeping figure. From a startling beauty, she had wasted into a pale ghost. The ash-colored hair spread across her pillow like old flax. She was thin, her cheeks gaunt and her eyes sunk deep into the circular ridges of her sockets. Her hands lay on the lace coverlet, the nails gray. Blue veins netted the backs of her white hands. Her translucent, cream-colored skin had become as dull as melted wax.

"Mother," he said softly. "It's me, Michael."

Her lashes fluttered as she slowly raised the lids, revealing the green eyes, milky as unpolished agates. "Ah, Michael," she whispered. "It's good you've come. I've something to give you."

Tears welled in Michael's eyes. His throat tightened at the feeble sound of her voice. She was fumbling, her hand weakly reaching for something on the bedside table.

Michael quickly wiped away a tear and then retrieved the object. It was a small ivory and glass jar. It had a silver lid etched with Celtic spirals. She made a motion with her hands that indicated she wanted him to open it. He did, catching the scent of aromatic oil. He handed her the opened jar.

"Bend down now to me," she said, dipping her thumb into the oil.

He closed his eyes and bent his head. He was surprised, for he assumed the sweet-smelling oil to be chrism. A final Christian blessing from his dying mother. And yet in all the years he could remember, Eileen McBride had never set foot inside a church. She had not refused his own participation in the Catholic Church, but she didn't go to mass, had not been there at his baptism, nor his first holy communion and confirmation. It was Mary, with her long strand of black rosary beads clicking between her fingers, who had seen to his instruction over the years. The priest had come often in the last three months hoping, Michael thought, that the nearer death approached, the more willing Eileen McBride might be to unburden her soul. But Michael had not thought the priest successful.

He could hear her whispering in Irish, the sound of it like the dry rustle of autumn leaves. But her thumb did not trace the sign of the cross on his forehead. Instead she planted it on the lid of his left eye and drew a little smear of oil over the rounded hump of the lid. She can't see, he thought, anguished. He said nothing, not wanting to shame her pride, but submitted quietly to her awkward ministrations. His eyelid tingled; the oil as it penetrated the skin grew warm and then smarted like a burn.

Michael straightened his head and wiped his eye carefully with his handkerchief. When he opened his eye, his vision was unfocused and his eye felt scratchy. A tear welled up, and his mother's room seemed to swim. He looked at his mother, and from his right eye he saw her clearly, a smile on her wan lips.

She spoke, her voice barely a whisper. "Once, long ago when the Tuatha Da Danann rode their fairy horses over the green hills, a mortal man fell in love with Etian, the second and much-neglected wife of Midhir, King of the Fairy Hill of Bri Leith. This man came one night into the King's court and challenged the King to a game of chess. Foolish was Etian, for she looked upon the mortal man and saw his desire. Flattered, she said nothing to the King, but she knew in her heart that the man would win and that she would be the prize he would claim."

Eileen paused in her story, and Michael saw on her

cheeks a flush of color, her lips parted in expectation. Her eyes gazed out at an unseen place, her gaunt face animated by a spark of light from within. And then just as quickly the spark was extinguished, and he heard the long-drawn sigh of her final breath. Her body seemed to shrink beneath the coverlet, as if the solid core of her flesh had escaped with her last exhalation.

Michael stared at her, terrified by the empty face. And in the sudden quiet of the room, Eileen McBride's voice silenced by death, all the magic of his childhood ended.

"No!" he cried, clutching her limp hand as the huge silence surrounded him. The tears started freely, and the salty drops stung his left eye. A knock startled him with its noise, and as he turned to the door, James McBride entered, followed by the doctor.

Michael lowered his mother's hand to the coverlet, gently placing it alongside the remains of her frail body.

"She's gone," he said thickly.

"Gone, is it?" his father mumbled.

"Just now."

"Get Mary then. She and Bridget will prepare the body."

Michael stared bitterly at his father. The man's face was a hard mask, his heavy-lidded eyes unreadable. He stood firmly in the center of the room, his feet apart, his hands clasped behind his back. He seemed utterly lacking in grief; there was no hint of a hidden sorrow, no emotion save a cold pragmatism. Even the doctor, who held Eileen's wrist as if hoping to find again the beat of an errant pulse, sagged unhappily.

And though she had not been called, Mary was there suddenly, filling the room with her cries.

"My lamb, my lamb," she called to the woman on the bed.

Then she fell to her knees beside the bed, and clasped her hands together. Weeping quietly, the tears streaming over her grieving face, she leaned her forehead against the foot of the bed and began to pray.

James McBride went to the window and, pulling back the heavy drapes, he stared down into the street below. He did not look at his wife or son. He did not venture near the bed. Grief and rage locked together like iron bands around Michael's chest. He couldn't breathe or swallow, his hands clenched in white-knuckled fists. He wanted to strike his father, lash out at the man who even now in their common loss denied his son as he had denied his deceased wife. And then, abruptly, James McBride turned away from the window. He reached into the pocket of his jacket and silently withdrew a rusted iron spike. He laid it down on the desk near the silver letter opener and, without another word, left the room.

Michael went quickly to the desk and scowled at the spike. It was a luck token that came from the rail yards where his father had worked and earned his fortune. But lying here on his mother's desk, it was an obscenity to Michael. His mother had hated the rail yards, hated the trains belching black smoke and the screech of their wheels on the iron rails. She would not go to Grand Central Depot, not even when his father was among the dignitaries celebrating the meeting of the Union-Pacific Railroad from New York to California. To her only travel by horse had dignity, and she flinched at the sight of the railway. Michael snatched the offending spike from her desk and placed it in his pocket. He would throw it into the East River that very night.

Michael clambered down the stairs, his legs as unsteady as a drunken man's. He felt a violent surge of energy as he rushed to escape the silence of his mother's death. His hands trembling with haste, he grabbed his overcoat, opened the front door, and stepped out onto the stoop.

The night air was cool, mist hovering around the lamplight. The streets smelled dank, and the carriages that rattled past sent up sprays of dirty water from the flooded gutters. Michael put on his overcoat, inhaling mouthfuls of the cold damp air. It tasted oily on his tongue. He shoved his hands into his pockets and found a half-full flask of whiskey. It had been there since the previous month, when he had gone with two college friends to the Belmont Stakes to watch the four-year-olds race. Impulsively, he had bet on a horse called the Faery Queen. It had lost, and in the aftermath he had drunk a fair amount of his flask. He hadn't a head for whiskey, and later that night his friends had dumped his nearly unconscious body on the stoop before they'd made their own staggering way home.

Which way? he thought, his head turning right and then left. To the left, he saw a man in a red cap and jacket hurry past the lamplight, dragging a bleating goat behind him. Michael paused, confused by the sight, and then promptly forgot the odd pair as they were swallowed in the darkness of an alley. Michael set out left to walk along the perimeter of Gramercy Park. As he walked his stride lengthened and his pace quickened, his coattails flapping in the wind. And before he knew it, he was running, his shoes thumping hard on the cobblestones. The urgent need to flee overwhelmed him. He wanted to flee his father's unyielding coldness, to flee the stale odor of his mother's illness that clung to his nostrils, and, last of all, to flee the mounting silence that swelled like a huge wave and threatened to drown him if he moved too slowly.

Michael ran until he thought his lungs would burst. And then he flopped down on the sidewalk beneath a spreading elm tree, regained his breath, and began to drink steadily from his flask. It wasn't long after, in the dulling haze of drunkenness, that a man loomed over him out of the drifting tree shadows.

"Look at the gombeen," a raspy voice sneered. "Piss drunk he is and she not even cold."

From the shadows a fist crashed against the side of Michael's face. Stars sparked in his eyes as pain lanced through the thick blanket of his drunkenness. His arms flailed wildly as he tried to strike back at his assailant. But he was ineffective, and the man kicked him savagely in the ribs with the sharp point of a boot. As Michael contracted in pain, he felt the man's hands rummage in his pockets. The searching hand touched the iron spike and, hissing a loud curse, abruptly withdrew, leaving Michael alone.

Michael dragged himself home, rang the bell, and Mary let him in the door. Her nightdress on and her hair hanging loose down her back, she scoured him with angry words; called him worthless, feckle, a drunkard, and him with his mother not even cold. The last words stopped him with a chilling memory. How did the man know about his mother?

But he had no time to think further, for Mary led him by the lapel of his dirty jacket into his room. She pushed him onto the bed and pulled off his shoes. Then she wrangled him out of his jacket and shoved him back against the pillows. He had just closed his eyes when she reappeared with a basin of water and a towel. Calmer now, her face growing softer with sympathy, she gave him a cold compress to lay against his cheek.

"Eileen McBride was a good woman, praise God. Quiet in her ways, but generous. And now you'll do the right thing by her and mind yourself," she said firmly.

With the cold compress numbing the throbbing pain of his cheek, Michael nodded a weary consent.

"Good lad," Mary said, patting him on the shoulder. "It's sleep you need." And she pulled the coverlet over Michael and left him.

Eileen McBride's wake lasted three days according to the old custom. Mary and the cook, Bridget, had washed and laid out the body. The undertaker had met with serious opposition from Mary when he tried to have the body removed and prepared for burial. Mary remained firm, her lower lip jutting out aggressively as she told the undertaker that Eileen McBride had not wanted those strange tamperings with her body that were the fancy of other Americans. She was to be washed and dressed by her own women and otherwise left in peace. The undertaker tried to appeal to James McBride, but there he met with even less success. In the end, frowning like a man unjustly maligned, the undertaker consented to measure the body for a casket, which he then had sent over by carriage.

Mary and Bridget dressed Eileen in a white linen shift and crammed cloth slippers over her stiffened feet. They combed out her hair to lay across her stilled breast and folded her hands around a bouquet of white lilies. The oak casket was lined with white silk, and to Michael it seemed as if his mother's diminished figure floated in a ruffled cloud.

They placed the casket in the parlor, lining the walls with chairs for the mourners. The clocks had been stopped, and all the mirrors draped with black crepe. Mary and Bridget kept themselves busy in the kitchens preparing food, cutting bread for sandwiches, and baking cakes. The kettle steamed constantly as tea was brewed and poured into cream-colored teapots. Mary dusted the insides of the blue-and-white Minton teacups, laying them upside down on their saucers in readiness. Cut crystal glasses for port and whiskey were laid in neat rows beside the teacups. The curtains were closed to keep out the light, but the windows were opened to keep the room as cool and fresh as possible. Black crepe hung from the windows, and Mary sewed black armbands on James's and Michael's suit jackets.

The first two nights of the wake were gloomy affairs. Only a few mourners arrived, and they were people more inclined to be curious than grieving. His father received them, saw they were fed a bite to eat and had something to drink. They stayed for a short time, murmured the appropriate words of consolation, and left.

Michael spent his time sitting at the kitchen table, with his head between his hands, staring at the grain of the wood. His head still hurt and his eyes were bloodshot. A bruise darkened one cheek and was tender to the touch. Around him, he heard the bustle of the women as they worked and Mary's occasional sniffing as the tears came to her. There was always a hot cup of tea placed in front of him, and every now and then a plate of food would appear and he would force himself to eat.

On the third night of Eileen McBride's wake the mourners turned out in surprising numbers. Michael was in the kitchen, sullenly gazing into a teacup, when Mary came rushing in.

"They've come," she announced. "Put the kettle on, and I'll get the cakes and sandwiches." She reached into the drawers for butter knives, teaspoons, and salt shakers, loading them on a huge tray alongside the plates of sandwiches and sliced cake. "And you," she said, turning smartly to Michael's languishing figure, "get out there now and help your father to greet them."

Reluctantly Michael stood up, not wanting to leave the security of the kitchen. But Mary waited until he was ready, her blue eyes piercing him with a disapproving stare. He pushed the door open for her and then followed her into the parlor.

She was right: A crowd had come on the last night to pay a final respect to the corpse of Eileen McBride. Michael was astonished to see the parlor filled with people. There were still more people pressed together in the foyer, waiting to enter the parlor. Mary's arms were full of scarves, hats, and gloves as she went to store them away in the study. They were mostly men who had come, and the parlor was darkened by the brown and black hues of their wool serge suits. Smoke rose in a fine blue haze as cigars were passed around and then lit. They held glasses of whiskey and gathered in tight knots, their voices low with murmured conversation. A few had brought their wives, and the women roamed the edges of the room, fingering the lace curtains and running their fingers appreciatively over the smooth linen tablecloths. Mary and Bridget passed out cups of tea to them, and Michael saw one woman turn over the saucer to peek at the maker's stamp.

Michael leaned against the wall, suddenly shy of so many strangers.

An older man with white hair and a very flushed face approached him. He shook Michael's hand. "Very sorry about your loss," he said with a soft lilt.

"Thank you," Michael replied uncomfortably.

"John O'Neill," the man introduced himself, "and this is my brother, Frank." He motioned to a younger man who was just lifting a small glass of neat whiskey to his lips. Frank O'Neill nodded his head in greeting, his breath catching on the pungent taste of whiskey.

"I'm sorry for your trouble," he said.

"Thank you," Michael murmured.

"She makes a lovely corpse," Frank added before taking another hurried sip of whiskey.

"Are you working, then?" asked John.

"College."

"Ah, college, is it? And what are you studying?"

"Engineering."

"Oh, that's grand," Frank said, with an impressed pout. "Very like the father, I'd say. Good with industry."

Michael stiffened at the mention of his father.

John hailed another man to join them, and Michael found himself being introduced to Sean O'Neill, John's eldest son.

"Sorry for your trouble," he said, not too convincingly.

Sean O'Neill was close in age to Michael, though he was shorter and stockier. His features were of a rougher cut, his skin blotchy. Dark hair had been plastered across his forehead with cream. His eyes roamed across the room with a barely concealed envy. When he raised his glass to drink, Michael saw the black rim of oily grime under his squared-off nails.

"Do you work in the railway yards?" Michael guessed. He saw instantly that it was a mistake. Sean stared back, his eyes narrowed with malice.

"For now," he clipped. "I plan to go west soon."

"Ah, Sean here is a great man for the gold," explained John with an apologetic smile.

"There's more than gold out west. There's a future, which is more than I'll say for this place."

"But the Indians, Sean. Have you no fear of them? They say those savages will skin you alive if they catch you."

"Bad cess to them," Sean replied scornfully. "They'll be old history in another year. Don't you read the paper? The army'll finish them off."

Michael was growing impatient with their chatter. He excused himself brusquely and saw the offended expressions of the older men. Sean O'Neill glared at him with contempt.

Michael shouldered through clots of men, accepting condolences and refusing offerings of whiskey and cigars. The conversations around him swung easily from death to politics, and Michael was shocked to discover that, along with yard workers and laborers, there were influential politicians who had made a special point of coming to Eileen McBride's wake. He saw his father surrounded by a group of well-dressed businessmen and the Swallow-tail Democrats of Tammany Hall. They were speaking in earnest voices, cigars plied between their fingers. Younger men hung on their words, waiting to be acknowledged. His father was smiling, conversing easily with them. His hand clapped amiably across the back of one man and stretched out to take a welcoming handshake from another. It was hard for Michael to reconcile the stern visage of his father with the man before him who moved easily through the gathering, his features relaxed, his manner open and gracious to all classes of men.

Not a man in grief, Michael thought angrily.

Mary passed him bearing another tray of sandwiches. He grabbed her by the sleeve.

"What is all this anyway?" he asked bitterly.

She looked at him impatiently, one eyebrow arched with annoyance. There were small drops of sweat in the mustache of fine gray hairs on her upper lip. "What are you on about?" she snapped.

"This," Michael said, waving his hand at the crowded room. "These people didn't know her. What are they doing here?"

"Keep your voice down," Mary hushed him impatiently.

The woman who had peeked at the china mark of her tea saucer came to Mary, her hands outstretched.

"Ah Mary, let me help you now. I don't like sitting here idle."

"Great, Marion. Thanks. I could use the help. And how is your child? Whooping cough, was it?

"Yes, whooping cough. But she's right enough now."

"Just so, just so," Mary agreed, handing the heavy tray to Marion.

"She looks lovely," Marion said wistfully.

"Aye, that she does. Even dead there's a softness about her."

"She was a good woman," Marion said to Michael. "I remember well the time when my man Dennis and me first come from Ireland. I was scared here, me just after coming from the country and sick with the long crossing. Mr. McBride gave Dennis his work at the yards. And it was the missus that gave me comfort. She sent me new sheets and linens, and when my girl was born a christening gown of good lace so I'd not be shamed in church. She invited me to tea, and we sat in this very parlor and talked. I can tell you it did much to ease my longing for home. I know how you miss her, but she's with God, I'm sure of that."

Marion left, taking the loaded tea tray to the sideboard and settling the new sandwiches on the half-empty plates.

"Do you see now?" Mary asked Michael, her hands resting on her hips.

"No," Michael replied.

Mary pulled Michael by the arm into the privacy of the hallway. "Then you're a fool, my lad. The wake is for her, lying dead there; and it's for the living that go on after her, you and your father. People come, they eat and drink, and have a bit of socializing. It's to distract those in grief and help them through this time. But there's only so much you can say about death before the words turn to other things: a sick child, politics, or who's announced the banns. But through it all, we remember our dead and in this last celebration they're still with us. Tonight the priest will come and that roomful of men will get down on their knees—something God knows they should do more often—and they'll pray the rosary for your mother's soul. It's not our way to die alone, and praise God there'll be a wake for myself when the time comes. And no stinting either of the whiskey or the tea."

"I need some air," Michael said.

"Go on then, but mind you come back before the priest gets here," she admonished.

His ears red and burning with embarrassment, Michael shrugged into his overcoat and left the house. Once on the street he looked back up at the tall, narrow face of the house. From the opened parlor windows he could hear the drifting conversations and then a shushing sound as the room was quieted. Over the quiet rose a quavering soprano voice, singing a slow, sad air. It was a song so soft and full of sorrow that its hollow sound reso-

nated in his chest. He moved away from the voice, his
shoulders hunched.

On the street, Michael shivered with his loneliness. He
walked slowly toward the locked gate of the park, his
eyes fixed on the moving tips of his shoes. As he neared
the entrance to the park, he heard the sudden shrill sound
of someone whistling a reel, the notes spilling gaily over
the street. As the tune grew louder and more insistent, he
raised his head, curious to see the whistler. A tall, lanky
man, a red cap pulled low over his eyes and his hands
shoved in his trouser pockets, was nearly on him. He had
no time to change direction before the man collided with
Michael, his angled elbow driving into Michael's side.

"Excuse me," Michael said, thinking it was his own
distraction that had caused him to stumble into the man.

"Eh, what's that, you gombeen?" snarled the man,
stopping in his tracks. He pushed back the brim of his
cap, and in the lamplight Michael saw him clearly. He
had a narrow face with a sloping forehead and high-
ridged cheekbones curved like cathedral arches. His nose
was long and pointed downward over a small chin. His
lips were pulled back, exposing a set of white teeth in a
feral grin. But it was the eyes, filled with the hard gleam
of cold lamplight, that trapped Michael and rendered
him speechless.

The man slowly withdrew his hands from his pockets,
and Michael saw he held a silver dagger in one closed fist.

"I know you," Michael stuttered. "You attacked me
the other night."

"Is that so? And tell me then, from which eye do you
see me?"

Michael frowned, confused as he realized that when he
turned slightly to the right and focused his vision in that
eye only, the man before him disappeared. He saw the
street, and passersby giving him wary glances as he appeared to them to be talking to himself. But when he
turned his head to the left and peered from his left eye, he

saw plainly the man in the red cap standing before him.

"The left eye," Michael blurted out, frightened by the double vision.

The man slashed out toward the left side of Michael's face with the silver dagger. Reflexively Michael raised up his left arm and ducked his head. The blade sliced open the fabric of his overcoat and nicked his forearm. Pain seared his arm and he danced back, his arm still held defensively over his face as the silver dagger continued to slash at him. Michael cried out loudly for help, but people on the crowded street avoided him, circling widely around him.

The man in the red cap gave a shrill whistle between his white teeth.

A dense gray mist thickened in the night air, and out of the boiling clouds came three ghostly warriors. Their feet drifted above the ground and, as Michael stared up at them with mounting horror, they raised their long pikes topped with skulls. The warriors gave a raucous cry of delight as they rattled the skulls on the ends of their pikes. Then they swooped like birds of prey over Michael, filling the air with their harsh laughter. He was lifted from the ground by their driving winds and then slammed against the pavement.

The flask in his jacket pocket smashed, cutting his skin through the fabric. Blood and whiskey stained his trouser leg at the thigh. Dazed, Michael lifted himself unsteadily on his elbows and rolled to his back. The man in the red cap was on him, pushing him down again to the pavement. He place a booted foot on Michael's throat and leaned hard against it. Michael grabbed the man's ankle and tried to twist the foot away. The ghostly warriors hovered above the man's shoulder, their eyes cold white light in their misted forms.

"And now for that eye," snarled the man, his silver dagger poised over Michael's face.

Through his terror, Michael remembered the spike in

his overcoat pocket. In his drunken stupor, he had never made it to the East River that night. Now he reached frantically for it. He pulled it out from the depths of his pocket and rammed the blunted point of it into the man's calf.

The man in the red cap reared back his head and howled. His foot released its hold on Michael's neck. Michael clung to the iron spike as the man jerked his leg free of its shaft. Blood dripped from the point and the drops steamed where they fell on Michael's chest. The ghostly warriors gave a cry of rage, and as the hovering mist was shredded by a fresh wind, they suddenly vanished. The man in the red cap staggered away from Michael, toward the shadows of the park, clutching his leg and moaning with agony. He crouched near a sheltering of trees, and Michael saw the reflected glint of his animal eyes before they winked out of sight.

Trembling, Michael raised himself from the pavement. He swayed on his feet, aware of the stench of whiskey and the throbbing pain of his lacerated thigh. He put the spike back into the pocket of his overcoat. Then he withdrew the shards of broken glass from his jacket and tossed them into the gutter. A well-dressed couple passed him, and the man shot him a disgusted look from beneath his silk top hat. Michael inhaled a long ragged breath and then limped back toward his house.

Pain flared in his leg as he took the steps. He waited on the landing for the worst of it to stop before he went into the house. He summoned his strength and pushed open the door. Inside the house he was greeted by quiet. Then he heard the low, muttered chant of the rosary. The priest had come while he was gone. He listened awhile from the foyer wondering how much of the recitation he had missed.

He swore softly as he removed his overcoat and examined his trouser leg. His black wool jacket hid the worst of the tear, and the dark fabric of his trousers camouflaged the damp blood. But there was nothing he could do about the odor of spilled whiskey.

He creeped softly to the parlor, hoping that no one would see him enter. The priest was at the center of the casket, his back to the doorway. Behind him, fanned out across the parlor, the mourners were kneeling, their heads bowed over their folded hands. As Michael knelt, Mary looked up at him from her station at the foot of the casket, her cheeks flaming with anger. A slight dip in the rhythm of the chanting told him that his entrance had not gone unnoticed. Neither had the smell of whiskey. Eyes glanced sidelong and heads tilted to catch a glimpse of him. Only James McBride remained impassive, his broad back hunched, his voice steady as he recited beside the priest.

Michael squeezed his eyes shut and ignored the raised eyebrows and accusing stares. He was shaking and sick inside, confused by the terror he had experienced on the street and wrenched by the murmured prayers that signaled his mother's eternal departure. He concentrated on the recitation, allowing the repetitious prayers to calm his threading pulse. The words were soothing on his tongue, like water flowing over stones. By the time he was finished reciting two decades of the rosary, he felt drowsy, exhaustion replacing the ebbing adrenaline in his body. He told himself that it hadn't happened. His misery had unmanned him for a moment. It was a child's fright, a thing from one of his mother's tales that he had conjured in his grief. The man in the red cap was no more than a figure for his rage at his father.

The priest intoned the final Hail Mary of the rosary. Michael lowered his hands, convinced that he had stepped briefly into madness. But it was past. He looked around the room, grateful for the first time for the people who had come to the wake. Knowing glances from some of the older men seemed to forgive the stench of whiskey. Joints cracked, followed by weary sighs, as the mourners rose from their knees and filed past the casket for a final salute before it was closed. Michael waited at the end of the line, just in front of his father.

His head was bowed over clasped hands, and he stared vaguely at the pin-striped trouser legs of the man in front of him. The peppery smell of cigar smoke wafted back from the man and helped to lessen the alcoholic odor of whiskey. As he came alongside the casket, Michael raised his head and stared down at his mother.

Without intending it, his head tilted to the left. The breath strangled in his throat and his eyes widened in renewed terror. From his right eye he saw his mother's waxy face, pale lids closed over her eyes and her lips set in a stern but straight line. From his left eye he saw a block of wood, a hastily carved face emerging from the rough bark. The eyes were plain stones set in knotholes. Her long combed hair was no more than a withered vine of mistletoe, and the white hands that clutched the lilies a bunch of gathered twigs. It was not his mother the women had dressed for burial, but a block of wood.

Michael shook, fearing the return of madness. In a panic he looked to his father. But James McBride's dark eyes were fixed on the corpse of his wife. His skin was ashen, his clenched lips bloodless. A nervous twitch rippled across the cheek, forcing one eye closed. His hands held the side of the casket, the huge red knuckles bled white with the powerful grip.

He sees it too, thought Michael wildly. He knows it's not her! Slowly and with effort, James McBride raised his eyes from the corpse and met his son's gaze. His dark eyes sunk deeper into the sockets, the sparkling black pupils dulled by anguish. His whole face sagged, growing haggard with defeat. He pried his fingers free from the rim of the casket and stiffly turned away. He walked with an old man's gait, his shoulders slumped and his head drooping as he stumbled out of the parlor.

Alone with the corpse, Michael placed a hand over his left eye and looked again at Eileen McBride. She's dead, he told himself. But then his hand fell away from his left eye and the wooden face returned to mock his grief.

TWO

Michael lay on his bed and stared up into the ceiling, his eyes following the outlines of old cracks. Two thin cracks arched away from a long oval stain on the gray-white paint. The form hovered over his bed like the poised body of a dove. When the sun shone through his window, the delicate wings strained against the dry plaster. Flight; that's he wanted, Michael thought, imagining the flutter of wings on the ceiling; flight from the emptiness left by his mother's death, flight from the silence of the house that was broken only by the clocks that had resumed their ticking and chiming, now that Eileen McBride had been laid to rest.

Three days after her burial, Michael still could not shake the black mud of the Greenwood cemetery from his shoes or the hem of his wool coat where it had spattered from the horses' hooves. There had been a soft rain the night before, and the carriage wheels had driven ruts into the damp earth. And though the horses' hooves had been muted on the muddy driveways through the cemetery, their harnesses had creaked loudly against the straining animals.

It had disturbed Michael to see the huge stone James McBride had erected over the remains of his wife. On the brow of a large granite block rested a carved angel, white alabaster wings lifting heavenward. The hands were folded across its chest in supplication, the tilted face wearing an expression of translucent sorrow. Michael had kept his gaze averted from the dates chiseled in the stone that imprisoned Eileen McBride forever between two set moments of time. The grave cut a deep cavern into the greening spring grass, smelling strongly of humus. As the black soil thudded on the lid of his mother's coffin, burying her and the white roses they had cast in to join her remains, Michael fixed his eyes to the angel's wings spread wide to catch the morning sunlight. Away, he cried to himself, his heart beating wildly; away from here, and he rocked back on his heels into the soft earth, fearing that he might be unable to resist the urge to flee, his top hat knocking from his head and his coattails flapping as he ran away from the grave.

He and his father had shared a carriage ride home, the silence heavy and solid as the granite headstone. James McBride sat staring at his gloved hands, his breathing rumbling slow and deep in his chest, his face empty of emotion. Only once, as they passed through the north entrance of Greenwood, did Michael see his father lift watery eyes to settle on the carved figures of Faith, Hope, Memory, and Love that adorned the stone gateway. But after they had turned into the street again, James McBride seemed to abandon comfort and returned his gaze to his hands. They rode home to Gramercy Park without a word uttered between them. Away from the budding trees and green expanse of the cemetery, Michael watched the city gradually close in around them, the buildings growing taller and closer together, the streets cluttered with carriages and people, and he mar-

veled that the world could continue without the low singing of Eileen McBride's voice to give it life.

In the silence of his room he could hear the lilt of her
song as an echo of his own misery.

"Oh, if I was a small bird, with wings I would fly, right
over the salt sea, where my darling does lie. And with my
fond wings I'd beat over her grave, and kiss the pale lips,
so cold in the clay. Brokenhearted, I'll wander, brokenhearted I'll remain—"

"Michael, the tea's on the table!" Mary's gruff voice
broke the spell of his mother's lingering song.

Michael lifted himself from the bed with a sigh and let
his feet dangle over the sides before setting them down to
take the weight of his body. A whisper of dust scattered
under the closed door as Mary's skirts brushed past in
the hallway. He heard her knock at his father's door; he
strained a moment longer to hear the thump and tread of
his father's footstep. The door creaked open and Mary
softened her voice to a murmured request. Would he
come for tea in the parlor? He would.

Michael stood, his fists clenching and then unclench-
ing. Nervously he ran his hand through his tangled curls,
not wanting to leave the privacy of his room. For the last
three days they had avoided each other. Michael didn't
want to see his father, to sit facing him with no words
between the two of them. But Mary knocked again, her
rapping insistent on the door. "It'll go cold, Michael,"
she warned.

"I'm coming," he answered. In spite of his apprehen-
sions, he couldn't refuse Mary or she'd give him the
rough edge of her tongue. She still hadn't forgiven him
for stinking of whiskey on the last night of the wake. And
he guessed she meant to force them together. Michael
sighed deeply. He shouldn't refuse his father at least the
attempt at companionship. There had to be more between them than chess. It frightened him to confront his
father's stony face, and yet he longed to talk to someone

who had known his mother. Who might have loved her as he had. He would try again with his father. Try to make the words come that might help them both.

Michael straightened his waistcoat over his trousers and went to the mirror to reknot his loosened tie. He stared at his reflection, perplexed by what he saw. Something had changed since his mother's death. A stranger's face peered back at him in the glass. His fair skin was pale beneath the dark hair in which sunlight brightened stray rust-colored streaks. One eye gleamed brown as earth, but the other one, the left eye, swallowed the sunlight and shone out from the socket a deep-green jade. Had he always looked like this? he wondered. Or was it only now, with her death? He searched his own features to find the resemblance to her: her high forehead, wide-set eyes, and her ears like fragile shells. "My mother is dead," he announced to the face in the glass and watched as the features winced with pain. The pain, at least, he recognized as his own.

As he descended the stairs he heard a knock at the front door. Mary answered it and admitted to the house a man with long legs and a somber expression. He gave Mary his hat, and the thinning yellow hair drifted over the top of his narrow skull. He gave her his coat but kept hold of his leather satchel as he muttered his name to Mary. Michael stayed on the landing as the man fidgeted alone in the hallway, straightening his coat, brushing the lint from his trousers and smoothing stray wisps of straw-colored hair. Mary returned to the foyer and led the man down the hallway and into the parlor.

Michael continued down the stairs and grabbed Mary by the elbow at the landing as she made her way to the kitchen.

"Who's that in the parlor?"

"Solicitor, I expect. Got that lean look about him. Now that she's buried, they'll be reading the will, I suppose." She looked him over closely, then added more gently, "Go on, then. Your tea'll get cold if you stand here talking to me. There's some sandwiches; see that you have one."

"Thank you, Mary," he replied, his eyes on the closed parlor door. He could hear the subtle murmuring of men's voices, followed by the rustle of paper. But it sounded more like the conclusion of a conversation, and as he pushed open the door he nearly collided with the long-legged solicitor.

"Excuse me," Michael said, surprised to see him ready to leave already.

"My mistake, I assure you. Good day to you, sir." And he passed through the door, his satchel closed tight.

"Mary," his father called out to the hallway. "Get Mr. Curran's coat and hat." Then he turned to Michael, his expression unreadable as always. "Come in, boy. The tea is nearly cold."

"Was that a lawyer?" Michael asked.

James McBride didn't answer but crossed the parlor to the small ornate chess table. He looked down at the pieces arranged in tidy rows, waiting for their battle to begin anew. He stood with his legs apart, his hands clasped behind his back, as he studied the potential in every piece.

"What did he want?" Michael tried again.

"Hmm. Not much."

"Did it have to do with Mother?" Michael asked, growing annoyed. Why did every conversation take so much effort? Why couldn't his father share these things with him instead of treating him as if he were a child?

James McBride lifted a white pawn in one hand and then a black pawn in the other. "Will you crows or swans?" he asked in a husky voice.

"Father—" Michael protested, his cheek flushed red.

"Well boy, which is it? White or black?" He opened his hands, the pawns appearing small where they nestled in the huge palms.

"He came to talk about Mother's will, didn't he?" Michael insisted. *Tell me, Father, share something of her death with me!*

"I'll take the swans, then," James answered, setting the two pawns down. "Come, boy, and watch while I make the first move."

Michael felt his heart go leaden. He walked slowly to the gaming table and stared down at it resentfully. He knew that his father would speak to him only when pieces were put into battle. If he wanted a conversation with the man, even an unsatisfactory one, he'd have to play. Eileen McBride's death had done nothing to change that.

James McBride pushed out his pawn to knight four. Automatically, Michael replied with his own pawn to knight four. Then white moved pawn to king's bishop four.

"So, Father. Are you going to tell me why the lawyer was here?" Michael asked as he moved, a white pawn capturing the black pawn.

"Soon, soon," James answered, his eyes glittering white and black as the pieces clicked and bumped over the board, felling a pawn, then a bishop.

Michael watched the board, his father's moves seeming erratic and without careful attention. A cold thought struck him, and he looked up sharply into his father's scowling face.

"Are you in trouble, Father? Is that why the lawyer was here?"

His father's eyes darkened for a second, the pupils contracting. But the shadowed lids closed halfway, concealing whatever answer lay there. "No," he said gruffly, "but you are, boy. Mind how you play that bishop, for he'll be mine in the next move!"

Michael glanced down again at the board, surprised to see an attack laid out, an attack he had played into without seeing. His father had tricked him. He swore softly under his breath for being so easily fooled. Then he rallied his pieces and made a momentary counterattack. But he was too late. In two moves, his bishops were gone. Michael made one more attempt and almost succeeded.

"There!" shouted Michael stridently, "I have you," as his rook challenged the white king.

"Steady, steady," cried James. "You've nothing at all." And he played a king's side attack, driving his major pieces after Michael with an unexpected flourish. Michael frowned, seeing his attack shortened and himself on the run. And then it was over. His black queen stood before the king, herself a sacrifice to his father's rook. He would lose his queen, and he would lose the game.

Michael leaned back in the chair, disgusted with himself. "I've lost."

"You'll be back at college soon," his father said. It was a statement, not a question.

Michael gave a tight shake of his head. "No," he said, "I want some time away."

"Ridiculous. You need to finish your studies and get on in the world."

"Get on in the world?" Michael repeated. "Is that supposed to make me forget Mother's death?" he asked, his voice rising. "Is that supposed to make me feel comforted?"

James McBride's thick eyebrows knitted together into a frown, and if he'd heard the rising anger in Michael's voice he paid no attention. "And will you remain here and weep over what can't be changed?" He gave a tight shake of his head. "You must get on with it now." He reached into his fob pocket impatiently and fingered a gold watch, checking the time on its face. He closed it with a snap and looked out the windows. "She would have wanted it that way."

"How do you know what she would have wanted?" Michael said, rising from his chair. His mother's beautiful, sad face swam before his eyes. He was certain now. Only *he* had loved her, not this cold bastard sitting opposite him. "How do you know what she would have wanted, Father?" he repeated. "You never spoke to her. She died of loneliness, Father. Of loneliness." The words tumbled out, flung from his lips like stones. "Dammit, it was all your fault."

"That's enough!" James McBride bellowed. "You . . . you . . ." he stammered to say the words. Then abruptly he stood up and with one hand he scattered the chess pieces on the floor, sending the armies flying to the far corners of the room. The teacups rattled on their saucers. He gripped the edges of the table, breathing hard with effort, as though choking on words that would not, could not issue from the silent working of his mouth. Across his broad face the skin burned red and white. The clenched fingers shook the gaming table.

"Jesus, Mary, and Joseph!" Mary blurted out as she pushed open the parlor door, her hands filled with a tray of sliced cake and her expression horrified at the sight of James McBride doubled over the gaming table. She set the tray down and quickly came to him, her hands reaching out to hold the shaking shoulders, pulling him firmly away from the table. She glanced at Michael, her eyes black with fury. "Don't stand there like an eejit! Get him a chair," she commanded.

Michael jerked into motion and brought Mary a chair. Slowly and with patience, she resettled James McBride into its seat. His eyes were moon white and roving, his forehead sweating, his pallor gray.

"A gra, a gra, mo croi," he whispered hoarsely.

"Shush now," Mary said softly to him. "Shush, it's done."

Mary left James slumped in the chair and went to the sideboard. She pulled out three small glasses and a bottle of whiskey. She poured them quickly and brought one to James and one to Michael. The third glass she raised high.

"Now we'll drink to her," she said sternly, "and there's

an end to your quarrel." She threw back her head, the glass to her lips, and the whiskey followed neatly into her mouth.

Slowly, Michael did the same, swallowing the stinging mouthful of whiskey. It burned, and as he inhaled he tasted it a second time on numbed lips.

"It's all gone, Mary," James said, his voice hard and flat. "It was no more than fairy gold."

"It's no matter," Mary answered. "We'll manage."

Michael felt his heart contract, his arms pressed close to his sides. He drew away from the pair, his feet backing toward the door. He had wanted something from his father, some words or a gesture that would admit to their shared grief. He had wanted to offer the man comfort and instead he had fought with him, opening some hidden wound in his father's armor. It unnerved him, and in the brief display of James McBride's weakness, Michael discovered he had been repulsed by the man's anguish, repulsed by the notion that his mother's death might serve as a bond between them. Michael had never shared her with his father before. He would not share her with him now. Even in death, Eileen McBride did not belong to the iron-fisted man seated in the chair clutching his glass of whiskey.

"I'm going out," Michael declared, and he left the room without waiting for a reply. In the foyer he grabbed his coat from the hook, swinging it over his shoulders as he bolted through the door.

Once on the stoop, he took a deep breath, sucking in the cool spring air quickly to stop the heat roaring in his veins. He walked down the stairs and, turning on Twenty-third Street, walked along the gated edge of Gramercy Park. The black bars of the fence flickered in his vision, white and black and white again like the rolling chess pieces. He stopped before the gate and hesitated, fingering the key that lay in the bottom of his pocket. He had not been inside the park since last fall, before his mother had taken ill. They used to come here often, for she liked to sit in the shade of its lindens and chestnut trees and listen to the water running in the small fountain. If the weather was good she would tell him stories, the noisy babble of the fountain accompanying the lilt of her voice.

He used his key and entered the empty park. He followed the footpath to the fountain, where the statue of a nymph poured water into the basin. The fountain had been turned off for the winter, but a thin layer of muddy water and dead leaves filled the bottom of the basin. Michael peered into it and heard a sigh, no louder than the wind rustling through the dry privet hedges. He looked up into the face of the nymph and saw its features change. The classical stone face softened into his mother's likeness, and the still hands moved in the motion of washing. Between the white fingers a cloth rippled into the basin, stained a rust-colored brown where it touched the dead leaves. A sigh exhaled from the stone lips, now flushed a pale pink.

Michael backed away from the fountain. The nymph lifted her eyes to him, and he saw faint green tears that streaked her cheeks like a thin trail of moss. She sighed again, and the remaining leaves of last year shivered on the branches above. She lowered her eyes to the cloth between her hands and with slow, steady gestures washed it in the basin. The rusted stains on the cloth bled into the dirty water.

"No! You're not real," Michael said to the nymph. "A banshee, out of her stories. Not real. Go away, I say!"

At once the nymph's features hardened back to stone. In the quiet of the park, Michael watched the rippling shadows of the chestnut trees cascading over the nymph.

"A trick of light," he said aloud. It was no more than moving shadows that had animated the stone nymph. That and the memory of his mother's stories.

He turned abruptly and left the park, the gate groaning

on its rusted hinges as he shut it behind him. Too many memories to rest comfortably here, he thought.

In which direction, then, should he go? Michael wondered. Downtown toward the noise and the bustle of the city streets? Or uptown, where the brownstones stretched into residential streets and hotels and the carriages moved with a slow, easy pace? He turned north, suddenly needing a quieter street in which to think.

The world seemed tipped at odd angles as he walked, and he himself was sliding to the edge of its rim. He wheeled his arms but caught at nothing that might prevent him from falling. His feet barely touched the hard stones of the street, and the March winds hurried him along the avenue, past the ornate iron lampposts, past the shops, past women pushing babies in prams, their long skirts billowing like thick clouds.

At the corner of Fourth Avenue and Thirty-first he looked up, hearing the hammering of scaffolds. A sign announced the construction of a huge new hotel, the Park Avenue, that was being erected by A.T. Stewart. Already its shell was nearly seven stories high and shadowed the Brandes Hotel at its side. He walked past it, wondering how much such a building would change the quiet avenue that he had known since childhood.

At Fortieth Street he finally stopped and decided it was time to return home. He was hungry; he had eaten nothing since dried toast and tea that morning. It was now late afternoon, and his body protested at being ignored.

"Hot corn! Hot corn!" trilled a woman's voice.

Across the street from him, Michael saw a young woman hunkered down beside a basket and small smoking brazier. She looked up at Michael, and through the haze of gray smoke her eyes shone a bright, hard green. She was dressed only in a white cotton shift. She'd no shoes, nor stockings, and her hair, a dull oatmeal color, hung loosely over her shoulders. She stood up and arched her back wearily. In the afternoon sun, the light shone through the thin fabric and outlined her shapely body.

"All you that's got money, poor me that's got none," she continued to sing, a hand beckoning to Michael. "Come buy me lily hot corn, and let me go home!"

Michael shoved a hand into his pocket feverishly, looking for money. He felt compelled to buy corn from this woman standing so nearly naked on the street corner, her skin shining like spilled cream and her gaze pulling him toward her.

He set a foot in the street and heard the screel of a grindstone. "And you, laddybuck," a man's voice growled, "will you have any knives that need sharpening?"

Michael spared a glance behind him and saw the grizzled face of a knife sharpener seated at a small turning whetstone. The man was grinning widely, a few stray teeth remaining in his mouth. A bright gold earring glittered in one earlobe. He held a boning knife against the edge of the grinding wheel, the sparks from the silvery blade flashing over his fingers like stars. The man wore a black coat over a deep red vest and a wreath of mistletoe around the brim of his dirty bowler.

"No," Michael stammered at the man, backing away. He turned quickly, looking for the woman selling corn, but she was gone and the corner was empty. Even the black smoke from her brazier had disappeared, and along with it the burned papery smell of roasting husks. He spun on his heels to face the knife grinder and ask if he had seen where the girl had gone. The grinder was gone as well, yet if he listened hard, Michael was certain he could still hear the whirling sound of the whetstone.

Someone gave a low, throaty chuckle. "Do you mind yer man there? He looks a right eejit thrashing this way and that like a stuck rooster! He's only to stand still and he'll see it all!"

"He can see, but he can't know!" answered a breathy voice a little sadly.

Michael turned slowly to the sound of voices. A photographer had set up his tripod beneath an elm tree across the street. He fussed over the plates, carefully settling a black cloth around the back of his camera. Michael frowned in confusion, unable to place the voices with the solitary photographer who seemed unaware of Michael's presence.

"What good is it then? Has he a chance at all?" grumbled the first of the voices.

"I'm thinking not," replied the breathy voice again. "Red Cap will have him in end."

"Not our lookout, then, is it?"

"Could be . . . if only for her."

"No!" said the grumbling voice vehemently. Above the photographer, Michael noticed the dried leaves in the branches of the elm begin to tremble. "We'd be bucked! Skelped if we was to get into it. No, no, I'm telling you, we've no more to do here than a tailor's cat to the price of wool. It's up him, entirely. Away now, before any knows we've come this far!"

The leaves rustled again, and just along the greening edge of one branch Michael caught a glimpse of two small figures with no more substance than knotted twigs running nimbly on bent legs over the outstretched limb. He held his breath and saw them shimmy down the trunk, using the head of the unsuspecting photographer as a footstool before scrambling down the back of his coat. They dropped to the ground, standing no higher than the man's knees. The first figure fled into the bushes, but the second stopped, crouching by the photographer's heel and tilting a head toward Michael. It had small face and thistledown hair peeking out of a spiked brown cap, like the half-open seedpod of a chestnut. It gave a shy salute to Michael, who found himself raising his own astonished hand in reply.

The photographer turned in time to see Michael's upraised hand and immediately gestured to a chair placed beneath the tree.

Caught like a fish in the rippling waves of a dream, Michael crossed the street and sat in the chair. The photographer spoke to him, but Michael never answered. He sat in the chair, wondering if the whole scene might suddenly vanish before his eyes and leave him sitting in the dirt. A puff of smoke, a blinding flash, and at once the photographer moved toward him again.

"Sir?" he was asking.

"Excuse me?" said Michael.

"Your address, sir. Where may I send the photograph?"

Michael gave the man his address and paid him for the photograph. He returned to the sidewalk, his footsteps slow. He shook his head, as if that alone might be enough to free him from the strange inventions that invaded his thoughts. He had convinced himself that it was the immediacy of his mother's death that had caused him to see phantoms where none existed that night at the park gate: the man in the red cap, the corpse of carved wood. None of those things could have happened; they were images and pieces out of the treasure trove of Eileen McBride's tales. They had come to him in his despair as a way of keeping her voice alive. The last three days, most of the time spent in his room, had been empty and quiet. He had come to believe that those phantoms had left him.

And now it was happening again.

Michael nearly walked into a man who carried across his shoulders a long pole strung with oranges for sale. He had stubbornly refused to believe the man was real and intended to pierce yet another shadow. But the man was real, and he gave a loud shout at Michael, who clipped his shoulder painfully on the tip of the pole.

"Why don't you watch where you're going!" the man shouted, struggling to maintain his grasp on the heavily

ladened pole. The oranges bobbed brightly, their skins
giving off a sweet perfume.

"I'm sorry, I just didn't see you," Michael said lamely.

"Not see me!" the man cried. "Man, wake up and
open your eyes, or you'll wind up under the wheels of a
trolley. Not see me!" the man repeated, shaking his head.
"Well, it takes all kinds. Say kid, want to buy some
oranges now that you see them?"

"No, thanks," Michael answered, edging away, his
face flushing with embarrassment.

"Says he didn't see me," the man muttered to himself
as he continued on his way down the street.

Michael shoved his hands into his pockets, his shoulders hunched as he walked, kicking out long-legged
strides. His ear caught a myriad of sounds just beneath
the city's roar: an insect's rasp, the rapping of a drum,
and the shrill call of a flute firing notes into the brisk
wind. He shook his head, not wanting to hear these
sounds, his eyes trained on the black tips of his shoes,
fearful of looking up into another vision.

A horse whinnied and Michael's head jerked up. He
thought of the orangeman's warning, believing for a moment that he had wandered into the path of an oncoming
carriage.

There was no carriage standing before him, but as he
turned to look behind him, Michael tensed. There, waiting on a black horse, was the man with the red cap. Only
now Michael saw it wasn't a cap, but long red hair
slicked down close to the sides of the man's narrow face.
Surrounding the man were other mounted horsemen
spread across the street, their spears and axes held upright. On the pommels of their saddles were skulls tied
together, festooned with red and green ribbons and the
glint of twirling gold coins. In the shadows of the building, the horsemen's faces were a deep mottled brown,
their bodies thick and strong like carved oak. But in the
open street, the sunlight drenched the armor and the war-

riors shone transparent as a sheet of gold rain. They were attended by wraiths whose pale gray faces wore masks of misery and who stared at Michael out of haunted eyes. Hands soft as dust clung to the bridles and held the mounts steady. Shadowed substance and shining light, they appeared to Michael at once solid and threatening as a closing storm and as vaporous as a misty dream. The man with the long red hair nodded at Michael.

Red Cap. That's what the tiny stick creatures had called him. And Michael recognized him at once. The man was hunting him, and this time he'd brought an army.

A crow cawed loudly overhead and the horsemen shifted in their saddles, their eyes trained upward toward the sound. Out of the blue sky, a huge black crow flapped her wide wings, driving a black shadow over the street beneath her gliding body. The horsemen stirred, clutching the reins as their mounts became restive. The wraiths bowed their heads into the deep valleys of their bony shoulders. Red Cap broke away from the line of waiting horsemen to confront the crow. He pulled his long bow from a case in his saddle and nocked a long arrow of yew, its red fletch a streak of blood.

The crow continued to advance, tilting her body downward until the black arch of her beak challenged Red Cap. He raised the bow and let loose the arrow. At once the crow reared, her wings flapping madly as she straightened her body in the air to receive the arrow. She hovered and the arrow hurtled in her direction. In the instant before the arrow reached her breast, the shaft burst into a harmless switch and merely brushed her with tiny stems of shivering leaves and red berries.

At Michael's ankle he heard a sharp twang. Looking down, he saw the same two small creatures from the elm tree, bows arched before their twiglike bodies. Loosed arrows, as small as tavern darts, buzzed angrily like wasps when freed from their strings. The small points found a purchase in the thighs and calves of the attending wraiths. They fell at once, a white foam gathering in their mouths and their bodies stiff and unmoving.

"Git, will you!" shouted one of the small creatures. "The shot will hold them only for a while, but not near long enough for you to stand here gapping. Go on, go on!"

Michael spared another glance over his shoulders and saw the cawing crow wheel her body high into the air. She was leaving! The horsemen urged their terrified animals to step over the downed bodies of the wraiths. The horses balked, some refusing to move as more tiny arrows shot through the air. Red Cap roared out in fury and raised his own bow toward Michael. At that the small twig creatures scattered, running and then rolling like tossed seeds.

"You're on your own," one cried. "Shite we're bucked if yer man catches us!"

"To the iron beasts," shouted the second. "They'll protect you!"

Michael heard the cold clink of the bridle and the rapping of horses' hooves over the cobbled street. He didn't turn to look but began to run, his eyes trained on the empty street in front of him, while behind him the storm thundered.

Michael ran, his knees raised high and his feet pounding along the pavement. He could hear shouting behind him, the huffing breathing of horses, and the rattled spears. A stone flew past his ear and landed hard in the street, where it burst into flame. A second stone shot out and he swerved to avoid it, his feet stumbling over the trolley tracks embedded in the street.

Michael's arms wheeled in the air to keep his balance and he glanced behind him at the advancing hunt. His feet teetered on the rail of a track. Red Cap pulled the reins of his silver bridle, and the horse reared back in alarm. White foam lathered the animal's neck and steam issued from its nostrils. The advancing line of horsemen careened into each other, the horses neighing shrilly as legs and arched necks collided in the sudden stop. Red Cap glared at Michael but waited, his horse straining at the bit.

Michael's lungs burned from the fearful run, and he gasped hard, sucking in the taste of steam and coal in the air. He looked down at his feet balanced on the trolley track and something of his mother's stories came to him. Iron. The cold touch of iron. Only that and the cross could repel a fairy host. He looked again at the horsemen waiting, their forms shifting unevenly in the afternoon light. Sometimes he saw them clearly, the red cloaks flaming, the sheen of the gold coins and the sweating hides of their mounts. And other times, they faded into color and light. Fairies. Eileen's fairy host come to haunt him.

Red Cap raised up in his saddle and barked out an order. From the assembled riders a figure sprang awkwardly into the air. It was partially human, but lifted upward by huge raven's wings sprouting from her back. Between the feathers of her chest jutted a small pair of women's breasts. The hands curled into talons, and beneath human eyes, the face was split by a short hard beak. A second creature rose from between the horses and took to the air. This one was female too, her sagging breasts visible through the dense plumage of black feathers. Her sparse hair was twisted into a gray braid, tied with knotted, sinewy ribbons. She'd no eyebrows but round yellow eyes, and she clacked together three huge upper teeth, sharpening them against a jutting lower tusk. Her black wings were tattered, and beneath her rising body dangled webbed feet.

They circled above Michael, diving low as if to grab at him with their claws. Their wildly beating feathers filled the air with the stench of carrion. Michael crouched, arms over his head as he tried to shield himself from their clawing hands. But as close as they came, they did not touch him, and in spite of his fear, Michael guessed that it was because his feet remained on the iron track. They meant to scare him, drive him off the track and set him running before the horsemen like a hare before the hunt.

With his arms sheltering his bent head, Michael walked the iron rail like a man on a tightrope. Overhead the creatures screamed in frustrated rage, angling their attacks even closer. One of them brushed him with her wings, and immediately the air was peppered with rusted smoke as her wing sizzled. She screeched at Michael, and he saw his own terrified face reflected in her round, mirrored eyes. Then he ducked his head again into the crook of his arm and continued, slowly making his way along the trolley track while the creatures harried him at every step.

Over the din of their screeching Michael heard the whistle of a train preparing to depart. The creatures scattered at once to the air and Michael looked up. Before him were the three rounded domes of the Grand Central train depot. The trolley tracks terminated at the station, and it was only a short distance across Forty-second Street to the train shed. In the shadow of the open doorways, Michael could see the graceful wrought-iron arches that spanned the roof of the train shed.

The twig men at his heels had told him to go to the iron beasts. Michael realized that they must have been speaking of the trains. Within the body of an iron beast, he'd be safe from Red Cap and his horsemen. The creatures flying overhead lifted themselves higher into the air and cried noisily as they returned to Red Cap.

Michael cast one last look behind him as he prepared to run. Red Cap had raised himself up in the saddle again, a long bow held in his hands, an arrow loosely nocked. As soon as his feet left the iron rails, Michael knew he would have but a moment and luck to pitch himself into the safe confines of the train shed. Michael crouched, trying to time the instant when he would hurtle himself forward. A hansom cab clattered up Forty-second Street, a big bay horse snorting as it pulled the black cab. As it neared, Michael took his chance. He darted out in front of the cab, the driver shouting as he jerked hard on the bay's reins. Michael heard the snap of the bowstring and threw himself on the ground to the other side of prancing bay.

The arrow struck into the horse's front flank and the bay reared in startled terror, the muscles spasming along its withers and down its sides. At once the bay's knees buckled and the horse collapsed forward, dragging the harness down with it. The horse gave a small nicker, and behind the blinders the eyes had rolled upward into white moons. The body shuddered, the front legs kicking, and then stilled. The cabbie was shouting, cursing, desperately trying to undo the tack and free the stricken horse. Seeing Red Cap nock a second arrow, Michael picked himself up quickly and fled into the train station.

From the bright sunlight of the street, Michael was plunged into the cool shade of the station. Several rail-yard workers in dark wool clothes brushed past him as the cabbie's shouts attracted attention. At the end of Fourth Avenue Michael could just make out the colored outlines of the horsemen where they rippled in the sunlight, unnoticed by anyone else across the street. A crowd was gathering around the fallen horse, and a police officer had appeared. Michael moved away from the doors, seeing the cabbie point angrily in his direction.

Once inside the station, Michael inhaled deeply, letting the moist steam coat his mouth and throat. Tobacco lingered in the air, and the faint hint of a woman's perfume. He had grown up with that smell. It had clung to his father's clothing, to his hands, to his exhalations. He smelled of the railways, of people traveling whose colognes and hair creams, whose cigars and pipes, bags of food and rotten fruit, mingled with the damp coal steam.

Eileen had despised the smell, and every night Mary laid a bowl of cold clear water for James McBride to wash in before joining his wife at their dinner. Michael had learned to associate that smell with the tension between his parents. He knew the moment his father returned from the yards, for his mother, even sitting in her study, would cease her storytelling and hold a lace handkerchief to her nose. Then the house would grow chilly and quiet.

Michael leaned wearily on the black railings with their grid of bars and iron roses, his breath still ragged after his desperate escape. Unexpectedly he felt a tiny shock, like a dart of lightning, strike his left arm. He lifted his arm away from the iron and the tingling pain went away. Michael touched the railing again with a tentative finger. Again the small shock of discomfort. He looked at his hand, the skin on his fingertip white where it had touched the iron. His left eye watered as if it hurt, and he put his face against his hand. From behind the closed lid, he saw the horsemen limned in red and gold.

Michael lowered his hand again and saw the world blurred through his left eye. He shut it, and at once the world focused with hard edges in his right eye. What was happening? He started to shake, terrified of what seemed his fearful imagination and at the same time a certain threat. If he thought as a rational man, he must accept the possibility that he was mad. But the danger seemed so solid and real; and he could see with his right eye the fallen horse and the gathered crowd.

No, he thought, shaking his head after a pause. He must not think as a rational man. Then there could be no answers as to why Red Cap had leveled his horsemen against him. Michael took a deep breath. He would find his answers in his intuition and from the knowledge gleaned from his mother's stories. His intuition told him that the horsemen led by Red Cap could wait forever for him to reemerge from the train depot. That there was no way he could go safely home from here. And even if he did make it home, they would not rest until his skull joined the other trophies hanging from Red Cap's saddle. But why him? he wondered. What offense had he committed to attract their attention?

A train waited at the end of its track, porters, and workers preparing it for departure. It was a Pullman, the lines sleek and powerful. Stretched out behind the engine were the passenger cars, the sleepers, and the dining car. From between the wheels it exhaled clouds of white steam. Last July it had been a spectacular event when Frank Leslie of the *Illustrated Newspaper* had departed, with his wife and an entourage of reporters, for a five-month excursion to the West Coast. Michael had been there with his father for the noisy send-off, breaking bottles of champagne over Pullman's latest elegant design, the Wagoner car. And amid the exuberant atmosphere, Michael had experienced for the first time the feverish excitement that such a journey might offer. As the train had pulled out of the station, firecrackers laid on the tracks exploded with a farewell salute.

"Are you about your father's work, then?" a man asked.

Michael turned abruptly and stared into the grimy face of a rail-yard worker. The man looked familiar, but Michael couldn't place him. "Sorry?" Michael asked, confused.

"Are you here to work?" the man tried again. He turned away from Michael and looked out at the train. From his pocket he took out tobacco and papers and rolled a cigarette. At the sight of his squared hands, the nails rimmed with grease, Michael remembered him: Sean O'Neill, the son of one of his father's workers.

"Not to work," Michael said.

Sean gave him a curious stare. He offered the cigarette to Michael, who refused it. Sean put it between his lips and, after striking a match on the iron railing, lit the cigarette. Smoke trickled from the sides of his mouth.

"Thinking of leaving?" he asked.

"I—I don't know," Michael said. Until that moment, it hadn't entered his mind that fleeing by train might be a choice. But now . . . He hesitated, the questions still hovering in his mind. "Tell me," he said brusquely to Sean, "what do you see when you look out at Fourth Avenue?"

Sean frowned from behind a curtain of smoke, but he turned his head to gaze out the open door of the train station.

"A horse dead on the street. A slaughter cart. People. Cabs."

"Anything else? Anything unusual?"

"Why, what is it I should see?" Sean asked, turning back.

"Nothing, I suppose," Michael answered. He was the only one who saw them, Red Cap and the horsemen. But he knew he wasn't crazy. Red Cap was there. And his horsemen had chased him up Fourth Avenue, and Red Cap had killed the horse while trying to kill him. And Michael could not go home. His thoughts quickened. "Perhaps I will leave. What time does this train go out?" he asked.

"Eight this evening. But wait—"

"And where to?"

"First north, to Rochester, Niagara. Then to Chicago and across the plains west. All the way to California."

Michael reached into his trouser pocket, letting the idea of flight tumble out with the folded wad of money. He started to count it. How far away would it take him?

"Do you mean to go now?" Sean asked, growing more curious. "What about yer man?"

"Who?"

"Yer father? Won't he mind you leaving kinda sudden like?"

Michael thought of his father, the silence and then the unexpected attack at the chess table. How could he ever understand his father? How could his father ever understand him? They were better off apart. "That's his look-out," Michael replied with a shrug. He refolded the money back into his trouser pocket and made to leave for the ticket office.

Sean grabbed him by the coat. "If it weren't for my aul fella being ill just now, I'd be away sooner myself. When he's well, I'll be on that train too," he said, almost belligerently.

"So you will," Michael answered and started to pull himself away. Then he stopped. "Would you do me a favor and tell Mary that I've gone? I don't want her to worry."

"I'm no errand boy," Sean snapped. Then he lowered his head. "Shite," he swore softly. "She's a decent enough skin. I'll let her know you're away west."

"Thank you," Michael breathed and started again for the ticket window. He turned once to see Sean, leaning against the railing, staring hungrily at the train. "Sean," he shouted back, "I'll look for you out there."

Sean raised his chin proudly. "In California. I'll be the one with all the money!"

The golden afternoon sunlight slanted through the high glass ceiling and lit the black flanks of the train. The train whistle sounded, and high in the arches the pigeons fluttered away in terror. Michael thought of the dove ascending on his ceiling, straining its wings against the light. Here was what he wanted. Here was the only path to take. He'd shake off the silence, he'd shake off Red Cap, and most of all he'd shake off the memory of Eileen McBride buried in the earth. And when the shrill whistle sounded again, Michael leaned into the gold spears of falling light and let the momentum of flight carry him into the waiting body of the train.

•

Three

Do you mind the tale of Kirwin of Galway?" Eileen asked in her soft, lilting voice. Ash-blond hair tumbled untidily down her back from underneath the straw hat. In her hands she braided cornflowers, cowslips, and primroses into a wreath.

"No," Michael answered, his young legs dangling over the sides of the stone bench in Gramercy Park.

She smiled at the flowers in her hand. They both knew he was lying. "Well then, I'll have to tell it again, won't I? And this time you'll have to listen," she said, her golden eyebrows raised over bright green eyes.

Michael nodded, the sun warm where it spilled on his lap, the scent of her perfume sweet in the summer air.

Eileen McBride looked up into the spreading branches and began. "Kirwin of Galway was riding home one night when he met with another horseman on the road. Well dressed and handsome the man was, with a horse as black as night and a gait as smooth as cream. The stranger was a well-spoken man, and in a short while Kirwin found himself at ease as the pair shared the road and conversation. They talked of horses and of racing, and it came about that Kirwin himself had a horse he was thinking of racing on the following day. . . ."

A long whistle pierced the tune of Eileen's voice, and Michael's head pitched against the train window. Michael awoke from his dream, a sharp pain rapping his temple. His body was pressed against the iron flanks of the train as it rounded a narrow bend, crying out its shrill warning. He clung to the fading sound of his mother's voice, refusing to let himself wake completely, wanting, needing the distant solace of his dream. He closed his eyes again, dimly aware that the warmth on his lap came not from the dreamed sun but a child crowded into the bench and now sleeping, her head on his thigh. Michael left her alone, crossed his arms over his chest, and twisted his torso, the better to lay the flat of his cheek against the window.

Down he went, into sleep, straining to find again the soothing magic of his mother's voice.

"The handsome stranger gave Kirwin the lend of his jockey, which he told Kirwin would bring him victory in the following race. And on the next day, just as promised, the jockey turned up in bright green and yellow silks. But there was something about the jockey that put worry into Kirwin's mind. The man was spry right enough, but he'd the look of a changeling, an old face in a youthful body and a limp. But by all accounts he rode the horse like it was a wind, and in a flash Kirwin found himself holding the silver cup of victory. That night, the handsome stranger invited Kirwin to feast with him in his hall."

The train lurched again in the night and shuddered to a stop, shunted to one side as a second, faster train hurtled past the window like a hurricane. The child on his thigh whimpered and curled herself into a tighter knot, a thumb stuck in her mouth. Michael awoke with an ache in his crooked neck and glanced wearily over the sleeping inhabitants sprawled throughout the passenger car. In the near dark they lay tumbled like old clothes over the backs and benches of the hard wooden seats. Some had rigged their suitcases as tables for their feet. A tattered quilt all but covered a woman up to her forehead; only her hat with its decoration of white bird wings was visible above the faded pattern. Small oil lamps glimmered at intervals along the walls, casting a dull smoky light over the huddled sleepers.

Michael looked out the window, but there was nothing to see. Only a handful of stars in a moonless sky and the sketched lines of unfamiliar terrain beyond the track. Another lurch, and the train chuffed into motion. The clackity-clack shook Michael's stiff body, his backside sore where it hit the wooden bench. With a sigh, he leaned his chin on his chest and tried to sleep again.

How did the story end? In his sleepy haze he couldn't remember, and a panic rose in his chest as he struggled to find his mother's voice again in the loud hissing of steam and clacking of the rails. The dream caught him anew, a fish on its silvery hook.

The sun shone on Eileen's cool skin, the leaves cast a stain of green on her graceful neck. The water from the fountain of Gramercy Park trickled and babbled sweetly.

"Oh, it was a fine time that Kirwin had in that manor, I can tell you. There was nothing wanting in either food or drink. And the music was grand, the pipers and fiddlers all in good form. Kirwin's eye fell to one young woman, certainly more beautiful than all the others, for she made his heart ring at the glad sight of her face. But still something troubled him. For when he looked at the dancers closely, he saw the faces of his friends who had died before him. And when he looked again at the beautiful young woman, he saw the string of pearls around her neck. It was himself that had given her those pearls years ago when he had asked her to be his bride. But she had died before the wedding could take place. Now she took him by the wrist and tried to draw him into the circle of dancers.

" 'Dance with me, again,' she whispered. 'Look at me, for you loved me once.' And her hand burned on his wrist like a ring of fire.

"Kirwin danced with a heavy dread, for he knew at last where he was. He went to the handsome stranger and addressed him as Finvarra, lord of the dead. He begged permission to return home. Finvarra bade him have more courage and to drink again from a glass of wine. But when he drank, Kirwin fell into a deep sleep. He awoke the next morning in his own bed, his head splitting with the drink and a mark burned into the skin of his wrist; the clasp of a woman's hand."

The train skipped on the track, the jerky gait throwing the passengers into new huddles, groaning and cursing. Slowing and bucking, the train squealed to a halt, and the oil lamps swung their dim light over the wave of rolling bodies. Michael awoke with sweat on his brow, his heart racing at the hot feel of a hand clasping his wrist.

He looked down in fear and saw the child, her body at his feet, her long yellow hair trailing his lap, her small hand gripping his wrist. He reached down and pulled her up, sleepy-faced and cranky.

A woman dressed in faded brown wool and a thick scarf about her face thanked him and then mumbled softly in a language he didn't know. She scooped the girl up into her lap and held on to her. On the other side of her was a boy, his hair too long and hanging in his eyes, his trousers too short over gangly legs. Squeezed out from the tiny space between the woman and the man sitting next to her on the narrow bench, the boy clambered into the girl's empty seat, stretching his thin legs. The man roused and nudged at a second child on his other side. A younger boy escaped from beneath the man's arm and joined the gangly boy on the bench. Michael moved over, the space on the bench growing increasingly tight.

"Goddamn these immigrants' trains!" a man behind him swore. "They stop for every goddamn sonuvabitch train that goes by. Goddamn hog could get to Chicago with fewer stops than this!"

"Well, that's what you get when you travel cheap!" answered a woman testily. She had a slight accent, similar to his mother's but flatter and less musical. "I told you, we should have spent the money and taken the Central Pacific."

"Too dangerous. Either you or me would've been spotted before we reached Niagara."

"You worry too much."

"I gotta get some air. Goddamn stinks in here." The man heaved himself forward out of his bench and, picking his way through the tumble of sleepers, headed for the end of the car.

Michael stared at him as he passed, a black ill-fitting suit covering a tall angular frame. At the open door he sucked in the fresh air, his cheeks long planes of pale flesh. Michael turned around in his seat, curious about the woman. She was small and well dressed in a neat black dress with rose silk trim. A white lace collar rose on either side of her neck, and a trim hat with black velvet ribbons rested atop her piled blond hair. She crooked a welcoming eyebrow at him and smiled. Older than him, he thought, but not by much.

"Traveling far?" she asked.

"Yes. I think so," Michael stammered.

She laughed, her voice girlish. "Don't you know where you're going?"

Michael shrugged. "Chicago. That's as far as my ticket will take me."

She gave him a wistful look, the eyes appraising him. "Join me. Over here." She pointed a gloved hand to the seat her companion had just vacated.

Michael hesitated, uncertain about this forward invitation. But he discovered he was glad of the opportunity to talk to someone. For three days he had been silent, keeping his own counsel. But now he needed to drive away the night's journey and the long dream of Finvarra, lord of the dead. He edged out of the bench, excusing himself after stepping on the older woman's foot. She hissed and slid her booted feet out of the way. In his emptied space the two boys sprawled out their weary limbs.

To get to the next window seat Michael had to step over the sleeping body of another man, his huge leather coat embroidered with bright red wool. He snored softly, his mouth ajar, exposing rotting teeth beneath the fringes of a long black mustache. A black felt hat was pulled low over his eyes. There was an odor about him of wet wool, leather, and garlic.

Michael sat down in the space opposite the young woman, who continued to smile at him.

When he was settled, she stuck out a small gloved hand. "Alice," she said, introducing herself. "Alice Ivers."

"Michael. Michael McBride," he answered, shyly taking her hand in his. For a small woman she'd a firm grip, the fingers curling purposefully around his palm. She gave his hand a squeeze before she released it.

"Are you Irish?"

"No," he said. "Well, yes," he stammered again, then blushed.

"Which is it?"

"My parents came over from Ireland. But I was born in New York."

"Explains the suit. Most Micks setting out on an immigrant train look as if they've just climbed out of the bog." She smiled and fussed with a small crocheted purse on her lap, opening and closing the drawstring as if she couldn't quite make up her mind about something.

"And you?" Michael asked. "You've an accent. Where are you from?"

Alice grinned and tugged the drawstrings shut. "Everywhere now," she said. "But England once. Now those folks," she said, nodding toward Michael's sleeping bench companions, "they're all Ukrainians. And they may look poor, but rumor has it the women have bars of gold sewn into their petticoats. I talked to a man once who sold land down in Kansas, and he said a whole village of them come and paid up front for all their land and livestock in gold. So who knows? A poor yokel getting on this train may just as well turn out rich. And a dandy in weskit and gold watch riding a Pullman train out of New York may be nothing more than a cardsharp," she finished, smiling. "Just never know out here."

She fell silent, studying Michael, half waiting, he thought, for him to say something revealing about himself. He fidgeted a little on the bench. He wanted company, but he had no idea what to say, much less how to try and explain why he was here now.

Alice sighed and chuckled into her purse. "So what'd you do? Ruin the reputation of some high society dove?"

"What?"

She lifted her sharp gaze. "I'm just trying to figure out what makes a man like you bolt and run from a good situation. Couldn't be you killed a man. I know what that looks like." Her glance shifted for a moment to the man in the black suit standing at the open door.

"What makes you think I'm running?"

She shrugged, a little annoyed. "You've got no bags about you, not even a blanket roll, and over the last two days of travel I've seen you count your money over and over. Just wondering, I guess, how far it'll take you. And wondering maybe what to do when it runs out." She opened her purse again and took out a pack of playing cards and laid them in her lap. She slipped off her gloves, tucked them into her purse, and then began to shuffle the cards.

Michael watched fascinated as the cards slipped easily

between her fingers, folding and refolding like a fan.

"Well?" she asked, her tone nettled. "Are you going to say?"

Michael leaned back in his seat and thought for a moment. It would be easy to keep quiet, or even to lie. But she was watching him, studying his face as he pondered, and he suspected that she could hear the truth from the lie.

"My mother is dead," he said, surprised at how dull his voice sounded.

She stopped shuffling the cards, her head tilted as if the answer caught her off-guard.

"She died two weeks ago. And nothing's been the same since."

"Father dead?"

"Sometimes it seems like it," Michael grumbled. "Dead to me, anyway."

"Grief's a powerful thing. Can turn one man inside out, make him gamble like there's no way he can lose; and it can make another fold his hand on a royal flush and just walk away."

"I don't understand," Michael said, shaking his head.

"Do you play poker? Vingt-et-un? Monte?" Alice asked, fanning the cards out across her lap and then flipping them to reveal their brightly painted faces.

"No. Just chess," Michael answered sourly.

Alice gave a short, barking laugh. "Not much call for that out here. But a man that can hold his cards close to his chest and play them right can make a few dollars. At least it might save him from losing all of them to someone like me," she said softly, looking up at Michael with an impish grin.

"Is that what you do?" Michael asked, shocked.

"Poker Alice, they call me. And there isn't anyone better on the Central Pacific or the Union Pacific at getting those swells to part with their money in a friendly little game."

The train lurched into motion once more, knocking Michael forward into Alice's lap. She gave a giddy laugh and sat back, the cards folding into a disorganized pile in her skirts. She pushed Michael back into his own seat, her strong hands shoving against his shoulders, her eyes smiling openly into his face. Michael felt the heat of a new blush stain his cheeks at her familiar touch.

"Hey, that's my seat and I want it back," snarled the man in the black suit. He held on to the bench over Michael for support as the train bucked down the track, his jacket falling open to reveal the pearled butt of a pistol stuffed into the waistband of his trousers. His eyes narrowed with an unspoken challenge.

"Oh, don't get yer knickers twisted, Jack," Alice said with a wave of her hand. "We were just talking."

"I want my seat back," Jack said slowly.

"Of course," Michael muttered, and he fumbled unsteadily as he tried to stand and maneuver out of the crowded seat on the moving train. Jack dropped his shoulder and hit him hard with the point of an elbow in the ribs as Michael squeezed past.

"That wasn't necessary," Alice said angrily as Michael groaned with the unexpected pain.

"Just remember who you're traveling with. I've killed men for lesser insults."

"And look where it's gotten you," she retorted. "You've been dealt the eights and the aces, Jack. A dead man's hand, and don't forget it."

"You and your cards," he growled. "They didn't prevent you from winding up here either, remember."

"Maybe, but then I've a different reason altogether for being here," she said softly.

Back in his seat again, Michael turned to look at Alice Ivers once more and found her staring sadly at him, the cards shuffling in her strong fingers. Then all at once she smiled brightly at him.

"In the morning, I'll teach you poker, Michael," she

offered. "Who knows, you might find it useful."

"Thank you," he replied, wondering why it was that people seemed determined to teach him one game or another. With his father it was chess; with his mother it had been the horses, the four-year-olds at Belmont; and with Alice Ivers, poker. As if life were a game in which one gambled the outcome.

In the morning the sun shone through the windows and lightened the muted colors of the passengers' clothing. Michael found himself staring eagerly at the moving landscape outside, green with thick forest and then breaks of rolling farmland. Moisture clung to the windows where the exhalations of sleepers met the cool rushing air of morning. The two boys that shared his bench were stretching like young dogs, their limbs rigid as they lengthened their cramped forms. They yawned, the roofs of their mouths pink. And then they straightened in the bench and wiped their sleepy faces.

Around him in the car the passengers awoke slowly to the moving daylight. The woman, hidden but for her winged hat, rolled back her quilt into a small bundle and stowed it in a carpetbag. She pulled out a pair of gold-rimmed spectacles from the pocket of her skirt and perched them on her snubbed nose. Michael smiled at the way her mussed hair uncoiled down the sides of her neck, and at the winged hat pitched at an angle on her head. She must have looked elegant when she started out, he thought, and then dimly wondered if he was looking as faded himself. A burning itch beneath his jacket made him scratch, and he noticed that the boys beside him were scratching vigorously as well. Around their wrists they had a red stain, and Michael was suddenly reminded of his dream of Finvarra.

A tap on his arm made him look up, and the older woman opposite was nodding to him and repeating something in her language. She had a small jar with red-colored ointment that gave off a pungent medicinal smell. She was waving it toward Michael, who had no idea whether to sniff it or taste it.

"She means for you to put it around your wrist," spoke the woman in the winged hat, peering over the top of a book at Michael, her spectacles low on her nose. "It's a sublimate of mercury, intended as a barrier for vermin, though I couldn't say with any certainty it will work." She scratched her side discreetly. "Still, I wouldn't refuse anything now that might offer any assistance in that matter. Except maybe burning every article of clothing you own." Then she lowered her head again and returned to reading her book.

Michael took the jar of red ointment and with a fingertip ran a red line around each wrist. The ointment stung his skin, burning as the dead woman's grasp of Eileen's story. Thanking the older woman, he handed back the jar and settled uncomfortably into his seat, trying to ignore his burning wrists and the itching on his back.

The sun rose higher over the gentle swells of green hills, and though he was tired and hungry, the rising sun once again lifted his spirits. Four days before he had been in New York, the world close and dark, haunted with violent fears and cold silences. Now he was on his way to Chicago. Michael gave no thought to what he might do there. He didn't seem able to summon up an idea or even a vague plan. He felt stuck, caught between action and stillness. In the stillness he could find his mother's voice and recall the image of her face, animated in the storytelling. If he tried hard enough, he could even forget that she was dead. But without warning, the sharp pain of that moment would lance him, and his body would jerk to life, seeking escape in movement. But it was only motion, and try as he might, Michael could not imagine his life, or shape it into meaning beyond this aimless flight. He sighed and heard his stomach growl in hunger. One of the boys next to him heard it too and laughed, a hand patting his own flat belly in sympathy.

The train pulled into a whistle-stop station in the middle of a large empty field. Alongside the track was a plain narrow building whose doors opened into a huge dining room. Michael joined the rest of the passengers as they bustled quickly off the train and onto the platform. They would have no more than thirty minutes in which to eat and then reboard the train. Michael had learned, watching another passenger left behind on the platform, arms waving frantically, that the train would offer no warning of its imminent departure. As the passengers rapidly ate and drank, they kept a worried eye on the smokestack and their watches.

Standing on the platform, Michael savored the stillness of the earth after the motion of the train. The wind blew a cool morning breeze against his warm, sticky face, and he could smell newly cut hay. A cow lowed somewhere unseen beyond the brow of a small hill, and if he cocked his head to one side he could hear the clank of a bell. He stretched his legs, hands dug deep into his pockets, and wandered into the dining hall.

The passengers were huddled over tin plates of food, scraping down the remains of fried potatoes, fried eggs, fried beefsteak, and biscuits. Michael sighed, his stomach hungry, but his mouth bored by the sameness of the fare. For the last four days it had been this meal only, and unless he looked at his watch, he might never have known the difference between the morning meal and the evening. Still, it was cheap—only a dollar—and the tea wasn't so bad.

He found a seat next to Alice and sat down at a plate of food. Alice was eating daintily, though there was a light sheen of grease on her upper lip. She licked her mouth like a cat cleaning its whiskers and smiled at him. Self-consciously, Michael glanced around him worriedly as he ate.

"Looking for Jack?" she asked.

"I just wondered that I didn't see him," Michael answered.

"And you won't see him anymore neither," she finished, wiping her lips with a lace-edged handkerchief.

Michael's eyebrows rose in question.

"The law was hereabouts this morning, checking the train over. He took one look at those stars and hightailed it out of here fast. Jackie's a wanted man in more than one place. So I guess I'll be making my own way to California without him." She shrugged her delicate shoulders. "Not so bad. He always did mess up my game."

Michael took the news calmly, but inwardly he was shocked. Alice seemed so sure of herself, as if she had no worries about her future, even alone. And he envied her quiet confidence.

"Come on, Michael, finish up and I'll teach you the game of poker, the way kings play but only queens win."

Michael swallowed the last bites of tough beefsteak and washed them down with lukewarm tea. He pocketed three biscuits for later, even though he knew they'd be dry as chalk by the time he got around to eating them. But if he was lucky at one of the station stops, the news-butches sometimes sold lemonade or fruit.

Back on the train, Alice had pulled her small trunk in front of her feet and was using it as a table. The cards were whirling through her fingers, shuffling like feathers over a bird's back.

"Can you keep a straight face, Michael McBride?" she asked, cutting and recutting the cards.

"I think so," he answered, amazed at the slippery speed of the cards shuffling through Alice's fingers.

"It's all in the face." She smiled, pointing a finger at her dimpled cheek. "A game of bluff and courage. I've held nothing at all in my hand and walked away a rich woman because my face never revealed a thing." She fanned her fingers over her smiling face, and her impish features became still and empty of expression. Her eyes were flat gray stones, her mouth a carved line. Not a blush or even a flicker of amusement wavered over her face. "Never let them know the worth of what you hold," she said softly. And then the steely gaze fractured and the wide smile returned. She swiftly dealt five cards to each of them. "Pick them up and show them to me and we'll begin."

Beyond the sooty window the fields unraveled as Alice taught Michael the intricacies of poker; the ranking of hands, from nothing to a pair and on up to a straight flush, with its crowning royal flush. She taught him how to manipulate the wild cards and how to gauge the odds of improving one's hand in draw poker. Michael's head spun with the possibilities, the bright face cards laughing at his clumsiness and inexperience. But in Alice's hands, every card played a part in winning, and like a hawk soaring above him, she watched in amusement as he fumbled his cards down below. Throughout the day and then the night they played poker, listening to the slap of cards and the whispered groans as he continuously lost to Alice.

Late in the evening, when many of the passengers had sprawled themselves out in an attempt to sleep, Michael found himself nodding over the cards in his hands. As he stared at a pair of queens, their prim faces softened to the likeness of his mother's face before his tired eyes. Without intending it, his face sagged with sorrow.

Disgusted, Alice threw her hand face down on the trunk. "Haven't I told you a hundred times today not to let me see you've a lousy hand!" she said, annoyed. "Your face is halfway to your shoes."

Michael looked up, confused, his eyes swimming with a thin film of tears. "But I don't have a lousy hand," he stuttered.

Alice threw her hands up in the air. "Oh hell, don't tell me. Just ante up, you goose."

But Michael couldn't. He laid the cards down carefully, the faces of the queens staring up at him. He closed his eyes and waited for the image of his mother to drift away.

Alice leaned forward, a hand on his arm. Michael could smell the faint fragrance of rose water and the prickle of female sweat.

"What is it?" she asked, concerned.

Michael opened his eyes and looked at the cards. They were just women's faces, painted in garish colors. He shrugged.

"My mother. I think of her sometimes. See her dying all over again."

"I'm sorry for that," Alice said, settling back against her bench. "I've been on my own a long time. I forgot what it is to grieve. Tell me about her. What was she like?"

Michael cocked his head to one side uncertainly. "Are you sure you want to hear?"

Alice smiled. "Why not? We've the rest of the night. And I surely don't think I could sleep anymore on these damn benches. So tell me, what was she like?"

Michael drew in a deep breath and began to talk, slowly at first, of Eileen McBride; and as the train rushed forward into the night, the words rushed from him, gathering strength and steam. Until the week of her death. And then the words came slow and halting. Alice leaned forward, her elbows to her knees, her chin resting on her palms, to hear Michael's low voice intoning the misery of the days and hours before Eileen McBride died. His left eye watered painfully and reminded him to tell her of the strange chrism with which his mother had anointed his eye.

Alice's expression grew somber, her eyes shadowed in the dim light of the oil lamps.

"The left eye?" she asked in a hushed whisper.

"Yes," Michael answered weakly. "She couldn't see too well. I think she meant my forehead."

"Maybe," Alice murmured.

Beyond the black edge of the horizon, Michael could see a narrow band of gray, hinting at the dawn that was coming fast. They would be in Chicago finally that day, and then he would have to think about what he was going to do with his life. He looked at Alice, sleepily shuffling her cards in her hands, her weary face turned toward the glass, and realized he would miss her companionship. In a short time he had told her more about himself than he had ever told anyone. How strange that he could be so anonymous, so alone one moment, and then close, straight to the bone with a generous stranger. To neither Mary nor his father had he ever confided much. But to this slim woman, with her cards drifting from one hand to another, he had poured out his heart. On impulse, Michael wanted to tell her everything.

"The real reason I left New York in such a hurry was because I'm being haunted by the demons of my mother's stories."

He looked at Alice hard to judge how she would take this piece of news. Her face was still, her eyes hooded. But she sat quietly to hear the rest.

"Since the night of my mother's death I have been attacked by creatures that I thought only existed in her stories. But they were hunting me on the street as I walked in New York, and it was only by taking shelter in the train station that I was able to save myself. I left New York to escape from them. I know it sounds crazy, but believe me, they were there and they meant me harm."

The cards in Alice's hands stopped shuffling for a moment and then slowly, without a word, she set down the pack on her trunk.

"Cut the cards," she ordered.

Michael cut them, watching with curiosity as Alice laid out the new pile of cards in a strange configuration. Over the queens were black knights, in the corner a pattern of eights, on the side the ace of hearts.

"What are you doing?" he asked, as the pattern of cards wove black on red, some upside down, emptying their numbers over the scatter of royalty.

"The cards never lie. The face yes, the tongue too often. But not the cards," she answered softly. Then Alice sat back, her face pensive. "I believe you, Michael McBride," she said. Then she sighed and pushed the cards together into a single pile again. "I believe you. But there is more ahead of you to come."

"Are you reading my fortune in the cards?" Michael asked.

"The possibilities, that's all. Every man must play the hand he is dealt, Michael, whether it is high or low. But if you are wise to yourself, the cards will do as you would have them."

"I don't understand."

"Don't worry, most folks don't. Take my friend Jack. He'll be dead before next year because he thinks he holds a winning hand and will throw it away by being arrogant."

"And you?"

She smiled ruefully. "Too many queens and wild aces in my hand. I'll do well and I'll do worse." Then she reached into her purse and pulled out a wad of dollar bills tied with a ribbon. She peeled off about half of the wad and handed the bills to Michael.

Michael started to protest, but she stopped him with her steely gaze.

"Listen to me, Michael McBride, and do what I say. When we get to Chicago, don't stop there. Take the Santa Fe and go south. Way south down to Texas, all the way to a town called Redwing, near the end of the line at San Antonio. Outside of Redwing there is a ranch called Aces High. It's run by a man named Jordan Paul Moore." She stopped and knitted her brow in a question. "You did say you know how to ride?"

"Yes," Michael answered, growing more confused.

"Well? Really well?"

"Yes," Michael said more confidently. His mother had seen to that.

"Good. Tell that to J.P. He'll be hiring hands for a new roundup. You can get work there. J.P. owes me. So you tell him that I said to hire you and then we'd be quits."

"Alice, that's impossible. People don't make deals like that."

"Out west they do. A man's word may be all he has to offer at the time, and most of the time it's as good as money in the bank. J.P. said he'd pay me back any way I wanted it. And this is how I want it."

"But why should I go south?"

Alice gave him a sad smile and folded her hands together on her lap. "I'm just trying to buy you some time, Michael. The cards are crowded, the space around you showing narrow as a coffin. Down in the desert you'll find more room, and with luck, Red Cap may not find you so quickly. And there may be more to protect you down there than in the northern cities."

"What do you know about this? What do you know about Red Cap?"

Alice shook her head. "Same as you. Old stories learned at my grandmother's knee. But the cards . . . the cards tell the danger right enough. I'm just offering a helping hand."

"How can I repay you? For even just believing me?"

Alice grinned widely. "That's what J.P. asked, and see how I'm collecting now!" She laughed and then grew serious. "Just don't embarrass me down there. You may be a tenderfoot, but keep your eyes open and your wits about you so J.P. doesn't curse the day he met me. I may need his friendship again one day."

"All right," Michael answered, a new thread of excitement pulsing through him. He had begun his journey with no thought of the future. And without effort a future had been handed to him like a gift wrapped with a string. He had but to pull the knot and watch what would unravel.

"Thank you," Michael said, "thank you very much."

Alice gave him a tired smile, her skin wan in the pale morning light. "No need for thanks. Just remember to play the game carefully."

The train whistled shrilly, the smoke belching as it rounded a long slow curve. They were approaching Chicago. And from there, he would go south, to Texas. Michael looked out eagerly, smiling at the low bank of clouds that hovered over the horizon and partially concealed the city beneath it.

Four

The sun was high in the bleached sky when the train pulled into the station at Redwing, Texas. Michael disembarked from the smoking black hull of the old train and stared out, dazed, at his surroundings. The iron tracks ran alongside a ramshackle dining hall, its wooden planks gray and warped on the southern side. There was no platform, the tracks digging furrows into the hard-packed soil of the dirt street. An old yellow dog stood on bowed legs and barked at the train, his barrel chest rising and falling with the hoarse sound. Michael walked slowly away from the train and directly onto Redwing's main street.

To Michael the ten-day journey from Chicago to Redwing had seemed like an ocean crossing, the huge prairie an endless sea of gray-green buffalo grass, broken by patches of yellow, white, and lavender flowers. As Michael watched the land undulate with waves of sun-ripened green, he remembered Mary's stories of her crossing from Ireland and imagined the sails of her ship gliding like gulls over the prairie. How similar her tales o the weeks at sea to his own days on the train west: th monotonous sameness of the view, the horrible food, an the loneliness that penetrated far deeper than the damp Except that on the train there had been no damp, jus dust, and it had permeated every article of clothing Mi chael wore until he could feel it trickle into his pant leg and down the sleeves of his jacket. He scratched it out o his scalp and blew it free from his nose.

Passengers had come and gone, a few making smal talk and some even lifting Michael from his loneliness b acts of generosity and kindness. Outside of Topeka, young Dutch engineer shared his food and precious ba of soap with Michael. For fifty cents Michael bought thin shuck mattress which enabled the two of them to li across the otherwise too hard benches and sleep. Michae also contributed copies of cheap novels he bought fron the newsbutchers, and they took turns reading then aloud to each other to pass the time.

When Michael switched trains, traveling the Katy, line that served the small towns down through Texas, he found himself more often than not the only follow through passenger. Most were cattlemen or miners, only taking the train for the day or an overnight. The miner were burly-looking men, their denim clothing rough an dirty, their faces scarred by exposure. They chewed thick wads of tobacco plugs, which they freely spat only some times into the spittoons that grew more numerous on the trains the farther south Michael traveled. They also car ried bottles of whiskey tucked into their vest pockets.

"Smile?" one miner asked Michael, a bottle held up right in a gnarled hand.

Michael shook his head, puzzled by the question.

"He's asking if you want a snort of his liquor, son," a man in a large white hat drawled beside him. Beneath the hat, the skin of his face was a polished oak. His clothes gave off the faint odor of saddle leather.

"Thank you," Michael replied to the miner, and he took a deep swig from the bottle. Then he doubled over, coughing violently, as the harsh whiskey scorched a ragged track down his throat.

The man in the white hat thumped Michael hard on the back, while Michael coughed and wheezed.

"Now take it easy, son. That's Red Dynamite, guaranteed to blow yer head off. Plain to see it ain't what yer used to."

With tears streaming from his eyes and his nose filled with the pungent fumes, Michael returned the bottle to the grinning miner and thanked him in a hoarse whisper.

Later that same day two cowboys boarded the train and Michael watched them nervously as they strutted noisily up and down the aisle, their broad-brimmed hats pulled down over their foreheads and revolvers slung behind them like short stubbed tails. Every now and then when the train slowed, one of the cowboys would lean out an open window and shoot at anything moving on the prairie, swearing loudly when the target was missed.

The man in the white hat leaned over to Michael and winked a watery blue eye. "Never mind them fellers. If you leave them alone they won't meddle with you. As a rule, they mostly shoot at their friends." The man gave a low chuckle and then, resetting the brim of his hat low on his forehead, promptly dozed off.

On the last night of his journey Michael gave up trying to sleep and instead stared out the window at the widely flung stars burning across the huge sky. He had never seen so many in New York, never imagined that the horizon of the world could stretch so far as to make it seem they traveled with an infinite slowness across its broad face. In the weeks it had taken him to journey across the continent from New York to Texas, he had acquired a mixture of emotions: pride at the sheer size of his country and a humbling shame at his own ignorance of it. The streets of New York had been large enough when com-

pared to the compact world of his mother's green-tinted
stories of Ireland. But this country of endless plains, of
deserts shaded by the lavender ridge of distant mountains
made him feel set adrift in a vast sea. For once Eileen's
stories paled, her voice a whisper as it was carried away
by the wind over the sweeping grass.

Standing at the entrance of Redwing's main street, Michael shook himself awake from the dream of flight. He
was here now. He had arrived at a destination, though he
had no idea what that might mean.

The air was dry and smelled of hay, dust, and cattle. A
bird trilled, and he saw the bright red flash of a cardinal's
wings as it alit on the upper branch of a slender cottonwood tree. Michael could still feel the rattling vibrations
of the train, hear its deep residing hum in his ears, and
despite the slow motion of his feet, his legs trembled. His
clothes clung to him, the fabric heavy with the weight of
accumulated dust and soot from the train. His face
itched, the skin brown with grime. Michael took off his
coat in the heat, and the trickling sweat on his back ignited the fiery itch of vermin bites beneath his yellowed
shirt. The red rings around his wrists had faded quickly
and, along with them, any hope of preventing further in-
festation. He ran his fingers through his hair, the curls
lank with dirt.

Suddenly Michael hated the feel of himself. What he
wouldn't give for a bath, towels of white linen, the feel of
a clean shirt freshly ironed, the collar smelling of starch
and Mary brushing the lint from the back of his jacket.
What he wouldn't give for the sight of a city street that
wasn't diminished beneath a huge arid sky. A wave of
homesickness hit him, and he squeezed his eyes shut.

Then he snapped them open with a fierce determina-
tion and took a sharp breath. There was no going back.
He'd be all right. He had a name given to him by Alice; a
man that owed her one. Michael looked about him, turning to the right and then, with more caution, to the left.

From his green eye the landscape remained quiet, the trees sighing in the heat but empty of threat. There was nothing here to fear. Straightening his clothes as best as he could, Michael marched up the street in hopes of finding someone who could direct him to the Aces High Ranch.

After days of watching the landscape roll past with a confirmed sameness, Michael was stunned by the simple but available details of the town. There was a raised sidewalk of wooden planks, low two-story buildings with dirty glass panes, and hand-painted signs that creaked on rusted hinges as the wind set them flapping. He passed a hardware store, its window filled with bolts of calico cloth, white enamel dishes, rakes and hoes and little packets of seeds. The old yellow dog at the train tracks now slept in the street and lifted his grizzled muzzle to whuff at Michael's passing before returning to sleep. Horses were picketed at posts and Michael studied them, taking note of the different tacks and saddles used on these working animals. Not the sleek creatures of Central Park or his mother's own stable, but solid, sturdy beasts nonetheless, their ears pricked forward with curiosity at the sound of his walk. He heard the sharp staccato rap of footsteps and looked up to see a woman in a faded print dress marching toward him, a bolt of fabric clasped in her arms.

"Excuse me, madam," Michael said, and she stopped, looking him up and down with steel-blue eyes. Her face was browned except for a web of fine white wrinkles at the corners of her eyes. Light red hair had been piled into a loose knot at the top of her head, and a few strands of it clung to her damp neck.

"I'm trying to find the way to Jordan Paul Moore's ranch. It's called the Aces High. I was told it was in Redwing."

"Not in Redwing exactly. But hereabouts," she corrected him.

"Can you tell me how to get there?"

She squinted her eyes as if considering him.

"You just come in on the train?"

"Yes," Michael answered, feeling uneasy beneath the woman's scrutiny.

"Seems like you been on the road a spell," she declared.

Michael hunched his shoulders, suddenly wondering how ragged did he look, how offensive did he smell. He rubbed his hand across his cheek and felt the stubble of a beard. If he had been in New York, would he have even stopped to answer a man that looked as destitute as he must to this woman right now?

"Yes, actually, I've been traveling quite awhile."

"You see that rooming house over there? The one with the gold letters painted on top? And the wagon out front hitched to the pair of bays?"

Michael looked across the street and saw the words BURDEN'S ROOMING HOUSE painted in red and gold letters above the door. On the window was painted the price for a shave, a haircut, and a bath. By the porch there was a wagon, its bed half filled with brown sacks. In the harness a pair of bay horses waited patiently, tails flicking out to brush away flies.

Michael nodded at the woman.

"Tell you what, you go over there and get a bath and a shave. J.P. isn't fussy about most things, but he don't take too well to train tramps. When you're done, meet me by that wagon. I'm riding out near the Aces High and I can take you there."

"Thank you, thank you very much." Michael smiled gratefully. And then he remembered that he had no money left. He had bought a pear from a newsbutcher with his last dime. He shoved his hands into his pockets and looked away, wondering if there was a dignified way to refuse the offer.

The woman waiting before him sensed that something

was wrong and shifted the bolt between her arms.

"Um, I am afraid I must refuse your kind offer," Michael said.

"You tell Miguel that Hattie Burden said to give it to you on the house," she said briskly.

Michael looked up at her with relief and ran his dirty fingers through his hair. "Thank you. I'll pay you back at the very first chance, Mrs. Burden."

"It's Miss Burden, and that's fair enough. Call me curious, I guess," she said, a friendly smile opening her face. "Just want to see what you'll look like cleaned up some."

"I'm Michael McBride, from New York City," he said, sticking out his hand to shake hers. But the bolt of cloth came between them, and she couldn't let go of it. "Can I carry that for you?" Michael offered.

She laughed and shook her head. "Well, nice to know your mama taught you decent manners. Nah, I'll manage fine on my own. You go and get that bath and shave before the smell of you takes anymore starch out of my skirts." Then Hattie Burden continued on her way down the sidewalk, the heels of her boots rapping smartly.

Eagerly, Michael crossed the street and through the front door of Hattie's rooming house. It was difficult at first to convince the man Miguel of what Hattie had generously offered. The man spoke little English and regarded Michael with a sullen dislike. But Michael, imagining the water, the soap, and long-denied cleanliness, grew determined. At last Miguel consented and, bringing Michael into a backroom filled with wooden tubs, proceeded to fill one up with buckets of lukewarm water.

Michael stripped off his clothes, shook the dust out of them in front of an open window, and hung them over the sill to air. He stared down at himself, astonished to see his naked white legs after so many days of being smothered under clothing. The grime was everywhere, etched in all the creases of his skin. His feet had blisters and sores from wearing shoes and socks that were stiff with dirt. Along his thighs and across his belly were the red raised marks of vermin bites, scored with the hours of scratching. He eased himself into the water and sighed deeply.

Miguel, grumbling in Spanish, appeared, lugging a bucket of steaming water, which he added to the already half-filled tub.

"Thank you, thank you," Michael murmured as the hot water scalded his bites and peeled away the scabs. He lowered his body deeper into the tub. Hunching his knees close to his chest and holding his breath, Michael submerged his head completely. He stayed there, letting the warm water muffle all the sounds except for the slow, contented beat of his heart. He shook his head and the dirt swirled away from his hair. And then, unable to hold his breath any longer, he surfaced and spouted water into the air. It seemed a century ago that he could have taken so simple a pleasure as bathing for granted. The porcelain tub of Gramercy Park with its smooth white interior and clawed brass feet was not half so fine as this wooden tub.

Later, Michael sat stiff with terror, his hands wrapped around the arms of a barber chair, as Miguel scraped a straight-edged razor across his lathered throat. Miguel continued to grumble in Spanish, stopping every now and then to look Michael square in the face, his deep chocolate-colored eyes troubled by what they saw. Michael was afraid to say anything for fear of further upsetting the man holding the razor to his throat. But Miguel finished the job, yanking off the white linen cloth with a furious tug and fairly pushing Michael out the door again.

Hattie Burden was waiting in the seat of the wagon, and she motioned Michael to come up beside her. She was wearing a wide-brimmed straw hat trimmed with faded blue silk flowers, and beneath its shadow she smiled broadly, her teeth white in the tanned face.

"Damned sight better," she said with a deep chuckle.

A blush rose to Michael's cheeks as he pulled himself up onto the wagon's buckboard.

But Miguel, standing by the front door, began to speak quickly in Spanish. He pointed an accusing finger at Michael.

Hattie frowned at him and answered back in a short angry burst.

Miguel threw his hands up in the air and, though defeated, was clearly annoyed with her. He took a last unhappy look at Michael and made the sign of the cross over his chest.

Hattie briskly snapped the reins over the backs of the bays, and the slow-turning wagon wheels groaned beneath the buckboard. Michael clutched the seat to keep his balance as the wagon swayed and pitched over the uneven road.

They traveled in silence, Hattie fuming in her own thoughts. Just outside of town, Michael summoned his courage.

"What made Miguel so angry? Did I do anything wrong?"

"Nah. He's just a superstitious old buzzard, that's all."

"About what?" Michael asked.

Hattie turned from the reins and regarded him with a half smile. "Yer eyes," she said softly. "Miguel doesn't like it that they aren't the same color. *Ojo de mal,* he called it. Evil eye. He says you'll bring trouble." Hattie watched him, seeing how her words might affect him.

A chill touched Michael's clean neck and the skin of his arms prickled with warning. He shrugged and looked away.

They rode on. Michael watched the thin purple line of the far horizon as the afternoon heat quavered in sheets of rippling light over the spare grassy plains. Once Michael tensed, imagining he saw the figures of Red Cap and his horsemen emerge from the curtain of gold light.

He started to say something, his hand half raised in a question. Hattie's low laughter stopped him.

"That's a mirage out there. The heat and sunlight play all kinds of tricks. Keep watching and you'll see it fade before we've gone much farther."

Michael leaned forward to watch the rippling light. Thin shadows of high clouds passed overhead, and the light shifted as it cooled. He could have sworn he saw a line of riders, and then just as quickly the vision dissolved and he thought he saw a solitary figure beckon him: a woman in a flowing gown of green, her white arms opened to receive him.

"Over there's the Aces High Ranch," Hattie said, and Michael tore his gaze away from the mirage to where Hattie pointed.

A small indentation in the land offered a shallow valley, and in its center was a low ranch house, surrounded by several outbuildings. Two corrals were filled with milling horses kicking up clouds of dust. Beneath a faded tile roof the front doors of the main house opened out onto a long narrow porch that was deep in shadow beneath ribbed eaves. A well lifted water from far below the sun-baked ground and spilled it out into a long trough. The fresh water sparkled invitingly in the dry heat and Hattie's horses, smelling it, picked up their pace. Bougainvillaea vines grew around the entrance of the door, and they bloomed with a rich profusion of papery magenta blossoms.

Hattie drove the wagon down the gentle slope and through an open gate over which was mounted an arch with the Aces High name hammered out in wrought-iron curves. A black dog raised himself from the cool shade of the porch and barked a greeting to the oncoming wagon. The ears of the bay horses flattened with annoyance at the sound, but Hattie held them steady.

"Shut up, you mangy cur," someone shouted from inside the house. A tall angular man appeared at the door, waiting in the dark shadows of the porch. He stepped forward, one booted foot planted in the sunlight and an arm upraised to shield his eyes. Michael saw him smile as Hattie waved her hand in greeting. The man came down the two steps of the porch and out into the yard to meet them.

He moved with an easy gait. Heeled boots scuffed at the loose soil and small roweled spurs made a soft clinking noise. He was plainly dressed, but the heavy trousers and white collarless shirt were clean and well pressed. He wore a vest over the shirt and a gold watch chain draped across his chest that disappeared into a watch pocket. His dark hair was short, combed to one side, and he had a large salt-and-pepper mustache that all but hid his upper lip.

"Been awhile, Hattie, since we've seen you hereabouts," he said amiably, taking hold of the bays' harness and steadying the animals.

"Could be I haven't had an invitation, J.P.," Hattie replied tartly.

"Since when do you need one?"

"Since the day I realized you put women and muleys in the same damn corral."

"Aw, that ain't true," J.P. said gently.

"Then how come you never come calling into town? You know I can cook."

"Been working. We start the roundup tomorrow, and then we're driving cattle in a week or so. There's no shortage of things that needs doing."

"It's always going to be something, J.P.," Hattie said, waving him off, but Michael could see the disappointment in her tightly closed lips. J.P. Moore wasn't a bad-looking man, and he was close in age to Hattie Burden. Their eyes spoke more to each other than the lightly offered words, but it was clear that J.P. kept a polite distance. J.P.'s slate-gray eyes settled on Michael with interest, but he said nothing.

"Come on down," J.P. offered, a hand held up to assist Hattie down from the buckboard. "Water your horses and stay awhile. Tefa's put on a decent feed."

"Well, maybe just some of her coffee," Hattie relented with a faint smile. "I've got to get some supplies over to Missus Riley. That baby came early and I think she could use some extra help." Hattie gave her hand to J.P., who helped lift her down from the buckboard. As her feet touched the ground, Hattie held his hand a little longer than necessary. J.P. smiled at her and waited a moment before he lightly released her grip. He looked over Hattie's shoulder to where Michael stood.

"I see you got yourself a partner," J.P. said softly.

"He's not mine," Hattie answered. "He's come looking for you."

Hattie stepped to one side, and Michael spoke up.

"My name is Michael McBride, Mr. Moore. I was told to come to the Aces High Ranch and that you might have a job for me."

J.P.'s eyebrows went up in surprise. But he shook his head and chewed on the fringe of his mustache. "I'm sorry, son, for your having made the trip out here for nothing. Whoever told you I was hiring wasn't right. I've hired on all the hands I need for this season. And besides, meaning no offense, but from the looks of you, I'd say you're a stranger to cattle country."

"Alice Ivers told me to come to you. She said you owed her one and giving me a job would make you quits with her," Michael said quickly, trying not to sound as desperate as he felt.

"Poker Alice sent you?" J.P. asked, his voice surprised.

"Yes. I met her on the train."

J.P. settled back on his heels, and as his expression softened, a smile took the corners of his mouth. "Well I'll be goddamn. I should have known I'd be settling up with that woman one day."

Hattie's blue eyes flashed like summer lightning. "I just

remembered that I got other things to do besides taking those supplies to Missus Riley. Don't think I'll stay for that coffee after all." She whirled around from J.P. and pulled herself back up into the wagon with an angry jerk of her arms.

"Now Hattie, wait a minute. It ain't what you think. Don't go off sore like that—"

"Good luck, Mr. McBride," Hattie clipped. "And good day to you both."

She snapped the reins hard over the backs of the bays and they snorted, startled by the blow, before lurching into motion. The wagon rumbled and groaned as Hattie drove it around the well and then out through the arched gate, dust raising up behind the turning wheels.

J.P. watched her leave silently and then turned at last to Michael. "Damned techy woman. Redheads is the worst. Jealousy makes them loco."

"I'm sorry," Michael apologized. "I didn't think that mentioning Alice's name would upset her. She's been very nice to me."

"Yep. I'm sure she was. Hattie Burden is a good woman, jest techy is all. You might as well come in and have some grub and let me see if I can figure out what to do with you."

They entered the house and walked through a cool stark room nearly empty of furniture except for a pair of heavy wooden chairs placed in front of a huge stone hearth. On the mantel were tall candlesticks and a stamped silver plate. The walls were smooth inside, colored a pale pink plaster, and the deep window recesses shaded the sunlight that filtered through the room. The floor was laid with dark green flagstones and the doorways seemed narrow and low.

Michael followed J.P. into a small and crowded kitchen. The room was dominated by a long wooden table that held a large selection of food in the midst of being prepared. Red and green chilies waited on a tray beside a mound of coarsely ground meat. A wooden bowl of yellow-skinned onions sat beside a pile of chopped onions, the flesh white and moist. A black cast-iron stove threw off fragrant sparks of burning mesquite wood. A white enamel coffeepot steamed on one of the burner plates, while on the two other burners, pitted cast-iron kettles were filled with a bubbling thick stew, the aroma hanging heavily in the close air. The back door to the kitchen was thrown open to a vegetable garden, and chickens scratched near the entrance, picking out the tossed grains of rice and corn. A scrawny ginger tomcat slept on a barrel, his scruffy head lying in a patch of sun while his body rested in the cooling shade.

A short, heavyset woman with a dark face and long black braids came through the garden and entered the kitchen, her apron filled with ripe tomatoes. She wore a loose white blouse with bright red embroidery worked across the yoke and sleeves. Her black cotton skirt was heavily pleated at the sides and held up with a bright red-and-green woven belt. She was barefoot, and a white dust coated her brown ankles and feet. She smiled at J.P. and said something in Spanish. J.P. answered her and disappeared into a side pantry.

She set her apron down on the table and began to empty out the harvested tomatoes. Some of them rolled away from her grasp and she laughed, trying to catch them. Michael swooped down and retrieved one just as it fell over the side of the table. He handed it back to her and she took it with both her hands, smiling and thanking him in Spanish. And then she stopped as she looked up and her eyes met his. Michael saw her startle, blink in surprise, and then withdraw uneasily from him, the tomato held tightly between her palms. She turned abruptly to the cast-iron stove and, with a quick furtive gesture, crossed herself.

"Here's a cup," J.P. said, returning from the pantry with two cups hanging off a forefinger and in his other hand a pie plate with golden cornbread. "When did you last eat a real meal?"

"I don't really remember," Michael answered, his stomach grumbling at the sight and the smell of so much food.

"Thought so," J.P. grunted. "Tefa, get the boy some stew."

Tefa nodded, her head turned sideways to J.P. but still hidden from Michael's gaze. She took a tin plate down from a rack and from one of the kettles ladled a large serving of meat stew. To this she added another serving of the mashed pink beans cooking in a second pot. She brought the plate to the table, keeping her eyes averted from Michael's face, and scattered raw onions on the top and a few green chilies. She set the plate down in front of Michael, along with a fork. J.P. cut a piece of cornbread and handed it to Michael.

"I'd watch those chilies if I was you," J.P. said. "If you ain't used to them they could go off like a yearling colt in yer mouth. But there's nobody 'round here can make a stew like Tefa," and he smiled appreciatively at the woman.

"Thanks for the warning," Michael murmured, wondering what Mary or Bridget would make of this dark stew with its strange pungent aroma. It was a long way from boiled beef and yellow potatoes in their jackets. He let the savory steam touch his face as he picked up his fork. Then he took the first bite and tried to chew slowly. His eyes watered, tearing as the heat of the chilies burst in his mouth and coated his tongue with a scorching flame. He inhaled quickly, hoping to cool the fire on his lips. Though it was hot, as the unfamiliar spices filled his nostrils, Michael discovered the stew was also delicious. He braved the second bite. It was better than the first; the heat of the stew had scalded his lips and now instead of just a fiery mouthful, he could taste the meat and the soft pulp of the beans.

"It's good," he mumbled, sucking short cooling breaths into his full mouth. And at once he was ravenous, eating the food rapidly as though it might vanish before he had a chance to finish. J.P. poured him a cup of coffee so black that Michael couldn't see the bottom of the white cup. Then J.P. put in a spoonful of brown granulated sugar, and when Michael drank it, the bitter coffee was laced with a heavy sweetness.

As Michael ate, J.P. watched him with quiet amusement. Michael's fork dove again and again into the food, scraping across the surface of the tin plate, up into his mouth, and then returning to the food before he had even finished chewing the previous mouthful. Soon Michael's jaw began to ache with the fury of his eating, but once started he couldn't stop himself. It wasn't until he was wiping the last of the thick brown sauce from a second plate of stew with a piece of cornbread that Michael felt the hunger in him abate. He slowed his hand a little and, between sips of hot coffee, slowly chewed the piece of sopping cornbread.

J.P. nodded with frank admiration and drank his coffee. Even Tefa stared at him with wonder, giving him a watery sidelong glance, as she continued to chop onions.

"Well, son, I don't remember when I've seen a feller eat like that before. You want some more?"

"No thank you, sir. I'm pretty full right now," Michael answered, embarrassed, feeling the unexpected pinch in the waist line of his clothing. "It was really good. I've never eaten this kind of food."

"Where are you from?" J.P. asked.

"Out east. New York."

"That far?" J.P. shook his head and stretched his legs under the table. "I've been as far as Chicago. Went there one year to strike a deal with a rich cattleman. Can't say as I enjoyed it much. Too many people and too little room to move around in."

"It's very different from here," Michael agreed. "May

I ask you how you met Alice?"

"The same way you did, probably." J.P. grunted and stood up. He went to the stove and poured himself another cup of coffee. "It was on the train coming back from Chicago. I was a mite rollicky from expensive liquor and feeling flush, having made a couple of promising deals. I had a lot of expense money in cash on me for the cattle drives I was arranging. Well, there were two other gents on the train. Real high-class looking, and they offered to play a friendly game of monte just to pass the time." J.P. sat down again heavily and stirred some sugar in his coffee. "Damn fool I was. In about two hours those black-eyed buzzards had won every cent off of me. So I had to bet the ranch 'cause I'd lost all the money for the drives, and without it I couldn't even consider fulfilling those contracts. I'd a been flat busted."

"Did you lose the ranch?" Michael asked.

J.P. nodded with a sour grin. "Yessir I did. Right in the next hand. But lucky for me Alice happened to be sitting nearby, just watching the game. When I lost the ranch she came over and asked if she might be able to join in. Well, you know Alice, nice-looking woman and a smooth sort of charm. Those two must have figured they had what they wanted anyway, so they let her in on the game."

Michael started to laugh, thinking of Alice's trim figure and her easy smile. J.P. joined him and tugged at his mustache.

"She's just like a cougar, sleek and determined, and those two never knew what hit 'em. She played them like they played me. They started pushing each other to see who'd take up with her but she kept her eyes on the cards and damn if she didn't win back my money and my ranch before the night was over. It sobered me up watching her.

"And it sobered up those two fellahs. I thought there was gonna be trouble at one point because I saw one of 'em get kinda red in the face and stand up like he was going to start something. But damn if that woman wasn't as cool as they come."

"What did she do?" Michael asked as he cut another piece of cornbread. Tefa poured him more coffee, still taking care, Michael noted, to avoid staring directly at him.

"She pulled out a small pearl-handled gun and set it on the table. Those things ain't good for much, but at close range they can mess you up good, depending on where you're shot. She said she didn't tolerate gambling with a one-eyed player and she was prepared to shoot the sonofabitch if he didn't get out of the game. By this time most of the passengers were huddled around watching, and Alice's words set them to complaining."

"A one-eyed player?" Michael asked.

"A card cheat."

"Which one?"

"Probably both. 'Cause both of them scattered out of there fast. And Alice, well, she come over to me and handed back my title and my cash. Told me I was damn fool, which by that point, I pretty well knew was true. Told me to go home to Texas and spend my time looking down the backs of longhorns instead of cards. You know, I asked that woman why she had done it, stepped in like that and helped me out. And she said if they'd a won the money off me fair and square she wouldn't have bothered. But they were working together to cheat me, and it hurt her professional pride to watch them rob me so easily. So I told her I owed her, and she told me she'd collect one day." J.P. looked Michael up and down and then shook his head. "Well, I'm obliged to make good on my debts. Tell me, son, you know anything—anything at all—about cattling?"

"No sir."

"How 'bout horses? Can you ride?"

Michael smiled. "Yes. I can ride fairly well, actually.

My mother kept a stable in New York. Raised thorough-breds."

"Well, horses out here ain't fancy. Jest hard working. But at least you know which end is which. We'll start with that. Come on, I'll take you out to the corral. We've just rounded up a new herd of wild mustangs to break for the drive. Let's see what you know."

J.P. got up quickly, his chair scraping across the stone floor, and headed out to the main room again. Michael gulped down the last of his coffee, the sugar a thick syrup at the bottom of his cup, and then got up. He lingered at the door, turning to Tefa.

"Thank you for the food," he said, hoping the woman would look at him.

Tefa bent her head lower at the sound of his voice, her eyes trained on the knife that was chopping onions.

"De nada," she murmured, refusing to meet his glance.

"You coming?" J.P. called from the other room.

Michael bowed his head, a tiny dart of worry lodging itself between his shoulder blades. He thought he had outrun his trouble. But twice that day strangers had seen something in his eyes. *Ojo de mal,* the evil eye, Miguel had called it. It bothered Michael, but there was nothing he could do about it except hope that he would prove their fears wrong.

J.P. was leaning against the porch railing, waiting for Michael. He wore a tall white Stetson with a wide brim decorated with a band of snakeskin. As Michael approached, he tugged the brim down over his eyes to shield them from the glare of the bright afternoon sun. Michael hurried to follow him as he headed across the yard to the corrals.

A soft whistling sound made him glance up. Even J.P. stopped in his tracks and tipped back the white brim. He squinted up at the house. The sound called again, and this time Michael saw the small brown-feathered body of an owl perched on the roof of the house. The creature looked confused, crying into the light with eyes that were transparent circles of gold. It ruffled its feathers, the wings opening and closing noiselessly.

As the owl gazed down at them from the roof of the house, Michael saw a small pair of hands reach from beneath the wings and raise the ruffled bird's mask. A pale, sad face with a small, pouting mouth appeared. Green eyes stared first at J.P. and then at Michael. The creature shuddered, seeing Michael, and hissed in surprise. The mask was quickly lowered and the owl took flight, drifting down from the shallow roof. It grazed the top of J.P.'s head before it swerved off into a stand of oak trees.

"Well I'll be goddamned," J.P. muttered, straightening. "Don't see that much. A screech owl in the middle of the day. Wonder what flushed him out of his hole?"

Michael stared after the retreating wings of the bird, watching with held breath until the moment the bird's form faded into the dull brown background of the oaks. The lid of his left eye itched.

Tefa came to stand at the porch, her brow pulled together in a worried frown as she wiped her hands on her apron. She called out to J.P. and then looked fearfully at the oak trees.

"It's nothing," J.P. said quietly. "Nothing to worry about." But still Tefa remained at the doorway, scanning the skies. "Let's go," J.P. said to Michael, "before Tefa gets any more upset."

"Why would she be upset?" Michael asked as they crossed the yard, heading for a group of low buildings and the corrals. He brushed his left eye, soothing the sudden itch. Dust, he told himself. Just dust.

"Oh, it's an old superstition. Seeing an owl in the daytime is bad luck."

"What kind of bad luck?"

"Some say it means a person's gonna die. I don't hold much with those stories, but you'd be surprised how many people 'round here do."

"Including Tefa?" asked Michael.

"Especially Tefa. If she thought there was a screech owl on the roof of her kitchen in the daytime she'd be off to the hills in a flash, doing God knows what ritual to set things right again. And I need her here to help out with the cooking. Tomorrow I got an army of hands coming from three ranches to work the roundup, so I don't want Tefa getting all panicky and taking off. Don't say anything 'bout it, all right?"

"Of course," Michael answered, only too glad not to have to talk about it at all.

They continued walking behind a long building that was put together with roughly hewn logs, caulked with plaster at the seams and joints. Windows and doors had been cut out, but there was no sheltering porch on which to linger out of the sun.

"This here is the bunkhouse where you can bed down 'til we hit the trail," J.P. said, jerking his thumb in the direction of one of the two opened doors. "I'll find you a spare bed somewhere. And I suppose you'll need a bed-roll too."

Michael looked through the opened door into a long dark room. Lining the walls were small narrow beds, no more than hammered frames and cord netting barely able to hold up the lumpy shuck mattresses. The floors, though, were laid wooden planks, and at one end there was a table and chairs gathered around a wooden stove. The dark room smelled of oiled leather and horse sweat.

At the sudden sound of men shouting and the shrill neighing of a horse, J.P. pulled away quickly from the bunkhouse door and headed for the corrals. Michael followed, hearing a defiant rage in the strident squawls of the horse.

They reached the corral where men perched on the wooden fence shouting angrily. Inside the pen a man was lying on the ground, blood slowly seeping from his downturned face into the hard-packed dust. A white stallion stood over the man, head down, snorting like a bull and scraping furrows into the ground. A thrown saddle lay in the dirt to one side. Hugging the edges of the corral, a man was waving his hat to distract the stallion, while a second man was trying to throw a rawhide rope around the animal's neck. Each time the noose came down the stallion tossed his head away from the rope and stamped harder into the ground. The man with the hat suddenly rushed in, shouting, but the stallion reared up and brought his sharp front hooves down on the fallen man's back, with a loud bellow.

"Goddamn, get back!" J.P. shouted. "Don't push him further!" he warned. "What the hell happened here, John!" J.P. demanded of an older man leaning against the fence, cursing under his breath. "I thought I told you to leave that goddamn stallion alone. You were supposed to shoot him if you had to once the mares were brought in."

"I got here too late to stop it, boss. I was out working on the grub wagon when Ned came and got me. Told me that damn hotheaded Striker had roped in the Ghost and was bragging about how he was gonna put on the saddle and screw it down. I came as quick as I could, but not quick enough," the older man concluded.

"That stallion's a killer all right," a younger boy with wheat-colored hair said. "Turned on his own when he realized we'd trapped them in the corrals. Killed two mares and near busted through the fence before we could get the rawhide on him and cut him out. Even that took four men. But you know Striker, sir. Don't see a horse like the Ghost very often, and I know he's been itching after that stallion ever since we seen him two years ago. So he started bragging about how he was a good enough buster to bring the horse down. With three men holding him he got the bit on all right. The stallion sort of went hame-headed and just stood there. But you could a'known there was gonna be trouble jest by the light in his eyes. Full of fire. Soon as the saddle went on and Striker in it, all hell broke loose. Striker tried, but he was slow hitting the saddle, that horse was bucking so fast, sunfishing one minute, piledriving the next. You could see daylight between Striker and the saddle. Striker was clawing the leather, but it was too late. Lost his grip and I lit out for John. Almost seemed like that horse was waiting for Striker to get on just so he could get him."

Michael looked at the man Striker, lying facedown in the dust, the deep imprint of a hoof on his back, the pooled blood near his face turning brown. Over him the stallion continued to snort, shaking his body furiously, the long mane whipping back and forth. The white flanks were gray with dust and sweat. Foam lathered his neck and gathered at the corners of a steel bit. There was no mouthpiece to the bit but a wide noseband, which was intended to curb the horse by cutting off his wind at the nostrils. The horse tossed back his head, his eyes rolling wildly, as he fought against the hard steel.

The bit made Michael angry, and he took a careful look at the stallion. "That's not a wild horse. Breeding's too good," he said, appraising the long sleek head, the clean white legs, and the fine hair of the mane and tail. The mares, milling in a second corral, were of stocky build, their hides scrubby, their tails and manes long and shaggy. Almost all of them were colored shades of dirty brown and sorrel.

"Happens out here sometimes," J.P. explained. "A Mexican estate will lose a good thoroughbred to the plains. The horse starts running wild, gathering up a herd of mares, and sooner or later you get one of these powerful creatures. Raised on buffalo grass and free range, they're something else again. Every man as sees him wants to own him. But there's too much spirit and too much intelligence in a horse like that to be brought under the saddle. They'd just as soon kill as be broken."

"My mother kept horses like that."

"Did she?" J.P. said without much conviction.

"That's a stupid piece of tack for a horse of that temperament," Michael said angrily.

"What the hell do you know about it?" J.P. snapped.

"Enough not to use a breaking bit on any good horse."

"Who's the tenderfoot?" John asked under his breath.

"Get my shotgun, Ned," J.P. ordered.

"No," Michael blurted out, grabbing the boy's collar to keep him from moving.

"Think you can do better, son?" J.P. snapped, his eyes narrowed.

Michael remembered all the afternoons spent watching his mother gentle her fierce horses, sitting on the fence as she coaxed and cajoled, charmed them with her words. He remembered her slender white arms as she pulled herself up onto the back of a tyrant horse, its head bowed respectfully. And on them she had ridden, small and slight as thistle down, the reins held lightly in her confident hands. There was much in the West that was strange to him, but here was something he knew how to do. Eileen had taught him well.

"Yessir. Give me a lighter bit."

J.P. gave him a searching look, surprised by the confidence in Michael's voice. "Out here a man is only as good as his nerves," he said gravely. "You sure you got enough?"

"Just let me try before you shoot him. I know what to do," Michael answered and released his hold on Ned's collar.

"That cowboy out there thought so too," J.P. pointed out.

"The stallion is worth it." Michael turned to the boy Ned. "Get me a lighter bit. Something nicer."

J.P. nodded his agreement to Ned. The boy raced up to the bunkhouse as the other men waited in tense silence. Ned returned a moment later carrying a racking bit in his hands. It was simple, engraved cheeks in dual graceful curves, and the mouthpiece was no more than a narrow bend. He handed it to Michael, who slung it over his shoulder with a small grunt of approval. Then Michael turned to the fence, his hand resting briefly on the post as he gathered his wits.

His confidence wavered as he faced the angry stallion. But when Michael looked into the stallion's smoky eyes, he found himself smiling, recalling his mother's horses. They had all carried the same shifting light in their eyes. The stallion raised his head, and along the arched neck the hide was smooth as silk. Around the quivering nostrils, steam from his heated breath curled over the steel bit. Instinctively, Michael turned his head slightly to the left. He paused, seeing the wild stallion shimmer in the light, vaporous as a desert mirage. The steel color of his body faded into the blue sky and only the flowing white of the mane and tail was visible, like the crest of a wave breaking to the shore. So it must have been with his mother's horses, he thought distantly; creatures of fire and air born out of her tales.

Michael climbed up and over the sides of the fence and into the corral. The stallion bellowed in warning, his head thrown back as he bared his teeth. He raised up on his haunches, pawing at the air, and then came down hard, pounding crescent-shaped indentations in the dust with his hooves. But Michael remained calm, walking slowly around the perimeter of the corral. When the stallion eased into a wary quiet, Michael began to speak in a low voice that rose from the pit of his stomach and through the hollows of his chest.

At first his voice sounded strange to Michael. All his life it was Eileen McBride who had spoken the spell-charming words of a story. It was the soft music of her voice that had seduced men and horses alike. But in his chest and in his throat the words had changed. They were his stories now. And from his mouth his voice issued in a dark murmur, like the rumble of thunder too distant to frighten but loud enough to command attention.

"Once in years past the Tuatha De Danann rode out on their great horses, and beneath a sun-starved sky changed the winter's gray into the spring's green. Their bridles were made of silver and their saddles of gold, and none but the old race of kings could ride upon their backs. But there came a time when the Tuatha de Danann were driven underground by their enemies, the Milesians. The great horses were scattered over the land to survive without masters and without peer. Though alone, they lived long, for by their own enchantments they could throw off the hand of death. There were none so fine and proud as these horses with flesh made of fire and wind, and their eyes gleaming bright to prove they were not formed out of the earth's dull clay."

The stallion lowered his head, the long white mane falling like water over the curved neck. His heaving breath left dark stains in the dry dust. His flanks trembled wearily. Michael edged closer and continued speaking.

"Once in Connaught a king had been fortunate to capture the last of these great horses. But he was wise enough to know that though he might possess such a treasure, only by the horse's consent would he ever be able to ride upon that royal back. But the king had a foolish groom and, not knowing the prize in his master's stable, was tempted. The arrogant groom tried to mount this magnificent beast. But the horse reared and, throwing off the base-born fool, trampled him under its sharp hooves. Blood and bone crushed into the earth. Then faster than a thought the horse broke free and galloped away to the sea's edge. There he plunged into the sea, the white waves breaking against his chest. Away he swam, away, away, his noble head no more than foam upon the water. And the last of the great breed was gone from Ireland, over the ocean to a land without men."

The stallion had lifted his white head, the ears pricked forward to catch the sound of Michael's words as the

man walked in a circle, the racking bit on his shoulders
and his hands resting quietly at his sides. He continued to
speak, his voice still no more than a low rumble. Tighter
and tighter Michael wove the circle around the horse, the
murmured words casting a net until at last he could reach
out and touch the creature.

A man at the fence cried out a warning but was
shushed instantly by someone else. Michael stared into
the horse's eyes and saw the white foaming crest of a
wave breaking behind the black-mirrored iris. He laid his
hand along the stallion's neck. The flesh quivered beneath his palm, but the horse permitted the gesture. Michael let his hand stroke the sweated hide, gentling the
proud horse with whispered words of praise; Eileen's
words to the great horses of the Tuatha De Danann. He
took hold of the breaking bit and removed it, dropping it
to the ground. The horse leaned forward, the great head
close to Michael's face, and breathed hot, moist exhalations into Michael's upturned palm. Then Michael carefully placed the racking bit over the stallion's head. The
horse bristled, but only for a moment, chomping down
on the thin metal bar more with interest than outrage.
Michael led the horse away to the other side of the corral,
still stroking his neck and speaking words of praise.
Dimly he heard behind him the soft scurry of men coming to get Striker's trampled body. Michael rubbed the
horse's nose and scratched him on the bony forehead between the wide-set eyes.

In the sky above, the screech owl called, the eerie whistle rising over the hushed quiet of the corral. Michael
glanced up quickly as it glided overhead, its body casting
a small shadow over the ground. Still crying, it flew over
Striker's limp body, held up between two men. Striker
stirred and lifted his bloodied head to the passing owl.
His battered face was purple with a spreading bruise, but
the lips were nearly gray as they parted in terror. Michael
saw a flash of gold, and a little hook tumbled out of the

owl's uncurled talons. It fell downward in the air and touched Striker on the lips.

Striker bucked against the men holding him, suddenly racked with coughing, the blood spattering over the front of his shirt. Michael stood still beside the stallion, watching with cold fear as Striker twisted and fought like a caught trout. A white-thread of light stretched from Striker's mouth and spiralled upward until it gathered in a faint mist under the outstretched wings of the owl. The owl banked into the wind, turned toward the open plains, and silently flew away.

The light faded from Striker's face and he sagged heavily. The two men holding him buckled with the sudden weight of Striker's unconscious body as they half dragged and half carried him to the fence. There other hands lifted his broken body over the fence and carried him up to the bunkhouse.

The stallion nickered softly, close to Michael's face. Michael released his tight hold on the halter and forced himself to calm his pounding heart before he spooked the horse further. The men remaining leaned on the fence, watching Michael and the wild stallion. It was hard to read their faces hidden in the shadow of their hats, but Michael could hear the expectation in their silence. They were waiting for him to mount up. Even J.P. had leaned his body into the fence, one hand tugging on his mustache.

Michael inhaled; from the horse's sweated hide he smelled the salty tang of sea foam. He remembered that Poker Alice had said the creatures he ran from would not leave him alone, but at least out here in the West he might find help. If Michael was right and this wild stallion the color of moonlight carried the old lines, then he might have an ally in this strange country. Michael stroked the horse's neck, sliding his body alongside the right flank of the stallion, his hands touching the withers, smoothing down the shoulders and to the middle of the stallion's back. There Michael braced his arms and raised himself over the back of the stallion, letting his legs dangle a bit off the ground, just enough to let the stallion feel his weight and make its own decision. The stallion pranced to the side, surprised. Michael held on and the stallion quieted and seem to accept the burden of extra weight.

Encouraged, Michael pulled himself up higher and swung his leg over the back of the horse. The stallion stirred again, his head thrown down between his forefeet in sudden confusion. But Michael held the reins steady and clamped his thighs firmly around the stallion's sides. He slowly eased himself down onto the horse's back, gradually letting the horse feel his full weight. The stallion jogged backward at first, his ears laid flat, his head tossing uncertainly as the metal rings of the bit clinked brightly. Michael leaned forward, his chest resting along the stallion's neck, and spoke into the twitching ears.

"I will not command you, but go as you would have us."

The stallion snorted and then settled in his stance. Lifting his head proudly, he began to trot around the corral, the tail held high and sprayed out in the wind.

Twice around the corral the stallion carried Michael, and when Michael pulled gently on the reins, the stallion halted and waited. With a grateful sigh, Michael dismounted and walked slowly to where the silent line of men waited at the fence. His hands were shaking as the tension began to leave his body. When he climbed over the fence, J.P. was the first to grab his hand and shake it.

"Goddamn. Goddamn, I guess you do know something about horses, Mr. McBride. You got yourself a job as a wrangler."

And suddenly Michael found himself surrounded by men, pumping his hand and slapping him on the back. "Mighty fine job. Ain't seen nothing like it. Tenderfoot and all. . . ."

Though embarrassed by their praise, Michael accepted

it, his hand aching where they shook it hard.

"And Striker?" he asked, though he knew the answer.

J.P. frowned and kicked at a stone with the toe of his boot. "Spurs have rung their knell."

"He's dead, mister," Ned offered, seeing the look of confusion in Michael's face. "They took him up to the bunkhouse already to lay him out."

"The owl—" Michael started to say and then stopped at the dark expression on J.P.'s face. Michael saw J.P. shake his head almost imperceptibly, warning him not to say anything more.

"Striker have any kinfolk?" J.P. quickly asked the older man.

"None as far as I know. Came out from Arkansas on his own," John answered.

J.P. turned to Michael. "You can take his saddle then and bedroll. No sense in it going to waste. Get Ned here to show you Striker's bunk and get settled in. John, will you see to the service for Striker later tonight?"

"Yessir," the older man replied and then turned to the men lingering by the corral fence. "All right, boys, back to work," he ordered, and around him men started moving away reluctantly.

A cowboy with a dark brown face and thick black hair stopped to vigorously shake Michael's hand. In his other hand he held a battered black hat. *"Muy bien, muy bien."*

"Come on, Ramon," John barked. "There's too much to do to stand here jawing."

Ramon smiled, and in the brown face his teeth were a gleaming white. "There's always too much to do, Señor O'Connor." Then he shrugged and replaced his hat on his head. *"Los muertos al pozo y los vivos al negocio,"* he said evenly as he left.

"What did he say?" Michael asked.

"The dead to the grave and the living to their business," J.P. answered. He strolled away from the corral, heading back to the main house and shouting orders across the yard as he went. Michael found himself alone with Ned and John.

"I'm Ned Darling. Got a name, mister?" Ned asked, leaning back on his heels to gaze up at Michael. Light brown freckles speckled his cheeks and nose, and a thin white scar crossed his chin. His pale, sun-bleached hair fell in a loose fringe over earnest dark blue eyes.

"Michael McBride," Michael answered.

"Knew you had to be an Irishman," John said. "I ain't heard those stories for thirty years since my pa died. He was a great storyteller back then. Name's John O'Connor. And it seems you picked the right time to come, Mike. We can use a good wrangler right now." John stuck out a hand for Michael to shake. A thin, wiry man, he had powerful forearms but hands that were small and neat. His hair was gray and thick, cut long over the collar of his white shirt. His face was finely boned, but the sun had browned the skin, and it was wrinkled and folded over light gray eyes. A white beard and mustache hid most of his mouth.

"Wish it could have been sooner," Michael said softly. "That man might still be alive."

"Well, Striker always was one for living risky. Good buster and worked hard. Just didn't have much sense most of the time. Probably how he would have wanted to go. Had his boots on, anyway."

Michael glanced back at the bloodstains seeping into the dry earth and recalled the look of fear on Striker's face. Probably not how he had wanted to die at all. It wasn't the stallion that had killed him. Michael turned back, aware that John was talking to him.

"Go on up now with Ned to the bunkhouse and get squared away. Then the two of you come down to the far corral. The boys'll be cutting out their choices for the drive soon and I want 'em rounded up together. Every man will be riding range tomorrow, including the pair of you. I expect you'll keep the stallion?" John asked Michael. "Though can't say how good a cutting horse he'll make."

Michael looked at the white stallion waiting silently, but ears held alert as if listening.

"He'll do all right for me," Michael answered.

"And probably no one else," John snorted. "Still, he's a fine-looking horse, and if he's got a lick of sense you'll do all right on him. He'll need a name. Around here he's been known as the Ghost. But I guess he's got too much life in him for that name."

Michael scratched his head and then smiled. "Mo Neart."

"What's that?" Ned asked.

"Irish. Means 'my strength.' "

"You're gonna need a lot of that just to get through the next few days. The roundup is hard work, and you best be ready to wear off the hide on yer backside," John said with a faint smile.

"I'll do my best," Michael answered.

"And maybe some more," John muttered, walking off to where two men were laying out branding irons.

"Come on," Ned said. "If you're gonna work you'll need to get out of those city clothes. They won't last a day around here."

"I don't have anything else," Michael answered.

"Let's see what Striker left behind." And then Ned stopped and touched Michael on the arm. His face held a concerned expression. "Don't bother you wearing a dead man's clothes, does it? Some folks get notions about such things."

"No," Michael lied. "It's all right." And he gave Ned a friendly shove toward the bunkhouse.

"Yessir. Dead ain't coming back, so might as well someone else use them."

Not coming back, Michael thought uneasily, and suddenly he wondered where Eileen had gone when she had left behind the wooden image in her place.

Five

Michael turned in his sleep and groaned. Every bone hurt, every muscle ached, and the narrow bed with its sagging shuck mattress did nothing to ease the terrible pain of his spine and hips. He opened his eyes and found he faced the open door of the bunkhouse, the gray light of false dawn giving way to a rosy blush across the sky. Why did he hurt so much? he wondered. And why everywhere?

He tried to close his hands into a fist but found he couldn't bend his swollen fingers. It didn't matter that he had worn leather gloves the last four days. The skin on his palms had been too soft for the work he was doing, and he had a row of pearl-sized blisters on each hand. All he could hope for was that they would break and then harden into calluses soon. Michael closed his eyes again, even though he knew that in another minute Ned would be standing over him, shaking his shoulder and calling him out of the lumpy bed to start the day's work. Michael curled deeper into the thin blanket, hoping to find a morsel of painless sleep.

He heard the soft footfall and braced for the touch on his shoulder.

"Hey, Mike, come on, Mike. Get up now. Joshua's got sinkers. Get up now and we're first in line."

Michael threw off the blanket and stretched his aching legs over the side of the bed. Around him weary cowboys slept, some snoring loudly, rolled like sausages in their blankets, some with their arms flung wide over the sides of the narrow beds, big-knuckled hands dragging to the floor. The crowded room stank with the odor of horse sweat and unwashed clothes. A thin, pallid cowboy whom Ned had called a "lunger" hacked loudly in his restless sleep, the cough deep and racking in his chest.

Michael squinted up at Ned and smiled. He was eating, a white biscuit in each hand. Bacon grease lined the edges of his shiny lips. In the four days they had worked together, Michael had learned that outside of horse wrangling and cattle, Ned thought only of food. "Tell me, Ned, are you always eating?"

"Always hungry," Ned answered with a grin. " 'Sides, Joshua's the best camp cook there is, and I should know. I've eaten at quite a few roundups. Joshua is generous with the sugar and packs extra canned peaches. Good thing J.P. signed him on to the drive. Long days out on the High Plains makes a man loco for good food. Work better when your belly's full!"

"Work better with sleep," Michael grumbled.

Ned laughed, hunching his thin shoulders, and took another bite of his biscuit. "Get plenty of that at the end of the drive," he said, little white crumbs spraying out. "Come on. Let's go!"

Michael finished dressing quickly, Striker's clothes still feeling strange on his body: the trousers too long, the width of the jacket too wide at the shoulders. The red bandanna and checkered flannel shirt were permeated with Striker's scent, and in the deep pockets of the vest,

Michael had found his tobacco and papers, a small folding knife, and a woman's gold earring. As they had buried Striker in his boots, John O'Connor had lent Michael an old pair of his. The boots were a little too large and rubbed against his toes where they curved into points. Michael was learning to accustom himself to the awkward feel of the boots; the high heels that pitched him forward when he walked and the narrow, pointed toes that pinched.

"Come on, Mike. Hell, if you ain't slow," Ned complained.

"I'm coming, I'm coming," Michael answered, wincing at the blisters on his toes as he slid his foot forward into the boot. Every step sent a pain shooting from his heels to his hips. Though he was an accomplished rider, he had never spent so much time on the back of a horse as he had in these last days. Now he walked with his legs bowed, knees turned out and his shins sore. He looked down at himself and gave a short barking laugh, thinking he looked like a man who'd been riding a barrel.

Outside the bunkhouse lay more sleeping men wrapped in blankets and quilts and scattered over the dew-dampened ground. After the first night, Michael had asked a pale red-haired cowboy why he slept outside instead of in the bunkhouse. The man had given Michael a huge grin, pushing back the wide brim of his white hat to stare at the clear morning sky.

"Bedbugs in them mattresses 'bout drive you crazy with itching," he replied. " 'Sides, too many years driving herd. Get's so a man likes to wake to the clean sight of the sky. Not some cowpoke's stinking foot in yer face."

Michael inhaled deeply, letting the fresh air cleanse his head of the sour bunkhouse smell. Ned waved to a man standing bare-chested before a small rectangular mirror. He was shaving, something that surprised Michael, as he had noted that few cowboys during the roundup took the trouble to wash much, let alone shave. His own face had begun to acquire the scratchy stubble of a beard.

"Who's that shaving?" Michael asked.

"Jim Delaney. He's a regular with the ladies. Got a mess a good stories to tell," answered Ned.

"Probably because he's well acquainted with water," Michael added.

As they continued walking toward the open fields, Michael could see the smoke rising from different cook camps. Three ranches had joined together to accomplish the task of rounding up the nearly wild longhorns into herds of trail-ready cattle. They would share in doing the hundred odd tasks that needed to be done before any ranch could send its own herd out on the drive heading north. Saddles and tack would be mended, rawhide ropes braided, horses broken and shod, cattle sorted by brands into separate herds, and the mavericks and calves with no brands marked with the smoldering irons. But perhaps as important as the work, Michael had discovered, was that in such a large gathering of men rarely given to close community, there would be an opportunity to talk and exchange news. And, Michael had learned to his unexpected pleasure, wild tale telling. On the second night of the roundup, a tall lanky cowboy with a boyishly honest face named Finbar Simons had kept a crowd of deadweary cowboys awake and open mouthed with incredulity at his tales. It seemed to Michael that the man had no end of amazing stories, all of them seeming almost true, but each bearing the colorful stamp of invention.

"I don't expect my stories to be believed necessarily," said Finbar with a wink when Michael protested, "just my ingenuity respected." After that Michael remained quiet and let the stream of Finbar's stories wash over him without worrying about the finer points of truth.

Though the sun had yet to appear in the sky, many wranglers and cowboys had already awoken to the day's tasks. They were gathered in small clots around the cook camps, wiping yesterday's dust and grit from their haggard faces, drinking coffee and talking in low voices. The orange pinpricks of lit cigarettes burned brightly in the gray light. The air carried the sharp smell of the tobacco mingled with the damp, sweet scent of mesquite trees and strong coffee.

They stopped in front of a neat campfire at the back end of a chuck wagon. The tail of the wagon was down, holding an array of pots and dishes and a small area for cooking. The back of the wagon was fitted with an elaborate warren of cubby spaces designed to hold tins of food, coffee, sugar, and flour. Joshua, the cook, was hovering over a Dutch oven that rested on the coals of the cookfire. He was whistling softly through his teeth and checking the contents that steamed beneath the lid. Joshua was an older black man, himself once a trail hand on two different ranches. He had salted hair, but his brown face was robust and his eyes, despite the smoke of the fire, clear as obsidian. And though his legs curved into a near circle from so many years on the back of a horse, his walk was spry.

Most of the cowboys and wranglers that Michael had met in the recent days were young, like himself. John O'Connor had laughed when Michael remarked on it after the first day.

"It's a hard life, son. Cowboys don't often get the chance to get old. If they don't die of drink, they die of the cold or get broken on some trail. And if they don't die on the trail, they go bust gambling. And if they escape all that, well, son, they become a cook. Which is why no man alive messes with a cook, not even the trail boss, 'cause cook's meaner, more ornery, and more cantankerous than a rattler. Just remember that."

Michael remembered and made a point of always being respectful to Joshua. At first he found it difficult to imagine Joshua being cantankerous to any man just in from the plains. Chasing cattle in the brush country or running down strays was long, hard work. Joshua seemed to know in advance the cowboy's need before he even dismounted, as if he still shared the weariness and hunger in his own bones. He always had coffee ready and a bite to eat for any hungry drover that came by his chuck wagon. But Michael had seen him curse out a cowboy stupid enough to ride his horse too close to the cookfire and spray fine ashes into the food. Joshua had pulled out a short-handled quirt and snapped it hard against the horse's flanks, driving both man and beast away with loud, swearing curses.

"Well, Mike, I see the boy done brought you 'round here at last," Joshua said, looking up from the Dutch oven with a smile. "I was thinking I was gonna hafta give these sinkers to those wranglers from the Lazy L. Ain't no good letting them burn waiting for you, now is there?"

"No sir," Ned said eagerly. "I could use another right now."

"Son, you got a hollow leg. Your mouth is everywhere hungry. But go on. If I don't feed you, you'll go around all day complaining."

Ned reached into the Dutch oven and pulled up two biscuits, still steaming. He was cursing at the heat, blowing on his fingers but unwilling to set the biscuits down.

Michael laughed and waited for Joshua to bring out the rest of the biscuits on a tin plate before he took one.

Joshua handed him a thick-handled mug of black coffee. "Take a good swig of that now. Got a long day before you. They're fixing to finish rounding up all the herds today over other side of the river. Heard the trail boss from the Double Triangle is heading out tomorrow. We won't be long behind."

"Come on, we got to bring in the remuda," Ned urged, heading for the rope corral where his horse waited. Michael gulped down his coffee and started limping after Ned.

"Hold on there, Mike," Joshua called, reaching into one of the smaller cubbyholes of the chuck wagon. He pulled up a small whiskey bottle filled with an oily brown liquid. "Here now, try some of this remedios on those aches and see if it don't help." Joshua handed the bottle to Michael.

"Thank you. What's in here?" Michael asked, uncapping the bottle and giving it a quick sniff. He grimaced at the rancid odor and pulled the bottle away from his nose with a sharp jerk.

Joshua gave a rumbling laugh. "That's rattlesnake oil. Don't drink it, now. Jest rub it on where it hurts. Do you good, son."

Michael recapped the bottle quickly, trying to ignore the queasiness in his stomach as the rancid odor lingered in his nostrils. But he inclined his head in thanks to Joshua and pocketed the bottle in his vest.

"Ned, wait," Michael called, and he hurried his steps to catch up to the boy. By the time Michael had reached him, Ned had already mounted up on his small grulla horse, Mouse, and was nervously watching the exposed brow of the rising sun.

"Shake yer leg, Mike. O'Connor'll be down here soon enough and get all riled if that remuda ain't brought in."

"Let Mo Neart do it then," Michael offered as he pulled himself up and over the back of the big white stallion.

"You're crazy. That horse ain't got that much sense. He goes where you tell him, is all," Ned answered peevishly.

"Come on, I'll prove it to you," Michael said, and he touched Mo Neart's sides with his heels.

They rode out over the open plain and headed east, into the sun that was opening over the edge of the earth like a golden eye. Mo Neart's coat shone a bright saffron color as it absorbed the warm light of the sun. After a short ride, Michael tugged gently on the reins to let the stallion know he wanted to stop.

"What are you doing?" Ned asked as Michael dismounted and whispered into the stallion's ear. He tied the loose reins around the saddlehorn. Then he patted the horse on its neck and the horse shot away from him, the sharp hooves thudding over the ground and casting divots of dry earth.

"Just watch," Michael said as the stallion disappeared, fading like a pale star into the rising curtain of gold light.

"If you ain't just the idiot," Ned complained. "It's too soon to be letting that horse loose on the plain. He ain't been broke long enough. He won't come back. And you'll be walking back to camp, 'cause I sure as hell ain't taking you, 'cause I'm gonna be off finding that remuda and aw hell, why'd you go and do that?"

"Be quiet, Ned," Michael said softly. He started to whistle a tune, one he remembered from the stables. Eileen could stand in an empty pasture, the horses nowhere to be seen, and whistle. Within moments they would appear, charging through the dark shelter of the trees and out from the hidden edges of the field. Michael whistled, letting the sound of the tune carry him back to the scent of damp earth and the sight of his mother laughing joyfully as she was surrounded by her horses.

"Well I be goddamned," Ned swore. Out of the golden horizon a herd of horses came thundering toward them. Mo Neart drove them, his head held high, his huge body commanding them to follow. One coyote mare broke loose and he quickly nipped at her flanks, forcing her back into the compact herd.

Michael kept whistling, letting the tune be carried over the drumming sound of the horses' hooves. Then he threw back his head and laughed as he found himself standing among the milling herd of horses, their gleaming flanks shining with sweat from their run. Dust rose up from their tramping hooves and they butted their heads against one another's shoulders and flanks, trying to reach Michael. He held out his hands, palms up, and rubbed their muzzles, greeting as many of them as he could touch. Mo Neart pushed through the throng of horses, and after rubbing the stallion's forehead in thanks, Michael got up on the stallion's back.

"Well then?" Michael asked the astonished Ned. "What do you think now?"

"That you'd better teach me that tune," Ned replied with a grin as he kicked Mouse. The grulla horse snorted, then lifted her dainty hooves into a trot.

"It's called 'The Road to Lisdoonvarna.' "

Ned frowned. "I can't say that. How 'bout we call it 'From Hell to Breakfast'?" Speaking of which, I sure could use some right now."

"Why are you always so hungry?" Michael teased.

"Back home I had eight other brothers and sisters, Mike. I was lucky if I got anything to eat at all when I was a young 'un."

"You're not that old now."

"Fourteen," Ned said with a shrug. "Out here that's old enough to do a man's job and get a man's portion on my plate," Ned answered brusquely.

"Do you miss your family?"

"No. J.P. runs the ranch good enough. And O'Connor's a pretty decent skin to work for. Don't drink or get nasty like my paw did when he was rollicky. Got me a place to sleep, wages, and food that I don't have to fight over. This here is my second drive. Another couple of years of wrangling and I'll be able to drive cattle instead of horses."

"Is that what you want to do with your life?" Michael asked, suddenly envious of Ned's confidence. Had he ever had such a clear vision of his own future? Michael wondered. He had gone through the motions of being educated, good schools, engineering training, but he had never associated the daily work that he had done with his future. It was as if he had spent most of his life waiting for it to begin.

"Yessir. What else is there? I like it out here. I'd like to work point, like Jim Delaney or Ramon, and then maybe be trail boss one day. Take over from O'Connor when he gets too old," he said with a grin.

"Isn't that O'Connor coming up to meet us now?" Michael asked, seeing the older man riding up on a huge cream-colored palomino. Next to him was a smaller man with long, flowing black hair, riding a compact sorrel mare with a white star on her forehead. The mare had no saddle but a blanket thrown over her back and a light arrangement of rawhide stirrups. The man rode easily, his body moving in rhythm with the smooth gait of the horse.

"Aw hell," Ned groaned. "We're gonna get cussed out for being late."

"Who's that with him?" Michael asked.

"Jake Talking Boy," Ned answered. "But most people 'round here just call him Jake. He's a half breed. Mother was Apache and his paw a buffalo hunter. He knows things, and that makes him a good man for the trail."

John O'Connor slowed his horse as Michael and Ned approached them, the remuda thronging around them.

"Glad to see you boys were fixing to join us this morning," John said, slowing his horse to a walk. He pushed back the brim of his hat and squinted into the light, letting the sun brighten his weathered face. Though he rested easily in his saddle, Michael saw that one hand was laid over the narrow butt of a rifle sticking out of a case on the saddle. The second man, Jake Talking Boy, was scanning the horizon, as if looking for something.

"I guess it's my fault," Michael said. "I'm still having trouble getting up early enough."

"Well you're lucky today, son," John answered. "Camp's been a mess over the last hour. Cowboy from the Double Triangle come in half bled to death, leg and side all torn up. Seems he met up with a panther just before sunrise and the two didn't take to each other none. Said he tried to shoot it but missed. Thing gave a couple of good swipes and then took off for the brush. Now I got cowboys more interested in hunting big cats instead of longhorns," John said with a frown. "Hell, they're all trigger happy and more than likely to shoot each other."

"That panther won't come out in the day," Jake said softly. "He's a night creature and his power grows weak in the sunlight."

"Well, maybe so. It's probably just attracted to the smell of so many cookfires. Won't be surprised if it don't walk into camp tonight and order up a plate of Joshua's stew. Always knew that cook had a good reputation." He laughed to ease the tension.

Ned cocked his head to one side and grinned. "Say John, that's why you come out here, ain't it? We ain't late, you just wanted to make sure me and Mike weren't meeting up with that cat on our ownsome."

"Huh," John snorted, but a smile tugged the corners of his mouth beneath the mustache. "You boys ain't much meat for that cat's breakfast. But I figured I wasn't about to lose my wranglers just yet. Come on now, best be heading back and soon, before those cowboys start forming a posse."

"We're there," Ned said, snapping his reins over the grulla's back. Mouse startled into motion, picking up her pace to a fast trot as the remuda dutifully followed.

Jake brought his horse alongside Michael's and tipped the brim of his black hat in greeting. He had a strong profile, his smooth skin earth-colored and the cheekbones high twin arches in the broad oval face. But his eyes were a dark green, and Michael saw that the long hair that had looked black from a distance held shades of deep auburn in the sunlight.

"Name's Jake," he introduced himself. "That's a fine horse you got there."

"Thank you," Michael answered, pleased by the compliment. "I'm Michael—Mike," he added, liking the simpler sound.

"Watched you the other day at the corral. My grand-father used to break horses like that, by talking to them. Said it was Kiowa magic. Where did you learn it?"

"My mother," Michael answered. "In New York City."

Only Jake's green eyes widened slightly to show his surprise; the rest of his face remained calm. "Hah." He nodded in agreement. "My mother too had wisdom and magic from her tribe. But I didn't learn it," he said almost apologetically. "Too much of my father in me, I guess. Be seeing you, Mike." He nodded again and then nudged his horse into a canter.

It occurred to Michael as Jake rode away that he wasn't at all sure what wisdom or magic Eileen McBride had given him. She had filled his head with stories of imaginary people and magical places. Michael had hardly known how to exist in the real world of New York. At the social events to which he went unwillingly, he would stand brooding along the wall. The studies at college seemed withering and dry compared to the rich, fantastic events of his mother's tales.

Even when he was with the few friends he had made, he could never escape the sensation of being alone. He laughed uneasily at their jokes, as a man trying to rapidly translate from one language to the next. He wanted to be one of them but was always more keenly aware of their differences rather than similarities. For the first time in his life, Michael discovered that he resented Eileen McBride. Resented the hold she had claimed over his life; resented the sound of her seductive voice making him deaf to the ordinary speech of his friends; resented the loneliness into which his own peculiarity plunged him.

Mo Neart huffed in the morning air, and Michael bowed his head, flushed with a sudden remorse, feeling the smooth gait of the powerful horse carrying him as easily as sunlight. His mother had given him this, he thought, as he stroked the neck of the stallion. This love of horses, this touch. The stallion's silky hide was warm beneath his palm, the pulse solid and steady. Michael looked up into the horizon and saw the morning sunlight cascading to the ground in a hot, shimmering curtain. A mirage shaped itself before his eyes. Thin figures twisted like black tendrils of smoke in the rippling haze, and one by one a row of spear-carrying horsemen emerged to spread themselves along the edge of the earth.

In the air overhead, black birds flapped their wings, spiraling upward in the heat. Michael tensed, seeing the legs and webbed feet that dangled from beneath their elongated forms. His hands closed into tight fists around the reins. This too his mother had given him: the curse of sight. How long, he wondered, before the distant mirage of Red Cap's warriors caught up to him again? He lightly kicked Mo Neart's sides, driving the stallion into a canter and then faster into a gallop, as he felt the urge for flight overtake him once more.

Two days later, amid the flurry of constant work, the roundup was complete, and each ranch had established its herds of cattle and horses on the trail that led to the northern cattle towns. In the early evening, Michael stood wearily, looking out at the remuda of a hundred-odd horses grazing quietly along the banks of a slow-moving river. Spread out behind the horses were two thousand head of cattle, lying contentedly on the grassy bedding ground. Michael faced north, staring at the faint depression in the dirt that marked the northern trail. His long black shadow was cast across the new grass that reached up out of the dried thatch of last year's growth. The sun was slow to set, as if reluctant to leave its daily vigil. Over Michael's head, the sky glowed a furious red and orange. In the east, the horizon was streaked with tongues of lavender and deep blue. There was the faint glimmer of the first evening star.

"Pretty, ain't it?" Standing next to him, Ned sighed.

"Never get tired of seeing the sun go down 'round here."

Michael nodded. "Everything out here is so farflung."

"Wait till we're out on the staked plains. It's just like they say: A man can look farther and see less. You coming?"

"Be there soon," Michael answered, breathing in the cool evening air. The river gave off a fresh odor of clean water.

"Don't wait too long, or food'll be gone," Ned warned.

"I won't." Michael laughed. "Just don't eat my share if you can help it," he said, tugging at the boy's hat brim.

Grinning, Ned straightened his hat again and walked quickly toward a small stand of willow trees that sheltered the chuck wagon and the night's camp.

Michael turned to look out at the river, washed a fading orange in the dying light. It still took awhile to lose the shyness that came over him in the evenings. It wasn't just the old feeling of being a stranger that haunted him. Here it was also being a foreigner to a way of life that all of these men had been born into. He felt sometimes like a fraud, like an actor dressed for a part he didn't really know. Most of the men were friendly enough toward him, though they held him in polite reserve. They might grudgingly respect him for his skill with horses and his prized stallion, but he was still a tenderfoot, asking too many questions and needing too many explanations for what they regarded as simple things.

A calf bleated for its mother and was answered by a deep maternal bawl from somewhere amidst the sea of resting cattle. Michael looked over the horses that were slowly fanning out along the narrow banks in search of tender grass. It was almost easier for Michael to know the men he traveled with by the horses they had chosen for their string. Every man on the drive needed ten horses to carry him through the day-and-night work on the drive. The best horse out of the ten would serve as his most trusted night horse, a calm and intelligent companion in the dark hours of watching cattle. John O'Connor had shown his practical good sense by choosing a string of solid-colored horses, their lines clean and strong. "A good horse is never a bad color," he told Michael. "Stay away from those pintos. They're all inbred." Fox Sumner, the foreman and second in command, had picked out a mixture of rugged horses, including a stout bay big in the chest, that could carry a man across the river without panicking. Jake Talking Boy had favored the smaller, lighter mares, round in the jowls and bright-eyed, their foreheads often starred, their legs in white socks. Ramon had a buttery palomino for his night horse that he called El Mecedor, the "Rocking Chair," and the rest were a mixture of grullas and blacks. Finbar had chosen for his night horse a blue-black gelding he called Black Kettle, which he claimed could find its way back to camp in the darkest of nights, no matter how far a stampede might carry them. "Had enough practice, bringing you home dead drunk," Sumner had retorted.

Jim Delaney, the cowboy Michael watched shave every morning at the ranch, was a handsome man with a narrow long face, framed by thick black hair that swept back from a high white forehead. His eyes were a cold blue, but his mouth was soft, the lips full beneath the fringe of a well-trimmed mustache. He was vain, Michael thought, but also practical. He had chosen a string of mostly roans and sorrels, their hides shades of mahogany red. But his night horse, Tuck, was a scrubby coyote color with a black lobo stripe down the center of her back. Ugly though she was, the mare was smart, and Michael had watched Tuck deftly cutting out cattle and calves from the milling herd without Jim saying much of anything. In fact, Delaney bragged that the horse was smart enough to cut out a jackrabbit from a herd of longhorns. "But is she smart enough to get you out of the way of some jealous husband with a shotgun that's fixing to drill daylight into your liver?" Finbar had asked. Jim had just smiled and smoothed down the sides of his mustache. "Ain't been caught yet."

The brothers Ludie and Barney Strayhorn, were the last two cowboys hired on out of Redwing. They would work drag, bringing up the rear of the herd, and spend their days most likely covered in dust kicked up by the tramping hooves. They were both young, not much older than Ned, and Michael found it difficult sorting out which one was which. They shared the same dull flax-colored hair, hazel eyes, and lantern jaws. When they smiled, their teeth fanned out like picket fences. Though lean in the torso, they were big boned, their wrists and long hands absurdly outsized where they exited the too-short sleeves of their coats. They wore identical hats of a dirty gray color, and when they walked side by side, or rode their matching dun-colored mares, it was near impossible to tell them apart. As far as Michael knew, Ludie was older by a year or two; but he guessed that only because on Ludie's face rough blond hairs had started to show on his upper lip, while Barney's cheeks were still smooth.

"Hey Mike!" Ned called, and Michael turned to see the boy standing by the chuck wagon, waving a tin plate at him. From this distance the warm glow of the campfire looked inviting, and against the huge, nearly naked horizon, the chuck wagon sheltered beneath the willows had a homey appeal. Smoke rose from the cookfire into the fading lavender twilight and carried with it the aroma of Joshua's stewing pot. Michael started walking toward the camp, smiling as he heard Jim Delaney's laughter and caught the soft pleasant sound of a guitar being strummed.

This was their last night of relative comfort before they hit the trail. Ned and Michael had ridden out the day before with Joshua and the chuck wagon and the remuda to join up with the herd that was waiting by the river's edge. Sumner wanted to give the animals a day on the banks of the river to get rested and to eat and drink their fill before the start of the drive. One by one, the cowboys had turned up in camp throughout the day, checking over the last details of the drive before settling into this, the first of many nights away.

Michael entered camp and tipped his hat clumsily to the men already seated around the chuck wagon. He still hadn't gotten used to wearing a hat, and this simple gesture always felt awkward. Why couldn't they just shake hands? he grumbled to himself. He got himself a plate of stew from Joshua and sat down beside Ned.

Finbar sat with his back leaning against a wagon wheel, a small Spanish guitar held across his knees. He was strumming it quietly, singing mostly to himself. Michael was surprised to hear his light tenor voice. Ramon smiled at Michael and nodded in appreciation.

"Finbar is the best at settling the herd at night. He sings to them as if they were babies. Not like you, Delaney, with your crow's voice."

"I ain't never yet heard a longhorn complain," Jim snapped, and he reached into his vest pocket and pulled out a packet of tobacco and papers.

"I have," Finbar said. "Didn't I tell you about the time—"

"Stop," Sumner growled. "I want to fix the watch before you get to jawing Finbar, or there'll be no stopping you."

Finbar shrugged goodnaturedly and was quiet, his fingers resting on the neck of his guitar.

Michael straightened up when Sumner started speaking. As foreman, he was in charge of delegating duties to the trail crew and answered only to John O'Connor for his decisions. He wasn't a tall man, but the harsh tone of his voice carried authority. He was ruggedly handsome, with thick blond hair and piercing blue eyes. He was strong in the arms and as sturdy as his bay horse, with a barrel chest and narrow waist. Michael had watched him over the days of the roundup and knew he was hard working and very demanding.

"It'll be me and Jake first watch. Jim and Ludie second watch." The brothers glanced at each other with concern, and it occurred to Michael they were not used to being split up.

Ludie started to speak. "Mr. Sumner, meaning no disrespect but me and my brother—"

"Would like to ride watch together," Barney finished.

"Time you boys split off each other," Sumner said brusquely. "You ain't even had a piss apart since I've known the pair of you. And I need at least one man with experience riding night herd."

Though clearly unhappy, the Strayhorn brothers accepted Sumner's call without further argument.

"Finbar, you and Barney make up third watch, and Ramon, I'm putting you on with Mike here. Teach him how it's done."

"Can you sing, Señor Mike?" Ramon asked. "Like Finbar here?"

"Not too badly," Michael replied.

"Good. I'll teach you real songs then, the *corridos.*"

"What's that?"

"Blood and spilled guts, son," Jim Delaney answered.

"And honor," Ramon said proudly. "Something I will teach you about, Jim, when you get tired of running from women's husbands."

Jim Delaney grinned as he licked the edge of his rolled cigarette, sealing it. "Well hell, son. By then we'll both be too old to give a good goddamn about something as useless as honor."

Ramon inclined his head and gave a small shrug. *"Si dejas de ser horada, bien pagada.* If you must lose honor, Jim, at least get well paid," he advised with a smile.

"You know, seeing you there in Striker's clothes reminds me of something," Jake said softly to Michael.

"Did you ever hear about Coyote meeting the white man?"

Michael shook his head. "Who's Coyote?"

Jake flashed him a smile for a moment, and then his face was serene again. He put his tin plate down beside him and took up his cup of coffee, wrapping his long fingers around the cup. "Old Coyote is a trickster. Not one to wrangle with if you meet him on the road."

"Go on then," Finbar said, leaning in to hear the story. "Tell it."

Jake nodded. "Well son, it happened one day that Coyote was traveling on the road, minding his own business for a change. As he come over a hill he saw a white man riding up on a big stallion.

"The white man stopped Coyote and said, 'Son, are you that lowest-thieving sonofabitch Coyote feller? I'm out looking for him.' Coyote shook his head. 'Why no, sir, I'm not that Coyote.'

"Well, the white man started insisting. 'You sure you don't know that old Coyote? I am aiming to prove that I can outsmart and outtrick him any day.'

"This boast was too much for Coyote, so he held up one paw and said, 'Mister, I think I can help you. Jest let me go home to my house and get my medicine bag. Then I can take you to that Coyote. But as my home is a long way off, maybe I can use your horse so I can be quick about it?'

" 'All right,' the white man says, and he gets down off the horse. Well, Coyote goes to mount up, but first he secretly pokes that horse with a stick so the horse give a jump. Coyote turns to the man and says, 'Mister, this horse won't let me ride unless I got your hat on.' So the white man gives Coyote his hat. Coyote turns again to the horse and pokes it. Horse jumps. Coyote turns to the white man and says, 'Mister, this horse won't let me ride it unless I got on some clothes. How about giving me your coat?' The white man gives Coyote his coat. Coyote puts on the white man's coat and turns again to the horse and pokes it. Horse jumps again. 'Mister, I think I need all your clothes to make this horse take me home.' So the white man gives Coyote his shirt, his vest, and, last off, his trousers.''

Ned bent his head and started snickering into his sleeve. "I heard this one before," he whispered to Michael.

"Coyote gets all dressed in that white man's clothes. He looked good, too. And then he gets up on the horse and starts to ride off. But at the top of the hill he turns around and shouts back at that white man: 'I am that thieving Coyote you were looking for, mister and I just beat you at your match.' And with that off he rides, leaving that white man standing there buck naked by the road." Jake looked over at Michael and nodded. "Yep. That's what I think of when I see you in Striker's clothes. You done got the clothes, so boys, beware Mike here don't get your horses."

Around Michael, the men laughed; even the Strayhorn brothers erupted into a choking fit of giggles. Michael didn't mind their laughter; being teased made him feel accepted. Their politeness had been more a measure of their distance than good manners.

"So have you heard the story about the buzzard that got his own shadow caught in the swamp?" Finbar asked. "I seen it myself."

Michael shook his head and caught a glimpse of John O'Connor rolling his eyes in mock annoyance. But the trail boss settled down on a log, his legs stretched out before the fire. Then he reached into his vest pocket and pulled out a stubby pipe, which he started packing with tobacco.

"Go on, Finbar," Ned encouraged, giving him a shove with his elbow.

Michael took a sip of his cooled coffee and felt the newly darkened sky beginning to close in around the camp with a cloak of intimacy. Tiny stars began to wink into light. He ate his stew slowly and listened to Finbar with half an ear, his thoughts quieting into a weary peace. Finbar's voice was light and expressive, his hands moving to shape the story, demonstrating the plight of a buzzard stuck in the muck of a swamp by its own shadow. Michael grinned at Finbar's face, mugging the discontented bird.

"And I am telling the truth now, the mud was so thick that even this struggling bird—"

Finbar's voice was suddenly drowned out by a loud squalling scream that shattered the softness of the night.

"Goddamn, what in the hell is that!" Jim Delaney said, standing up straight and staring out beyond the rim of the camp.

A second cry was heard, a long wailing scream, and the silence that followed was eerie and crushing.

"Panther," said Jake, standing up and going to the chuck wagon. He reached under the covered tarp of the wagon's side and pulled out a rifle. "He's out hunting."

"Damn cat. Thought we were shunt of it," John O'Connor murmured, putting down his pipe. He pulled out a partially burning log from the campfire and walked to the dark perimeter of the camp. The smoldering torch threw out an oval of orange light into the darkness.

He walked a few steps out into the darkness, the torch spluttering above him. He cocked his head and listened to the quiet sounds of the night. A horse nickered in warning, and Michael recognized it as Mo Neart.

Michael got up quickly. "The horses—"

"Settle down, son," John said, a hand held out to stop Michael from moving beyond the light of the campfire. "If that cat was after horses he'd a taken one already. They'd all be hollering. Fact is, I can't figure out why them cattle ain't going half off right about now. Almost like we're the only ones as can hear it," he said, peering out at the dark shadow of the riverbank. Michael stood beside John O'Connor and felt a cold band of fear tighten around his chest.

Out in the deep shadows of the night, Michael could see the dim outline of a man walking upright among the cattle. Michael said nothing, afraid to trust his vision and just as afraid not to. The figure wove its way among the sleeping cattle, touching one here and another there. It bent down and then suddenly looked up as if sensing Michael's hard stare.

Michael stumbled back at the pair of burning eyes that glowed bright red in the dark. The black form of the man fell to the ground on all fours. Outlined against the starry night, Michael saw the rounded skull of the panther, the flash of white teeth. The panther screamed. Michael swore he heard the sound of his name beneath its rage. And then without so much as disturbing the cattle around it, as though they were spelled into numbness, the panther grabbed a calf in its huge jaws and bounded away, the white spindling legs dragging over the ground.

And still John O'Connor stared out into the night, brooding but otherwise unmoved. He returned to his seat, leaving Michael standing on the dark border of the camp, his heart pounding wildly against his rib cage.

"Get the watch out there, Sumner," John ordered quietly. "I don't want those cattle getting spooked before we even get off the riverbank. And keep your eyes open."

Sumner and Jake took their night horses from the rope corral near the chuck wagon and rode out quietly to the herd. Joshua rattled the pots and pans of the dinner loudly as he cleaned them and stowed them away for the night. He was muttering under his breath, and every now and then he'd look out in the darkness, shake his head, and give the tin plates another rattle as if to scare off an offending evil.

The rest of the camp fell into an uneasy silence, each man listening to the night. Barney and Ludie whispered, their heads leaning in together. Ned was quiet, but his grim face showed he was determined not be scared. Finbar strummed the guitar but even that had lost its appeal, and he put it away again. Soon Michael could just make out the low, throaty baritone of Sumner singing. He couldn't hear the words, but the tone was soothing.

"Get some sleep, boys," John ordered, still sitting up by the campfire, chewing on the stem of his pipe. "You'll want to be awake come your shift."

Michael went to the chuck wagon where his oilskin and blanket were stored during the day. He rolled them out on the hard ground, his saddle serving as a pillow. Ramon pushed his saddle near Michael's and laid his blankets down on the ground next to him. Then he took a handful of something from his pocket and sprinkled it on the ground.

"What are you doing?" Michael asked quietly when Ramon had finally lay down, his head resting on the canticle of his saddle.

"Hmm?" Ramon murmured, his eyes closed.

"What did you toss on the ground?"

"Mustard seed. To keep away the panther," Ramon answered. "Among my people we call him Tezcatlipaca. It means the 'smoking mirror.' He is a death spirit and very dangerous. But the mustard seed is a strong magic, and he will avoid it if he can."

"Ramon, can I ask you something?" Michael whispered.

"Sí, Señor Mike. There's much you don't know, so ask."

"All the other Mexicans I've met are afraid of me. They don't like my eyes."

"Ojo de mal," Ramon answered knowingly.

"Why doesn't it bother you?" Michael asked, getting up to lean on one elbow.

Ramon sat up and brushed back the thick waves of his shining black hair. His square-sculpted face was half hid in the shadows, but his dark eyes glittered with spears of gold. "That is a long story. But I will tell you. I am a *co-coua,* Señor Mike, one of a twin. But in Mexico when twins are born one is always killed at birth."

"Why?" Michael asked, shocked.

"Because it is believed that if both twins are allowed to survive, one will murder their own parent. So when twins are born the parents will kill one to prevent this. But the twin left living has the magic power of both within its breast. I may walk into a room, Señor Mike, and see the warp of a loom destroyed at my glance, the food burned in the fire at my touch. And yet if I take water into my mouth until it is warm and breathe its purity on all that is in the room, it will be made right again. Your eyes do not scare me because, like me, they have both power for good and bad. In this we are alike. Except that I know what I am and will not cause harm if I can. But do you know yourself, Señor Mike? Do you know how to look with those eyes and not bring harm?"

"No," Michael stuttered. "I don't understand it very well at all."

"Then you should begin to search the answer. Or you will know nothing but trouble." Ramon closed his eyes again and settled his hands over his chest. "But first, sleep. The fourth watch comes too soon."

Michael lay down again on his hard bed and stared up into the swaying branches of a willow tree. He felt as if a door in his heart were opened, just a slight movement, but enough to make him catch his breath. It was true: He hardly knew himself. He had lived as a spectator to his mother's stories and as an unwilling partner to his father's endless games. He knew little enough of his parents' lives, but it was an equal shock for him to discover how much less he knew about himself.

He put his hand to his face, covering the left eye. The slender leaves of the willow tree shivered in the breeze. He moved his hand to cover his right eye and saw, in the branches above, the quick and jagged flight of a small white bird. It sighed and gave a hollow cry, its face hidden behind an outstretched wing. Then it lowered its wing and Michael saw his mother's face, contorted in grief. Two eyes reddened with weeping gazed sadly back at him. Tears stroked the feathered cheeks, and as they fell from her pointed chin they remained suspended among the tangled leaves, glistening like stars.

Six

N o, Mike, you gotta relax your hand when you let
the rope go," Ned was saying, the thin rawhide lariat in
his hand gliding out expertly and dropping over the neck
of a tired roan mare. The mare swished her tail with annoyance at flies that had settled on her flanks and returned to grazing. Ned walked over and loosened the
rope, giving the mare an absent pat on the withers for her
trouble. "You're jest trying too hard."

Michael retrieved his rope from the ground and coiled
it up again in one hand. In the other hand he lightly held
the slack noose and began twirling it over his head as
Ned had shown him.

"That's it, now don't rush. Get it slow and it'll come
fast later. Aim with yer eyes but feel it in the hand."

Michael released his hold on the rope and sent the
noose flying through the air. It landed on the mare's
flanks and slid off to the ground, empty of its catch. The
mare looked up from her grazing, her teeth bared, and
shook her head in derision.

"Aw hell," Michael swore. "I can't even do this standing. How in the goddamn hell can I do it on horseback?"

Ned grinned. "Well, son, you may not be able to throw a hoolihan like a cowboy, but you're starting to cuss like one."

Michael used his thumb to push back the brim of his hat and squinted down at Ned. "Yep, son, after two weeks riding herd," he drawled, "there ain't much I don't know about dust, cow shit, and those crawlie things that keep on trying to join you under yer blankets. I done sing 'til I croaked to a bunch of plug-ugly mealy-nosed sonuvabitch longhorns, and then stayed awake the rest of the night listening to some other drover's godawful noise 'til daybreak. I kin build a smoke to take yer lungs out but ee God, Ned, I cain't throw a rope over a fat old mare standing still."

"Tried running yet?" asked Finbar, coming up behind Michael, a cup of coffee in his hand.

"Who, me or the mare?" Michael said disgustedly. He retrieved his rope once more, coiling it up for later.

Finbar gave a tired laugh and wiped his face with a wet bandanna. They had come in from the drive for lunch, the cattle grazing slowly as they drifted with an easy pace over the sunbaked land. All around them the sky was a faded blue, the sun relentless as it shed its dry white heat. No clouds, no hint of moisture touched the air.

Michael gazed out over the quietly moving herd and sighed. "Doesn't it ever rain out here? Is it always so dry and hot like this?"

"Ain't you never heard about the man that owned hell and Texas both?" Ned asked.

Michael shook his head.

"Well sir, he lived in hell and rented out Texas."

"I believe it," Michael answered grimly.

Finbar rocked back on his heels, an earnest expression on his newly washed face. "And then of course there was the two cowpokes that came off of Noah's ark."

"Noah's ark?" Michael repeated, raising a skeptical eyebrow.

"Yessir. First thing they did was ride around looking for a good dry plain on which to settle down. And after they found it one of them says, 'Grass'll come along fine.' And the other turns to him and says, 'Yep, if we get another rain before the drought sets in.' "

Michael laughed, and the sound cracked in the back of his parched throat. Finbar looked modestly into his coffee cup and took another sip. But when he looked up again, his expression had changed. The eyes gazed out into the glaring sun with a silent longing, searching over the distant horizon.

Finbar sighed, his boyish face suddenly aged, narrow lines creasing the weathered skin of his cheeks. "It's always the same out here. Looking for signs of rain. Watching the sky in hopes of a cloud, listening for the rain crows to cry out their warning that rain is coming, watching the dance of cocks before sunrise. Everyone thirsty; men, cattle, the land . . ." Finbar shook his head and kicked at the dry soil. "In dry weather, all signs fail, my maw used to say, and the only proven prophecy in a drought is that every dry spell ends with rain."

"And then when it does come, it ain't always a blessing," Ned said loudly. " 'Member that one night last year, rain come so hard, the whole trail was swept with gully washers and fence lifters. Lightning spooking the cattle into a stampede and the swollen rivers was too damn dangerous for crossing. Had to wait days for the trouble to end." Ned crossed his arms over his chest, his head lowered, as if shielding himself from the memory. "Cold and soaked to the bone. That's how I remember it."

"But when the sun did come out, it was something to see, the plains burst open blooming," Finbar remembered. "All at once, grass and flowers everywhere. Almost broke a man's heart to see the dry trail look as pretty as a woman's hat."

"Hey, here comes one of the Strayhorn brothers," Michael said. "Alone." At that Ned and Finbar looked back at camp with curiosity. "Which one do you think it is?"

Finbar chuckled. "Lay you odds it's Barney. See, he's got a little jig to his walk that turns left. And Ludie's got one that turns right."

"No, it's Ludie," said Michael, watching the lanky, dun-colored figure approach, arms flapping at his sides like a loosened scarecrow. He walked with his head down, only the crown of his dirty gray hat visible on his head as he appeared to study the dust swirling into little clouds around his ankles.

"How can you tell?" Finbar asked.

"Crease in Ludie's hat," Michael answered. "What'll you bet?"

"My portion of Joshua's peach clabber."

"You're on. Ned, you're a witness," Michael added.

"Only if I git a share of the winnings," Ned answered quickly.

"All right," Finbar agreed.

The three men stood silently, watching the shambling figure approach them, head lowered. Just before he reached them, Ludie Strayhorn lifted his head, his pale eyes blinking at the waiting trio.

"Damn, son, how'd you do that?" Finbar exploded, and Michael started laughing. Ludie's mouth gaped open and then closed in a frown, uncomfortable with the unexpected attention he was receiving.

"What the hell's matter with you all?" Ludie asked in a hostile voice. He took off his hat, his fair hair plastered to his skull with sweat, and nervously rammed the side of his hand into the top of the battered gray hat, forcing a deep crease.

"He's been doing that ever since Sumner put him on night watch with Delaney," Michael explained in a low voice. "I think he's about worn it through."

"Do what? What in the hell are you jawing on about?" Ludie complained, digging a deeper furrow into the almost folded hat.

"You sure do notice a lot, Mike," Finbar said with a tone of respect. "Must be those piebald eyes of yours."

The smile on Michael's face stiffened. He shrugged at Finbar's remark, flustered and annoyed to be reminded of his eyes. Michael knew that Finbar had meant no harm in what he had said; if anything, it had been intended as a compliment. But to Michael it had seemed, standing among friends in the dry heat of a Texas afternoon, as if he had almost imagined himself someone else altogether. But the past was there on his face. Wherever he went, others could see it, no matter how hard he tried to ignore it.

"Sumner says Mike is to ride drag for the afternoon. He wants him to get a hand at herding," Ludie said, taking his hand out of the valley in his hat. He shoved it back onto his head. "Must think you got it too easy wrangling. Time to do a real job." With that Ludie spun on his heels and sauntered back to the camp, his shoulders thrown back.

Finbar clapped Michael on the shoulder warmly. "Well son, now don't that jest make you eager. Riding drag on one of the hottest, dustiest days of the year with the Strayhorn brothers to show you the ropes."

"Well, at least there'll be that extra portion of peach clabber waiting for me when we break trail tonight," Michael answered. "The day won't be a total loss."

"And maybe you'll find it easier to throw a rope over them sad-eyed muleys dragging their heels in the dirt instead of these fleet-footed horses of Ned's," Finbar ventured, bowing his head toward the roan mare, who was still placidly ripping up mouthfuls of dry grass.

"Aw hell," Michael muttered and started toward camp.

"No, Mike," Ned shouted. "Not hell. Texas."

From behind the dust-laden bandanna Michael swore and impatiently kicked the mustang's ribs. She stamped her hooves into the dirt. Grinding her teeth on the bit with irritation, she refused to obey the command. Before Michael a calf sprinted away, slipping out of sight between dusty bushes in the dry, narrow gulleys, just the flag of its tail flicking in panic. Michael snapped the reins over the mustang's neck, but she laid her ears flat and only reluctantly followed after the fleeing calf. Michael blinked furiously, his eyes tearing with the harsh grit blown underneath his eyelids.

The calf bawled loudly, but as Michael chased after it, it darted away again. Hot and dirty, Michael had grown frustrated with the calf that refused to be caught and returned to the trail, with the mustang beneath him resisting his every move. The horse was a cinnamon-colored mare, with a long shaggy mane and broomtail, the hallmark of a once-wild mustang. Michael had selected her because her compact body was fast and strong and her eyes seemed to hold a quick intelligence. But she was proving stubborn, jerking back on the bit and slow to follow his commands.

Michael relaxed his grip on the mare's reins and sighed wearily. As he inhaled, dust seeped through his bandanna and he started coughing. He pulled off the bandanna and shook it, spitting out the dirt on his tongue before retying the scarf around his neck. Then he took off his hat and knocked off the layers of trail dust that had collected on the crown and brim. The bawling calf sprinted away out of sight again. Farther down the trail, Michael could see the dust clouds of the passing herd. He sat there wondering what to do. He had tried for the better part of an hour to catch one straggling calf and bring it back to the herd. So far he was failing miserably. Yet he couldn't abandon the task. Ludie Strayhorn had told him to go after the calf, and Michael's pride prevented him from admitting defeat.

As he prepared to try again, Michael saw Jake Talking Boy riding back from the trail to join him. Michael groaned, guessing that someone had decided the tenderfoot needed help.

"Heard Ludie sent you out after a calf," Jake said when he reached Michael.

"Yes," Michael answered sharply. "I'll get it."

Jake cracked a small smile. "Son, those boys was playing a dirty trick on you. No cowman wastes his time and a good horse chasing after calves. When they get hungry, they find their maw on their own. Come on back to the herd and let that critter be."

Michael squeezed his scratchy eyes shut and lowered his head. "All this time," he muttered. "Even the mare knew better. She was pulling me back and I was pushing us forward."

"Yep," Jake agreed softly. "Good horse will often do most of the work for you if you let it."

They rode back together in silence, Michael feeling the anger well up inside of him. He could taste it on his tongue, no less sour than the dust he had swallowed while chasing after the creature. They'd played him for a fool and nearly worn him out. He'd get them for that.

"I'd forget about it if I was you," Jake said. "No harm was done. Jest a little wounded pride is all."

Michael looked up in surprise. Jake grinned back.

"It ain't hard to see something mean building up in a man. I know that look. But I'd let it go lest you choke on it. Too many men been put under 'cause of hate." Then he looked away to the west, his face absorbing the afternoon sunlight like polished wood. "Too many dead under the plains," he said more softly. "Ain't good to hold hate."

"I just feel stupid," Michael answered.

"Babies ain't born knowing how to walk. Why should you know everything about cattling? I 'member I did worse when I was first out here. I was so hot to show how good a cowboy I was, I threw out a rope, four-footed a cow, and broke her legs. They had to shoot her."

"I thought you were born here," Michael said. "Brought up to this life."

Jake shook his head, and Michael saw a shadow of pain darken the green eyes. "No, not here. Farther north. My father was a buffalo hunter that managed to fall in with a band of Kiowa Apache. He was a good hunter, and he was good with languages. So was I. That's how I got my name. I could rattle off in Kiowa and English by the time I was four. I lived with my mother and her people 'til I was about ten. Then things got too dangerous. Kiowas were kicking up a fuss, sending out raiding parties against white farmers. Army was coming in after the Kiowas. Killings on both sides. My mother got scared, so I was sent down to Texas to live with my father's relatives."

Jake's smile turned bitter. "Yessir, I know hate. Seen that look most of the days of my life. White men that hate out of fear of me, and Kiowa that hate 'cause they think I've betrayed them. I'm cursed and blessed by both bloods. Can't hide it. Can't run from it." Jake shrugged. "Though I've done all right staying on the trail. Out here every man learns to depend on another for survival. Don't matter what he looks like, if he'll do for you on the trail. Those Strayhorn brothers is jest having their fun. Don't pay them no mind."

As they reached the drag end of the trail again, Michael looked up and saw the flicking tail of the calf he had been vainly chasing. It was walking beside its mother, the stately heifer, lowering her head from time to time to lick at the calf's back. Ludie and Barney Strayhorn turned partly in their saddles to glance curiously back at Michael. At the sight of the gangly pair, Michael started to laugh, at them first and then at himself. They pulled down their bandannas and grinned back, their open mouths overfilled with their picket-fence teeth.

Sumner rode up quickly to Jake, the big bay horse forcing a path through the herd of moving cattle.

"Jake, I want you to scout ahead out to the northwest a ways. Ramon says he's seen a circle of buzzards flying over. Just check it out. Mike, you go with him. Make sure you have plenty of water with you."

Jake pulled down the brim of his hat and then tested the weight of the canteen hanging off his saddle. Satisfied, he gave a light flick of the reins and headed off to the northwest, riding away from the herd. Michael followed after him, wishing he was riding Mo Neart. The wild mare was a good pacer, with a quick, light step, but Michael would have preferred the solid feel of the stallion underneath him when he ventured out on the open plain.

About a mile ahead of the trail they saw the dark circle of buzzards gliding in the updrafts of warm air. Huge birds with large shaggy wings, they carried themselves aloft until it seemed that either gravity or curiosity tugged at them and they dove back to earth. Michael watched them landing awkwardly, their wings flapping over the ground as they see-sawed, trying to stand upright around a mound of dull white bones. Their serpentine necks were pink and naked of feathers; their sharp beaks snapped at others that lumbered too close.

"What are they after?" Michael asked, disliking the ugly birds.

"Carrion, most likely. But whatever it is, sure is big," Jake said. "Look at how many have come to feed." Jake pulled out his rifle from the saddle holster and fired several shots into the dense cover of birds. The black wings fanned the air in terror and a dozen birds lifted in angry and noisy flight. They refused to go far but remained hovering overhead, watching with malice as Jake and Michael approached a mound of bones.

"What the hell . . ." Jake said softly, and he rode his horse slowly around the collected pile of bones. Gathered into an untidy heap were the remains of cattle, mostly calves, the small arrow-headed skulls picked clean of flesh but still shrouded with veils of shedding hide. Hollowed sockets stared back at Michael as he followed behind Jake. Some of the carcasses were newer, and beneath the upturned ribs, the drying fragments of flesh tempted the birds. The mare stepped nervously over the ground, and Michael could feel her tremble beneath his thighs.

"These are all calves. Like they've been slaughtered. But what in the hell are they doing out here in the middle of nowhere?" Jake asked out loud. He slid down from his horse, a hand reaching up to scratch the back of his head beneath the black hat. Holding onto the reins with one hand, he stared down at the ground around the piled remains. Walking slowly, he studied the marks in the dirt. Michael saw him stop and squat down, a hand touching the hardened indentation of a print.

"What is it?" Michael asked.

"Paw marks. A big cat. But this far out on the plain? This ain't its country. And why'd it bring its catch here?"

The image of the panther's red eyes sparked in Michael's memory. He saw again the dark shadow of a man lowering itself to the ground, and the dangling white legs of the calf as it was carried away. Michael's heart banged against his ribs. The breath caught in his throat, and he looked out over the horizon where the heat rose in its shimmering curtain of light. There was no mirage this time, just a thin line of slate-gray that darkened the rim of the earth.

"A man's footprints too," Jake said softly. "But no horse. It don't make sense."

Suddenly Jake stood up and looked at Michael with a worried face. "This ain't right. Ain't natural. We got to get back."

"What are you going to tell them?" Michael asked.

"To move the herd farther east." Jake dropped the reins of his horse and started walking backward around the circle of bones, murmuring under his breath. When he reached his horse again, he pulled out an eagle feather from his shirt pocket and braided it into his long hair.

"What are you doing?" Michael asked, a fist of tension seizing the back of his neck. He tried to shrug it off, but it clung to his spine. The buzzards overhead screeched at them, their wings driving a hot wind over the bones.

"Protecting myself from sorcerers," Jake said flatly as he remounted his horse. Then he snapped the reins hard across the mare's shoulders and she bolted across the plain. Michael gave his horse a kick and she bounded after Jake, seeming almost grateful to be retreating from the piled bones and the drifting shadows of the black birds overhead.

"Yessir, I'd say it's gonna rain tonight," Joshua announced as he ladled out a helping of salt pork and beans onto Michael's plate.

"Go on," argued Delaney. "It's been hotter and drier than hell today. It doesn't feel like rain to me."

"Well, that's 'cause you don't know where to look, Jim," Joshua said confidently. "You think the only sign is dark clouds overhead."

"It's never failed before," Delaney scoffed.

"Well sir, there is other signs to be reckoned with. I been watching dust devils stirred up in the distance, seen the ants digging in, and heard that rain crow moan just before sunset. And if that ain't enough, Mike and Jake come into camp with feathers all tangled up in their horses' manes. Now that's a sure sign of coming rain." Joshua sat down on a small stool and took out his tobacco and pipe.

At the mention of feathers, Michael looked nervously over at Jake, who continued eating, his calm face empty of expression. When they returned to camp, Jake had reported quietly to John O'Connor about his findings. O'Connor had listened gravely and then chewed the fringes of his mustache as he considered the news. Jake had insisted that they travel farther east, that it was dangerous in a way he couldn't explain to travel too close to the heaped bones. O'Connor had agreed reluctantly to shift the herd on the promise that neither Jake nor Michael worried the others with their findings. They had moved the herd off the trail as Jake concocted a story about finding an old horse carcass and the remains of an Indian, probably Comanche from the dress. Out of respect for the dead and hopefully not to anger any Indians that might be around, Jake had recommended moving the herd east a ways.

But the truth stuck in Michael's throat and made it hard to eat. The tension remained coiled in his body, without a hope of being released. The dryness of the day had given way to a sluggish heaviness that bore down on the trail from the cloudless sky above. The air grew dense with the clinging dust, coating men and cattle. Michael had watched the far northern horizon and seen the thin line of dark gray expand. Joshua was right: There was rain coming, but the light winds that preceded it carried a bitter taste.

"First watch goes to Delaney and Mike tonight," Sumner was saying. Michael shook himself from his worry and nodded. "Take yer fish, boys," Sumner advised. "Joshua ain't never wrong about rain."

"Too bad too," John O'Connor added, reaching for another cup of coffee. "I was hoping we could cross the Red River before the rain set in. Hate to do it when the river's high."

"Hey Mike, can I have your peach clabber?" Ned asked eagerly.

"Take it," Michael said, forcing a smile at the boy. Slowly Michael finished eating his plate of beans, using a biscuit to soak up the last of the pork gravy. Ever since they had found the piled bones, Michael's worried thoughts had worn away his appetite. He ate now only out of a sense of duty to his body, to keep it prepared against whatever would come. He had spent the latter part of the day at the drag end of the herd, trying to deny his fears. But in the end he couldn't. Red Cap was coming. He could feel it, knew it in the bitter taste of the wind.

It didn't matter that "fairy" here wore a different face from his mother's stories: mirages wavering on the horizon, a death-dealing owl, and a man's shape shifting into the body of a panther. It was all part of the same flowing river of magic, and sooner or later, as long as Michael remained in the world, the current would bring Red Cap to him.

Michael glanced up at the circle of men, sitting wearily eating their plates of pork and beans, mugs of coffee close at hand. Delaney had deftly rolled a cigarette and was licking the paper closed. He scratched a match against his boot and sucked in a long breath of smoke from the lit cigarette. The Strayhorn brothers sat side by side, their almost twin heads bowed over their plates as their forks scraped up food. O'Connor and Sumner were discussing the herd in low voices by the chuck wagon, Sumner occasionally looking out at Jake and then Michael. He didn't look too happy. Jake was sitting quietly, his eyes heavy-lidded as he stared dreamily into the flames of the cook-fire. Finbar had returned his empty plate to Joshua and took out a small harmonica from his vest pocket. He started playing a bright tune that sounded off-key and broken in the failing twilight. Finbar stopped playing and looked at the reeds with a questioning face. He tapped the harmonica against his thigh and put it to his lips again. This time the tune was slow and sad, the reeds crying the melody, until Delaney kicked Finbar with a booted toe.

"Gods, man, give it a rest. You're sorrier sounding than a whore on Sunday morning."

Finbar shrugged. "Came from somewhere, I reckon."

Ramon sat down beside Michael and, smiling, gave him a nudge.

"Do you miss your soft bed?"

Michael put his plate down. "I don't think I can remember what a soft bed feels like anymore."

"A buen sueño no hay mala cama," Ramon said with a quick smile, brushing back his shining black hair. "There is no bad bed for a good sleep," he translated.

"Though if it rains—" cracked Ludie.

"You'll at least wish it were dry," finished Barney, looking over at his brother. The Strayhorn brothers had finished eating their beans and were now attacking their servings of peach clabber in unison.

"Then it's missing home that makes your face so long," Ramon ventured.

"Haven't thought much about home," Michael said sharply.

"A girl? Your parents?"

"No girl. My mother's dead—" Michael stopped, wishing he hadn't said the words.

Jake's head jerked up, his burnished cheeks glowing with firelight. "How long she been dead?" he asked.

"Not long," Michael replied, uncomfortable with the intense look in Jake's eyes.

"Is that why you came out west?"

"Partially," Michael replied. Jake continued to hold Michael's gaze as though waiting to hear more. The tension coiled tighter in Michael's body, and suddenly he wanted to tell them. Tell them everything as he had once told Alice: his mother's eerie death, Red Cap chasing him, and the line of warriors that he had seen stretched out in the shimmering mirages. He wanted to tell them also of the white bird with his mother's voice that had mourned in the willow tree by the river; and to warn them of the shapeshifter out on the plains, changing from a man into a panther. The need to confide welled in him, and he parted his lips to speak.

"Better git out there, boys," Sumner ordered, and the words went unspoken in Michael's mouth. "Don't forget yer fish," Sumner said to Michael.

Michael averted his eyes from Jake's hard stare and went to the chuck wagon. Alone again, he exhaled with relief that he had kept quiet and said nothing after all. He realized how much it mattered what this circle of men thought of him. It was too dangerous and too strange a truth to admit to these trail-hardened cowboys. They would think him crazy, and it was their respect that he wanted, not their mistrust. He would have to find the answer to Red Cap's threat himself.

Michael reached into the back of the wagon and brought out the yellow oilskin slicker with the image of a fish stamped into the collar. The slicker was wide and loosely cut, long enough in length to cover his legs once seated in the saddle. He put it on, and his nose wrinkled at the rancid scent of fat from the oil-saturated fabric. It rustled stiffly when he walked and slapped against his ankles.

Michael then went out to where the night herd grazed close by the camp and whistled for Mo Neart. In the pale light of a new moon, he saw the horse trotting toward him, the white vaporous mane flowing over the arched neck. The stallion came to him, butting his bony forehead and long nose against Michael's chest in greeting.

Michael smiled at the huge horse and affectionately scratched the space between the pointed ears. "Mo Neart," he whispered, taking courage from the stallion's name.

"Señor Mike," Ramon called from the edge of camp. "I've something for you before you go out tonight."

"Be there in a moment," Michael answered, and he quickly put the saddle and bridle on Mo Neart. As Michael swung his leg over the stallion's back, Mo Neart startled abruptly, the hind legs kicking out. "Hey boy, easy, easy does it," Michael said, holding the reins firmly, perplexed by the stallion's skittishness.

Delaney rode up beside him and gave a dry chuckle. "Horse ain't never seen a fish before. Spooks 'em sometimes 'til they get used to the feel of it over the saddle. You coming, son?"

"Wait," Ramon called, walking out to meet them. He stopped before Michael and reached into his pocket. He pulled out his fist and motioned for Michael to put out his hand. Michael did, and Ramon released a small handful of thorns into Michael's palm. The thorns were thick and fleshy, the points long black-tipped spears. "These are thorns from the agave plant, and they have a strong magic in them. Keep them in your pocket. I don't like the feel of the coming rain." Ramon turned to Delaney. "How 'bout you, Jim? Will you take some with you?" Ramon offered.

Frowning, Delaney shook his head. "You know I don't hold with that stuff, Ramon. Been lucky all my life. Got no cause to think it'll end now jest 'cause you got a bad feeling. No, son, I'll look after myself," Delaney said with finality. He tipped his hat in farewell and nudged Tuck, his night horse, with his knees. The scrubby coyote mare took off at a brisk trot, her brindled hide capturing the sparse moonlight in a dappled pattern of gray and black.

"Vaya con Dios," Ramon said lightly as Michael turned Mo Neart's head and followed Delaney out to the herd.

Jim Delaney rode Tuck clockwise while Michael traveled on Mo Neart in the opposite direction, gathering the widely scattered cattle into a compact herd, no more than four or five acres across. After so much time on the trail, the cattle had come to know what was expected, and each found a patch of grass in which to make its bed for the night. A small herd of muleys, cattle without horns, huddled together for protection deep within the herd. The sight of drowsy cattle contentedly chewing their cud and blowing over their full stomachs beneath a quiet night sky was restful. The tension uncoiled slowly in his body, and Michael's eyelids grew heavy. His shoulders began to sag with weariness and his head bobbed over his chest as Mo Neart circled around the sleeping cattle.

"Hey son, you asleep already?" Delaney chuckled softly.

Michael yawned to rouse himself as Delaney came riding up to him out of the dark shadows.

"No. I'm still awake," Michael replied, but his voice was groggy.

"Don't sound like it. Sounds like it's your horse doing the talking for you."

"Well, I am," Michael said irritably. "Don't you ever get tired, Delaney?"

"Did you ever get laid, son?"

Michael guffawed in surprised laughter at the abrupt question. "What's it to you?"

"I'll take that for a *no*," Delaney replied dryly, leaning his forearms on the horn of his saddle. "Figured as much out about you. Well, maybe this trip we'll fix that. I know a couple of good houses where all the gals are clean."

"What makes you think I want it so much?" Michael asked.

"I was your age once. And I don't remember thinking about much else. Why, getting laid was how I learned to stop sleeping altogether. I was with this gal one night and we were going at it tooth and claw. Never seen such a wildcat in bed and never know'd it could be so damn good. Well, after a few hours, I closed my eyes, jest fell off the face of the earth I was so worn out. It was only luck I'd say that made me wake in time to hear her husband charging up the stairs to the bedroom. I had jest enough time to grab my britches and duck out the window before that Colt forty-five went off into the headboard of the bed. Shot his wife, he did, right between the eyes."

"And you?" Michael asked, slightly repulsed but still fascinated by Delaney's story.

Delaney shook his head and smoothed down the sides of his trim mustache. "I got out without even a creasing. I've tumbled a lot of gals since then, but I ain't bothered much with sleep. I can do that enough when I'm dead."

Delaney leaned back in the saddle, the stars overhead sparkling in his eyes. He rolled another cigarette, and in the orange flare of the struck match, Michael saw that he was smiling. In the silence, Michael considered Jim Delaney's story and decided he didn't believe it.

"You're lying," Michael challenged.

"What don't you believe?"

"He didn't shoot his wife," Michael said flatly.

Delaney gave a laugh and took a quick drag of his cigarette. "So you'd like to believe the part about banging away at her for a couple of hours? I'd say you need to get laid, son. Seems like it's on your mind after all. Let's get moving again. You gonna sing, or do I torture them with my voice?"

"I will," Michael said, glad that the darkness hid the red flush he felt warming his cheeks. He hadn't spent much time with women beyond the few high society doves that he had been asked to escort to various charity functions. He had been shy and awkward in their company; they had seemed strident and much too calculating. And yet in the privacy of his dreams he thought often enough about women; imagined the feel of a small hand in his, the curve of a scented neck and the feather-soft touch of lips against his own. He had imagined a girl, one with a pale face and a lilting voice. He frowned in the darkness, realizing that it was a version of Eileen's face and Eileen's body that had dominated his dreams. Even there, he thought, she held him prisoner.

Delaney continued on his way, riding in a wide circle

around the herd. Michael watched him go and shrugged off the unwanted memory of Eileen McBride's soft hand pressed against his shoulder as she whispered into his ear. He started to sing. "Oh, if I was a small bird, with wings I would fly, right over the salt sea, where my darling does lie. And with my fond wings, I'd beat over her grave, and kiss the pale lips, cold in the grave."

A low rumbling sounded far in the distance. The cattle stirred, a subtle movement rustling the dry grass as they anxiously shifted their bodies. Michael looked out over the far horizon and saw the first silvery flashes of lightning streak across the underside of a low shelf of clouds.

He started singing again, hoping to calm the worried cattle.

"Brokenhearted I'll wander, brokenhearted I'll remain . . ."

A second flash of lightning brightened the sky again, illuminating the approaching ridge of clouds. The heavy growl of thunder rumbled more loudly. The low tremor vibrated in Michael's sternum and thrummed the ribs of his chest. He looked up and saw that the storm was moving quickly across the open plains. One by one, stars winked out of the clear black night as the bank of thick clouds rolled in, covering the high-domed sky. The lead cattle had risen to their feet, their snouts raised to the gusting wind as they sniffed the air. Calves bawled, frightened by the noise, and were answered by the deeper calls of the heifers. Michael tried to keep singing, but the words were lost in the steady rumble and clap of thunder.

Between the darkening night and the bright flash of lightning, Michael saw Jim Delaney riding toward him at a fast pace.

"We got one hell of a storm on the way. Keep close to the herd and keep circling," he shouted. "The lightning might spook the cattle and send them stampeding. Keep your eyes open and your foot in the stirrup," he warned.

Michael gave Mo Neart a kick, but the stallion was already moving more quickly around the herd, standing at times shoulder to shoulder with a longhorn that had staggered to its feet and was trying to flee the bedding ground. A loud sizzle of static split the air with the sound of shearing metal. A blinding flash of lightning brought the herd to their feet, bellowing in fear, and the loud canyon boom that followed nearly knocked the wind from Michael's chest. The long, curved horns of the milling herd were etched against the flashing night sky like thousands of upraised spears. The horns clattered noisily as the cattle pushed and shoved against one another in a confused frenzy. There was no rain yet, only the sharp taste of ozone and the heavy weight of the clouds moving rapidly overhead.

Long jagged arrows of blue-white lightning were shot from the black clouds and stabbed at the dry earth. Then the lightning arrows shattered and the incandescent fragments coiled into balls of silvery-white snakes that were sent wheeling over the ground toward the herd. They bounced and pitched, whirling over the rocks and bushes. Sparks ignited the blades of dried grass and a shrill whistle pierced the low-throated rumble of thunder.

Delaney rode up beside Michael, Tuck snorting in fear and her ears laid flat against her head. Foam gathered at the corners of her bit, and her nostrils flared at the metallic scent of the wind. Jim was having trouble holding her steady as the careening balls of lightning rapidly approached them.

"St. Elmo's fire," he shouted at Michael over the din of bellowing cattle and shrieking light. "Heard of it, but ain't never seen it before. I'll try and hold 'em over on the south side, you stay here." He let go of the mare's reins and she took off, galloping away from the charging balls of light.

Michael rode Mo Neart back and forth along the wavering edge of the herd, keeping the frightened cattle bunched together, as overhead the sky continued to flare more brightly with each new surge of lightning. Anxiously he watched the wheeling balls of St. Elmo's fire draw closer to the herd, the cold white light trailing behind the whirling forms like shooting stars.

The balls of light exploded at the edge of the herd; leaping nimbly into the air, they balanced like spinning globes on the upturned horns of the cattle. Tumbling from horn tip to horn tip, the spinning balls of light showed the white-rimmed eyes of the terrified animals. Their horns struck against each other with the crash of battle spears as the bawling cattle clambered over one another, trying to escape the shrieking light. Michael stared in astonishment as the balled lightning bobbled and danced over the jostling field of horns, moving, it seemed, with a determined purpose. One passed near him and Mo Neart reared back on his haunches, squalling in angry defiance. Michael crouched along the stallion's neck, clinging to his mane as the horse continued to rear and kick out with his front hooves.

Michael raised his head from Mo Neart's neck and saw the balls of lightning suddenly uncoil and drape long, flaming tendrils over the herd. The air stank of burning hair and flesh. Cattle bellowed as a gray cloud of acrid smoke lifted from the flanks of the panicked herd. A fierce gust of moist wind shredded the billowing smoke, and Michael cried out as he saw Red Cap's warriors riding astride the backs of the longhorns. Their armor shimmered with the white heat of lightning, and blue and green streaks carved the features of their cruel faces. Naked swords and curved lances exhaled bolts of light from their bladed edges.

A warrior confronted Michael and laughed, his mouth coated with blue flames and the sound rumbling deep as the thunder. He pointed a long-handled dagger toward Michael, the razored blade an undulating fang of blue light. Then, still laughing, he kicked the longhorn beneath him into a staggering run. Terrified, Michael reached into his pocket and pulled up the agave thorns that Ramon had given him. The shining black points glowed a brilliant red and a sweet smell like incense burned from the thick flesh.

Michael forced Mo Neart to ride close to the warrior, shouting as he went to thrust out the fear from his heart. Mo Neart shoved against the lumbering cattle, and Red Cap's warrior slashed at the air with his dagger. Light from the falling dagger arched over Michael's head and he lunged away from its driving point at the last moment. Still bent, Michael stabbed a thorn into the warrior's thigh and then a second thorn as he heard above him the loud howl of pain. The dagger fell and was trampled beneath the prancing hooves of the longhorn. The agave thorns tore a long gash across the shimmering white flesh, and a fountain of red flame burst out, striking Mo Neart across the chest.

The stallion stumbled back, twisting his huge body away from the scorching flames. Then, lowering his head, Mo Neart began to gallop away from Red Cap's warriors, his long white body stretched out over the hard ground of the darkened plains as he ran.

Dazed, Michael clung to the fleeing stallion until he was roused by a terrible realization. Delaney! Where was Delaney? Michael thought quickly and pulled hard on Mo Neart's reins, to slow the horse in flight. The stallion neighed shrilly in protest, the proud head tossing wildly to resist the downward pull of the reins. But Michael held on, his arms nearly wrenched from the sockets, as the powerful horse battled against him. "Turn! Turn, damn you!" Michael cried to the slowing stallion. Still bellowing in rage, Mo Neart spun about and galloped back toward the herd.

Ahead of him, Michael could just make out the black form of Delaney's body mounted on Tuck's back, his arm outstretched against a sheet of white light.

Michael reached into his pocket, grasping for more

thorns, but Mo Neart stopped abruptly, his back haunches buckling with the effort. The stallion refused to
move any closer to where Delaney's horse stood unmoving in a shower of light.

"No!" Michael shouted, "No!" His voice was ragged;
his mouth and throat were filled with a thick cloud of
stinking smoke.

They were on Delaney and Tuck, a warrior at his back,
one at his side, stabbing him over and over with daggers
of lightning. With each thrust, Delaney cried out and
blue-white flames shot from his mouth. His hat was gone,
blown away in the rising wind, and his hair blazed white,
curls of smoke drifting around his ears, his collar, and
from the sleeves of his outstretched arms. His wide-open
eyes glowed like hard emeralds, then changed to blue,
and at last a diamond white. In desperation Michael
called Jim's name and cast an agave thorn in his direction. It was caught by one of the warriors, who held it up
in the blazing light with a malicious smile. And, still smiling at Michael, he stabbed the thorn into Jim Delaney's
back.

There was a crack, and a blinding light flowered over
Jim's shoulders. It rose like a high-pointed collar around
his neck and then wreathed his head with a brambled
vine of thorns, each sharp point tearing at the skin of his
face. The vine and thorns grew stronger, encasing the
body of Jim Delaney and his horse in a thicket of stabbing light. He wailed, and along the branches the color
shimmered a soft blue with his exhaled breath, and then
hardened white as the thorns continued to tear his skin.
Tuck shuddered awake and began to trip out of the circle
of light, stumbling closer to Michael and Mo Neart.

Mo Neart reared up once more, refusing to remain;
spinning around, the stallion galloped back over the
plain. Michael released his hold on the reins and let the
powerful horse run. He turned his head long enough to
catch a glimpse of Tuck's white shimmering body slowly

following after. The high pitch of Jim Delaney's wailing stayed in Michael's ears, and only the roaring thunder overhead deafened him to its awful sound. Looking forward again, Michael saw that Mo Neart was headed for the distant firelight of the camp. He had to warn them, Michael thought. Red Cap's warriors were coming.

A new gust of cold wind brought the damp smell of rain. The air curdled into a fine mist. Mo Neart shook his head and water sprayed from the whipping mane. Rain began to fall, battering against Michael's slicker like tiny pebbles. Michael could see the cookfire begin to splutter and he could hear the men loudly cursing. The dark shadows flickered against the firelight as they moved quickly to stow blanket rolls and supplies into the covered belly of the wagon.

Michael and the stallion burst into the circle of camp, Mo Neart's sharp hooves trampling the wet earth into mud. Michael slid from the horse, breathless and scared, trying to frame the words to explain what had happened. His legs were shaking, his hands weakly holding onto the dragging reins. He leaned against Mo Neart's side, the lathered foam wetting his cheek.

"Hold on there, son," O'Connor was saying, holding him upright by the shoulders. "What in the hell's happened? Where's Delaney?" They crowded around him, their faces filled with apprehension.

"Out there . . . The lightning," Michael started to say.

"Ee Gods, look!" Finbar shouted. "It's Delaney."

On the shadowy edge of the camp, Delaney's horse limped toward the light, the dark figure on her back slumped to one side.

"You all right, Jim?" Sumner called out.

There was no answer, but the figure stiffly dismounted from the back of the mare and slowly walked toward them. Freed from the burden of her rider, Tuck's knees buckled and she collapsed to the ground, her chest heaving noisily with her labored breathing.

Sumner started toward Delaney, but Michael grabbed him.

"Don't get near him!" he warned.

"What the hell—" Sumner barked angrily.

"Oh sweet Jesus," Joshua moaned, "he's been struck."

Jim Delaney entered the camp wearing a cloak of thick gray smoke. His yellow slicker was burnt black, the brittle remains of the fabric crackling into flecks of ash as he lumbered toward them. His hair was gone, the soft folds of his ears fused into the sides of his blackened skull. But in the hollowed sockets, his eyes still blazed with a cold white light. Threads of light whip-stitched across his lips and sparked in the hollows of his charred throat. He raised his black and smoking hands, and blue sparks cascaded from his fingertips like tiny stars collected in the burned hands. He opened his mouth to speak and tongues of lightning snaked out, his words strangled by plumes of smoke.

The rain was falling in scattered drops and then more steadily, each drop hissing with steam as it landed on Jim Delaney's blue-black body. No one moved before the swaying figure of the blackened cowboy as the rain fell more heavily, sheets of cold water washing over them.

Jim Delaney was still standing, the white light dimly flickering around him with an angry static charge. Finally, as they stood waiting, huddled together and shivering in the lashing rain, the cowboy crumpled dead to the slick, muddy ground.

"There's nothing to be done tonight." John O'Connor broke the silence at last, raising his voice over the keening wind. "Get under cover. And we'll settle it in the morning. Sumner, you and Jake take the herd. Ramon and Finbar, you ride next. Give me Jim's bedroll," he said to Joshua. Joshua handed him the thin blanket and he walked slowly toward the dead cowboy. "Goddamn night," O'Connor swore, as he laid the blanket gently over the smoking body, covering the charred face.

Those remaining scuttled for cover from the rain under the wagon. The blankets were damp and offered little warmth. But it wasn't the penetrating rain that caused Michael's teeth to chatter; nor Ned, lying close beside him, to shiver throughout the long night. It was the cold sight of Jim Delaney's body shrouded by smoke in the pelting rain, one glittering white thorn piercing the palm of his upturned hand.

Seven

The morning came quietly, the pale sunlight brightening the soft air. Broken storm clouds scudded across the blue sky, chased by a dry wind to the far horizon. Waking to the touch of a fragrant breeze on his face, Michael opened his eyes to see the dark wooden slats of the chuck wagon's belly. His clothes were damp and musty smelling, his hair stiffened with dried mud. Ned was huddled close to him, his knees drawn up and his head wedged under Michael's arm. Mud streaked his forehead and the sides of his smooth cheeks. On the other side of Ned, the Strayhorn brothers slept, their faces turned into each other. Ludie Strayhorn had thrown a protective arm over the shoulder of his younger brother. Michael moved Ned, who whimpered before curling again into a sleeping knot. Then Michael slid out from beneath the wagon and leaned against the wheel. He sat, dazed by the contrast between the clear light of the morning and the horrors of the night before.

Looking out beyond the chuck wagon, Michael was

astonished at the sudden transformation of the plains.
With just one night's rain, the hard-baked earth had softened; in the breaking sunlight the grass was turning from
dying straw into a fresh new green. On the gnarled
branches of mesquite shrubs, rows of tiny leaves had
begun to unfurl, and the sagebrush was tinted a silvery
gray. The last clouds were fading, no more than white
ribbons against the blue sky. The grass waved enticingly
in the scented breeze and the cattle, already woken to the
day's march, had stepped out from their bedding ground
into the calm ocean of grass to graze.

Michael looked back toward the camp and saw the
body of Jim Delaney lying covered by his wet blanket,
only his burned trouser legs and outstretched arms visible. It seemed as if the man had withered, the shape
beneath the blanket narrow and flattened. Long gray fingers were bent upward, rigidly grasping at the empty air.
Michael shuddered and looked away. Nearby, he could
hear shovels coughing up spadefuls of wet earth. He
stood and leaned against the wagon, lightheaded as the
blood drained from his face. When he swallowed, he
could taste the sour residue of ashes in the back of his
throat. He peeled off his slicker and laid it out on a bush
to dry. He rubbed his chapped hands together and then
tucked them into his armpits for warmth.

The cookfire had been relit, the damp wood hissing as
the flames spluttered with green-tinted smoke. Hung on a
tripod over the fire was Joshua's huge white coffeepot.
Michael took a mug off the wagon's buckboard and
poured boiling black coffee into it. He drank it quickly,
the hot, bitter drink scalding his tongue and washing
away the taste of ashes. Standing close to the cookfire,
his clothes began to heat, steam rising off the damp fabric
around his knees and thighs. As he drank the coffee, Michael grew more steady, the blood returning to his cheeks
and the warmth into his cold hands. The digging stopped
and Michael listened until the sound resumed. Then he

put his cup away and went out to help dig Jim Delaney's grave.

Jake and Ramon were standing shoulder-deep in a rectangular hole they had dug on top of a small grassy knoll. They lifted the filled shovels high over their shoulders as they deposited the red-colored earth beside the open grave. Though the morning was still cool from the retreating storm, their faces were sweating with the work. Joshua was sitting on his stool, pipe in hand, as he waited for them to finish the task. On the ground close by were Jim Delaney's things piled into a neat bundle. On top of the bundle was the shaving mirror and his razor.

"May I help dig?" Michael asked, trudging up the slope, his legs swishing through the wet grass.

"We're almost done," Jake answered, grunting as he hoisted another shovelful of red earth out of the grave.

"What happened to Tuck?" Michael asked, sitting down on the grass next to Joshua.

"Weren't good for much. Blinded by the lightning and scorched full of burns. Sumner took her out yonder and shot her," Joshua said. "She'll be buzzard food by now."

"And the cattle? Did we lose any to the lightning?"

"A few. And a good many of 'em have blackened horns. Like the devil himself came through and marked 'em all. Strangest thing I ever did see."

The sun's rays warmed Michael's back where he sat and he inhaled the sweet scent of grass. Down by his feet Michael saw the woody stems of white flowers, the new buds already beginning to open. "How quickly it all changes," he breathed, "from last night to this." Idly he picked up Delaney's shaving mirror, remembering how fastidious Delaney had been about his appearance.

Michael tilted the small rectangular mirror toward him and gasped at the reflection. His own face was there, haggard and dirty looking, his eyes full of quiet fright. But behind his shoulder, Michael saw another man reflected in the mirror. Jim Delaney's gaunt face gazed back at him, watery blue eyes just watching him. His hair and mustache were a fragile white floss and his skin an ashy gray. The clay-colored lips were speaking. Michael leaned in to the mirror, his eyes trapped by the sight of the moving lips.

Abruptly, the mirror was jerked out of his hand and the haunting image of Jim Delaney disappeared.

"What the—" Michael started to say, but Joshua put a firm hand on his shoulder and shook him hard.

"Ain't no good to be looking in a dead man's mirror, son. Ain't no one ever told you that's the surest way to get haunted by the dead?" Joshua replaced the mirror on the piled bundle of Jim Delaney's things and turned it glass side down.

Mary and Brigit had covered the mirrors at Gramercy Park with black crepe when his mother died. Michael had thought it was a show of respect, to deny vanity while in mourning. But maybe it had been out of fear of seeing Eileen McBride's face staring back at them from the other side of the glass.

"I grew up double-sighted," Joshua said suddenly, scratching the gray stubble of a beard on the side of his cheek. "That means I can see into the spirit world. Done seen my share of unhappy ghosts wandering from the other world."

"Why do they come back?" Michael asked. "What do they want?"

"Mostly it's unfinished business. I s'pose most folks die with unfinished business, but fer some, they can't leave this world 'til it's done. My pappy, when he died, his ghost done hung on for three days, jest crowding 'round the rain barrel, complaining 'bout his unplowed field. Had to go out and do it afore he'd quit the rain barrel. Most ghosts'll stay by water if they can," Joshua explained, "that's why I done emptied out all the dishes of rainwater early this morning, so Jim here won't think of following after."

"When my mother died," Michael said softly, "I saw her washing a cloth in a fountain near my house."

Joshua nodded, his face somber. "Yessir. That 'ud be right." Joshua put a heavy hand on Michael's shoulder, and Michael looked up into the man's dark brown face. "Did you fix things with her, so's she could move on?" he asked sternly.

Michael gave a small shake of his head. "I didn't know what to do. I got scared and ran."

"Ran, huh? And didn't stop 'til you done reached Texas?" Joshua said sharply.

Jake and Ramon had stopped digging the grave and were watching Michael, waiting for him to reply.

"Yes," Michael answered, "I guess so." Their somber expressions made him uncomfortable, as if they knew the truth about Jim Delaney's death. He should tell them what really happened, he thought miserably. But he held back, fearing that they might blame him for the night's events. He tried to remember; Had he done all he could do to help Delaney?

Jake pulled himself out of the grave and brushed off little clods of dirt that clung to his trousers and boots. Then he smoothed back his long black hair, his fingers finding the eagle feather. He touched it, as if making sure it was secure.

"Among the Kiowa, when someone dies it's important to mourn. But it's also important to let go of the dead, because we believe that while you mourn, you are swept into the land of the dead and travel with them. You must accept your loss so that you can be reborn, brought back from death's side to life. If you don't, then the dead'll follow you and you'll become a danger to everyone around you."

"What are you saying?" Michael asked warily.

Jake shrugged. "What do you know about last night that you aren't telling?"

Michael stood up, angrily resisting the stab of guilt. "I

don't know how your people mourn, but I did my share of it when my mother died. Eileen McBride was waked, prayed over, and then buried in Greenwood Cemetery. And that's all there is to it."

"But you said she come back," Joshua pointed out, a finger held to his pursed lips. The pipe in his other hand went unlit. "Something ain't been done for her."

Michael felt the weight of their gaze on his shoulders. "Delaney's death wasn't my fault," he insisted, glaring back at Jake. Michael's hands balled into fists and his voice rose. "I didn't kill him."

"No one's accusing you of anything, Señor Mike," Ramon said, leaning on his shovel. "But when a man fears the world of the spirits, they will hunt him down. A man must be brave and battle those spirits. Then he will get riches and magic power. But if he runs away, only poverty and disaster will be his reward."

"It's late. I have to get the horses rounded up," Michael said brusquely. "I haven't the time for talk."

He stormed away in long strides, the grass crushed down as he dug his heels into the softened earth.

"Tell Sumner, grave's done been dug," Joshua shouted after him.

Michael raised his hand but didn't turn around. He couldn't look at them, couldn't face them, as guilt bathed his skin in a shining layer of sweat. Though his mouth was dry as chalk, his face was hot and sticky, his sides slick beneath his shirt. He could smell the rank odor of his fear. It was his fault. Red Cap's warriors had come for him in the lightning. And Jim Delaney had died horribly because of it.

Why had his mother cursed him so? He had loved her, loved her more than anyone when she was alive. And now in her death it seemed she held him captive, haunting him with her white, weeping form. And the stories that had seemed a harmless pleasure between them had become a source of danger. What did she want? he asked

himself. How far did he have to flee before her ghost and
the demons of her stories left him alone?

He came into camp and found Sumner and Finbar
rolling up the remains of Jim Delaney in his groundcloth.
John O'Connor was standing by the cookfire, a mug of
coffee in his hands. Ned was beside him, his mouth
screwed tight as though he were trying not to cry. The
Strayhorn brothers were standing close together, clutching their dirty gray hats in their hands as they watched
Sumner and Finbar hoist the body of the cowboy.

"Joshua says they're ready for him," Michael murmured.

"Come on, then," O'Connor said gruffly, spilling the
dregs of his coffee onto the ground. "Let's get this over
with and get back on the trail."

They walked slowly up to the grave site, Michael following behind them. He couldn't watch as they lowered
the body into the black hole but kept his eyes trained toward the last wisps of clouds. He ached at the memory of
his mother, buried like this beneath the earth, the thudding sound of dirt cast back into the hole and the hollow
ring of the spades tamping the top of the filled grave.

John O'Connor spoke briefly of Jim Delaney's life and
even more briefly of God. But Michael scarce heard him,
for in his head he whispered his apologies to the dead
man and begged him to forgive him. Joshua sang a
hymn, and his deep resonating voice rolled over the
blooming plains as soothing as the thunder had been om-
inous. Then they filed away from the grave, each cutting
a narrow path though the waving grass back to camp.
There the chuck wagon was quickly packed, the cookfire
doused, and the ashes scattered. Michael and Ned
rounded up the horses, bringing the remuda back to
camp to join the herd. Delaney's horses were split up
among them, and each man carefully examined his own
horses for injuries or burns. Michael brushed the palms
of his hands down Mo Neart's sides, reassured by the

silky feel of the horse's glossy hide. There was no mark, not so much as a scratch on the horse's body. The stallion leaned his long head into Michael's head, the stiff chin hairs tickling Michael's ear. The stallion snorted lightly with affection, his breath warm and moist.

"Thanks, boy," Michael whispered gratefully, as though the horse's loyalty had returned to him a sense of worth in himself.

Sumner and Jake took point, giving direction to the lead cattle, which were already briskly pulling the herd behind them on the trail north. Ramon and Finbar rode swing; riding up and down along the sides of the herd, keeping them together. In the swirling dust of the drag end, Ludie and Barney Strayhorn whistled, shouted, and hurried the stragglers. Joshua had packed his chuck wagon and hitched his team of horses before the camp had fully broken. He had ridden out ahead of them, preparing to set up the next camp on the banks of the Red River, which they would reach by the end of the day. Michael rode with the remuda on an energetic black horse that Ramon had named Cuervo, the "Crow," because of his blue-black hide. Mo Neart followed close behind him, occasionally breaking away from the remuda to run freely over the open plain before turning around again to come trotting back to the plodding herd. Michael watched the stallion with envy as the wave of his white mane sprayed out along the long slope of his neck and the powerful body moved gracefully over the ground. Mo Neart could leave if he chose to, gallop away so fast none would ever catch him again. But he always returned, and Michael realized that whatever else happened, Mo Neart would remain with him, his ally and his protector.

They reached the Red River late in the afternoon. The cattle could smell the fresh water long before they could see it and they hurried their steps in anticipation of a cool drink. Around Michael the flattened plains rose into gentle hills covered thickly with gray sagebushes and mesquite shrubs, blooming with small yellow flowers. Trees appeared again, tall stands of cottonwood and a few hardy scrub oaks, providing a rare line of green shade. From the brow of a rock-crusted hill Michael stared down into the wide river valley. The long rays of the afternoon sun spilled across the surface of the smooth-flowing water, dying it a reddish gold. Joshua had set up the chuck wagon near the spreading branches of an old oak. The smoke from his cookfire spiraled high in a single gray plume into the clear sky.

The cattle bawled at the sight of the river and rushed down the hill toward the water. They spread out in a dense crowd along the riverbank, all trying to wade into the water. The lead cattle were standing up to their chests in the river, dipping their snouts in and then raising their heads to bawl at their companions waiting impatiently on the bank. The horses too were eager, and Michael and Ned led them down the long incline to the river's edge. Only Mo Neart kept his distance from the muddy banks. When Michael looked back, he saw the stallion waiting at the top of the hill, his head held high, his ears pricked forward, alert.

"That stallion's a regular ridge runner," Ned said.

"A what?"

"Some stallions'll keep to the high ground as a way of looking out for predators. Seems like your horse always wants to know what's around him. He's smart," Ned said, turning back to gaze at the river. "Aw hell! Smarter anyway than some in this remuda. Looks like Finbar's horse got itself bogged in the mud!"

As Ned and Michael approached the struggling horse, Michael saw that his first impression of the serene river had been deceived by distance. Out in the middle of the river the current was fast, the waves in the silent water turning and rolling swiftly. A torn tree branch swept past them, moving as quickly as a fallen leaf. The banks held their own hazards. They were mostly a thick red-colored mud, and the horses and cattle, their heavy weight balanced on the small surface areas of their hooves, were sinking rapidly into the yielding earth. Finbar's horse took fright, and the harder it struggled in the mud the more deeply it sank. Ned roped it around the neck to hold it steady and stop its thrashing. Then between gently pushing and pulling, Ned and Michael were able to free the horse from the muddy wallow. The red clay sucked at Michael's boots as he trudged out from the bank.

All along the bank cattle were becoming bogged down in the mud churned up by their hooves. O'Connor and Sumner rode along the stretch of river, looking for a dry bedding ground on which to turn out the herd for the night. They drove those cattle that were still milling on the drier banks out onto the plains again, keeping them for the time being away from the treacherous river. Jake, Ramon, and the Strayhorn brothers began the arduous task of pulling bogged cattle out of the mud.

At camp that night, each man stood by the fire, drying out his wet and muddy clothes. The stench of wet denim and steaming flannel mingled with the aroma of Joshua's beans and dried pork. In the branches overhead, a jay chucked loudly at the intrusion of Joshua's wagon into his territory. He streaked in and out of the tree, his blue wings the color of the evening sky.

The men ate quickly and silently. The only sounds were the jay squawking overhead, the crack of firewood, and the fierce scraping of forks on tin plates.

Ramon was the first to look up and, giving a slight smile, nodded at Sumner. *"A buen hambre no hay mal pan,"* he said, and he eased his legs out in front of him, his boots still full of mud. "Hunger is the best sauce," he said in English.

Sumner laughed dryly and set his plate down with a

sigh. "Tailing up bogged cattle all evening don't hurt none either," he added. "Damn this river. How long, John, before you think it'll go down enough for us to cross?"

O'Connor bent his head to consider his pipe, packing it slowly with the shag tobacco. "I'd say another day at least. Tomorrow Jake and I'll head upstream a ways, see if there's a better place to cross. Channel's too deep here, and with the sides so slick I'm afraid the cattle'll start panicking. I don't want to lose any more than I have to. In the meantime, we'll stay put. Ramon, take the boys out with you in the morning and cut down some of those smaller cottonwoods. If we lash some logs beneath the chuck wagon wheels we ought to be able to float it over."

Ramon gave a slight frown of displeasure, and Michael knew that most of the job of chopping wood would fall to himself and Joshua. One thing he had learned in the weeks on the trail was that few of the cowboys would ever consider doing anything besides eating and sleeping that brought them down off a horse. Once when Joshua had needed more wood for the cookfire, Delaney had returned a short time later dragging behind his horse a huge fallen stump lassoed in his rope. But it was to Joshua and then to Michael that fell the task of chopping the stump up into usable firewood.

"We're a man short now, so John and I will take first watch tonight," Sumner said. "Ramon, you and Ludie take second, Jake and Finbar third, Barney and Mike fourth watch into morning. Got that?"

Everyone nodded, but Michael saw the look of panic in Barney's eyes. Ramon got up quickly and found the half-finished rope he had been braiding on the trail. He bent his head to the job, his gaze lowered to the rope in his lap. Jake came over to Barney and spoke quietly to the boy. He gave him an eagle feather, tucking it into Barney's hatband. Barney gave Jake a grateful smile, but every time he looked at Michael, Michael could see the apprehension in his face. Joshua busied himself at the chuck wagon, banging dishes into a tub.

Were they avoiding him? Michael wondered, suddenly aware of the gloomy quiet. Even Finbar had grown somber during the day, and now he placed his attention on the guitar he was strumming. Except for Ned, no one spoke to him directly. Michael felt the subtle way they closed him out of their shared communion, as if an unspoken fear made them wary of him. Had Jake and Ramon said anything? Michael didn't think so; it wasn't their way to talk much about private matters. And while it was true that the trail gave one the habit of silence after a while, Michael was certain he sensed a distancing in their silence, as if he stood outside an invisible circle. Jim Delaney's death had given him the taint of disaster. Michael chewed his lip and then sighed wearily. Perhaps it was just his own fears fueling his imagination. Perhaps they were all just tired from the day's ride and the gruesome shock of Delaney's death the night before. They didn't grieve or say much about his death, but each man must have quietly turned over the events of last night in his mind more than once.

Joshua lifted the tub of dirty dishes and headed down to the river's edge to wash them. Michael followed after him, wanting to talk.

"Here, let me take that," Michael said firmly, grabbing hold of the tub. Joshua looked at him with a mild surprise but relinquished the tub into Michael's arms. They continued walking down the hilly bank to the river, Joshua's freed arms swaying loosely at his sides.

"What's on your mind, son?" Joshua asked once they had reached the river.

Michael set down the tub and Joshua squatted beside it, pulling out the dirty dishes and dipping them into the flowing water. He swabbed them down with an old cloth.

"What did you mean when you said you were double-sighted?" Michael asked.

Joshua shrugged. "I can see more than most folks."

"What exactly do you see?"

"Dead folk, mostly. Though once I seen a coyote on trail turn from a dog to a man. And I seen an owl sitting on a stump one night with a woman's face and a pair of long black braids hanging down either side of her wings. Mexicans call them *brujas,* witches." Joshua stacked the clean dishes. "I done recognized her as my neighbor's wife," he added, smiling.

"Does it bother you? That you can see those things and other people can't?" Michael asked, bending down beside Joshua.

"Is that it, son?" Joshua asked quietly. "Are those eyes of yours double-sighted some?"

Michael nodded. "Yes," he whispered. "Ever since my mother died, I see things. Sometimes terrible things, but I don't know what to do about it."

"Got to stop running away, for a start. Being double-sighted is a gift, boy. Got to use it!"

"How?"

"Whatever's needed," Joshua said plainly. "I don't look for it, son; it comes to me. One time a woman called on me 'cause her little girl was missing. Well, I could see that little girl's ghost just a hanging on to her mammy's skirts, but the woman was seeing and feeling nothing. Girl was dead, see, drowned in the river. I followed that child's ghost and showed 'em all where to find her body down among the weeds."

Joshua stood up, his knees cracking. The dishes were piled up in the tub again. Michael picked up the tub and held it in his arms, hesitant to return to camp.

"Is that all there is to it?" Michael asked. "Finding ghosts? Am I to be haunted by them always?"

Joshua frowned, suddenly agitated. He pointed a finger at Michael. "You got to find the answer for that yourself, son. Ain't no man can tell another what his responsibilities should be. You have to know that for yourself."

"Look!" Michael said softly, his chin pointed to the river.

Joshua turned, hands on his hips, feet firmly planted in the mud. "I don't see nothing," he said irritably.

"Nothing?" Michael said in a shocked whisper.

"And if you do, then it's your calling, son, not mine!" Joshua grabbed the bucket of dishes out of Michael's arms and started up the hill toward camp.

Michael stayed at the river's edge, staring out at the far bank. An incandescent figure, shining as brightly as the full moon now rising over the eastern horizon, was calling out to him. He saw her more clearly as the sky darkened into the royal blue of twilight. It was a woman who called him. She was dressed in a long white flowing gown, her pale hair streaming down her back and swirling around her waist. She dipped a white cloth into the river and pulled it up, stained a blood-red. She was weeping, her sobs the low keening of grieving women. She dipped the cloth in the water again until the whole river was a dark wine-red. She looked up at Michael, and his heart ached at the familiar face.

The ghostly woman called him by name, her voice a whisper on the breeze. He took a step forward, wanting to dive into the water and swim against the current to the other side. The water penetrated his boots, the cold slicing his ankles. He stepped in farther, his eyes holding on to the radiant image of Eileen McBride. Michael stumbled in the current and looked down alarmed at the red river lapping at his thighs. The rushing water tugged him, loosening the soft ground beneath his feet and threatening to send him sliding into the water.

He looked up in panic but the ghost was still there, the hem of her white skirts dyed red where they dragged under the water. The breeze rippled her image, and she seemed to have no more substance than a quavering re-

flection glancing off the water. She released her hold on
the billowing cloth, and once in the water it broke into a
path of floating light. The woman was fading beneath the
rising moonlight, her voice growing softer and more distant. Michael quickly took another step and felt something thick and muscular coil around his legs. His knees
buckled, and his arms thrust out to keep his balance in
the rushing river.

A horse neighed shrilly. Michael glanced behind him
to see Mo Neart careening down the hill. The stallion
charged into the water, blood-red waves splashing high
on the horse's white chest. The coils around Michael's
ankles squeezed tightly and a weight shoved against the
backs of his legs. He reached down to free himself and
quickly drew back his hand, feeling the cold hard plates
of scales. He was falling, his arms windmilling in the
open air. But Mo Neart was there at his side, and Michael made a grab for the horse's mane as he fell. His fists
clutched handfuls of hair and he strained to free his legs
from the coiled prison. As he clung desperately to the
horse, Mo Neart trampled the ground, waves foaming
around his body. The churned mud thickened in the
water and the coils scraped against his legs, tearing the
fabric of his trousers.

Then, all at once, the coiled grip relaxed and unwound
from his ankles. A long dark shadow floated away. As it
drifted down the river, a pair of yellowed eyes stared up
through the red murky water at him and then winked out
of sight. Michael hoisted himself up onto Mo Neart's
back and let the horse carry him out of the water. On the
stony crest of the hill, Michael slid off the stallion's back
and lay on the ground, his chest heaving as he tried to
slow his panicked breathing. Above him, the huge sky
was peaceful, stars splashed against the dark like drops
of spilled milk. The moon was a round pewter dish
against the black cloth of the night. Mo Neart's head
loomed over him, stars tangled in the strands of his lumi-

nous mane. He bent his head low, his warm muzzle touching Michael's face. The stallion's teeth nibbled lightly at the buttons on his shirt. Michael reached up and patted the horse's smooth cheek and then scratched him firmly beneath the rounded jowls.

"I'm all right," he sighed. "I'm all right."

He pushed the horse away gently and stood up. Looking back at the river, there was nothing fearful to be seen. The moon's reflection lay like torn lace on the surface of the flowing water. Small leather-winged bats had appeared and were diving and swooping at the insects that hummed noisily above the muddy banks. A mourning dove called, hidden among the branches of the oaks, and the water lapped softly at the banks. The weeping woman and the coiling dark shadow were gone. Michael was alone on the hill with Mo Neart. Joshua had said this ghost was Michael's calling. His calling, all right. But what was he supposed to do with it? What did his mother want? Michael bowed his head in weary confusion. He was sure he didn't know. Slowly, he limped back into camp, wincing at the pain in his ankles.

John O'Connor and Jake returned by midmorning saying they had found an easier crossing about two miles east down the river. The water level was lower, the channel wider and slower. Finbar, Ramon, and the Strayhorn brothers immediately mounted up and rode out to join Sumner, who was out watching the herd. Together they would drive the cattle along the river to the new site. Ned took the remuda and joined them, leaving behind the chuck wagon team and Mo Neart.

Joshua and Michael remained in camp, finishing the job of cutting logs from the slender cottonwood trees to use in ferrying the chuck wagon over the river. Michael's shoulders hurt from swinging an ax at a cottonwood that should have fallen over. But he didn't have the smooth swing required to send the ax cutting deep into the bark.

Instead he chipped away at the trunk, and Joshua gave him no end of grief about his lack of skill.

"We'll be here 'til next week waiting for you to figure out I don't need toothpicks," Joshua complained. "Let me do it, for godsakes, or we'll never get anywhere."

"I can do it!" Michael said with gritted teeth and took another swing. He tightened his arms, his fists clenched, slowing the movement of the ax as his body anticipated the pain of the impact. The ax hit the trunk unevenly and the force rebounded back up into his hands and arms. Once more Michael felt the shock of the blow in his aching shoulders.

"Don't try so hard, son. Jest let it out easy like. Let the weight carry it into the tree, not back up yer arm," Joshua counseled. "Like this." He took a swing upward, and at the apex of the arc he let the ax swing down of its own, weighted by his body. It sliced cleanly into the trunk and was buried to the hilt. Joshua jerked it out of the tree and handed it back to Michael. "Now try it again."

Michael did, trying not to force the ax but letting the weight of his body follow the downward swing. The ax landed squarely in the center of the wedged cut and the tree began to wobble. Michael smiled and struck again. A few more good blows to the trunk, and all his earlier wasted effort vanished as the tree toppled with a loud tearing sound.

" 'Bout time," Joshua muttered. He tied a rope to the branched end so as to drag the tree and its felled companions behind the wagon.

"Let's go and join up with the others," he said to Michael. "And bring that ax with you, son. You ain't done chopping."

"That's all right," Michael answered, his face flushed and sweating. "I got the hang of it."

"Well praise God," Joshua said. "Now let's git." He slapped the reins over the back of his team, and the horses strained in the harness, dragging their heavy load, until the groaning wagon wheels slowly began to turn.

They arrived at the river in time to see Sumner, mounted on his bay, loudly cursing the lead cattle and slapping at their rumps with his black hat. The cattle were lined along the river but were refusing to enter the water.

"What in the goddamn hell is the matter with you boneheaded stubborn bastards anyway!" he shouted, riding his cutting horse among them.

But the longhorns were unimpressed, their hooves set defiantly in the bank, bawling their refusal to go into the water no matter how much the man on horseback shouted and prodded them.

John O'Connor, waiting on his horse at the top of the hill, called to Sumner. Sumner, red in the face from shouting, rammed his hat on his head and rode back up the hill.

"I don't know what's gotten into them. Yesterday I couldn't get the bastards out of the water, now I can't get them in!" Sumner grumbled.

John pushed up the brim of his hat and looked over the river with an appraising eye. "Let's get the wagon over first. Maybe they'll change their minds."

Joshua and Michael lashed a cross-hatching of logs under the wheels of the chuck wagon and, after Ned had released the horses from the harness, pushed the wagon to the river's edge. Ramon rigged up two different sets of guide ropes; one held the wagon from the back and was looped around the trunk of an obliging cottonwood. More ropes were tied through the wagon's tongue and carried across by Ramon on his horse to the far shore. There, Ramon, Jake, and the Strayhorn brothers tied the ropes to their saddlehorns and waited for the wagon to begin its journey. Joshua sat on the buckboard, muttering nervously, as Michael and Ned pushed the wagon into deeper water. The logs lifted it gently and it began to float, straining against the ropes as it struck the current. With one foot braced against the cottonwood's trunk for support, Michael and Ned slowly eased out the length of rope that held the wagon from behind. As the wagon drifted farther into the river, the cowboys on the far shore backed up their horses, taking up the slack of their guide ropes as they pulled the wagon toward them across the river's current.

As soon as the wagon reached shallow water, the Strayhorn brothers waded out and helped pull it to shore. With Joshua's help, the logs were untied from beneath the wagon and set adrift downstream. Then Joshua's team was brought up, the wagon's tongue lifted out of the water, and the horses set in the harness again. Amid the cheers and whoops of the cowboys, the horses pulled the wagon the rest of the way out of the river and up onto the dry bank on the far side.

"Nice job, boys," O'Connor said to Michael and Ned.

The cowboys returned from the far bank, swimming their horses across the deep water. Wet and tired, they took a short break, changing their mounts for fresher animals as they considered the problem of the herd, as the steer were still showing their reluctance to cross the water.

At last John O'Connor shifted in his saddle and turned to Sumner, who was still cursing under his breath. "Here's what you do," he said calmly. "Cut a small herd of calves and drive them over to the other bank. When they start bawling for their mothers, we'll see how long it takes before those heifers find the courage to cross. If the heifers go, it ought to shame the rest of them into moving."

Sumner nodded with a half smile and briskly turned his horse's head into the herd of cattle. He called out to Jake and Ramon, and the three men began cutting out calves from the herd, separating the frightened youngsters from their mothers' sides. When a small herd had been thrown together, Sumner's big bay drove them into the water. Jake and Ramon whistled and shouted, their horses driving the youngsters into the water and forcing them to swim on the current. The calves bawled in panic, their heads barely breaking above the surface. Their long legs reached out, splashing the water as they paddled wildly. Within moments they were on the other side, darting up on the bank and kicking up the mud with their heels. Sumner turned around and the bay horse plunged into the river again.

"It's deep, all right. But I think the current's slowed enough," Sumner said when he returned to John O'Connor's side. They waited astride their horses and watched the calves on the other side of the river. Aware that they were alone, and afraid to cross back over the river, the calves began bawling loudly, their cries answered by the frantic calls of their mothers. The heifers shoved and pushed their way through the herd until they reached the river's edge. Still they hesitated, dipping their heads as though afraid to enter the water. The calve's cries became more piteous, and at last one desperate heifer gingerly entered the river, her nostrils flaring in fright as the water surged around her chest and the current lifted her off her feet. But she was determined and so began swimming toward the far shore, to where her bleating calf waited. Behind her the other heifers took more courage and slowly, one by one, they entered the water, easing themselves into the current. As they dragged wearily out of the water on the far bank, the grateful bleating of the calves seemed to stir the remaining herd into motion. The lead cattle now took their turn, and soon the entire herd was gradually entering into the river and swimming across.

Every cowboy on horseback was swimming with the herd, guiding and encouraging them as they floundered in the deeper water. Michael saw Finbar slip from the back of his swimming horse and grab the horse's tail as it towed him to the other side of the river. Sumner made three trips back and forth from one bank to another, the big bay horse taking to the water like a huge dog and never seeming to tire. Astride Mo Neart, Michael approached the river's edge. The horse stalled, his ears flattened in disagreement. Michael remembered the dark shadowy thing from the night before and understood Mo Neart's hesitation. But the sun was shining now, and the bright day was filled with the loud cries of the cowboys and the constant bawling and snorting of the herd as they swam across the river. Churned mud from the many hooves clouded the water, turning it a clay-pink.

"It's all right," Michael said to the wary stallion. "Go on, boy, take us across. We'll be safe now." Mo Neart went into the river, stepping carefully. The water rose to meet him, swirling around his legs in pink eddies and then lapping against his white chest. Michael felt the stallion lose his footing as the water became deeper and he was carried by the current. To make it easier on the stallion, Michael followed Finbar's example and slipped from Mo Neart's back. The water was cold, and he shivered as he held onto the stirrups and kicked out his legs. It wasn't until they had reached the other side that Michael realized he had been as frightened of the river as Mo Neart and had kicked his feet strongly in the water against the anticipation of feeling the shadow's scaly grasp.

The herd was almost across; only a few stragglers were left that had to be prodded into the water. Barney was in midstream, astride a small dun mare, when the terrified bawling of a muley caused him to look back.

From the bank, wringing the water out of his vest, Michael saw a long shadow darken the pink muddy water to a deep rose. He glanced up quickly, hoping it was a cloud drifting overhead. But the sky was an empty blue, with only a light haze softening the sun's glare. Michael looked back at the water, seeing the shadow lengthen under the floundering muley.

Michael held his hand over his eyes to shield them from the sunlight. He hoped he was mistaken, that it was a trick of the light. But the terrified muley was kicking the water into a white froth with its forefeet as the dark shadow slipped beneath it. Michael saw the pale gold eyes floating near the surface, peering up at the struggling muley. Then out of the muddy water, the jaws opened wide and a circle of teeth tore a hole in the muley's side. Barney was almost there, the horse's ears flat against its head, the head rearing out of the water in fright. A look of puzzlement spread across Barney's face as the water turned bright red.

"No!" Michael shouted. "Get away!" Barney looked up at Michael on the bank, and the dark shadow stretched out beneath Barney's horse. "Get away from there!" Michael shouted.

But his voice was lost in Barney's sudden high-pitched screams as a silvery gleam flashed along the surface of the water. A long chinless head lunged out of the water and, locking its jaws into Barney's leg, pulled him under. A coiled tail followed, whipping through the water and encircling the heaving body of the horse. Razor-edged scales from its coiled back opened to slap the surface of the river, sending showers of bloody water high into the air. Michael couldn't see anything in the exploding fountain of water, but he could hear Barney's screams. Then it was silent, as the water fell back into the river and Barney and his horse sank beneath a whirlpool of foaming water, the long shining coils turning over after him.

"Barney!" Ludie cried out on the far bank. "Barney, I'm coming!" Before Finbar or Ramon could stop him, he had turned his horse back into the water and was swimming out to where his brother had disappeared beneath the roiling water. He shouted Barney's name over and over, his eyes darting over the surface for signs of his brother. The water was growing quiet again, red-stained waves rippling out from the once-churning whirlpool.

"Barney!" Ludie cried again in desperation.

His horse started to squall, struggling to keep its head above water as something dragged it down from below the surface. Ludie looked about him in terror, clinging to the drowning horse. He was shouting for Barney as a fierce jerk from below sucked him under the water, his cries strangled in a new fountain of spewing red foam. The sun glanced hard off the bristling water, flashing with the brilliance of a mirror. On the banks the cowboys looked away, blinded by the sudden light. Only Michael stared long enough to see the opening and closing of huge silvery scales that slapped the surface of the water with a wet smacking sound and sent a new fountain of bloodstained water into the air. And just before he turned away, his eyes seared by the light, Michael caught a fleeting glimpse of both Barney and Ludie Strayhorn, trapped in the crushing grip of a coiled tail that lifted briefly out of the water and then descended again into the river. Michael squeezed his eyes shut, the light bursting like the sun behind his closed lids. But etched in black, the lines burned into his retina formed the last sight of the Strayhorn brothers: Barney's white face, his torn side draining blood and his hand clasping Ludie's as they were carried together under the water.

"Oh, God, oh, God," Finbar cried, running to the riverbank and looking out helplessly as the water quieted, the strong current washing away the remains of a frothing pink foam.

"What the hell happened!" Sumner was shouting. "Where the hell are they?" He mounted his horse and rode to the water's edge, but the horse refused to enter the river. No matter how hard Sumner struck at the bay's flanks, it sat back on its haunches, its flanks trembling. At last, in frustration, Sumner got down from the horse. Once freed, the skittish creature bounded back up the bank to wait on the crest of the hill. Sumner stared out angrily at the river. "What the hell happened?" he repeated dismally.

"Ahuizotl," answered Ramon softly, standing beside him at the river's edge. He held the reins of his horse to keep the frightened animal steady. "A water spirit. You will not find them anymore, Señor Sumner. They are gone forever."

"Bullshit," Sumner answered heatedly. "I don't take to your Mexican superstitious bullshit. Something out there killed them. Something real!"

"Most likely water snakes," John O'Connor said evenly, coming to stand between them. He took off his hat, a gnarled hand smoothing down his graying hair. His faded blue eyes squinted as he stared at the quietly flowing river. "Seen it happen before. Cowboy swims into a nest of snakes, gets bit, and then paralyzed. Water pulls him under then and he drowns. That's what happened, I reckon. Snakes. Got 'em both." He put his hat back on, adjusting the crown so that the brim all but hid his eyes in deep shadow. "It's two more graves we'll mark before we get the hell off this bank."

"Who's going to recover the bodies?" Jake asked.

"No one," O'Connor answered flatly. "They've gone downriver. It may be days and miles away before they turn up again on some bank, and we can't wait. 'Sides, I expect there won't be much left to bury by the time they do surface again."

"Nothing left of them," Ramon said softly.

The men moved silently away from the river, stopping every now and then to glance back, as if hoping to see some final sight of the Strayhorn brothers. At the top of hill, Ramon stopped Michael with a hand on his arm.

"Did you see it, Señor Mike? From your two colored eyes, did you see Ahuizotl take them into the river?" he asked in a harsh whisper. The fingers gripped more tightly.

"Yes," Michael answered. He lowered his head. "I

tried to stop them," he said. "But they didn't hear me."

"Maybe Jake is right about you. *Te asusta la mortaja, te abrazas al difunto,*" Ramon said angrily, spitting the words. "You are afraid of the shroud, yet you embrace death," he repeated in English. He let go of Michael's arm and pushed him away. "Who is next, Señor Mike?" he asked. "Who is next?" Then he turned away, leading his horse up the bank to join the others at the wagon.

Michael stood alone, his face hot, his eyes still scorched by the glaring light. A cool river breeze gusted along the bank, fluttering the silvery leaves of the cottonwoods. The branches of the oaks swayed and their leaves whispered dryly. The yellow blooms of the mesquite scented the wind. But even the dusty, perfumed air was not enough to cool the shame that burned on Michael's skin.

Eight

The ceremony for the Strayhorn brothers was short. From the stripped branches of a cottonwood, Joshua lashed together two crosses with a length of braided raw-hide. They planted the crosses among the sagebushes and, with their hats held in their hands, listened as John O'Connor spoke a few words. Then they moved silently away from the bank, and each man mounted his horse and took up his position on the trail. Their faces were grim beneath the shadows of pulled-down hats, jaws set in hard, stoic lines. They hollered and whistled, kicking up dust, as they spurred their horses and set the cattle moving north again.

Michael took a position at the drag, his bandanna covering him from his chin to his eyes, hiding his face. The air thickened into swirling clouds of dust that filtered the sunlight with a reddish haze. All he could see through the rising dust was the long sloping backs of the cattle, bony hips swaying with their tread, and the rise and fall of the curved horns as their bobbing heads measured the pace.

They drove the cattle without rest throughout the length of the day and they were still driving the tired herd in the early evening. Michael guessed O'Connor had wanted to put as much distance as possible between his men and the tragedy at the river. The evening dew had dampened the worst of the dust and made the march at the drag almost endurable. An evening star winked brightly on the deep blue lid of the night.

"Do you really think it was snakes?" Ned asked Michael as he rode beside him. The remuda was scattered alongside the herd, only Mo Neart staying close at hand.

"I suppose so," Michael lied.

"Last year on the trail I seen a cowboy drown when his horse took cramps in the middle of a crossing and sank. Cowboy couldn't swim well enough on his own. But I ain't never seen anything like what happened back there. The river turned . . . so red," Ned finished.

"It's all right, Ned," Michael said, wanting to reassure the boy and wanting more than anything not to have to think about the dark slithering shadow at the river. One foot in front of the other. Just keep moving, he told himself.

"I'm sorry Barney and Ludie are dead," Ned said softly, "but I'm sure glad it weren't me."

Michael turned to Ned, for the first time seeing clearly the boy's frightened face. The wind burns on his cheeks had grown whiter as the skin of his nose had freckled and browned on the trail. The small white scar on his chin made him look more fragile, like a crack in a china cup. He took off his hat to adjust the band and his wheat-colored hair fell across his worried eyes. It could have been Ned at the river, Michael realized. It could have been any of them.

Ned put on his hat and gave Michael a brave smile. He squared his shoulders and pushed out his child's chest. The coattails of his too-large jacket flapped like wings over his thighs. "That's the cowboy's life, I s'pose. It cain't be all bad. Look at John and Sumner. I guess it'll be all right."

Ned gave his horse an enthusiastic kick and the horse broke into a canter, chasing the straggling mares of the remuda back into a compact herd. Farther up the trail Finbar slowed his sorrel mare, waiting for Ned to join him. Michael watched them for a while, as Finbar yanked down the brim of Ned's hat, teasing the boy. Ned responded by snapping his reins over the rump of Finbar's horse and startling the plodding animal into a brisk trot. Finbar had to grab quickly at the reins as he bounced from side to side, trying clumsily to regain his seat.

Alone with his thoughts, the terrors of the last two days crowding together in his mind, Michael discovered that it wasn't love or grief he felt for Eileen McBride anymore. It was hate. With her voice she had created a world for him that was small and full of wonder. But her death had abandoned him to a world that was as vast as this night sky looming over him, his life no more than the tiniest pinprick of light amid an ocean of stars. It was a world of violent death, full of a threatening magic he didn't understand. She had given him the power of sight. But she had given him no weapons of his own against what he would see. He felt betrayed. How could she have done this to him? He saw in his mind's eye the portrait of her hanging on the stairway wall at Gramercy Park. He saw the cream-colored skin, the graceful curve of her neck, and the green eyes that he imagined now as mocking and cruel. Is this what his father had known of her? he wondered. Is this why there had been such a coldness between them?

Michael lowered his head, his chin nearly resting on his chest, as his last image of James McBride returned to him. Had he misjudged his father all these years? Confusion and anguish swept over Michael as he tried to piece memories together out of the vague recollections of his childhood. Here, among the emptiness of the darkened plains, he tried to look again at the familiar scenes in the narrow rooms of the Gramercy Park house with the eyes of a man, not a child. What pain could there have been on his father's face that he had not seen before? What dark shadow lay in his mother's heart that she'd hid behind her lilting voice? But the faces of his parents wavered like a dream, and all he could see was the chessboard, James McBride bending over the forest of pieces, the queens and kings hidden behind a wall of pawns.

"You marching all night, son, or do you figure to stop with the rest of us?" Sumner called out, rousing Michael from his thoughts.

Michael's head jerked up, and he was surprised to discover that the herd had stopped marching and was spreading out slowly in search of soft grass in which to sleep. Even the muleys at the drag end had clotted together and were already bedding down for the night.

"You sleeping?" Sumner demanded, leaning his forearms on the pommel of his saddle.

"No," Michael answered. "Just thinking."

"Well get yourself into camp and get some food into you. Then do your thinking laying down 'cause you're on third watch tonight with Jake."

"All right." Michael nodded and rode his horse to the rope corral that Ned had set up to hold the night horses. He slid down from the saddle, exhausted, and went to the chuck wagon. Joshua silently handed him a plate of beans and salt pork. There were also two white biscuits, their fragrant brown tops dusted with a light coating of flour, and next to the biscuits a side helping of peaches, gleaming with syrup. Michael's shoulders sagged, weighted by an unexpected sorrow. Joshua had attempted, in the only way he knew, to bring comfort to the declining morale of the crew. Death had ridden hard on their heels, giving them no chance to mourn. But staring down at the lavish peaches and the biscuits, Michael could think only of a doomed man's final meal, as if Joshua were preparing them for worse yet to come.

"Ain't they good?" Ned said happily, his mouth full of peaches. The biscuits were already gone from his plate.

"Yes," Michael replied, "they're great." He ate one, but misery squeezed his throat so that he couldn't swallow anything as sweet and undeserved as a slice of peach. Without a word, Michael scraped the remaining peaches from his plate onto Ned's and gave him the two biscuits. The boy's eyes went wide, but he didn't disagree, and with a smile he finished them off.

Michael quickly finished eating what was left and returned his empty plate to Joshua. Then he dug out his bedroll from the wagon and found a place near the fire to spread it out. He lay down, the blankets pulled up to his chin, his head resting in the shelter of his arms. And though he was tired, he couldn't sleep. Each time he closed his eyes he saw again Delaney being stabbed in a curtain of electric light, the Strayhorn brothers broken and torn in the grip of silvery scales. He squeezed his closed eyes harder, trying to erase the horrible images. The grit from the trail scratched beneath his eyelids like tiny stones, scraping across the images until the welling tears came at last and washed his eyes clean again.

"Hey son." Someone jogged his shoulder. "We're on watch." Michael awoke with a start from a terrifying dream of falling, arms outstretched, into a black sky. He shuddered awake, comforted by the pull of gravity on his spine as he stood up. He rolled up his bedding, stowed it away in the wagon, and softly whistled for Mo Neart. The stallion came quickly, his white form ghostly pale in the moonless night. Out of his left eye Michael saw the stallion's body shimmer brightly, the mane curling like soft gray smoke over his arched neck.

"Hey boy," he greeted the horse, taking the long face between his hands. He saddled Mo Neart and then rode out to the bedding ground, where he could see Jake talking to Ramon.

"They are restless tonight," Ramon was saying. "The singing is all that is keeping them quiet."

"What do you think it is?" Jake asked.

"I won't say, for fear of calling it to my side," Ramon answered. "But be careful. *Vaya con Dios,*" he added as he rode away to the camp.

Jake took out a leather tobacco pouch and reached his fingers inside. He first sprinkled some on the ground. Then he took a second pinch and rolled it into a cigarette. In the brief flare of the match, Michael saw Jake's face lined with tension. Jake sucked in smoke and blew out the match with his exhalation. His face was hidden in the darkness, but against the starlit sky, Michael could see the silhouette of Jake's black hat turn toward him.

"I have to say it makes me worried being out here with you, son," Jake said in a low voice. "Seems there's something following you, and it don't seem to care much who gets in its way."

"What makes you think it's me?" Michael said gruffly. "Could be anyone on this trail."

"Right there's the reason I know it's you. You didn't disagree that something was following us. You might have said it was just our powerful bad luck to lose those cowboys. But you didn't."

Jake paused, taking another drag from his cigarette. He gently blew out the smoke and it formed a wreath beneath the brim of his hat.

"You know there's something out there, don't you?" Jake said.

"Maybe I do," Michael replied carefully. "But if there is, I know even less than you what it is or what to do about it."

"You fixin' on learning any time soon, or are you planning on waiting until we're all dead afore you give it some thought?"

Refusing to answer, Michael tugged Mo Neart's reins and turned away. He rode the stallion to the far side of the herd, away from the peppery stink of tobacco and the cold accusation in Jake's voice. The cattle shifted restlessly on the grass, lifting their heads to snort nervously at the wind. One steer rattled his horns against another and the clatter brought two other heifers lurching to their feet in panic. Michael started singing, his voice groggy with fatigue but clear enough to soothe the fretting cattle. The two heifers gradually folded their legs beneath their bodies and lay down again with heavy sighs.

Though Ramon's warning had made Michael anxious at the start of the watch, the night settled into a peaceful quiet, a breeze blowing down from the north and bringing a cool, dry wind. There was no moon, just the distant stars shedding a faint, dappled light over the humped backs of the drowsing cattle. Mo Neart's walk was smooth, the saddle shifting on his back like the gentle rocking of a cradle. On the other side of the herd, Michael could hear Jake singing in Kiowa, a low rhythmic song that slowed his pulse and lulled him into a near sleep.

It was later, when the night had stilled to an utter quiet, that Michael dimly heard a faint whirling. The sound tugged at his ear, rousing him out of a half sleep. Mo Neart stumbled in his walk and then picked up his pace as though uncertain. Michael lifted his head to the dark night, his eyes seeing only the stars and the mottled shadows of the cattle. More awake now, he listened intently to the odd fluttering noise filling the air. He could hear the sound but couldn't find its origin. Something furry and reeking of musk brushed against his face. Alarmed, he batted it away with one hand, and Mo Neart beneath him startled and sidestepped away. The thing screeched and darted in close again with a fluttering of wings. Michael raised his arm protectively and the creature slammed against his arm, clutching the wool of his jacket. A mouthful of sharp teeth bit Michael hard on the exposed wrist. Michael waved his arm as the creature let go and flew off with the sound of slapping wings.

"Goddamn," Michael swore in shocked surprise as he held up his hand, unable to see it clearly in the deep darkness. His wrist throbbed, and he could feel the blood trickle down his arm toward the elbow. The fluttering noises grew louder, a breeze whispering with the frantic movement. At once the air was filled with the soft clapping of leathery wings and the frightened bawls of the cattle. Bodies brushed against Michael, skeletal wings hitting the brim of his hat and shoulders, claws catching in the fabric of his coat. He ducked his head into the corner of one raised elbow as wings beat against his face.

They were bats. A swarm of leather-winged bats, sweeping and soaring over the cattle with a rapid motion of their wings. The dark cloud blotted the starlight, and the air was permeated with the animal musk of their bodies. They dove into the cattle, biting them on the necks, along their shoulders and rumps. The steers bellowed angrily, heaving to their feet. More cattle followed, pushing against each other, horns slicing the air angrily as the bats continued to hover over them in a malignant swarm.

Michael couldn't see, his head held down to keep the bats from hitting and scratching his face. One landed on his thigh and he grabbed it quickly in a gloved fist. The creature struggled wildly in his hand, screeching and then biting Michael's gloved thumb. Michael held it up to the faint starlight and saw its face. A man's face. An old man's face, with a twist of teeth reaching up from the bottom of its jaw to nearly cover the flattened nose. The struggling bat hissed and then spat at Michael.

"You're bucked now, boyo," it screamed. "Red Cap'll have you soon, but these fat bits are for us!"

With a burst of rage Michael snapped the bat's neck and threw the stinking body down to the ground. But it was already too late. The bats had goaded the terrorized cattle into motion.

They had risen to their feet, bawling as they anxiously milled about, looking to escape the claws and stinging bites of the bats. Several cattle were bucking and kicking their heels, goring the air with their horns, as the bats continued to attack them. Then, at the sudden impulse of the lead cattle, they all began to run. Trotting at first, then gaining momentum, the herd bunched together and started stampeding.

Michael hunkered down in his saddle and grabbed a firm hold of Mo Neart's mane as the stallion bolted after them, galloping hard to keep pace. Sumner had once instructed Michael to stay near the lead cattle in a stampede and try and direct the charging herd away from camp. If they stampeded through camp at night, too many sleeping cowboys could wind up dead beneath the trampling hooves. Mo Neart poured out more speed, his long legs tearing at the ground as he angled his huge white body against the lead cattle, gradually forcing them to turn away from the camp. Behind them, the other cattle followed the gentle curve, flowing after the lead cattle like a river flooding its banks and spilling out across the dried earth.

Just stay with them, Michael told himself; running was not a natural gait for these large beasts, and they would exhaust themselves soon. It was his job now to keep them together, keep them out of danger and slow them down as much as possible. The sound of the stampede thundered in his ears, hooves drumming, bawling cries echoing out over the night. Amid the rising dust, Michael could just make out the black outline of Jake, riding on the far side, his free arm whipping at the animals who tried to break ranks with the herd.

As Michael looked ahead of him he saw that the herd was coursing over the plains, away from the camp. But the noise of the stampede would be enough to bring the other cowboys out riding to help them regain control of the herd. Michael looked worried about him, the bats having abruptly disappeared. A cowboy dashed by, firing rounds off an old Colt, and Michael recognized Sumner. O'Connor and Ramon quickly appeared around the flanks of the running herd. The cattle flinched at the sounds of the guns going off but would not stop their desperate running.

Suddenly Michael felt uneasy. There was something not right, something he was missing, as the herd thundered away in terror.

Two shots sounded, the reports like the crack of a whip. Not a pistol, but a rifle. Michael glanced quickly behind him. Far back at camp, he saw the glow of the cookfire and the vague shape of the chuck wagon. Another rifle shot cracked, and Michael pulled hard on Mo Neart's reins to stop the galloping horse. Caught up in the frenzy of the careening cattle, the stallion shrieked angrily, falling back on his haunches and wheeling awkwardly as Michael forced him to change directions.

Michael released his hold on the reins but kicked the stallion hard in the sides. He leaned his head forward and shouted to the stallion over the sound of the stampede. "Camp, boy, take us to the camp!" he yelled into the twitching ears and slapped the reins against the stallion's neck. Head lowered, Mo Neart galloped toward camp, his hooves scarcely touching the ground as he crashed through the low bushes.

Michael's heart was pounding, the sweat hot on his face and his breath coming in ragged gasps by the time he reached the camp. He found Joshua first, sprawled on the ground near the campfire. His arms were thrown wide, his rifle lying near the wagon wheel. His legs were bent at an odd angle, the feet turned out. His black eyes were open but unseeing, only the flames of the fire animating the huge, dark pupils. His throat was torn, a ragged gash that drained blood in a thickening rust-colored halo around his head.

"Ned! Ned!" Michael shouted as he scrambled from Mo Neart's back and began to feverishly search the camp. Please, he prayed, please let him be all right!

"Mike!" Ned called out from the dark, his voice thin and high with terror.

Michael ran to the edge of the camp, just where the light of the campfire blended into the darkness. He peered out, seeing two figures stumbling amid the sagebrushes.

"Mike, help me!" Ned cried out.

"Stop there!" a voice ordered.

Michael had taken a hurried step forward and now stopped with a sharp intake of breath. In the dim light of the cookfire he saw Ned turn toward him, white-faced like one of the calves. The boy was waving his arms wildly, trying to wrestle himself free from a man who gripped him tightly around the chest. Michael recognized at once the tall, gaunt man with the feral grin and the red gleam shining in his eyes.

"So, McBride, are you wishing you'd given that eye when I first asked for it?" Red Cap laughed coldly.

"Take it now," Michael said quickly. "Take it. But let the boy go."

"Ah no," Red Cap said, shaking his head. "Too late for that. It won't be finished without blood now. It was she that started it. Tried to break the curse, she did, by giving you that eye. But it won't work. And now, me boyo, one by one you'll watch them all go down, no matter if you cut the eye out and give it me on a golden plate. It's the price you'll pay for who you are!"

"No!" Michael shouted. "No. Let him go!"

"Mike, help me," Ned pleaded, thrashing harder in Red Cap's grip. He kicked his legs, his heels finding a target in Red Cap's shins.

Red Cap threw back his head and howled to the sky.

At once his body changed. Ned was lifted off his feet as
Red Cap arched his back into a deep curve, his head upturned to the sky. Red Cap's pale skin absorbed the
night, becoming as black as the moonless sky, black as
padded velvet. His gaunt face grew round in the jowls
and flat on top, with two tufted ears. The red eyes continued to glow like burning coals; his mouth opened wide
and a pink tongue uncurled from a jaw of gleaming sharp
teeth. Then Red Cap cried out with the exalted scream of
a hunting panther.

Too late, Michael rushed forward to help Ned. Red
Cap flexed his claws and raked a black-pawed hand over
the boy's chest. Three lines appeared across Ned's shirt,
the torn fabric etched with spilling blood. For an instant
Ned looked at Michael, his mouth rounded in dismayed
surprise. Then his eyelids drooped, and Ned slumped like
a rag doll, his fair hair falling forward over his bent head.

"No!" Michael shouted. "NO!" He rushed to the
wounded boy.

Red Cap released his grasp on the boy. Moaning
softly, Ned tumbled heavily to the ground. Half man,
half cat, Red Cap crouched over the crumpled body and
spat at Michael. Then, dropping to all fours, the arms
changing as he pitched forward, Red Cap bounded away
under the cover of dark bushes, only the curved tip of his
tail twitching once to mark his passage.

"No," Michael cried again, his voice hoarse. He
reached Ned and gently turned him over. The boy's eyes
were almost closed, his mouth gaped open. A sticky
breath snagged in his throat, wet and choking. A thin
trickle of blood flowing from the corner of his mouth
dyed the old china scar on his chin. His chest rose and fell
unevenly, the blood pumping from his wounds. Michael
picked up the limp body of Ned Darling and cradled him
close to his chest, Ned's head resting against Michael's
shoulder. He heard the boy's last drawn-out exhale, no
more than a weary sigh. The body collapsed in Michael's

arms, growing heavy. The blood was warm where it seeped through Ned's shirt and soaked into Michael's vest.

"Not you, Ned. Not you," Michael whispered fiercely. He looked down into Ned's face, the fair hair stained with blood, the pale eyes half lidded and opaque. Then Michael hugged him close, wanting to give warmth to the boy's quickly cooling face. "Don't go, Ned. Don't go," he said, tears stinging his eyes. Far away Michael could hear the low rumble of the cattle, running out across the plains. But the sound faded, and in the sudden quiet hush of the night, Michael bent his head over the slain body of Ned Darling and wept.

The cattle were returned to camp in the early morning. The sun was breaking through a low bank of clouds, shafts of falling light creating gold rainbows over the blooming mesquite bushes. The cowboys came back to camp, their horses foot-sore and limping from the long night run. Michael heard them dismount behind him, the creak of the saddle leather and the bridles clinking as reins were dropped. He heard the harshly whispered curses and the scuff of their boots as they came out to where he sat, still hunched over the cold, stiff body of Ned Darling. But he kept his head down. He couldn't look into their faces.

"Señor Mike," Ramon said, his quiet voice hard. "It is enough. Give me the boy."

Unfolding his arms, Michael let go of Ned Darling, the dried blood cracking into a powdery dust as they pulled him out of his lap. Freed of their burden, his arms fell stiffly into his lap. He stared at his hands, stained with Ned's blood, mixed with his own where the bats had bitten him.

"Get up," Jake ordered.

Michael moved slowly, his body aching, his limbs feeling aged. He looked down and saw the river of blood that had dried on his vest, the lap of his trousers, and all the way to the tips of his boots. How could a child bleed so much? he wondered distantly. Why couldn't he have stopped it?

"Pick up your head and look at me," Jake snapped.

"I can't," Michael groaned. "They all died because of me."

"Then be a man, Michael McBride. Stand up for yourself and stop letting others die for you."

Michael raised his head and looked into Jake's unforgiving gaze. The stern face did not offer sympathy. But there was in the severe glance the hint of understanding.

"You've been walking in death's world, and you've dragged us all with you. You've got to get away. Get out."

"How?" Michael asked him. "How?"

Jake shook his head. "I don't have the answer to that, but somewhere in you is the way back. You have to find it. But you'll have to search for it on your own."

As Jake was talking, Ramon, Finbar, Sumner, and John O'Connor came and stood before him. They had tied his yellow oilslicker and bedroll to Mo Neart's saddle. A canteen and a leather pack hung down one side of the saddle, tied by a rawhide rope to the horn.

Michael's heart sank. He knew what they were asking, and he knew he couldn't refuse.

"Son, I think it's time you left the outfit," John O'Connor said, his voice a rasp as he struggled to get out the words. "I been talking to Ramon here. . . ." He paused, shaking his head in disbelief. "Ned was a good boy. He would have been a good man. So were the Strayhorn brothers and Delaney. Joshua and me . . ." He paused again, pursing his lips as his face showed the strain. "We went back a long way. Now they're all gone, just markers on the trail. I ain't never turned a man loose in a drive before, but this time I'm going to. You got something on your tail. And if it weren't for the death I've seen these last weeks I might never have believed it. But it's happened. And I can't let it happen again. To anyone that's here."

"I understand," Michael said weakly. "I should have left earlier. I didn't know it would come to this . . . to people being killed." Michael shook his head as he stared out at the quietly grazing cattle and the gentle roll of the land. "I don't know how to stop it."

"Listen to me, Señor Mike," Ramon said, taking a step closer. His dark eyes sparkled with the points of diamonds and his skin was flushed a ruddy color. "When I was a young man in Mexico, I heard one night the noise of wood chopping. No one cuts wood in the night, so I knew in here," he said, tapping his chest, "that it was Youaltepoztli, the night hatchet. Having heard him I must pursue him, for not to do so would mean misfortune, and any man brave enough to confront him would get power. So I ran into the woods, my fear falling behind me."

Ramon stopped, drew in a deep breath, and let it out slowly. "I found him at last. The night hatchet has no head. His body is an old stump, his throat a gash in the bark. On his chest are two doors that swing open and shut, banging like the chopping of wood when he runs. I stopped him and reached in the open doors where he kept his heart. I grabbed the night hatchet's heart. I held it in my hand, Señor Mike, and demanded payment."

Ramon reached into his vest pocket and pulled out a closed fist. He opened it to reveal a small black knife, its blade a smooth stone, chipped into a sharp point. "He gave me this obsidian knife, which will wound and kill the most difficult of spirits. Take it, Señor Mike. It may help you."

Ramon took Michael's hand and put the small knife in his palm. Michael carefully closed his fist around it and stowed it away in his vest pocket.

"Thank you," Michael said softly. "It's more than I deserve."

"It is little enough if you succeed," Ramon replied.

With aching arms, Michael heaved himself onto Mo Neart's back and eased himself down into the saddle. He looked around him at the huge, empty plains. "Which way?" he asked the silent line of men. "Which way should I go?"

"West," John O'Connor answered. "Toward the mountains and the higher ground. Some of it's desert, but among the rocks you'll find springs, and sometimes old Indian rock pools that are filled with rainwater. We've given you what supplies we can spare, but you're going to have to learn how to fend for yourself."

Michael nodded. Then he reached his fingers to the brim of his hat and tipped it to them in a gesture of farewell. They did not answer him, only stepped back to let Mo Neart pass between them. Without another word, Michael rode off on Mo Neart, through the sagebrushes and blooming mesquite, through the grazing cattle and out beyond to the western plains, where he knew Red Cap waited for him.

Nine

For two weeks he crossed the high plains, moving west toward the distant broken line of lavender mountains. Overhead the skies remained blue and empty, except for one afternoon when a pair of mating ravens filled the sky with their harsh and joyous cries. Michael watched them, amazed by their aerial play, the male swooping upside down in flight beneath the female to impress her. One night it rained a little, a light shower of cool water; and in the morning, as the damp ground was quickly drying in the rising sun, Michael heard the cheerful chorus of birds, their parched throats refreshed in small pools of water collected in the hollowed-out depressions of rocks. The brittlebushes were a drab olive green against the pale pink soil that was growing more gray with stones. An iridescent hummingbird, like a precious jewel, hovered in front of Michael's face one morning, curious at the bright red bandanna tied around his neck. Every night Michael made his campfire and watched the moon rise like a shield of bone in the night

sky. He sat close to his fire and waited in silence for Red
Cap to come. And every morning, when he rose bleary-
eyed and soot covered with ashes, he wondered how long
Red Cap would make him wait.

Gradually the land around him changed. Though it
seemed drier and more forlorn, the flatness of the plains
had given way to narrow valleys among rising cliffs and
pine-covered bluffs. Scrub jays chattered to Michael as
he rode past in the daylight, and at night he could hear
the distant cries of coyotes. Water had been scarce, but
he had found a spring that bubbled up between a pile of
granite stones. The stones had been marked with drawings, white lines carved into their immutable surface. He
stared at them, seeing the carved lines flow over the rocks
with the circular pattern of ripples. The water was sweet
and cold, and the grass around it surprisingly green and
lush in the dry earth. He had camped there, and as he
slept, the ancient drawings on the rocks turned in his
head until he saw the image of a bird, wings spread wide,
falling into the black center of the white circle. He awoke,
disturbed by the dream, and packing quickly, he left, the
evening star still glimmering on the low horizon of dawn.

Michael squatted beside his campfire, encouraging the
flames with small sticks of juniper kindling. They crackled noisily, sending up the thin trails of sweetly scented
smoke. His saddle lay on the ground, and from the sad-
dlebag Michael withdrew a small pot, which he filled with
water. He took a handful of coffee beans and ground
them between two pieces of cloth as he had seen Joshua
do on many a morning. The grounds he placed in the pot
and set it over the fire. The coffee would be strong and
bitter, but it would also quiet the gnawing hunger that
had begun to be his constant companion. He withdrew a
thin piece of dried jerky and chewed it slowly.

The days had passed so quietly and repetitively that
Michael had almost forgotten to fear. Almost, that is,
until yesterday. Michael stared dreamily into the flames,

a half smile on his lips. He had seen no other human beings on the trail, though the nights and early morning hours had been filled with the scurrying noises of small animals, taking advantage of the cooler hours to hunt for food. There had been lizards the color of gray rocks, which had almost gone unnoticed except for their swift escape when Mo Neart's hooves had strayed too close to their perch. Rodents and snakes rustled the dry branches in the evening, and black beetles made their slow, laborious way in the dark shade of the rocks. Though he looked often enough at the rippling heat on the horizon behind him, Michael had seen nothing from his left eye.

Then yesterday, as he was riding through a narrow gap between two wind-scarred bluffs, he had seen a coyote standing on a tall boulder as if waiting for him to pass. From a distance, the creature had appeared half starved and ragged looking, his tongue hanging out as he panted in the heat. His sides were dust colored and his tail covered with burrs. A sorrier looking animal Michael had never seen before.

But as Michael neared, the coyote changed. He sat on his haunches and the back legs stretched downward, while the shoulders rose and hunched over a caved-in looking chest. Two long hands tapped nervously at the tops of his thighs. By the time Michael reached him, the coyote appeared as a thin, hungry-looking man, wearing a hat that half shaded the pale yellow eyes. From his left eye Michael could see the dog's ears that poked up through holes in the man's hat.

Michael slowed Mo Neart, warily watching the silent coyote-man, who started smiling and beckoned Michael to come closer. Michael hesitated and then realized that there was no other way for he and Mo Neart to go through the narrow valley except past these boulders, where the coyote-man happily waited for him. Michael sighed and tightened his hold on Mo Neart's reins. A dram of Eileen's cautionary advice struck him. It was never safe to talk to a fairy. And remembering Jake's stories of the coyote, perhaps it were wise if he said nothing now. Coyote may not mean him any real harm, but Michael knew he would be foolish if he didn't regard the creature with a healthy suspicion. At least, Michael thought, he knew one of the coyote's weaknesses.

Michael quietly dismounted Mo Neart and, letting the horse graze, took out his food pack and opened it up. The coyote licked his human mouth with a huge pink tongue that had a spot of black skin on the tip and scrambled down from the rocks to join him. Michael let him take what he wanted without complaint and wasn't surprised when all the salt pork and most of the dried jerky disappeared in several huge mouthfuls.

Then coyote sat back, pleased, a hand with black fingernails gratefully rubbing his newly distended stomach. Long black eyelashes fluttered over golden eyes as he sighed and then belched. He sucked his teeth and picked at them with a juniper twig.

"I know what you've got dogging your tail, son," the coyote said when he had finished cleaning his teeth. He shook his head and gave a low whistle. "I've been there myself. But since you've been good to me now, I'll return the favor." Out of the air, the coyote produced three stiff and shining black feathers. He held them up for Michael to see. "I stole them off of a crow two years ago. They can make you fly."

He gave them to Michael, who took them, restraining himself from saying "thank you." The the coyote looked at Mo Neart, head cocked to one side, his spotted tongue lolling out. "Nice horse," he said, his yellow eyes gleaming again.

Though he guessed the coyote would have more trouble than he knew taking on Mo Neart, Michael became worried by the hungry look on the coyote's human face. He stood up, nodded his thanks for the crow feathers, and got back on Mo Neart. And as he rode away, Michael could hear the coyote calling after him, the short yipping barks smoothing out into one long, sustained note of pleasure.

If the coyote had stopped him to warn him about Red Cap, Michael thought, sitting by the campfire and feeding it sticks, then he knew it wouldn't be long before Red Cap showed up. Michael guessed that the coyote had wanted to make sure he got one good meal out of Michael before Red Cap stole it all. The green juniper sprigs crackled as they burst into flame beneath his coffeepot. But the coyote had not left Michael empty-handed.

Michael retrieved the crow feathers from his vest pocket and studied them. They were beautiful, the black color glimmering with a green and blue sheen in the firelight. The shafts were stiff and unbending, the quills sharply pointed and the delicate ribs of the black barbs tightly interwoven. As he turned them in the light, three names came to Michael from his mother's stories. Morrigu, Neman, and Macha, the three goddesses of war, together in the single form of a black crow. Neman was the confounder of armies, who caused bands in the same army to mistake each other for the enemy; Macha reveled among the slain of the battlefields; and Morrigu, the greatest of the three, had given Cuchulain supernatural strength when it suited her to defeat the enemies of the Tuatha De Danann, and later, when she had come to hate him, had sat on his shoulder as he was dying of battle wounds.

"Will you be crows or swans?" James McBride used to ask at the chess table. A crow, Michael declared. Swans were for men lost in enchantments. But crows were for battle, for blood, reveling in the carnage of the aftermath. Morrigu and her sisters had no fear of death, but embraced it, carried it aloft in their black wings. He could use their wisdom and their savagery right now, even if he wasn't as great or fearless a hero as Cuchulain, he thought as he watched the flames sparkle on the black-bladed edges.

Mo Neart raised his head abruptly from the grass, his ears pricked forward to catch a tiny sound: a rustle through the dried creosote branches and the snap of a twig. Michael stood up quickly and stared out into the night-covered ground. He had made their camp near an outcropping of rock, hoping the shelter might give their backs some protection. Michael's long shadow flickered against the wall of weathered stone. Mo Neart shook his head and gave a throaty murmur, the sound a warning to Michael.

"So, McBride, you've decided to go it alone, have you?" a voice cracked out of the darkness. "Or did those ones throw you out at last?"

Michael didn't answer but swiveled around, trying to find the origin of the voice.

"Can you not find me, then?" Red Cap taunted. "Can you not see me with that eye of yours?"

Beyond the circle of firelight the bushes were black shadows, joined by the smooth humps of boulders. A single pine tree raised its wind-twisted branches against the darker sky. The needles hissed dryly as a gust of wind shook them. Michael tensed, alert and afraid. Where was Red Cap hiding?

Red Cap laughed, a sound that swiftly altered into a low-throated snarl. Michael spun around and saw the crouched panther looming over the edge of the outcropping. The panther peered down at Michael and hissed, his ears flattened against his rounded skull.

Cold seeping into his limbs, Michael backed away slowly from the crouched panther, his trembling hand reaching behind him to find Mo Neart. The stallion nickered softly and leaned his shoulder into Michael's back to let him know he was there. Poised and ready to spring, the panther's red eyes followed Michael with a keen stare, black velvet muscles bunched at his shoulders and his tail switching back and forth in agitation.

Michael eased himself alongside Mo Neart, letting one hand follow the ridge of the stallion's mane, while in the other he gripped the crow feathers. He had Ramon's knife in his pocket, but he didn't think there was any way he could reach in and get it without forcing the panther to attack. Behind him, Michael could sense the eager stallion waiting impatiently to flee. A slight shudder rippled beneath the silky skin of Mo Neart's neck.

Then the panther screamed and launched his body into the air toward Michael. At the same moment, Michael turned and scrambled onto the stallion's back.

Mo Neart reared back on his haunches, his sharp front hooves knocking the big cat out of his flight. The panther crashed against the rocks and shook his head, dazed at the unexpected attack. With a loud shout, Michael kicked Mo Neart in the sides and the stallion turned and bounded away from the outcropping.

Michael clung to the horse, his hands buried in the flowing mane, his thighs gripping hard around the horse's heaving sides as he struggled to stay on the stallion's back. The wind whistled in his ears and his eyes teared, stung by the lash of Mo Neart's whipping mane. Small sparks of blue light scattered beneath the stallion's pounding hooves.

Michael could feel when the land changed under them as the horse left the open spaces of the plain and sought out the surrounding cliffs. A ridge runner, Ned had called the stallion, seeking protection from its predators on the higher ground. Michael turned his head, hearing the brittle snapping of twigs as something tore through the bushes beside them. The red eyes burned up at him, and the panther stretched out its front legs to keep pace with the galloping horse.

Mo Neart veered away and headed up a steeper incline. Stones kicked out around his hooves and rolled behind them. Michael bunched his body on the horse's back, holding on as the powerful stallion drove himself up the slope of a rocky hillside. The panther switched back and forth across the path behind them and, when close enough, striking out with his claws at Mo Neart's back legs. The horse was panting hard, lather foaming on his neck and chest, making his hide more slippery. But when the stallion reached the top of the hill, he lengthened his head and neck and, keeping it down against the wind, galloped along the cliff's edge.

To one side of him, Michael could see the racing panther, moving like a swift shadow over the ground. To the other side, the land dropped away into a steep ravine. The stallion poured out another burst of speed, his legs tearing at the land before them as he ran.

Michael looked ahead of him, feeling the stallion beneath him begin to tire, his breathing growing labored as he continued to gallop just out of reach of the panther's claws. It was dark, and in the dim starlight hard to see what lay ahead of them. Michael shouted a warning as he saw suddenly the curved edge of the ridge and the darker line where the land abruptly ended. They were trapped on a high promontory with nowhere to go but back the way they had come. Mo Neart saw it too and his legs stumbled, his knees buckling, as he tried to break his furious stride and turn away from the edge of the cliff. Behind them the panther leapt and clawed at Mo Neart's hind quarters. Mo Neart kicked out his hind legs to throw the panther off, his head dipping forward and revealing to Michael the long, perilous drop over the side of the cliff.

The panther lost his clawed grip on the kicking stallion and rolled away in the dust. He stood up and, shaking his body, prepared for a second attack. Close to the cliff's edge the stallion reared and spun around to face the panther, neighing with outraged pain. Michael cried out in alarm, his hands grappling to keep hold of the stallion's mane as the front legs reared up. His clutching hand pulled away, empty except for strands of Mo Neart's mane, as Michael lost his balance and was pitched backward.

Shouting, Michael tumbled over the haunches of the rearing stallion, one hand vainly trying to grasp the air, while the other hand held on to the crow feathers. His gripping thighs were not enough to keep him on the stallion's rearing body, and within a moment he was swept off the horse's back and over the side of the cliff.

And then he was falling, hearing above him the screaming panther and the bellowing stallion. But there was nothing to catch Michael as he fell over the cliff and into the air. Michael cried out Morrigu's name as the fluttering crow feathers were snatched from his grasp by the wind that rushed over him.

A fierce pain exploded in his chest, the bones of his sternum cracking. He looked down to see his ribs breaking apart, white bones tearing through the cloth of his shirt. His arms were pulled from their sockets, the elbows snapping as a force splayed the stretched limbs over the keening wind. Michael screamed in agony, his body fractured, his hips crushed, his legs curled like vines beneath him. And then from his skin black shafts sprouted. Along his back, his belly, and his chest, he felt the stabbing birth of feathers pricking his skin. His arms lowered in the air, heavy with the draping weight, and then he lifted them again, the air catching beneath the sail of black iridescent feathers. Michael's head jerked up to the stars, and his screams took on the harsh cawing of a crow. The feathers closed over his cheeks, his head, his chin. His mouth was lost behind the hard armor of a beak that snapped open and closed with his raucous cries. The outstretched wings took on their own momentum and began to pump like bellows.

His body slowed in its falling, hovered, and glided over the downward pull of the earth. He looked down, confused, not knowing what he saw. There was only the panicked urge to fly, to escape to somewhere else. He felt wounded, but he could not find the source in his body. He remembered pain, but it was gone now in the exhilarating rush of wind through his wings. He gave a harsh cry and then tilted his body against the wind.

Upward he flew, driving the wide sweep of his wings to catch the wind. The stars above him gleamed with invitation, and he flew toward them. A woman's face shown in the bright twinkling light. She was weeping, and the tears flowed in streams of cold light into her hands. She looked down and saw him, then opened her hands to receive him. The tears spilled from her fingers and formed a luminous silver river that spread like moonlight over his jet-black wings. He cawed with joy that he was at last returning home.

He flew into the night sky, each thumping beat of his black wings boosting his body higher, to where the stars waited for him. And among the stars he saw seeds of light swell into the fat buds of flowers and then open into radiant blossoms. Out of the shimmering folds of starlit lilies and hawthorns, men and women appeared, crowned with the diadems of royalty. On horses exhaled from the icy breath of comets, they set out riding across the black field of the sky.

He called to them in his crow's voice, and the harsh, urgent sound of it arrowed through the light and left a wake of turning, curious faces. One of the men offered his arm as a perch and the crow angled toward it, the sad smile on the man's broad face known to him. His wings flapped uncertainly, tearing the aura of light, until his talons finally secured a landing around the closed fist. Tired but pleased with himself, the crow preened, the tips of his wings catching the falling beads of starlight.

"And are you of my people?" the man asked in a voice as hollow as a wooden flute. His broad face was bearded, and tousled yellow hair curled over the rim of his crown. The light shivered, and the silvery bridles and tattle bells braided in the horse's mane jingled sweetly.

The crow bowed his head, the short bristles above his beak trembling with the greeting.

"And what have you there, Finvarra?" demanded a woman, her shoulders covered by a black cloak outlined with a web of stars. She was astride a black mare with opal eyes and a white star emblazoned on the forehead.

"One of yours, perhaps, Morrigu," the man replied.

The crow felt himself lifted up on the fist for inspection and he stood erect, the feathered crest of his brow raised aggressively.

The woman's face came close to his and the crow lidded his black eyes with a thin white membrane to show her respect. She too was known to him. Her hair was polished jet, her skin a winter snow that was chiseled into cruel and beautiful features. She turned to one side and her face was a hag's, gray-haired and bony; she turned again and it showed youth, full cheeks the color of buttermilk surrounded by glossy black hair. When she tilted her head back, to gaze at him down the length of her nose, her face changed again into middle age; the jaw line rounded, the wide brow shadowed with faint lines as, frowning, she studied the crow. She had a smell about her: the rust of blood and newly dug earth. She tore out a coarse laugh from the back of her throat. The crow lowered his body, his head bowed over the fist to show his submission to her greater authority. She stroked him, one cold finger riding over the back of his closed wings.

"A strange one if he's mine," Morrigu said. "But if he called my name and came here in this form, then he's at least of the blood. Let him stay for now, Finvarra, and later we will see where he belongs."

Finvarra settled the crow on the golden horn of his saddle.

"Tok! Tok!" the crow called, telling them of his pleasure to be traveling with them. Morrigu laughed again, and on her youthful face, the white teeth gleamed between her parted lips.

Throughout the night the long line of luminous noble
rode in procession, moving always toward a distant lin
of pale blue light. It beckoned on the night's horizon lik
the edge of the ocean, mist curling up from its cool rim
The crow opened wide his wings to gather in the sof
sheen of the distant light. Home, he was going home, th
light called with a sibilant voice, pulling at his breastbon
with the rawness of instinct. Behind him he could see th
field of night fading to a gray blanket of clouds, the fier
lip of a new sun burning off the starred path they nov
rode. Far below him, he could hear the day rising with
chorus of sound, the joyful and the miserable in one jar
ring clash of music. He shook his body, puffed out th
feathers of his chest and neck as if to drive away the ugl
noise of the world below. He was going home, where n
such disharmony existed.

A woman in a cloak of gray rode her white mare besid
Finvarra. She pushed back the hood of her cloak and
stared long at the crow. His eye met hers and he stumble
back, fearful and angry. She smiled at him, but her fac
held no happiness. In the rising dawn, her skin was a
gray as her cloak, but her eyes were lit by green leaves
and the hair that fell over her shoulders was the fallov
color of corn silk. She touched him and he moved away
troubled by the sight of her.

"I know this one, Finvarra," she said, and her voic
sighed through the darkness like a wisp of smoke.

He looked at her in surprise and then back at the crow
"He's fine enough looking. But who then are his people?"

"He's mine. Let him go, Finvarra."

Finvarra gazed at her with a mixture of pity and un
derstanding. "You'll not come with us, then?" he aske
her gently.

"Not yet," she whispered in reply. "Only when it'
fairly done may I return."

"Then we will wait with you to see how it is finished."

"Suit yourself," she answered.

Finvarra looked with interest at the crow on his saddle and nodded. He tucked his fist beneath the crow's talons, loosening him from his noble perch. "Away with you, then," he said sternly, "and be about your own work."

He launched the crow, releasing him to the gusts of warm air rising from the dawning earth below.

At once the crow was snagged by the rushing wind, turned over and over, wings splayed as he spiraled downward and into a bank of thick white clouds. Moisture collected on his wings, streamed from his beak as he tumbled headlong in the clouds. Abruptly he broke through the bottom of the cloudbank and fell into a hazy blue sky, water droplets spraying from his fanned feathers. He cawed in startled fright as the morning sun blinded him. The slanting rays coated his black wings with a patina of gold. He steadied his body in the driving wind and glided over the currents, searching upward for a path through the clouds that would return him to the procession of light. But the clouds were ships rapidly blown away across the skies, their wakes shredding into ribbons with the winds. The path to the stars was gone. And though he searched, he saw nothing but the blue bowl of the sky. On the far horizon the arch of a new moon hung stubbornly, its horns upturned to hold the remnants of a fast-fading night.

He could feel the longing for that blue-misted place still pull at his breastbone, but there was no way to find it. Hunger and fatigue overtook him, demanding that he return to the earth and seek food. His limbs ached with the pounding wind and he let them rest as he drifted downward again toward the earth. "Krawk! Krawk!" he called in dismay as he cocked his head, surprised to see that the world beneath him had changed. The land he was now soaring over was different, stranger than the one he had fled.

In the night's journey with the starry procession they

had traveled a far distance over the darkened earth. The wide-open plains of buffalo grass were gone; so too were the low-lying mesquite trees, the gray sagebrush, and the slender cottonwoods and scrub oaks.

The land below was a long strip of desert, the spreading sunlight reflecting off the near-barren land like a burnished, copper-colored river. He flew closer and saw strange trees; the bark was thick and shaggy, and along the uplifted branches the leaves clustered in spiked heads, topped with spears of greenish-white flowers. In the dryness of the morning the last exhalations of dew carried the faint fragrance of the trees' perfume high into the warming air. All around, struggling for a purchase on the hard soil, withered-looking shrubs waited for rain. Spine-needled plants squatted close to the ground, and the morning sunlight trapped among their thorns gave them a soft golden glow.

The crow saw a narrow lake and descended quickly, his throat parched by the long flight from the stars. The stilled water was like glass, and he was startled to see the sudden black outline of his own reflection against the blue sky as he hovered over its surface. He landed near the shore, his talons scrabbling to find a footing on the pebbled soil. Several clumps of brilliant yellow daisies greeted him with the nourishing promise of water. He strutted, his head arched forward to the silent lake. A white earth had bubbled and hardened at the edges of the lake, and he stabbed his beak into the twisting forms with curiosity. The shapes crumpled into powder and he shook his head to clean his feathers of the ashy residue. He dipped his beak into the water and sipped a drop of the water.

Then he cawed in anger, his throat burning with the taste of alkaline salt. He shook his head, the feathered crest of his forehead lifting in annoyance. He stalked away from the lake, thirst and hunger clamoring in his body. A slight scurrying noise caught his ear. He stopped, head poised to see the flash of a lizard's tail disappear between the narrow shadow of two rocks. He sidled closer, keeping his movements spare as he eagerly approached the lizard's hiding place. He leaned over one of the rocks and saw the gray-speckled lizard, almost invisible against the rocks except for the gentle heaving of its sides. The crow gave a quick dart of his head and snapped up the lizard in his beak. Trapped, the reptile wriggled violently, but the massive beak was closed tight around the twitching body. The lizard was too large and too awkward to eat in one mouthful, and its wild movements made it difficult to hold onto. Angrily, the crow held the twisting lizard pinned to the ground beneath his talons and began to spear it with his beak until the flesh pulled apart in smaller mouthfuls.

He shuddered, something in him resisting this meal of unfamiliar flesh. But the few drops of blood washed away the fierce burn of salt from the lake and the warm meat appeased the gnawing of his hunger. It wasn't much, but, having eaten something, the crow took to the skies again.

He saw now that the desert stretched out like the tattered hem of the mountains rising behind it. When he flew high into the air, he could see the faint hint of green amid the purple stain of rocks on the mountains. Down below on the dun-colored land, the world seemed quiet and empty of life. But as he traveled across its face, he learned that much went on in the rounded shade of the rocks and the strange branching trees. Brown wrens sheltered in prickled trees, and ruby-throated hummingbirds sipped at the long flower stalks suspended over plants composed of thick-bladed leaves. White-necked rats hustled mouthfuls of spiny plants beneath the tangled growth of brittlebushes. Ants made trails in the dust between their cones, and snakes coiled their dirt-colored bodies into the cooling shade of the rocks. The crow perched on a lichen-covered rock and watched the determined march of a black beetle before snapping it up in his beak.

But though he searched and cawed through the sky, there were none others like him. A red-tailed hawk chased him in the midmorning, driving the crow away from his mate sitting on their nest. And later he saw a roadrunner streaking along the ground, head down as the legs churned up little clouds of dust. He circled in the sky, letting the currents of heated air carry him aloft, lonely and lost.

It was near midday, when the sun's heat forced him down out of the sky, that the crow saw the old carcass of a rabbit wedged between two rocks. Its matted fur was peeling off in clumps of fine hair, and the exposed ribs tempted his hunger, which had returned. He came close to it, the stench lifting the stiff bristles over his beak. He jumped up on the rocks and, bending down, stabbed his beak into the carcass to pull out the thready sinews. But the body, dried and hardened by the sun, refused to yield its flesh easily. He moved closer between the rocks and stood on top of the body to get a better grasp while he tore at the old flesh.

Slowly the rocks began to move. They ground together with a dry scratching sound, the earth shifting beneath them. The rounded backs uncurled, and from the bottom of the rocks, the crow saw the stony faces of two creatures emerge. Their eyes were a pale pink, their foreheads and chins covered with an armor of mottled-colored horns. They hissed and squeezed together more tightly. Too late, the crow realized his legs were trapped.

"Kaaa!" he screeched in alarm, flapping his wings wildly as he struggled to free his imprisoned feet.

The rocks growled with laughter and dirt sprayed from their mouths. From a cleft in one of the rocks a stony hand appeared and began to pull him down by one wing.

He stabbed at the hand with his beak, shards of rock splintering into dust, but the hand continued to draw him closer to the stone faces. They were murmuring, little noises of pleasure that vibrated through the hand that clutched him. They ground their pebbled teeth and licked at the lichen-covered gums. Though he continued to flap his free wing and cry out, the crow, already weakened from hunger, was rapidly growing tired from the struggle. His eyes lidded over white and he gave a loud cry of distress. More stone fingers jutted from the rocks and tried to tear the feathers from his wing.

A raucous voice blared out from the sky and an angry cawing made the stone fingers hesitate.

The crow cleared his vision and saw above him another crow plunging through the blue sky toward him. It was a huge female crow, her black wings glistening and the spear of her beak shining like polished obsidian. "Kaaa!" she screeched in outrage, and the rock creatures raised their horned faces upward in concern to watch her approach. They hissed and chuffed out mouthfuls of dust. The hand clamped more tightly around the crow's wing, making him cry in pain.

Hovering just above them, the female crow tilted her body upward, her wings forming twin arches above her black head as she attacked the rock creatures. She raked her talons over their pale pink eyes and they groaned, pulling their heads down into the valley of their stone shoulders. Again and again she attacked them with her talons, even when their heads were buried out of sight, only the low murmurs of fright rumbling through their rock bodies. Standing on them, she stabbed the rounded shoulders with her beak, striking them hard until steel-colored sparks flew from the broken shards of gray stone. Groaning, the rocks opened a narrow space between them, and the hand released the crow's tattered wing. Feeling himself at last freed, the crow staggered away from the rocks, his legs unsteady and his injured wing bruised. A few of his pulled feathers had drifted on the wind and snagged in the thorns of a prickling plant.

There was a sudden flurry of wings, and the female crow took to the skies.

"Krackrackrack!" she cried in an invitation for the crow to fly with her.

From deep in his throat he answered, "Rawk!" and lifted himself into the air. "Rawk!" he called again in greeting, triumphant to be free and soaring once more above the earth. The female crow flew before him, higher in the blue sky, and he chased after her, glad not to be alone.

"Kukuk!" she chucked, urging him to join in an aerial chase.

In the bright air, he pumped his wings and then flipped over onto his back, flying upside down beneath her, the rushing wind curving his tail feathers up toward her. She slipped to the side and barrel-rolled in the open sky, and he tumbled after her in play. Through the wind he caught the rusty scent of spilled blood. His heart beat more strongly in his chest. He remembered her cold fingers stroking his back. He became happy then, knowing that he would not be abandoned by the shining host after all. She flapped her widespread wings and, rolling lazily to her back, let the wind pull her down toward the earth in a game of daring. He cried out eagerly and, folding his wings, passed her, straightening his body just above the tops of the shaggy-barked trees and shaking the blossoms loose from their spikes before swooping upward again.

Throughout the day they flew together across the dry face of the desert toward the mountains. The female crow showed him how to find the clear sweet water cupped in weathered hollows in the rocks so that he need not drink from the salted lakes. She brought him to the carcass of a deer, and after chasing off the gathered coyotes, she stood guard while he ate his fill. From the cool shade of some ironwood trees the yellow eyes of the coyotes watched with annoyance as she strutted possessively up and down over the deer's spine. They yipped and whooped, licking their lips and pawing at the dirt over their loss. But none would come close enough to challenge the strident female crow. Before they left the carcass, the female crow plucked from her back two long pinion feathers and, jumping down from the carcass, offered them to the coyotes.

One of the male coyotes, his spotted tongue lolling out of his mouth with his grin, snatched up the feathers between his teeth. And as they took to the sky again, the crow looked down and saw an old man sitting by the carcass of the deer, fitting two crow feathers into the band of a battered hat.

It seemed right to the crow; this world of giving and of taking. He didn't even begrudge the rocks that had torn at his feathers. They had acted out of their own need to survive, which was his need too. The sun was a golden ball balanced on the back of his outstretched wings, and he sensed the world was like him, bright and dark, woven together as sunlight and shadows fell over the earth.

He looked down and saw the red glory of an opened flower against the flat gray of the rocks. He watched the desert rat at work, the soft, furred belly pricked by the sharp thorns of the plant he carried to his den. He could smell the cold rivers of water that flowed far beneath the surface of the dried land. All of it vibrated with life, a beating pulse that whistled in the dry wind, ratcheted in insects' call and hummed a low song in the shifting rocks. All of it connected by one heart, one flesh, of which he too was a part. And when he looked to the far-distant mountains, he could hear the earth's blood coursing through gold and silver veins buried in the mountains' flanks. The trees whispered with rustled breaths, the spiny plants sighed from mouths wreathed with voluptuous flowers. Beneath the shade of warped rocks, the coyotes became men for a moment, and in a grove of ironwoods strangled by mistletoe, a gray dove mourned, crying with the sad voice of a woman. He banked his wings, turning in the sky to follow the female crow. He saw below him a white stallion breaking through the glass surface of an alkaline lake, the flowing mane scattering a powdery dust to the winds as it galloped over the crystalline banks.

The sun raised red and orange arms of farewell across the lavender sky as it began to slide lower on the horizon. The purple mountains opened to receive the ball of light, swallowing it slowly and letting the gold spill over its rim. A few salmon-colored clouds swam in the fading blue light. "Rawk!" the crow called to the female as her black wings blazed for a moment red as flame and then subsided into a smoky gray.

She answered him and then, stroking her powerful wings, angled her body upward to the darkening blue sky. She set her course for the evening star, glowing bright and hard as a new diamond. He followed her, feeling the sense of anticipation rise in his breast as the longing for the misted blue horizon returned. She continued to fly with a steady pull of her wings, and he struggled to keep pace with her, his wings aching with the effort. The air was cold and thin, and below him the earth curved away in a dark green line. But ahead the horned moon had turned over and was tipping out the shimmering light of the stars.

He saw them, gathered together, some seated around gaming tables, others playing instruments, a few examining weapons, their faces lit by starlight, their bodies a shimmering blur as they moved. He wanted to cry out a greeting, but he had no breath to spare, his body weary from the long flight. He followed the female crow until she came to settle on the back of an empty chair placed beside a gaming table. He joined her on the chair, his head bowed low to acknowledge the power of those gathered there.

The female crow gave a harsh cry that turned into a

woman's shrill laughter as she shook off the feathered
body of the crow. Morrigu sat in her chair, brushing the
starlight from her midnight hair with her fingers. She
placed her elbows on the gaming table and, resting her
middle-aged face on her fists, looked over the chessboard. She *tsked* loudly and shook her head at the battle
that was being lost among the white and black pieces.
Finvarra looked up silently from the game, his brow
creased in annoyance at her noisy disruption. He ran his
fingers through his curling gold beard, tugging it lightly.

"Losing again, are you, Finvarra?" Morrigu said
scornfully, her eyes darting over the battlefield. "Your
man there has you routed."

"Trust you to know the stench of defeat," he said
glumly.

Morrigu inhaled deeply. "Perfume," she cackled, and
her hag's face appeared like a quick shadow passing over
the surface of the moon.

"Who's your companion?" the second player asked.
The crow ruffled his feathers at the cold sound of the
voice, familiar and dangerous. He looked from one eye
and saw the man with a close cap of bright red hair falling over his shoulders. Small braids at the temples kept
the fine hair from his eyes as he bent over the playing
board. The narrow face was long and hungry-looking,
and the eyes that slanted over the high cheekbones
watched the crow with suspicion.

Morrigu sensed the crow's alarm and smoothed his
chest feathers, chucking lightly in the back of her throat.

"One of mine," she said.

"Liar," the man shot back.

"And why's that?" Morrigu asked, wearing her youthful face, milk-white and angry.

"He's no fit match for you," he replied, moving his
white knight to challenge Finvarra's king. "Check!" he
announced.

"He's more a fitting companion than the pair that follow you, Donn Feirine O'Conail of Knocfierna!" Morrigu said tartly. "Do you fancy that you need such messengers?"

Donn Feirine leaned away from the table and rested his head between a pair of dusky ravens guarding the back of his chair. They had partial human faces, their long necks a collar of dirty feathers between their hulking shoulders. They hissed softly. The crow sidled closer to Morrigu's head, taking protection in the blowing strands of her hair. The round yellow eyes of the ravens regarded him with hostility. They were females; their sagging human breasts were laid over the tattered plumage of their chest feathers. One had webbed feet and a woman's clawed hands. The other leaned forward, menacing the crow with the clacking of her tusks.

"It was you who gave the bananachs to me, Morrigu," Donn Feirine answered smugly. "A present for my wedding."

"More's the pity," she sniffed, and her face became that of a hag.

"They're your offspring. But not that one," Donn Feirine said, pointing toward the crow.

Finvarra gave a short cry of triumph and moved his bishop to the right, where it threatened Donn Feirine's black king in return. "Check!"

"You'll not call me a liar, Red Cap, and get away with it!" Morrigu shouted, the wind driving her hair around her face like the flurry of wings.

"And you'll not call me 'Red Cap'!" he shouted back. He stared angrily at the chessboard and, with a quick dart of his hand, moved a second unnoticed knight, knocking out a pawn guarding the white king. "And it's mate!" he exclaimed.

Finvarra leaned back heavily with a groan. Then he slammed his fist against the table. "Again!" he demanded. "Play me again!"

"No," said Donn Feirine. "I've other business to attend to and will not waste the time when I know in advance the outcome." He stood up in preparation to leave.

"And what's your hurry, then? Surely it's not to torment the wife who grieves her return to a cold marriage bed?" Morrigu said sharply.

Donn Feirine's eyes narrowed and his sharp teeth raked his lower lip in suppressed anger. "You mind your own sorrows, Morrigu."

"And isn't it my sorrow too for letting it happen? Your wife, but one of my sisters."

"No doubt it's where she's learned to deceive!"

Morrigu laughed, throwing back her head, the sound rising from the pit of her stomach. "It's easy enough to trick an army of bloodthirsty men into the death they didn't know they craved, but you, Red Cap, haven't the wit about you to keep one woman happy and living in your house. More's the fool, you."

"Bitch!" he snarled.

"So I am," she said proudly.

He raised his hand as if to strike her. She stood up and faced him squarely, her face wavering in the light between youth and age. And then the hag's face appeared, sharp as a skull, the eyes hollowed with night. The wind carried the reek of smoke and blood. Around the hem of her flowing skirts came the rumbling sounds of war carts and the groans of dying men. The bananachs behind Red Cap cowered, hiding their faces in their wings.

"This crow belongs to me," she said, "and is under my protection. Not even you would risk your armies against me. A waste of time, we both knowing the outcome in advance," she mocked.

Red Cap lowered his hand slowly, his face white and poisonous as mistletoe. With effort he silently regained his composure, then left. The bananachs lifted their dusky wings and with dismal cries fled the gaming table after the retreating figure.

Morrigu gave a long sigh, and the skull's head softened

into the comfortable expression of middle age. She sat down in her chair and lifted the trembling crow onto her fist.

"Arrogant bullocks," she muttered.

"But dangerous," Finvarra added. "You ought to be more careful," he warned her. "At least for her sake."

"As long as the boy remains my crow, Eileen has nothing to fear," Morrigu answered, giving her shoulders a delicate shrug. "He's under my protection. Red Cap'll not touch him."

"But he can't stay like this!" Finvarra argued.

"And why not?" Morrigu asked, her youthful face flushed moon-white.

"Because it's no future for a child of mine," the woman in the gray cloak said, coming to the table and sitting in Red Cap's vacant seat.

"But it is a life, Eileen!" Morrigu countered. "Better than what your murderous husband would have for your child."

"That one is not my husband; my husband lies elsewhere," Eileen said bitterly, picking up the white queen and king and rolling the two chess pieces between her palms. Her green eyes stared sadly out at the board and then up at the crow. "And a crow's life is no life at all for a man. And a man he is, though he wears the feathered cloak."

Morrigu's middle-aged face softened with concern. "You know, Eileen, I cannot change him back. It must be by his own will, or the will of another with wit enough to break the spell. Though I may welcome him as a crow and give him my protection, I cannot undo what has been done by his own hand."

Eileen sighed and looked away. "I know that. And my *geasa* forbids me speaking directly to him of his heritage. Even as a crow, he is still my son, and I am still cursed."

"Then what will you do?" Finvarra asked.

She turned to face the crow again and let fall the chess

pieces from her long white hands. "I gave him the sight, but without knowledge, I fear it is not enough. So I shall do what I have always done. Recite the tales and hope he will learn from them." She raised her fist, and Morrigu moved the crow from the back of her chair onto Eileen's waiting fist. The crow trembled, afraid of the gray-cloaked woman.

"Do you mind the tale of Cuchulain's birth?" Eileen said, her voice light.

"Oh, not that one," Morrigu complained with a frown.

"You loved him once, did you not?" Eileen said sharply. "You gave him strength in battle against the Fomorians and he fought for you."

"Yes, and then he betrayed me. And I sat my hate upon his shoulder when he was dying on the battlefields of Ulster. And that's what comes of loving mortals."

"Mortal by half. Cuchulain was son to Lugh, the sun god, and Dectera. He had both within his blood. It's what made him a great warrior, second to none."

Morrigu sat back angrily in her chair, her fingers wrapped over the arms in a taloned grip. "He was a warrior, true, but he was also a whoring, gambling—"

"No less than those of his father's people," Eileen snapped. She turned sharply to Finvarra. "And you, Finvarra, after Ethna, who else's wife must fear being seduced away?"

"Enough!" Finvarra growled. "I'm not in need of such an insult from you, the second wife of Donn Feirine, seduced yourself by a mortal."

"Not seduced. Given away, and by Red Cap himself!" Eileen said, raising her voice. "I was the prize in a game of chess! It hurts to speak thus," she said, a hand held to her throat. "Though it is to you and not my son I give these words, I may say no more."

"You wanted to go with that man," Finvarra reminded her. "We all saw the glad look on your face when the man proclaimed you his prize at the winning. Even Red Cap saw it."

"And, sore loser that he was, cursed me for his own foolishness," Eileen said bitterly. She laid a hand over her forehead. "Can there be no better road for a child of mine than to flee the wealth that both bloods have to offer him? Can he not be raised to see the greatness in both his lineages? I don't care for myself that I should be happy again. Too long I've lived with sorrow to know anything else. But for him . . ." She stroked the crow's chest lightly. "To know that this is all I may offer him torments me."

"Tell us of the story of Nemhglan," Morrigu said.

Eileen's sad face brightened with new understanding. "The king of the flocks of Conaire Mor."

"That's the one." Morrigu nodded.

"He could change himself from bird to man and back again and in that guise was able to render many services to Conaire Mor. There is one tale of him . . ."

As the gray-cloaked woman began to recite her story, the trembling crow grew calm. There was something in the soft, lilting music of her voice that was familiar; he remembered it as the sweet babble of water breaking free in a stream after the thaw. He closed his eyes and let his body settle comfortably on her fist. The whispered words were soft and warm as the dry desert wind, and her tale began to spin a thick cocoon of dappled light over his black, hunched shoulders. He felt himself grow drowsy and, closing his eyes, he slept as the words surrounded him, filling his feather-covered ears.

And so it went for days. First beneath the sharp spring sky and then the long stretch of the summer sun, he flew accompanied by the female crow during the day and, with the first winking of the evening star, returned in the night to the shimmering host. Perched on the gray-cloaked woman's fist, he preened his feathers, tucked his head beneath his wing, and listened to the soft babble of her voice. Sometimes they were alone, other times there were several of the royal host sitting nearby to listen attentively to the carefully chosen words. Finvarra would engage an opponent and play chess while he listened. Sometimes the crow watched with interest as the chess pieces tacked across the gaming boards, the fortunes of black and white armies rising and falling in complex patterns. Once the narrow-faced man with the red hair came close to him, his high, slanting eyes boring into his. He tapped a finger on the crow's sharp beak and gave a dry laugh that made the crow fearful.

"Leave him be," Morrigu warned.

"He'll trip himself, he will. And then there'll be an end to it," the cold voice said.

"Don't you touch him, Red Cap."

"Oh, not I," he said with a sneer. "Not I." And he moved away.

The crow, feathers ruffled and head arched in alarm, side-stepped closer to the gray-cloaked woman.

"Sh, sh," she whispered. "Will I tell you about Liath Macha, also known as Gray of Macha? He was one of Cuchulain's favorite horses, and he was white as the foam and born from a lake."

The crow listened, feathered ears inclined to catch the words. And at last, growing calm again, he slept contented.

When he awoke this time, lifting his drowsy head from the shelter of his wing, it was a chilly morning. He stared dazed at the new world around him. The washed colors of the desert were gone. There were no shaggy-headed trees, no drab olive bushes or spine-needled plants. He was cold, the dew clinging beneath his feathers like crystals of ice. A harsh driving wind blew in his face. He rustled his feathers, stretched the stiffness out of his wings, and then puffed his chest feathers to keep in the warmth.

He was huddled in the shelter of massive granite stones, their washed surfaces polished by wind and rain with streaks of bright silver. At his feet were the tiny pink blooms and leathery leaves of prickly phlox clinging to the hard soil. He jumped up onto the top of the stones and had to steady himself against the cold, gusting wind. He was on the top of the mountains, the landscape stark and naked of trees. Low blooming flowers, the pink phlox and yellow wallflowers hugging the bases of heavy boulders, offered the only color against the relentless gray stone. Small drifts of hard-packed snow filled the low depressions between the walls of rocks. The sky was a clear blue, the fading night a thin slice of purple light. The moon was full, and it hung like a polished mirror brightening the massive backs of the rocks.

The crow looked about for the female crow, waiting to hear her cry split the fresh cold mountain air. But there was only the sound of the wind like the rush of water flowing over cataracts. He opened his wings and lifted into the morning air, his black body absorbing the warmth of the early morning sun. Back and forth he drifted over the barren high country, waiting to see if the female crow would join him. One by one the last of the stars winked out of sight in the approaching daylight. The chilly winds hurried thick gray clouds over the sky. He could smell the dankness of snow and wet stones. "Krackrack," he cawed, hoping to hear the female's answering cry. The wind sucked at his voice and sent it blowing over the harsh landscape. "Krackrack!" he cawed again, wondering where the female crow had gone. Was he alone again, now that the world had changed once more?

Alone perhaps, but not as lonely as before, he thought. Instinct told him he needed to fly down from these forbidding peaks to the warmer climate of the lower mountains. There he would find trees to give him shelter and food. There the air would be warmer, the wind more benevolent. He flapped his wings and drifted over the sea of rocks.

He had become stronger over the summer, his lean body heavily muscled beneath the feathered cloak. The long flights to the stars had given him stamina and his wings an easy power. With the female crow's help, he had eaten well throughout the summer, and his thickly laid feathers were glossy with health. He knew how to cock his head to one side and listen for the scratching of beetles buried in the shaggy barks of the desert trees. His beak was sharp enough to bore a hole into a tree and take the hidden meal. He could pluck a snake up from the desert floor and then smash it quickly against the rocks, killing it before it could strike. He knew where to find water and where the small desert rats slept in the day and the coyotes hid their bones. His female companion had taught him well, and he had a confidence now in himself that gave him curiosity and daring.

But for all his daring, he was still cautious. Some creatures, he had learned, were dangerous indeed. He had kept his distance from the rat-faced weasels with their sharp teeth and claws. He had seen them transforming at daybreak into bony-framed women, swaying with gallows hips as they gathered baskets of withered plants in the desert. He had seen the silver scales of the twisting serpents in the alkaline lakes, sucking into their white-foaming mouths the thirsty deer that strayed too close to their borders. And once, as he rested in the heat of the day on the branches of an ironwood, he was nearly taken by a one-eyed man with a huge mouth and a hand that protruded from the middle of his body. As he flew away over the desert, he had seen the creature follow him, leaping vigorously across the sand on one leg as a ravenous hunger goaded it into pursuing him.

The crow looked down with interest as the mountain landscape began to change its hues. The stark gray of the rock slabs was broken apart by tiny veins of moss and scrubby grasses filling the crevasses. Mats of blooming stonecrop, a pale sunrise shade, softened the ground.

Along the high valley walls trees clung tenaciously with tangled roots, their gnarled branches bowing to the wind as they sprawled over the rocks. On the valley floor tall narrow pines sprang up like spears out of the barren land, dark cones clustered at the tips of their bluish-green branches. Splashes of red paintbrush flowers brightened the gray-green wells of the valley.

The air grew warmer, the wind softer, as the trees became denser and more numerous. The crow could smell the rich fragrance of pine resin carried in the moist breezes. He glided over the tops of stately red firs, their long-needled branches sweeping down to a grassy floor. Standing in attendance around the base of the elegant red fires were the smaller lodgepole pines, their thin trunks covered with a dark, wrinkled bark. Mountain streams rushed violently over tumbled stone beds, and along the wet grassy borders bloomed orange tiger lilies, their speckled throats opened to reveal the drooping stamens. The tall spikes of white corn lilies, nodded, still heavy with the morning dew, and the camas flowers opened their purple stars to the new day.

The crow landed on the outstretched branch of a red fir pine. Below him a stream cascaded over a fall, the booming splash of plummeting water echoing in the trees. Hungry, the crow cocked his head to listen for the click of beetle wings or the diligent boring of an insect beneath the fir's rough, plated bark. Instead, he heard the clear voice of a bird trilling behind the rushing water. He turned, curious and alarmed.

A small gray bird was perched on the lip of a soggy green nest, built of moss and hanging close to the curtain of falling water. The crow watched the bird dive into the rushing water of the stream and slowly move upstream beneath the water's surface in a bubble of water, turning over rocks and looking for insects. Then it burst out of the water and, with a wet flash of its gray wings, returned to its nest.

The crow opened his wings and dropped gently to the edge of the river, stalking up and down along the side of the rushing water uncertainly. He put one foot into the water and drew back quickly, not liking at all the feel of the driving current. The gray bird began to call again, this time his voice the high pitched notes of warning. The crow looked up from the stream's grassy bank and saw two bananachs drifting high in the air, their shaggy wings outstretched as the torn tips fanned wide to catch the wind. They hovered, heads down-turned as they searched for something. Against the brilliant green of the bank and the white-rushing water, the night-black crow knew he stood out.

One of the bananachs saw him and screamed in delight. She clapped her taloned hands together, alerting her sister. The other bananach clacked her tusks and tucked her webbed feet close into her body. Then the two ravens folded their wings and dropped with a scalloped flight, descending quickly on the crow.

"Kwak!" he called out in alarm and lifted off the bank, his wings flapping wildly in terror.

He flew recklessly, breaking between the dense branches of the red firs, the soft needles brushing against the tips of wings. Behind him, he could hear the bananachs whooping and laughing in their pursuit, matching his zigzagging flight. He pumped his wings and dove beneath the branches, searching for cover. The lodgepole pines tore at his wings and the frantic beat of his wings broke the spindled twigs. A bananach appeared before him suddenly, landing heavily on a tree, her eyes gleaming and her taloned hands reaching out to grab him. He banked quickly, dropping below the branch on which she waited. She reached out, screeching angrily, as her grasp missed him, securing only a few feathers that she had ripped from his wing.

The crow felt the terrified beat of his heart slamming against his breastbone. A sharp pain lanced the edge of the injured wing. He continued to fly hard, sometimes trying to lose them in the tangled branches of the trees, and then when they spotted him, trying to simply outdistance them. But the bananachs stayed dangerously close, goading him from above and behind until he could feel himself weaken with fatigue and fear. The bananachs clapped their hands and screamed with half-human laughter.

The sharp odor of burning wood stung his nostrils. Fire, he remembered dimly, hot and crackling. Something the bananachs feared. He followed the scent, letting a thin haze of blue-gray smoke cloak him in the trees. All at once the trees opened into an abrupt clearing, and below him the crow saw a small cabin, smoke rising from a squat chimney that rose over a roof green with moss.

The bananachs cried out in delight. They had him now, flying wearily in the exposed open air of the clearing. They harried him on both sides, blocking his attempts to reach the cabin, where the door stood open. One bananach came close to him and pulled at his wings, shrieking. He fell in the sky, nearly tumbling to the ground. He righted himself and tried again to fly toward the cabin door. The second bananach dropped her body in front of him and backhanded him, knocking him down again.

The crow heard a woman's voice shouting. He lunged upward, straight for the blue sky. The bananachs glided in the air overhead, waiting for him. He pumped his wings furiously, hoping to outfly them. But one wing was torn, the blood seeping along his side and the gripping pain making it impossible to flap with the strength he needed. The bananachs mobbed him, taking turns as they dived over him, one knocking him aside in the air with her webbed feet, the other tearing at his wings. He fell, rolling in the sky, and then tried again to straighten his bleeding body over the top of cabin's roof.

He saw the woman now, standing in the clearing and

staring up at the bananachs. Her arms hung low at her sides. She was shouting at him and the bananachs. With the feathers of his injured wing fanning out in the wind, useless with pain, he struggled to lift himself in the air again and fly toward her.

The bananachs saw her too and closed in on the crow quickly. He could hear their grunted exhalations as they approached and he could smell them, their dirty wings reeking of carrion. One clutched him from behind, her talons squeezing around his back, digging into his flesh. In a blaze of pain, he tried to free himself, but his wings fluttered uselessly as the bananach carried him upward into the sky.

Down below, the crow saw the woman raise her arms in a slow, deliberate arc. He saw the curve of a bow arched before her body. The bananach pumped her ragged wings harder, and the crow could feel the sudden thread of fear in her beating breast. He saw the sun glint off the black, shining arrowhead. As the rising bow reached its upright position, the woman released the arrow.

A hard *twang* snapped in the air and the freed arrow hissed upward. The crow cawed once as the arrow pierced his body where the wing and breast were joined. The bananach hastily released him, and the crow dropped toward the ground.

The arrow was made of ash. The rowan tree that breaks all fairy spells. The blessed tree that protected against the glamour of the sidhe. The crow, nearly blinded by pain, felt the ash arrow lodged in his breast transform him. The feathers fell away like coal dust, the curled limbs of the crow stretched out, and the wings became two arms. Turning and falling, blood streamed from a wound in a chest naked of feathers. He opened his beak to cry and his mouth swallowed air, tasting the scent of wet leaves.

He hit the ground hard, the air forced from his chest,

his ribs groaning at the suddenness of his landing. He lay sprawled on his back, feeling the cool earth, his heels digging into the mud. Atop the rapid rise and fall of his chest he stared perplexed at the slim shaft of an ash arrow.

A woman's face peered down at him, blond hair draping the sides of her face. In the sun's shadow her eyes were gray, fine gold eyebrows knitted together. She smelled of smoke and grain.

"Mister, if you ain't the derndest thang I done ever shot out o' the sky," she said in a thick drawl.

Words, he thought dimly, the pain in his chest spreading a cold numbness throughout his body. Words. Spoken with lips and tongues.

He opened his mouth to speak, but there was no sound save a long, scratching exhalation. And then he closed his mouth, sensing his tongue as though it were stitched to the roof of his mouth. His throat hurt with the effort of human speech. His vision blurred, and he felt the weariness of a long flight plant him into the soft, muddy soil.

The woman came close to him and laid a hand along the wound in his chest, gentle fingers trying to mark where the arrow had entered his body. A man's body. He turned his head to stare at his outflung arm, searching to find something remaining of his crow self. But the only feathers he could see were the stiff white fletches of the ash arrow, slowly rising and falling with his heaving chest. He closed his eyes and resigned himself to the white hand lying on his chest holding him fixed against the land.

Ten

He lay seized by pain, his body rocked by the violent waves of a storm. Water sluiced over his forehead, drowning his eyes and blurring his vision. The cross-hatched beams of a ceiling swayed, intersecting lines of black and gold. He gasped, snatching at air, his arched spine lifting from the wet sheets of a bed. A thick mud filled the hollow of his throat. He thrashed his arms in panic, choking on the rank taste of earth. His eyes rolled upward, and a white hand sloped out of the black horizon. The hand settled on his burning shoulder, pulling him over the side of a small bed.

"Git it out, mister," ordered a calm voice. "Jest puke it out. Lord, you been conjured too long. Done pizened yerself."

He closed his eyes, tears captured in his lashes as he retched into the circle of a white porcelain bowl. The hand on his back was dry and steady, holding him over the side of a bed while he vomited. The bowl filled with blackness; pellets of fur and bone, the twist of worms and the broken carapace of beetles. He shuddered, revolted and terrified.

He coughed, his cleared throat raw but the worst of it momentarily over. The white hand put a warm wet cloth to his face and wiped away the splattered vomit. He felt himself eased onto his back again.

He looked up into her face and remembered it. The woman with the bow and the arrows of ash. Her blond hair was tied into a braid that dangled over her breast as she leaned forward to study him. In the soft flickering light of a lantern he saw her pale eyebrows draw into a frown over worried blue eyes. She put her hand behind his neck and inclined his head forward.

"I hate havin' to make you puke, mister, but it's the only way. You got to purge your stummick. So take a little more." She held a small cup to his lips. He realized he was thirsty, his tongue thick with the lingering taste of the black mud. He sipped the drink and gagged. The woman chuckled softly and held his neck in a firm grip.

"I know, I know," she said sympathetically, "it ain't the best tasting. I done put in some long sweetin' but I know it's still powerful awful. You jest gots to drink it, though."

He closed his eyes and tried not to breathe as she settled the cup against his lips. A few more drops of the bitter drink filled his mouth, and he swallowed it with a shudder. She released her hold on his neck and laid him down again. He stayed there quietly, cold shivers raising bumps along his naked arms and thighs.

Then without warning, the violent storm gathered again in the pit of his body. He tried to fight against it, and it twisted him into a clutching knot of agony. He groaned as his stomach was gripped by a fresh wave of urgent pain. The hands were there again, palms of dry wood against his slick shoulders, turning him over the side of the bed. His head hung down, locks of his black hair plastered on his cheeks.

His stomach heaved and again he vomited. Throughout his body he felt his muscles spasm and then loosen, casting out the crow he had been. Along his shoulders and spine flashes of heat seared his smooth skin. Pores that had once held the shafts of his black feathers wept tears and closed. His toes curled into the soles of his feet, and he drew his dangling legs up, bony knees nestled beneath his sternum. His shoulders beat against the mattress, his neck arched and his chin thrust forward as he desperately sought the refuge of flight from his pain.

But his body refused to lift, remaining slumped in a bed, sheets damp with sweat and stinking of blood. The storm rocked him, heaved him into the rough swells, over and over, and only the dry hands kept him from slipping under the mud-churned water and drowning. It went on until it seemed there was nothing left within him that was crow; all of it turned out into the bowl, into the sheets, the floor. Foam dried into brittle salt at the corners of his mouth and his eyes.

There followed an uneasy truce, ending the wracking of his body but keeping him lightly rocking on soft waves that lapped against a shore. His shoulders relaxed into the sagging mattress. The drawn-up legs unfolded, reaching down to their full length. His hands opened and his feet splayed outward, the toes uncurling.

"That part's done and gone," the woman said with a tired voice. "Now to git you over the rest."

He heard the sounds of water being poured into a basin. Then he sighed when a warm wet cloth wiped his chest. She was talking to him as she cleansed him, but he couldn't understand her words. He could only concentrate on the warm cloth that worked its way gently over his battered body. It soothed his burning skin, eased the pain of his trembling legs. When she was done washing his front, she lifted him up enough to pull away the soiled bedding beneath him. She washed his back, a hand holding him upright while she worked. Then, as he lay down, he felt the rough ticking fabric of the mattress on his cold skin and was pricked by needles of shucks poking through the heavy cloth. She lifted him again, first his shoulders and then his legs, as she drew on clean sheets. They smelled of lavender and sage, and he had a memory from long ago of pressing his face against white pillows.

He slept fitfully, his eyes flicking from side to side beneath half-shut lids. He saw her at times sitting beside him, her face limned by firelight; at other times he woke to find the chair empty. He grew warm beneath the sheets and then feverishly hot. The sweat evaporated into salt on the surface of his skin. His mouth grew parched and he could feel the dried skin of his lips peeling away with each exhalation. He was out of the ocean, but she had cast him on the shores of a desert. He opened his eyes, the light of a white sun blinding him with pain. He closed his eyes again and inhaled a hot, shallow breath. Pain hummed in his ears, and the heat pressed down on his chest like a gravestone.

He was dying, he thought dimly, and he found that he had no will to resist. Instead, his mind wandered and he dreamed he was in the desert again, walking toward a hazy curtain of rippling light where black figures of smoke rose into the blue-white sky. His bare feet stumbled in the hot sand and he fell. His hands grabbed the outstretched branches of a prickling plant and the thorns scraped deep gashes in the papery-dry skin. His shredded palms were bleeding, the red blood quickly absorbed by a thirsting sand. He grew weaker, his body nestling deeper into the yielding sand as he let his life flow out of his hands in a slow river of blood. Soon, he thought, feeling the sand cup his cheek. His dry tongue curled like old leather in his mouth. Soon this would be over.

A slap of something cold and wet grabbed his face. He shuddered awake, and his eyes looked into the cool blue steel of the woman's eyes. It was her hands around his face, lifting him from the desert floor.

"Yer name!" she shouted. "You got to give me yer name, mister! I cain't heal you lessen you tell me yer name!" She shook his face between her palms, and stars exploded with the pain in his eyes. "Gimme yer name!" she demanded.

He stuttered to life, her icy cold hands stabbing his face and forcing him to answer. A name. He had had one once. He searched his mind and found it wadded up like crumpled parchment in the back of his throat. Slowly he opened the crackling paper, smoothing it as he unwrapped the once-folded words and let them settle on his tongue.

"M-m-michael," he said, shocked by the movement of sound in his throat.

"All of it," she commanded. "I gots to have all of it."

"J-james," he murmured, and the photograph of an old man sitting beside a cottage came to him. His grandfather. "Francis." A confirmation name, and there was Mary sitting in the pew beaming at him. "McBride," he exhaled, as the fleeting image of his parents rose to his eyes. They were standing as a couple, but with an narrow empty space between them and their faces turned away from each other.

"Michael . . . James . . . Francis . . . McBride," the woman repeated softly. "That it? That all of it?"

He nodded.

"Aw right then," she said. "I aim to stop your bleeding." She laid her hands on his shoulder, and as he turned his head toward their weight he saw the gaping hole of his arrow wound. The torn flesh was stained an angry purple, mauve streaks carrying the infection across his chest. Bright red blood pulsed from the open wound and coated the pale, rounded hump of his shoulder. She slid her hands over his wound and pressed down firmly. Pain shot through his chest, and he stifled a cry.

"Michael James Francis McBride," she whispered. "Michael James Francis McBride." She gazed at him, her black pupils widening to eclipse the blue in her eyes. "Michael James Francis McBride," she said a third time and then closed her eyes.

As she called him by name, it seemed a flurry of ghostly black wings fell away from him. Memory stirred and crackled, struggling to give a history, a story to his name. There were no words, only the faces and the stiffly posed bodies, dyed in tea-colored sepia and bordered with gold frames. And on each rigid face he could see the hidden anger and longing, the clenched jaws of fear and the shadow of bitter love. The faces turned to him, different strands twined into a plaited cord of memory, and drew him back unwillingly into his past. Not a crow's life. But a man's.

The woman lifted up her face. "And when I passed by thee, and saw thee polluted in thine own blood, I said unto thee, Live: yea, I said unto thee when thou wast in thy blood, Live."

She looked down again at Michael, her face radiant, and her yellow hair catching the light in a halo of gold.

"Upon Christ's grave, three roses bloom. Stop, blood, stop," she chanted.

Michael gasped, a sudden bloom of heat from her hands searing the wound in his chest. The bones of her fingers shone, luminous and white through the darker lace of her pale skin. His heart began to pound rapidly as though waking hungrily out of a dark gorge to feast on the offered gift of blazing white vitality.

Again she called his name three times, her voice growing louder each time. And deep within, his body roared an answer to her command. A surge of strength filled him, green and sweet like the running of sap. It coursed from the rooted soles of his feet, churning in his veins and rising into his trunk and limbs. Saliva pungent with the taste of pitch flooded his mouth, and his breaking sweat carried the sharp fragrance of burning cedars. His heart beat stronger, pumping out a burnt-orange amber to mingle with his blood. The thickened amber coiled in his blood, spiraling like honey poured into his veins. Amber filled the hollow well of his arrow wound, easing the pain and sealing the proud flesh with a molten gold. And still it flowed, thick and resinous from his pounding heart.

The woman cried out in surprise, but she did not move her hands away as the golden amber bubbled over the edges of the wound and oozed between her white fingers. It continued flowing up the narrow stretch of her arms, pushed along in pulsing waves. At her shoulders it ebbed and then ceased to flow. As it cooled, it crusted and dried into a hard cast. The woman stayed there unmoving, her hands sealed by the amber to his shoulder until her body sagged with fatigue, and the radiant light of her face dimmed.

Slowly, she leaned down close to him, her face open with wonder. As her arms bent, the dried shell of amber cracked and fell away from her skin in a shower of cornmeal-colored dust. "What sort of man are you, Michael McBride? One of God's chosen, or the Devil hisself come to tempt me?"

He couldn't answer her. He didn't know just then. But from her hands had come one power to heal; white and pure, sharp-tongued as juniper berries. And from within him had joined another: green and gold, giving him the grained flesh of oaks and the healing blood of pines. He closed his eyes, shielding himself from the intensity of her stare. His strength was returning again, and as his aching limbs became freed of pain, he remembered the other part of his past; born out of the spilled seeds of starlight, the shimmering faces, the hands that moved carved pieces over a gaming board and the whisper of stories. He was something in between, he thought quietly. Neither God's own nor the Devil's. He opened his eyes to her once more, wanting to tell her, to speak a truth that had been kept hidden from him.

"The Sidhe," he replied. And, seeing the frown of confusion crease her brow, he smiled. "Fairy," he tried.

Her eyes widened but never left his face. "Is that right?" she breathed softly. "I know'd right off you was differn'." She tilted her head to one side. "Them there wings done give it away."

A sound rose in Michael's throat, and he realized he was trying to laugh. It hurt.

Very gently, the woman eased her hands away from his wound.

"Hush now," she ordered. "Got to rest easy. You still got to heal some."

The heat from her hands lingered, and Michael shivered as a cool draft brushed the surface of his wound. He heard the sharp intake of her breath and turned to look at his shoulder. The worst of the gap was closed, the raw edges of the wound stitched in a circular pattern. It looked no more threatening than a rose lovingly placed at his shoulder, his fever-breaking sweat like dew on the petals. She touched the skin with her white fingertips and slowly shook her head.

"Don't you just take th' rag off'n th' bush?" she exhaled. "You ain't half a wonder, Mr. McBride."

" 'Mike,' " he said, closing his eyes. "Just 'Mike.' " Then he struggled to open his eyes again, sleep dragging at the heavy lids. "Who are you?"

She hesitated at first, then shrugged. "Well, it won't do no harm I suppose. You done give me your name after all. My name's Annie Mae Snow," she answered, pulling up a light wool blanket over his chest.

Looking into her calm, smiling face, Michael suddenly discovered a reason to worry. He reached out, closing a weak hand around her arm. "It isn't safe for you. . . . I'm hunted."

"Now just git yerself to sleep, Mike, and don't worry none," Annie Mae replied, gently taking his hand away and slipping his arm beneath the blanket again. "I ain't no acorn calf to be skeerd by h'its shadder. I know'd how to ward away evil. Them she-buzzards cain't ha'nt you in here. There's salt down at every window sill, owl entrails 'neath my door, and I done made the cross with sticks of hazel. You're safe as any newborn babe in my house," Annie Mae said confidently.

"Thank you," he whispered, letting his exhausted limbs relax again. He didn't quite understand the litany of strange tasks she had performed to ensure their safety. It was enough to know that she had understood the danger without needing an explanation. "Thank you, Annie Mae," Michael repeated, not wanting to forget her name as he drifted into sleep.

"T'ain't nuthing," she said, resting her hand lightly on his chest.

Michael nodded and, closing his eyes, let the warmth of her hand settle him deeper into the comfort of the bed.

"Well, Mike, I done tutored you long 'nuf," Annie Mae said brusquely. She stood by Michael's bed, her arms ladened with folded clothes. "H'it's 'bout time you was a-moving lessin' you get limber sick. Put on these here clothes. They orter do for you." She dropped the pile of clothes at the end of the bed and turned sharply on her heels, heading for the door. She left him alone in the cabin, the door swinging open to reveal a cool bright morning beyond its threshold.

Michael sat up quickly in the bed, swinging his legs over the side, and became dizzy with vertigo. He stayed there, waiting until the room stopped swaying, before going on. Annie Mae was right: He had to get up, remember how to walk, how to use his hands again. Hands. He looked down at his hands denuded of feathers, the long, squared-off fingers still strange to him. He had spent the better part of four days in this bed, watching Annie Mae come and go, bustling with human activity. But mostly he had watched with interest the movements of her pale hands. He thought that they resembled a pair

of finches fluttering over her work as she cut meat,
stripped the green husks from the corn she grew in her
garden, twisted the spindle, and sharpened her knives.
Light as a wing her fingertips brushed his forehead to
check for signs of fever and her little finger crooked like
an errant feather as she held the razor to his cheek and
shaved him.

He sighed to his upturned palms, resting in his lap.
"Get up, Michael," he said aloud, and dimly he heard a
voice from the past echo, ". . . and be a man." He fingered the rough wool of the trousers and the soft red flannel shirt. It seemed he was always putting on another
man's clothes and taking with it another man's identity.
His father's cut-down suits, Strider's work clothes, and
O'Connor's boots. So who had these belonged to first? he
wondered as he pulled on the flannel shirt. He winced, his
injured shoulder stiff and aching as he lifted his arm.
There had been no other signs of a man in Annie Mae's
cabin, and in all her talk, of which there was a lot, she
had never mentioned one.

Slowly Michael stood up, clutching the bed's wrought-
iron headboard for support. The ground quickly fell
away below his startled face. Too tall, he thought wildly,
his body lengthening, rising up like a spindle-legged
wraith from the floor. He was much too far from the
ground. But when he gazed upward and felt the weight of
the ceiling on him, his shoulders sagged. Not tall enough.
He would never reach the heights that he had had as a
crow. His feet were made of clay, meant only for the
earth now. He put on the trousers, amazed at the long
limbs and white feet that pushed their way through the
pant legs. On the table Annie had left a belt and heavy
wool socks, and, by the chair, a pair of old boots, the
black leather cracked over the blunt rounded toes. Well,
at least they weren't cowboy boots, he thought as he
pulled them on, glad not to have his toes squeezed into
pointed tips.

Moving unsteadily, Michael walked toward the open door, suddenly eager to be outside, where the sun sparkled in the dark green of the treetops. The wind was fresh and cool on his bare face. The clear song of a thrush rang out, proclaiming its territory among the trees. Without thinking, Michael lifted his head to answer it and then stopped, his mouth open but silent.

"Purty, ain't it?" Annie Mae said, smiling up at the trees. Around her feet scruffy hens cackled as they scratched at the tossed grain.

Michael nodded, unable to speak as a shadow of sadness wrapped itself around him, chilling him in the heat of the morning sun. He gazed up in quiet misery at the dark green arrows of pines spearing the blue sky. High above a hawk coasted in the sky, pinion feathers fanned to catch the wind. Lower down, skimming the tops of the pines, Michael watched the scalloped flight of a lark, remembering the feel of the wind's currents pressing against his feathered breastbone.

It was gone. All gone. The sense of belonging and the oneness of his world as a crow, when he could fly back and forth between the shimmering stars to the earth without ever crossing a border. As a crow nothing had separated him from the wonders of the fairy world. But he was a man again, blind in one eye to those wonders, and exiled from the shimmering host waiting far above him. His left eye itched and teared as if unable to contain alone all the radiant light of the Sidhe. And from his right eye, he saw only the muted shades of the earth, pale by comparison. The world had sheered into two halves. And as the road split apart, Michael stood paralyzed, not knowing on which path to set his feet.

Annie Mae came to him quickly, the hens scattering away at the brush of her skirts. She touched him on the shoulder. "You done look like you supped sorrow out of a big spoon, Mike. You all right?"

"Sure, I'm well enough," he muttered, lowering his

head from the green light of the trees to wipe his tearing left eye.

"I know'd how you feel," Annie Mae said softly. "There ain't nuthin' like it in th' whole world. When I done put my hands to a healing and feel that fetchin' power drivin' through my soul, it 'bout breaks my heart ever' time. Ever'thin' 'round me gits to gleamin' so, gits to singing almost. Then, when h'its done and over, I cain't hardly stand it. There comes a hollowness in me, and looking out, the light done faded and ever'thin' goes quiet. I ain't there and I ain't 'actly here. That's 'bout the time I git to wondering whether I done been cursed or blessed."

Michael turned to Annie Mae, her words reaching into him and drawing him out of the shadow of his half-blind misery. He saw her clearly for the first time, standing beside him in the bright sunlight. She was much shorter than he had thought lying in his bed. Her body was thin, her collarbone rising in twin ridges beneath the cotton fabric of her faded print dress. She was also younger than he had thought, listening to her brusque throaty voice but not clearly seeing the fine skin tightly stretched over the delicate bones of her face. Her nose was snubbed like a child's, and light brown freckles were scattered over the bridge and dappled her pale cheeks. Her mouth looked full above the small pointed chin. In the sunlight her blue eyes faded to gray, her yellow hair a soft corn silk. As he stared at her, he saw the rosy stain of a blush rise up from the hollow of her throat.

"Work helps," she said with a slight stutter. "H'it makes it easier to git back to this here place and not be sorrowing so."

"What should I do?" Michael asked dully.

She laughed and gave a shake of her head. "There's a heap a work needs doing and I ain't half glad of the help. There's garden work, I gots to pack in some wood, draw water, do some greenin' and mebbe, if'n there's time, hunt for whitefish."

"All right," Michael said, giving a faint smile. "Tell me where to begin."

She nodded in the direction of the garden. Michael started toward the garden quickly, wanting desperately to move away from the sorrow he felt standing in the shadow of the trees. But he stumbled over the uneven ground, his weakened legs still unsteady.

"Just hold on, Mike," Annie Mae said, catching him by the elbow. "Ain't no use gittin' ahead o' the hounds. Corn'll wait for us to git there."

She put an empty basket on one of Michael's arms and, hooking her arm through his other, walked with him to the garden. He smiled down at her open face, distracted by the pleasant heat of her body next to his, her slim hip jutting into his as she guided him along. He leaned against her slightly and breathed in the dusty lavender scent of her hair. Work might help, he thought, but Annie Mae's knowing presence was the real salve for his aching sorrow.

They spent the morning working on opposite sides of the garden, he digging potatoes as she had instructed and she thinning and harvesting onions. The sun felt good on his back, and as he sweated the heat eased the soreness out of his shoulder. Spadefuls of warmed earth lifted fragrantly, spilling out the dirty brown potatoes over the surface. He dusted off the little clods of dirt and tossed them by the handful into the basket. From time to time he rested and watched Annie Mae at her work. Her thin body bent like a willow strand, her white hands disappeared into the thick green border of bladed onion leaves. Though he could hear the birds and the rustle of the wind in the pines, he mostly listened to her voice as she talked without pause.

"See, I know'd you was a-coming that day," she announced, pulling a weed from the row and examining it before putting it into a second side basket. "I done dropped a dishrag that morning and it fell all loose, 'stead of wadded up, so I know'd it was a man coming. And then just a while back I done found a stone with a hole in it in the run, so I figured to get good luck. And I done cast salt over my shoulder to make sure."

Annie Mae wandered through the garden, stepping carefully over the cultivated rows. She kneeled down beside a row of green beans and lifted the heavy leaves with a satisfied smile.

"Now looky here, ain't that a lolliper sight?"

Michael glanced up from the piles of potatoes he was cleaning and saw the thick cluster of long bean pods resting in Annie Mae's palm.

"See, I did what my momma done told me and planted these here in the morning following a new moon. That's why they all grew so good." She straightened up again and pointed to the nearly full basket of potatoes. "And those I dug in the light of a full moon in March. It were a little too cold for it up here in these mountains but I done it anyway. And it ain't done no harm."

"What mountains are these, Annie Mae?" Michael asked, leaning wearily on his spade.

"You don't know?" Annie Mae said, squinting her eyes in the sunlight to stare back at him in amusement.

He shook his head, embarrassed by his ignorance, as she contemplated him through half-closed eyes.

"These here are the Sierra Nevadas, smack between the desert t'oneside and California t'other. Now do you know where you are?"

Fragments of maps came back to Michael, and he remembered the spine of a long jutting mountain ridge cleaving the western half of the continent. He remembered something else.

"Is there gold here?"

Annie Mae frowned, her lips pursed as if tasting something sour. "Some thinks so. Some even found it. But most is just wastin' away huntin' for it, only to git it hornscriggled out o' 'em by gamblin' men. But you all cain't swade them to nuthin' differn'. They's all fritter-minded, always lookin' for one thing only, not seeing what all else riches is in these hills. It's purty here, and peaceable. Air's pure as God's breath. H'its 'nuf for me." Annie Mae reached into her basket and pulled out an onion. She peeled off the papery brown skin and grunted. "See this?" she said, rubbing the thin skin between two fingers. "Onion skin mighty thin, easy winter coming in," she recited. She looked up at Michael, who was still lean-ing on his spade, a half-full basket of potatoes at his feet. She gave a small frown. "Come on," she said, lifting up her basket of onions to her hip, "standing here jawing ain't buying th' baby a new dress, nor paying for th' one is already wore out."

Michael smiled and shook his head as he lifted the spade over his shoulder and picked up the basket of potatoes to follow after her. Though it was hard some-times to understand Annie Mae's speech, Michael was taken with her looping drawl that seemed to slather words with a thick coating of butter. And if he listened closely to catch the meaning, he found himself laughing at her sharp peppery wit that rattled off insults as easily as wisdom.

He followed her to the cabin and set the basket down inside the door. She stood by the fireplace, lifting a pot of steaming coffee off the grate. On the table was a plate of biscuits, left over from the morning's meal. She had opened a can of peaches and split them between two bowls.

"Here now, best to eat sumthin' afore we go into th' woods," she said, pouring out the coffee into two mugs.

Michael sat down and took one of the mugs between his hands. His fingers were dirty, earth clotted beneath the nails. He could feel a row of watery blisters swelling up on his palms. He sighed, feeling tired but content. Annie Mae's prediction that work would help had been right. Wearily he took a sip of her coffee, and his eyes widened at the strong bitter taste.

Annie Mae grinned and pushed over a squat jar of honey. "Take a little long sweetnin' for that, Mike. That there is wedge-floating coffee." She leaned forward on her elbows, her mug balanced between her hands. "That means my coffee's so strong, I kin float an iron wedge into it and h'it won't sink."

"Annie Mae, I worked a cattle drive where a man doesn't survive without strong coffee. But I've never had it quite this strong," Michael replied.

"You'd be surprised how little water it takes to make good coffee. 'Sides, ain't no such thing as strong coffee," she added, a gleam sparkling in her eyes. "Only weak people."

Michael spooned the honey into his coffee and sipped it carefully a second time. "Better," he said, smiling.

"So you rode trail?" she asked, looking at him over the rim of her cup.

"Yes."

"How long you been doing that?"

"Not long." He shrugged.

"And afore that?"

"Not much," he answered. "How about you?" he asked, wanting to swing the arrow of questions in the other direction. He didn't want to talk about himself. He needed time yet. Once she knew about him, he was certain she would be afraid of him and he'd have to leave. "How did you wind up here? Alone?"

She lowered her eyes. "Long story."

There followed an uneasy silence, and Michael felt her weighing something in her mind, as if wanting to trust him but remaining unsure of herself. He understood it; the hesitation that kept them silent when it came to talking about their pasts. They were very much alike, he thought, sitting together here, away from everything, and hiding.

"If'n I tell you," Annie Mae started slowly, "will you tell me 'bout you?"

"Yes," Michael promised, knowing that he would.

She sighed, her shoulders hunching forward. She took her braid in her hands and undid the leather tie. Then, weaving her fingers through the yellow hair, she combed out the little twigs and dried leaves that had become entangled in the braid.

"I come from Arkansas, the Ozarks. Far away from these here mountains. My kin was mostly pore ridge runners, and I was the last 'un born to a big family. But I was born with the caul, a skin of power laid over my face at birth." Annie Mae raised her white hands to cover her face. "My momma know'd then I was special. But my daddy, he didn' mind the same." She lowered her hands, and Michael saw her features harden. "He shore were a contrary 'un. If he'd a drowned, we 'uns would a looked upstream for him. An' he didn't like me none. I skeerd him 'cause I know'd things an' 'cause I could heal. In my holler there was differn' kinds o' power. My granny was a yarb doctor, healed with herbs, an' I had an auntie that was a wart witch. She must of had a hundred different cures for warts," Annie Mae said, flashing a quick smile. Then her face became serious again. "But only I was a power doctor. Didn't need no charms, no madstones in my hand. Just me and the Book's words, and the white healing come over me." Annie was quiet a moment, taking another sip of her coffee. She grimaced at the taste and gave a delicate shudder.

"Well, the worst is to be know'd as a witch. The Bible done say thou shalt not suffer a witch to live. Exodus Twenty-two. My daddy was havin' no luck at all. Crop done suffer and he weren't ketchin' nothin' in his traps. He got to reckoning that it was me spelt them on account of he done fisted me sumthin' turrible one day when he was angry. Figured I was gettin' back on him. Then when my older sister up and died, well he thought I'd kilt her to pay the witch's sixpence. They say someone has to die to the Devil 'afore a witch kin come into her full power.''

"Course, he was wrong," Annie said angrily, tugging at the strands of her braid. "I ain't no witch no how. And I didn't have nothin' to do with my sister's dying. That gal pizened her self to git shunt of a baby she had in her. Weren't a thing I could a done for her. She just sicken and died 'cause she wanted to. But there was talk and there was rumoring put out 'bout me. Momma wouldn't stand for it, but there weren't much she could do neither. So when Mr. Walker come through fixin' to buy a gal, well, they just figured it 'ud be best all 'round if I was to go away with him."

"You were sold to someone?" Michael asked, shocked.

Annie Mae nodded, her lips drawn tight. "Yeah, in a manner. Oh, they made us jump the broom all right, git married, but it weren't no marriage. Damned but I was just a little girl, so skinny I had to stand twice in the same place just to cast a shadder. That man near broke my bones first time he tread on me. But well, Mr. Walker had money and he needed a gal to cook and clean up after him. So he paid off Daddy and I tuck out here with him."

"How long ago?" Michael asked.

Annie Mae thought for a while. "Seems like it must be going on five years," she said softly.

"Where's Mr. Walker now?"

Annie Mae shook her head. "Don't rightly know. Walker came here to do prospectin'. Took off 'bout three years ago lookin' for his share o' th' gold and I ain't heard nor seen o' him since. Hell," she grunted, "hardly seen anyone since. Just the occasional Miwouk or You-kot Injun that come up into the mountains. That's how I done got my bow and arrow. Ain't got no gun. Miwouk traded it to me on account I healed his baby. Ever' now and then, some Injun that heared 'bout me will come over to get healed and mebbe eats a can o' peaches. Half o' them is starvin' most times. Still, they leave stuff I can use to survive on, deer hide, an' smoked venison, and seed corn. I know'd already how to set traps and I got me a bit o' livestock, coupla sheep, mule, and a milk cow, so I ain't made out too bad without a man. An' ever' spring and then late summer I ride the mule down to the nearest town, three days away, trade furs, and stock up on supplies.

"Why do you stay up here by yourself? Don't you get lonely?" Michael asked.

"Yeah, mebbe so. But I seen how other gals live in town and it's rough. Whorin' mostly, or cooking for half-starved and dead-drunk miners. I'm better off here on my ownsome for now. Leastways I can be myself and it don't carry no shame."

"Do you think Walker's ever coming back?" Michael asked.

"Don't care if'n he do. I'm done muling fer that man," Annie Mae said sharply. She rose briskly, sweeping the dishes from the table with a clatter, and took them to the sink. "What 'bout you, Mike McBride? You're a long way from home. And a man as travels in the likeness of a crow, well, that's gotta be some story." She turned from the sink to face Michael and stopped. The slanting light of the afternoon sun spilled into the opened door and illuminated the look of surprise on her face.

"Well, how 'bout that?" she breathed softly, a hand rising to catch at her throat. "Now where do you suppose he come from?"

Michael stood up quickly and turned toward the door. There, grazing quietly just beyond the garden, was a huge white stallion. Michael felt his heart leap at the sight of the foaming mane and glistening white flanks.

"Mo Neart!" he called out, and the stallion raised his head from the long grass and whickered in reply. Michael ran toward the horse, denying the distance between them. At his side, Annie Mae was breathing hard, trying to keep pace.

Mo Neart trotted over to meet them, his slender legs stepping gracefully through the waving grass. When he reached Michael the stallion lowered his head, affectionately butting his bony forehead into Michael's open arms. Michael shouted happily as he was nearly knocked over by Mo Neart's rough greeting. He clutched the stallion's head, holding it close to his chest before running his hands down the sides of the animal's rounded jawbone.

"I thought I'd lost you forever," he whispered to the horse's twitching ears. "But you found me, didn't you?" The horse huffed warm moist air into Michael's face and then lightly nibbled at his hair.

"Is he yours, Mike?" Annie Mae asked, timidly putting her hand up to stroke the high, arched neck.

"No," Michael answered. "He belongs to himself. But he is my one loyal friend."

"Well now, I'm 'stonished silent."

Michael looked at her face, serious with childlike amazement, and burst out laughing. "Annie Mae, I don't think I'd know it was you if you were quiet," he teased.

"You just hush now," she snapped. "I know I prattle some, but it ain't half a wonder how you git this far in life not knowing nothin' nohow." Her face flushed, the freckles darkening over the pale cheeks. "And 'sides, I'm just sort of ketchin' up for the times I ain't had no one to talk after."

Mo Neart shook his head, his lips pulled back as he bared his teeth, jeering at Michael. Annie Mae held up her hands to ward off getting hit by his thrashing mane.

"I'm being reprimanded on all sides," Michael complained with a smile. "Come on," he said to Annie Mae, locking his fingers together to offer her a step. "Let's go for a ride."

She held back, nervously glancing up at the stallion's

powerful shoulders and long sweeping back. "I do right
'nuf on th' mule. But I ain't much for horse-backing,"
she said shyly.

"For once something you don't know!" Michael said,
grinning. "But you're in luck. It's the one thing I do
know how to do. And besides, Mo Neart is an easy horse
to ride. And I'll be here."

Annie Mae hesitated and then, shrugging off her fears,
stepped a foot into Michael's waiting hands and lifted
herself over Mo Neart's back with a grunt. Once on top,
she tucked her skirts around her thighs and tried not to
look apprehensive while perched so far above the
ground. Michael heaved himself up with his arms, sliding
his leg over the stallion's rump.

"Hold on to his mane," Michael told Annie Mae, sliding his body in close behind hers. He held her sheltered
against his chest, nestled in his arms, as he reached forward to take handfuls of Mo Neart's mane. Their thighs
lay side by side over the back of the horse, and he smiled
down at the sight of her small feet dangling against the
stallion's belly. He looked out over Annie Mae's shoulder and gave Mo Neart a little kick to let him know they
were ready.

Mo Neart trotted lightly at first, and then slowly
changed his gait, loping into a gentle canter over the
grassy field. At the end of the field, the stallion turned
and started up a narrow mountain path that cut through
the lodgepole pines and the tall, sweeping firs. The stallion carried them up the sloping mountainside, shifting in
and out of shadows and then sunlight as the thick pine
forest thinned in the higher rocky valleys. The graying
rocks were brightened by the last waving rays of summer's Indian paintbrushes and the stately remains of the
lupines, their seed pods rattling in the wind and the few
faded blossoms clinging to the tips. The air was clean and
sharp, the breeze cold as it swept down the trail to greet

them. Michael felt a renewed sense of balance and hope settling in him.

It was right to be here at this moment, Annie Mae closed within his arms, trembling with excitement as the stallion carried them easily over the rocky trails. He didn't grieve for the crow's life, for as free and magical as it had been, it could not give him the simple human pleasure of this woman's company. Imperfect though his pied-eyed humanity was, something in his heart now supplied the vision hidden by his half-blindness. Annie Mae's laughter rang across the stony valley, and Michael knew that neither the singing of Eileen's voice nor the wild birdsong would ever sound as sweet as this to his ear.

A burning log crackled and spit out a fiery cinder across the hearth and onto the cabin floor. It smoked and hissed as it embedded itself in a rag rug. Annie Mae swore, jumping up and grabbing a brush broom. She quickly swept it back into the grate before it could do worse. The room was briefly filled with the scent of scorched flannel.

"We can expect the first snow soon," she announced, pursing her lips with annoyance at the fire.

"Why?" asked Michael, looking up from his plate of venison stew.

"Fire done spit and hiss. That's always a sure sign."

"Annie Mae, are there signs for everything in the world?" Michael asked, nettled by her confidence.

Annie Mae returned to the table and sat down next to him. Her face was sober, her eyes a midnight blue in the firelight. "How else to survive in this ole world?" she said simply. "Good and evil is all part of one thing. Both of 'em come from God, after all. But God done give us a choice, and He sent signs so as we uns can find the right way. Takin' up th' good and laying by evil. That's our burden in life. You got to open your eyes to the mysteries 'round you all."

"Weren't you afraid of me when you saw me in the sky as a crow and saw me change into a man? What signs could have explained that?" Michael argued. "How did you know I wasn't evil?"

"Well, I must confess, I weren't too sure at first. But you was lying there wounded, mother-naked in my garden and not up to doing much harm when I come over to you. But it was when I done seen the power coming out a you that I know'd for sure I'd been led right. I don't know nothin' 'bout what you called fairy, but I don't reckon h'it's too differn' than what I'm used to," she finished. She leaned back in her chair and, drawing a shawl over her slender shoulders, she gave Michael a hard stare. "So you gonna tell me now what you been hiding?"

Michael nodded. "The Sidhe," he muttered. "They're very different from you, Annie Mae. There are no signs, only stories. And they go on forever," he said bitterly. Michael pushed away his plate and began to tell Annie Mae everything he could remember: Eileen's deathbed gift, the flight by rails, the cattle drive and Red Cap hunting him, murdering those around him until he was forced to flee alone into the hills. There was little he could say about being a crow; he had only memories of flight, of a constant hunger and the search for food. He recalled the distant landscape of the desert and the starry faces of the Sidhe in the night sky beneath the ivory-colored moon. Eileen's words remained in his head like the murmuring babble of a stream, but the words rushed away too fast for him to comprehend them clearly.

He finished talking, his voice growing heavy with dread as a silence filled the cabin. He glanced up at Annie Mae, expecting to see fear or revulsion on her face. And he would deserve it. He had fled in the face of danger. He had let his friends die on the trail. And he might well have stayed a crow had she not brought him down from the sky. He had done nothing but flee since it all began.

Annie Mae leaned forward, resting her palms flat

against the table. The shawl slipped from her shoulders and draped over her elbows. Even in the gold spill of firelight Michael could see that her face shone pale with anger.

"T'ain't your fault!" she blurted out, slapping the table. "T'ain't none of it your fault alone, Michael McBride."

"How can you say that?" he argued. "After what I've just told you? Men died because of me."

"If'n you don't know nothin' 'bout what's happen', how can you be expected to know what to do 'bout it? Don't you see? This ain't 'bout you alone. Someone's done shivered you out in th' wide world, just waitin' for you to make a wrong turn right. But ain't no one done told you how to 'ccomplish that. Cain't you see that? That's why you been ha'nted by your momma, that's why you been hounded by this here Red Cap," Annie Mae said firmly.

"You might be right," Michael said glumly. "But it still doesn't tell me anything. I'm still no smarter than I was before and probably just as dangerous to be around."

"Hmpf," Annie Mae snorted. "That stallion ain't no fool. He come back lookin' for you for a reason. And I ain't one to be skeerd off neither." Annie Mae put a hand on Michael's wrist. "Think, Mike," she urged, squeezing his wrist hard. "Think. I cain't believe your momma un' daddy didn't give you nothin' for this here time. Think. Had to be somethin' you could use besides that green eye o' your's."

Michael thought back, remembering his parents, stiff and silent, the chilly space between them. He shook his head. "Just chess and stories. Not even love."

Annie Mae got up slowly from her chair. She walked over to the fire and knelt beside it, her chin resting in her hand. Michael's heart ached to see the spun gold of her hair laid softly against her cheek. Her brows were furrowed as she thought, staring into the fire and trying to pluck from the pieces of his tale the hidden signs. She fed the fire a new log, and sighing, she stood up.

"H'it's late. C'ain't think no more," she apologized. "Head's near to burstin' right now." She stood wavering in the firelight, and he could see by her face that there was something more she wanted to say. He waited, watching the glow of her eyes and almost hearing the words before she spoke them. "I done been alone a long time," she said and then blushed, her hands gripping the folds of her shawl. "So I'll put it to you straight. I ain't one to say no if'n you want to share the bed some." She lifted up the narrow point of her chin with a hint of defiance. Michael understood the gesture. She wanted him enough to ask, but not enough to sacrifice all her pride in the asking.

Michael rose from his chair and came to where she stood on the hearth. He laid his hands on her shoulders and leaned forward to kiss her hair. It smelled of woodsmoke.

"Oh, Annie Mae." He sighed. "I do want to share the bed with you." He lowered his head, his mouth seeking hers. He kissed her softly at first. Her lips felt dry from the fire's heat; but as she parted them, he felt the unexpected touch of her tongue entering his mouth like a darting fish. He held her close in his arms, the contours of her body pressed against him. He could hear the rapid beating of her heart and felt his own pounding hard against his rib cage. How could he tell her that he was more afraid than she was of this moment?

Annie Mae pulled away from his embrace and with shy, downcast eyes, slipped the faded print dress from her shoulders. Underneath the dress she was naked, and the firelight gleamed over white skin, turning her flesh gold as a ribbon of amber. She took his trembling hands and laid them against her breasts, the small brown nipples hardening beneath his palms. He groaned, surprised by the utter softness of her skin. He bent his head and kissed the cleft between her breasts, his fingers rippling over the surface of her ribs. She ran her hands through his hair, kissing his head and murmuring in his ear.

He sank to his knees, his cheek resting against the rise of her belly. His arms around her hips, he stroked the hollow space in the small of her back and let his hand cup her buttocks. Then he stopped, still holding her, his face averted as his eyes searched the floor. His heart was pounding so hard he could hardly breathe, hardly speak. His cheek was hot and flushed where it lay against her smooth skin. Sweat prickled his upper lip.

"What is it?" Annie Mae whispered. Her fingers tangled deeper in his hand, holding him. Her thighs trembled.

"Annie, I've never done this," Michael said, hating the words the moment they were released.

Her hands turned his head upright from the floor, and she stared down at him with a smile. Relief flooded her face. "That all? Hell, you had me skeerd it were somethin' much worse." She knelt down beside him and stroked his cheek with her white hand. "That's one thing that come on its own. Ain't no better teachin' of it than love itself. I done learned it once in a sorrowing way, with too much hurt and no pleasure. But it won't be like that now. It'll be new, like a first time. Come to bed, Michael McBride, and we'll both figure it out as one being."

She took him by the hand and sat him on the side of the bed. She pulled off his boots, his socks, and started to help him with his shirt. He blushed, flustered, his sweating hands slipping on the belt buckle. She stood up and chuckled deep in her throat. "Mike, I done seen ever'-thin' you gots to offer the first moment I laid eyes on you. Ain't no surprises there and no complaints neither."

Annie Mae got into the other side of the bed, drawing the covers down on his side. Michael hurried to finish undressing, his mind racing to keep up with the flood of sensations. The skin of his naked chest prickled in the cool night air. He shivered, taking off his trousers despite his quickened pulse that sent waves of heat down his legs. Once under the covers, Annie Mae wriggled close to him, her arms around his neck. He groaned as she pressed the smooth coolness of her body against his heated flesh.

Not wanting to hurt, not wanting to be embarrassed, they moved slowly over each other, their hands discovering pleasure by gentle strokes and soft caresses. But when Michael eased himself between Annie Mae's hips and she drew her legs up, her thighs pressed tight against his flanks, he knew he could not hold back much longer. His thoughts were buried beneath the immediate roar of his senses. When he laid his mouth over her breast it tasted of salt, and her musky scent filled his nostrils with a sweet odor. He listened for the sounds of her low-throated moans and the sharpness of her breathing. But it was the silkiness of the inside of her thighs and the heat that surrounded him when he entered her that made him forget everything else. Small and tight, it almost hurt him to fill her. He tried to slow down, but she called him by name and, wrapping her legs more tightly around, pulled his hips down to her.

It was easy, he thought fleetingly, a moan escaping his lips. Annie Mae cried out, half laughing, half groaning, and her body contracted, curling around him like a new fern, the flat of her palms pressing hard against his back. He held his breath, the growing heaviness in his hips suddenly released. Twin arrows of a sweet pain shot down the insides of his clenched thighs. He held onto Annie Mae, at once fearful and ecstatic as she rocked him in the cradle of her hips.

"I ain't lettin' go," she whispered as his head lay tucked in the hollow of her neck. "I ain't lettin' go."

It was much later in the night that Michael awoke, hearing a noise. Puzzled by the sound, he lay on his back and listened for it. He smiled, hearing at first only the com-

forting sound of Annie Mae's slow breathing in the
stilled hush of the cabin. He turned on his side and lightly
ran a finger down the side of her sleeping face. She stirred
and shifted her body deeper under the covers. He listened
again, this time hearing the wood shift in the hearth,
charred embers dropping into the grate with a powdery
sigh.

But something had woken him, brought him out of a
deep sleep. He was certain of it. He sat up and looked
about the quiet cabin, each thing still in its place, except
for Annie Mae's dress that lay in a heap by the hearth.
He covered his right eye and gazed again at the room,
still not finding the reason for the sound that had woken
him.

He lay back on the bed uneasily. And in the quiet
something knocked. There. There, he heard it again. But
what was it? he asked himself, searching for an explanation that would end the nagging fear. It sounded like
chopping. Someone chopping wood in the middle of the
night. The sound moved around the cabin, growing
louder and more insistent. Michael sat up in alarm, his
hands clenched into fists. He glanced down at Annie
Mae, but she continued to sleep, untroubled by the loud
noise. The door to the cabin rattled but remained closed.
A wooden shutter flew open and then banged shut again.

And then, abruptly, the fierce chopping clatter
stopped. There was a moment of silence. Michael leaned
forward, tense with waiting. The chopping noise began
again, but this time it was more distant, muffled by the
pines as it seemed to move farther away into the woods.
The cabin settled into a restful quiet once more. Michael
lay down again and, pulling Annie Mae's sleep warm
body into his arms, tried to find the peace that he had so
recently discovered. But he couldn't, and he passed the
night staring wide-eyed at the ceiling, knowing that Red
Cap had found him again.

Eleven

As Michael returned with water from the small stream behind the cabin, he heard the loud crack of an ax splitting wood. The crisp sound echoed through the trees in the early twilight. He hurried up the path, the cold water splashing over the sides of the pail. He tried to hold down the rising panic but he couldn't separate the sharp ringing sound from his fears. For nearly two weeks he had laid awake every night, hearing the nocturnal sounds of someone chopping wood outside the cabin. The window shutters had rattled as they were shook by an unseen hand and the barred door heaved against its latch. But nothing had happened beyond that. Annie Mae had slept on, oblivious to the racket and the mornings had risen peacefully, without further events.

Until now. Michael broke through the darkening line of trees and ran across the grassy field. In the clearing his eyes quickly scanned over the waving tassels of the corn and beyond it, the cabin. A pearl-gray smoke was winding out from the chimney, spiraling into the dimming lavender sky. The trees had etched a black line against the last streak of an orange sunset. Annie Mae was standing by the wood pile wearing an old black coat over her print dress. She raised an ax high over her head and brought it down neatly over the top of a propped-up log. With a clean crack, the log cleaved in two as easily as a comb parting hair. Annie Mae kicked the two new halves into a pile and set up another log for splitting. Nearby Mo Neart grazed, his tail flicking out from side to side over his rump. In the twilight his flanks shone with a blue-white iridescence. Michael slowed his step and tried to calm the rapid beating of his heart. He took a deep breath and let it out slowly. Annie Mae was all right, he reassured himself as he approached her. Everything was all right.

She glanced up at his flustered face as she prepared to swing her ax again. She tilted her head to one side, the ax poised in her hands. "What ails you? You look like you done been pulled through a knothole. I ain't wore you out already, have I?" she asked lightly, but he could see her worried eyes searching his face.

He put down the bucket of water and shoved his hands into his pockets to warm them. Looking at Annie Mae, her slim white hands folded around the ax handle and her small shoulders buried in a too large jacket, Michael felt a sudden resolve harden in his chest, lifting up a shield against his fears. Annie Mae was tough. In some ways, he knew, tougher than him. She knew who she was, had accepted it, even when it wasn't acceptable, and had learned how to use her power. She had searched for the good among her many omens and signs, and for the most part, she had found it. It occurred to Michael that the only reason the shutters and doors had remained closed against the night intruder was because of Annie Mae's charms buried beneath the threshold and the salt sprinkled over the window sills.

But for all her spirit, she was also vulnerable, Michael

thought; fragile as bone china and up here in the mountains alone. Like Ned, she loved him and she looked to him for help and companionship. And like Ned she was breakable, though he had let her strength of character and her stubborn independence mask the smallness of her frame. Michael didn't want to see her hurt because of him. And he didn't want to lose her. For the first time since his mother had opened his eyes to the fairy vision, Michael didn't want to run away anymore. He wanted to use his sight to free him from the threat of Red Cap.

"I need to talk to you," Michael said.

"Now?" she asked, squinting at him, trying to figure him out.

"Yes. It needs to be now. Come up to the cabin and sit with me."

Her face froze and the hard point of her chin came up defensively. "You fixin' to leave, ain't you?" she asked. Michael winced at the coldness in her voice. He could see she was scared, her lips a taut line and her eyes dark gray beneath a scowl.

"Yes," he answered truthfully, "but only so I can come back and remain here with you and not feel like I'm hiding and jumping at every shadow. Annie Mae, my trouble isn't over. Red Cap isn't just going to leave me alone. I can't kill him. The Sidhe don't die. But I need to find a way to fight back and finish this mess."

Annie Mae sighed heavily and sat down on an ax-scarred stump. She leaned her chin on the ax handle, rocking her body back and forth and staring at the ground. Then she stopped and looked up at him, her expression sad but resigned. "I always know'd you have to go out and do this. T'wouldn't be right for me to keep you here. Still, I hate to see you go. Ain't the same when Walker up and left me. I done figured I was better alone than lonely in that man's presence. But h'it's differn' wi' you. An' I think you know that."

"Annie Mae, I do know that," Michael said, kneeling

down beside her. "I don't want to leave you. But if I stay and do nothing, Red Cap will try to hurt me by hurting you. He's done it before."

"What are you fixin' to do?" Annie Mae asked, a hand gently pushing Michael's long black hair out of his eyes.

"When I was driving trail, I worked with a cowboy named Ramon. He told me once about a creature called the Night Hatchet. You can hear him chopping wood in the forest at night."

"I know'd him," Annie Mae said with surprise. "We call him the Night Wood Chopper. He ha'nts my hills back home. Hard to say whether he means trouble. Most folks is just too skeerd to find out, I reckon. H'it's eerie some, hearin' that sound out of a dark night."

"I've been hearing it every night for the last two weeks," Michael said flatly.

"But I ain't," Annie Mae protested.

"That's why I know he's come for me. Look, Annie Mae, everything in me is unfinished. I'm like a tear in the fabric, and magic, both good and bad, comes to have a look and pull at the threads. The Night Hatchet has come around as a challenge. And Ramon said that to any man with courage to confront the Night Hatchet would come power and strength. To the man who fled afraid, only bad luck and hard times." Michael stood up slowly and held out a hand to Annie Mae, pulling her up to her feet. "So I'm going to meet that challenge. I'm going into the woods tonight. I'm going to find the Night Hatchet and get what I need to fight Red Cap."

"Tonight?" Annie Mae whispered, shocked. "Oh Gawd," she drawled, hiding her face in her hands. Michael put his arms around her, wanting to hold her. Her shoulders were hunched, her arms tight against her ribs. He could feel her silent struggle not to cry, her ragged breath hot and damp on his neck. He clung to her, pressing her close to the warmth of his chest.

"I need to do this, Annie Mae," he whispered in her

ear. "Ramon told me that the Night Hatchet could not hurt me if I showed courage. I don't want to run anymore. I want to be with you, to know that there is a future for us that doesn't mean fleeing from terror."

He coaxed her out of his arms and lowered her hands from her face. His heart ached at the sight of her tense, stoic features. "I love you, Annie Mae. I won't leave you behind. I'll come back."

He watched her fight to maintain her crumbling composure, her skin ashen and her lips trembling. Her eyes gleamed with tears but she refused to give in to weeping. She wiped her face quickly with the back of her hand, and Michael smiled at the streak of dirt left on her cheek.

He wiped it away with a gentle brush of his hand. Then, cupping her cheek in his palm, he kissed her softly on the mouth, swallowing the taste of juniper on her breath.

"Well," she said in a hoarse voice, "I done suffered to wait before. Guess I can do it again. Do you need anything?" she asked, pulling the folds of her big coat more tightly around her body. She shivered as a chilly damp wind blustered down from the treetops.

"No. I'll take Mo Neart. That's all I need. The Night Hatchet won't be hard to find."

"And then?" Annie Mae asked.

"And then . . . then I'll come back," Michael said lightly. After he had taken hold of the Night Hatchet's heart, he thought, but he didn't want to tell her that. It would only make her waiting worse.

Her eyes narrowed as she sensed that he was keeping something from her. Then she frowned and shrugged her shoulders.

"Come on then, pack in that there wood and leastwise we can eat somethin' afore you're off." She loaded a stack of split kindling on Michael's outstretched arms and picked up the bucket of water. As they walked back to the cabin she nodded her head. "Well, you done stood for a lot o' this here foolishness, but enough's enough, I guess, an' too much is just dawg's bait."

In spite of his worry, Michael laughed, and the sound of it loosened the knot of tension between them.

"You finally gittin' the hang o' my talk?" Annie Mae asked, flashing a grin.

"When you git ta talkin' too deep I jes tuck fer the hills," he answered smugly, leaning back and swaggering with the heavy load of wood.

"Well, h'it's a sin ta th' dawgs how you do go on, Mr. Mike. I never heard such a sayin' in my whole life!" she retorted with a haughty toss of her head.

"Gal, yer purtier'n a spotted pup," he tried again.

"Hmpf," she snorted, crossing the doorway into the cabin and setting the bucket of water down by the fireplace. "Mr. Mike, if I could buy you for what you're worth and sell you for what you think you're worth, well I'd be a mighty rich gal."

Michael dropped his armload of wood on the hearthstones. "That's it," he protested, throwing his hands up in defeat. "You win. I can't out-talk you, Annie Mae."

She looked back at him with a half smile. "I'll miss you," she said quietly. Then, averting her head, she bent to feed the fire new logs.

"I'm coming back," he said firmly, lifting her up to gather her into his arms again.

He laid his cheek against the softness of her hair, inhaling its smoky scent. He remembered the last verse of song that he had often heard Mary sing at her work. He rocked Annie Mae in his arms, and while the fire steamed and flared to life, he sang: "Oh I will climb the high, high tree. And I'll rob the wild bird's nest. And back I'll bring whate're I find to the one that I love best." He stopped singing and looked into her blue eyes, fair and wide as the skies over Texas. "To the one that I love best," he repeated and kissed her.

Michael ducked low over Mo Neart's neck as another hanging fir bough suddenly swept out of the dark, nearly unseating him. He swore, cursing the velvety darkness of the woods that turned everything into dense black shadows. He knew there was almost a full moon, rising brightly somewhere above the canopy of the tall trees. He had seen it lifting out of the mountain peaks from the path when he had ridden Mo Neart away from the cabin. Turning, he had waved farewell to Annie Mae, standing in the moonlight, her face a washed silver. But once he had entered the forest, the pines had closed in together, the interlocking branches of the firs shielding the sky and hiding even the sparkle of the smallest stars.

All around him in the darkness Michael could hear the busy rustle of night creatures, the snap of dried twigs and the scrabble of claws against the tree barks. He heard the call of an owl hunting and the short, piercing scream of a hare, caught in the killing talons. And overhead, the constant rushing sound, like a tumbling river cataract as the night wind blew through the pines. A cold mist played against the bare skin of his face, and he pulled up the collar of his coat to protect his chilled neck.

Where was he? And where was the Night Hatchet? How long was he going to have to wander these woods, cold and damp and stumbling into trees like a blinded fool? After months of avoiding danger, of running away from it, Michael now could not bear waiting for its arrival. He wanted something to happen soon, he wanted his chance to prove to himself and to Annie Mae that he wasn't a pawn to be played in another's game. He heard a dry crack and raised his head to the sound, his pulse quickening. There followed a silence, and he wondered briefly if it had been no more than the bending of a branch, weighted by a scurrying animal. There was second crack, louder this time but from another direction. Beneath him Mo Neart whickered nervously, his ears twitching, flicking back and forth to catch the sound.

Another crack was followed by a fourth. Michael turned his head from side to side, trying to find from which direction the noise originated. He kicked Mo Neart, and as the stallion trotted forward another loud crack sounded behind him. Confused, Michael pulled hard on the stallion's mane, to turn him around the other way. But Mo Neart stalled, lowering his head between locked forelegs and refusing to turn. As Michael prepared to kick him again, a loud banging broke the silence like the slamming of a door from the other direction. The Night Hatchet was moving, circling Michael where he and Mo Neart waited, blinded by the darkness. The banging continued, the harsh rhythmic chopping sound bouncing off the thick canopy of the trees, booming and echoing everywhere in the close forest. Between each clattering burst of sound, Michael could hear a voice moaning, accompanied by a shrill whistling.

Michael slid off the stallion's back, turning his body around in a slow circle, trying to follow the moving sound. An eerie green light flared, glowing between the branches of a scraggled lodgepole pine. For a brief instant, the Night Hatchet appeared out of the dark. From his right eye, Michael saw the huge severed trunk of a fallen tree. But from his left eye, he saw the subtle movements of the trunk as a blighted tree groaned and then twisted around to face him.

The Night Hatchet, hunched beneath the greening light, was a creature of decaying and mold-blackened wood. The body was a thick-trunked oak, the deeply grooved bark pitted with wormholes and studded with shelves of a glistening orange fungus. Flaps of rotten bark were peeling away like old scabs from the trunk. Sprouting near the base of the crown were five or six pairs of withered branches that ended in gnarled hands. The hands were snapping the brittle twigs of the lodgepole pine and stripping the leaves from the low shrubs. The trunk was sheared at the crown, as though the head that should have been there between the huge shoulders had been blasted away by lightning. The torn throat was split, thrown violently open, the raw wooden flesh a pale red. The greening light hovered over the Night Hatchet's humped shoulders, illuminating the white berries of a clinging garland of mistletoe and a mottled cloak of stag-horn moss. The light tumbled down the length of the lower branches and played among the bark-covered fingers.

A bark hand fisted the ball of green light and the forest plunged into darkness again. Abruptly Michael heard the furious clatter of an ax splintering into wood. But Michael also heard the snapping of smaller branches and the swishing of shrubs as the Night Hatchet staggered unseen through the trees. Michael spun on his heels, trying to follow the sounds of breaking branches and not the echo of the chopping ax that circled around him from everywhere.

The green light glimmered again in front of him and Michael started running, following the path of torn branches and down-trodden leaves of the low-lying shrubs. Michael was closing in on the green light, better able to tuck his body beneath the waving branches than the cumbersome and slower-moving Night Hatchet. Again the noise stopped, the light flickered out, and the forest returned to darkness and quiet.

Michael stopped running, his panting breath curdling into cold steam around his face. He bent over, his hands braced on his thighs as he caught his breath. He could hear the dry, feathered breathing of another closeby in the dark. The cold air was dank, musty with the odor of humus and decayed pine needles. Michael walked slowly toward the soft sound, peering into the dark, a hand held protectively in front of him. His heart was banging in his rib cage and he was certain the Night Hatchet could hear it in the muffled quiet of the forest.

Michael's hand touched the rough-grooved bark of a

tree. He stopped, uncertain. His fingers closed around a loose piece of the bark, and with a tearing sound he pulled away a thin layer of rotting wood. Michael crouched as a loud groan woke the silence. The eerie green light flared high up in the branches of the fir trees, illuminating the Night Hatchet standing hunched over Michael. From the moss-flecked chest of the trunk, twin doors banged open and shut repeatedly with the cracking sound of wood being chopped. Within the hollowed cavity of decaying wood, Michael saw the curved bones of a huge rib cage, the tips sharpened into gleaming white spikes. The air gusted out from the banging chest doors, stinking of carrion, and on the spiked ribs were the torn remains of an old flannel shirt. Air whistled shrilly as it was inhaled through a knothole near the sheared throat. The Night Hatchet gave a loud moan and then lunged its split open body at Michael.

Michael backed away in terror as the gnarled branches thrashed around him, hands with skin of flaking gray bark scrambling to grab his coat, his hair, his legs, and draw him into the hollow of spiked ribs.

"No!" Michael shouted as he struggled to free himself from the Night Hatchet's many-handed grasp. The more Michael fought against the Night Hatchet, the louder the doors to the chest wall banged open and shut.

A hand clasped over Michael's face, tearing scratches into his cheeks and forehead. He tried to yell for Mo Neart, but the wooden fingers jabbed into his mouth, strangling his cries. Michael bit down on the fingers, gagging at the bitter taste of rotting wood. Michael flailed his arms, his fists striking out anywhere he could as the branching arms continued to pull him closer, toward the Night Hatchet's banging chest. His dragging feet plowed deep furrows into the soft earth. At the entrance to the hollow cavity, the chest doors opened wide, splitting the Night Hatchet from its wounded gullet to the dense tangle of its roots. From the knothole, the shrill whistle piped gleefully in Michael's ears and the moaning turned into a throated laughter as Michael's twisting feet tripped over the tangled roots and the hands pitched him into the hollow chest. He was slammed against an interior wall covered with slime that sucked wetly at his shoulders. The Night Hatchet's laughter shook the cavity, and the sucking walls began to creak as they shut, encasing Michael within the creature's spiked rib cage.

Michael pushed himself away from the slimy, clinging walls and pressed his hands against the closing sides of the open cavity, forcing the rotting wood apart. The spiked ribs tore into his clothes and scraped along his skin. One pierced the top of his thigh and Michael roared in terrified rage but still held on, resisting. His hands were slipping, the rotting wood surface crumbling away but the hard red flesh beneath it slowly closing with an undiminished strength. The air inside the cavity was moist, the pulpy stench of carrion overpowering. Michael reared his head up, gasping for a breath of air in the near darkness of the Night Hatchet's trunk. A thin line of greening light showed him the sharpened points of two bent rib bones inclining toward his head.

But above these two spears, Michael saw a small white oval, like a spider's egg case, suspended in a web of delicate white filaments. In the fading green light it throbbed gently.

Michael stared at it, hope and fear flaming through him. That's what he had come for, he was certain. The pale oval jewel was the Night Hatchet's heart. But to reach for it, Michael would have to free his hands and let go his resistance to the Night Hatchet's closing walls. If he moved too slowly, he would die, the spiked ribs piercing him from all sides. But his second choice was to cling terrified to these last moments of his life and die without even having tried. Ramon had told him that to any man with courage would come strength.

Michael slammed his booted feet hard into the spongy

sides of the cavity, ignoring the pain as the spiked rib embedded itself deeper into his thigh. For an instant, the closing walls hesitated, a thick coat of slime oozing out where Michael repeatedly kicked a splintered hole in the wooden flesh. With a surge of desperate energy, Michael let go of the closing walls and reached for the delicate white jewel. As soon as his fingers closed around it, the shrill piping turned to a wailing cry and the low-throated laughter broke in howls.

The Night Hatchet twisted its trunk, swaying from side to side. Michael was tossed inside the trunk, but he clung to the egg-shaped heart, and the sticky white threads of filament tore away from the slimy walls. At once the Night Hatchet's bark-covered fingers clutched the sides of its chest and pulled it open. Michael blinked, blinded by the hovering green light that shone in his newly exposed face. He held the egg, firmly but carefully, feeling its terrified pulse fluttering like a moth's wings against his palm. The Night Hatchet continued to twist and sway on its roots, rocking wildly as it howled. Smaller, agitated hands reached in and snatched at Michael, trying to find where his hands hid the pulsing heart.

"Let me go!" Michael shouted. "Let me go or I'll crush it!" He squeezed the heart slightly and at once the Night Hatchet moaned and stopped its frenzied swaying. The branching arms reluctantly withdrew, snapping and creaking as they folded back to clear the way for Michael's release. The rib cage opened wider, and Michael gasped as the spike slid out from the wound in his thigh. Blood gushed down his leg, which trembled with pain. He limped free of the Night Hatchet's trunk and stumbled down onto the forest floor.

"I let you goooo," the Night Hatchet groaned. "Now give it baaack to meee."

The wind rattled through its branches, and rustling pairs of hands stretched out, waiting to receive the stolen heart.

Blood trickled into Michael's right eye from a deep scratch in his eyebrow. He wiped it away quickly, trying not to think of the pain shooting up from the stab wound in his thigh.

"Not yet," Michael answered through gritted teeth.

"Whaat do you waant?" hissed the Night Hatchet, the hull of rotting wood shuddering.

"Help in defeating my enemy."

"Give it back tooo meee and I will dooo asss you asssk," the Night Hatchet replied. Eager hands stretched out farther, beseeching Michael.

"If I give it to you now you'll disappear. You must come with me."

The Night Hatchet began its violent swaying again, the branches groaning as they crashed against each other. The doors to the empty chest banged open and shut with a dull, hollow sound. Michael held the heart, feeling the terrified pulse of the creature. The branches swept against the forest floor, scraping away the dirt and pine needles, but unable to do more. And then, its rage spent, the Night Hatchet grew quiet again, the wooden husk sagging around its shrunken chest as it surrendered.

"Gooo, then. I will follow. But desssstrooy my heart and you tooo will dieee. For it knooows you nooow."

"I understand," Michael said soberly. "Help me to defeat Red Cap and I will give it back to you."

"The sstallion comess," the Night Hatchet announced, and a bark-skinned hand pointed a spindled finger at a ghostly white form quickly approaching from between the dark trees.

Michael gave a short whistle and the stallion was soon beside him, butting him lightly with his nose, noisily exhaling warm moist air over his face. "I'm all right," Michael reassured the stallion, taking hold of his mane in one hand and gently putting the Night Hatchet's heart into his coat pocket. "Well, more or less all right," he croaked, the pain flaring in his thigh as he pulled his leg

over the back of the horse. Michael ripped the hem of his
flannel shirt and tied a makeshift bandage around his
thigh. He kicked Mo Neart with his other leg and the
stallion began trotting slowly through the night forest.

Behind him, Michael heard the Night Hatchet follow,
a mournful whistle lamenting over the hollow banging of
its empty chest.

"I did it," Michael said aloud to the stallion. "I did it."
And as relief and amazement washed over him, he
thought of Annie Mae and the look of happiness that
would show on her face when he came limping home.
And then her sharp frown of concentration as she would
fuss over his wound, instructing him in her thick drawl.
He would show her the Night Hatchet's heart, and together they would decide how best to use its power
against Red Cap. "I feel like a hero out of one of my
mother's stories," Michael said to the stallion. "Maybe
that's what I was supposed to be all along."

In the quiet night, fear ebbing from him and the gentle
gait of the stallion making him drowsy, Michael thought
about Eileen's stories, each one a lesson in the heroic as
well as treacherous ways of the Sidhe. "Surely your
momma and daddy give you somethin' to help you?"
Annie Mae had insisted. Until now Michael had refused
to believe that James and Eileen McBride had thought of
anything but their own private misery. But in Michael's
mind dozens of Eileen's stories sparked to life, their
meanings husked open, revealing golden kernels of hidden knowledge. There were tales of ill-fated love between
the Sidhe and mortals; tales of shape-shifters, men turning into swans and crows; the white, foam-flecked steeds
born out of the ocean waves and the fates of fairy queens
determined by reckless games of chess. It was more than
repetition that made it ring with familiarity, he thought,
suddenly awake.

What else? he asked himself. What else had his mother
told him in her stories that might explain her life, his fa-

ther's, and in the end his own? Michael recalled the stories of Lassa Buaicht, the fairy druid forced by the Sidhe to a life of gambling, and his *geasa,* a taboo, that forbade him from ever speaking of it to anyone, sealing him in a vow of silence.

A fairy queen lost in a game of chess. A mortal man fleeing with a fairy woman. A jealous husband and a *geasa* of silence. The stiff faces of his parents rose before him, his mother's shade weeping by the Red River and the memory of his father choking at the gaming table, trying to speak words that were not allowed to be uttered. As Michael rode home to Annie Mae, he let his memory dip into Eileen's stories, mining them for the wealth of knowledge that she had stored in every one. Annie Mae had learned her magic through a reading of signs: the skin of an onion, the final shape of a fallen cloth. Michael would learn the measure of his fairy magic through the memory of his mother's lilting voice shaping the knowledge she could not speak of directly into stories she had told him over and over.

Twelve

Michael could smell the smoke of a fire long before he could see its destruction. It was the hour before dawn, and the velvet blackness of the forest was bleeding into a soft, hazy gray. The green boughs of the fir trees were shrouded with a cold mist that carried the acrid stench of burning wood. Though he was exhausted and the wound on his thigh throbbed, Michael kicked Mo Neart, urging the horse to travel more quickly through the forest. He may have succeeded against the Night Hatchet, but Red Cap was far more cunning and treacherous. And as the stench grew worse and the mist thickened with fragments of pulpy ash, Michael felt the dread in him return. "Annie Mae," he whispered, and, leaning over Mo Neart's neck, he drove the stallion into a fast run.

Michael cried out in anguish as Mo Neart broke through the line of fir trees at last and galloped across a fire-scorched field. The corn had withered and curled into black stalks; the black husks were peeled back, revealing the blighted seed. Over the smoking field of burning grass the sky hung a dark gray, the air clouded with thick plumes of smoke. Except for the brick chimney standing forlornly amid the ruins, little of Annie Mae's cabin remained. Shattered glass from the windows lay scattered over the packed dirt floor, greasy with soot. Annie Mae's possessions were strewn about in blackened heaps of broken crockery, smoking blankets and quilts, smashed jars of preserves, and broken chairs, all trailing wisps of smoke. Only the wrought-iron headboard was recognizable, and that was sagging in the middle where the heat of the flames had caused the metal to soften and bend. The shuck mattress was a blackened slab of soft gray charcoal that exhaled ashen flakes into the gusting winds.

Michael slid from the stallion's back and began running toward the cabin. His injured leg buckled with pain but he ignored it, staggering over the field of scorched grass. "Annie! Annie Mae!" he shouted, frantic for a sight of her or the sound of her voice answering. He prayed that she had managed to flee to safety, that her foresight had protected her from being caught by Red Cap.

Michael tripped over something lying half hidden in the burned grass. He cried out, pain shooting through his thigh as he sprawled across the blackened earth. He rolled over, horrified by the feel of a body lying beneath him.

He turned over the black, smoking figure, feeling a surge of relief as he realized that it wasn't Annie Mae's body. But the fear returned when he saw that it was one of Red Cap's bananachs, a white-fletched arrow shot through its forehead. The twisted black face was covered with dried blood, the tusks a sooty yellow in the gaping mouth. The dirty raven wings had burned and were a black crumbling dust in the grass. Long strands of bright yellow hair were tangled in the curled talons.

Michael stood up, moving slowly with shock and pain. He limped over to Mo Neart and leaned his sweating forehead against the stallion's side. He could hear the Night Hatchet lumbering through the trees and then into the clearing. The chest doors had continued to bang open and shut through the night, haunting Michael with their empty sound. Now it stopped. Michael lifted his head and saw the Night Hatchet settled like a huge blasted oak in the middle of the scorched field. In the gray dawn it had lost its aura of threatening danger and seemed to be only an ancient and dying tree that had been growing a century in the field. Only from his left eye could Michael see the hands dangling wearily at the end of the twisted branches, and these were concealed by drooping, leather-brown leaves.

The quiet dawn was broken by the harsh call of a crow, greeting him from the pale blue sky. Michael looked up quickly and saw a large female crow, her shining black wings catching the morning rays as she banked down the rocky slopes of the peaks and skimmed over the treetops. He watched her approach, her uplifted wings flapping noisily as she prepared to settle on the field.

As soon as her grasping talons reached for the charred grass she was transformed. Her legs lengthened and her black wings stretched into white arms. The long oval of her body became a slender torso, and the hard obsidian beak disappeared into a woman's youthful face. She glanced around at the burning remains of the cabin and inhaled deeply, taking in the smoke as though it were a perfumed incense.

She came toward Michael, her legs gliding easily through the smoking grass, her arms swinging loosely at her sides. Tendrils of smoke blew into her eyes like thin clouds passing over the bright face of the moon. She smiled at him.

"Do you remember me, then?" she asked in a husky voice.

Michael nodded. For at the sight of her face he did remember. He had lived as a crow, traveling with her by day in the deserts, seated over her shoulder at night among the court of the Sidhe. He was kin to her, and she was powerful and dangerous. Her face never stayed the same but shifted with her mood and intent. "Morrigu, goddess of war," he said, bowing his head respectfully.

She gave a sparkling laugh as bright and gay as the charred ruins of the cabin were dreary.

"Good man," she said, openly pleased. "Do you know why I've come?"

Michael wanted to say no, but the answer suddenly seemed obvious. Red Cap had been here but was here no longer. And Annie Mae was missing. "Have you come to deliver Red Cap's message?"

"You feckle brat, you," Morrigu spit. "What makes you think I'd do a deed for that worthless bastard?" The white skin of her round, youthful face shrunk into the sagging folds of a gray-headed crone. "It's to you I've come. As favor to my sister. But I can leave again in a tick if you can only think to insult me."

"Wait," Michael said quickly. "I'm sorry. I'm sorry. I didn't mean that. I should have remembered, but it's still not all clear to me what is happening. I didn't mean to give offense."

Morrigu hesitated and then released her sudden anger with a sigh. She came closer to Michael, and he saw her crone features soften, the black sheen returning to her blowing hair. Beneath a firm brow, dark, intelligent eyes regarded him sternly, measuring his worth.

"I've come to tell you this: Red Cap has your friend. She's alive because he finds her amusing. Even I found her worthy of a second glance. She killed my bananach with a single shot and raised no small trouble to those that carried her off. So he keeps her a prisoner for now, because she is spirited and he is bored by most things except games of torture."

Michael clenched his teeth and his hands closed in fists of rage. Since his mother's death he had been chased and hunted like a hapless chess king imprisoned on the checkered squares of the gaming board. The pawns and mounted knights had died around him. The rook had been destroyed, and now the queen was taken captive. A game of chess, that was all this was to Red Cap, and all it had ever been.

Michael stared into the blackened grass and saw in his mind the gaming board at home, then the one at Red Cap's table. Chess was a game of cunning and power. He closed his eyes, hearing his father's gruff voice ordering him to the table, drilling into him the rules of the game and the brutal strategies; who to sacrifice and who to save in order to win at all costs. Michael sighed and opened his clenched fingers. He understood his father's obsession with the game at last. He had won a fairy wife by such a skill, even though it had brought them both pain. But he had tried in his own way to reach beyond the *geasa* of silence to Michael, to teach him a king's skill even as his mother had tried to prepare him through the telling of tales.

"Do you know who you are, then?" Morrigu asked, looking at Michael's somber face.

"Yes," he answered with quiet pride. "Yes, I do know. I am the son of James McBride, who won a fairy wife from the Sidhe, Red Cap, beating him at a game of chess. And I am the son of Eileen McBride, daughter of the Sidhe and your sister. I am half mortal and half fairy, sighted in one eye and blinded in the other, but whole at last in heart."

"Good. Good," Morrigu replied with satisfaction. "What will you do, then?"

"Will you take a message for me to Red Cap?"

She cocked one eyebrow, momentarily irritated. Then she shrugged it away with a bright laugh, her youthful cheeks filling out like the moon. "For you I will carry a message back to Red Cap."

"Tell him that I challenge him to three games of chess.

The winner claiming their prize. Tell him I will meet him at the gray stones of the high peaks where I first landed here as a crow."

"I know the place," Morrigu said, nodding. " 'Tis cold and forbidding."

"Just like him," Michael replied.

"When?"

"It'll take me at least a day by horseback."

"Sooner as the crow flies," she argued.

"I don't know how to do that," Michael answered. "The last time was because of Coyote's gift. I've nothing like that now."

"But you don't need them," she scoffed. "You didn't need them then. It's in your blood, man. You've only to command it of yourself and the change will come. Last time it was to me you called, and so you changed but lost the power of your own will and had to have the spell broken by someone else. Ask it of yourself now and you will be able to remain human here," she said, tapping her forehead, "even as your body goes forth as a crow."

"No. Not this time," Michael answered firmly, looking out at the ancient tree hunkered in the field. In his pocket the warm heart pulsed. He had an idea and needed time to think about it and time for the Night Hatchet to keep up with him on the journey to the peaks. "I'll be there tomorrow morning, waiting."

"What makes you so sure Red Cap'll come?" Morrigu asked.

Michael gave a dry laugh. "I'm a better player. Just like my father before me. Tell him I said that."

Morrigu threw back her head and laughed. "Oh, he'll come for that, all right. And hoping to tear you limb from limb if you should lose, Michael McBride."

"Maybe," Michael said grimly.

"Give us your leg there," Morrigu ordered. "Leastways I can make the journey easier." She spit into her palms and rubbed them together. Michael undid the bloody bandage from his leg, his stomach rolling at the sight of the swollen puncture wound. It oozed with caked blood and pale green pus.

"It's nasty, to be sure. But I've seen worse," she chuckled. Then she slapped her spit-covered palms on his wounded thigh.

Startled, Michael swore loudly, his voice raising into a sustained shout of agony as Morrigu's fingers burrowed through the wound. Clutching his knee between her thighs to hold his leg steady, she worked, her head bent to the wound and oblivious to his loud cries. Like needles of molten iron her fingers prodded the deep wound, searing away the infected flesh, cleaning and cauterizing the wound. Foul-smelling smoke from burned hair and flesh filled Michael's nostrils, making him retch. He pressed his sweating face into Mo Neart's foamy, sea-smelling hide, clinging to the stallion's mane as he tried to remain upright.

"There," Morrigu said finally, releasing his leg and stepping back. Her face was pale, her eyes smudged with deep shadows, but she smiled weakly. "Good man you are. You didn't even call out His name. That would have made trouble."

Michael's head swam with the lingering pain, his tightly shut eyes squeezing out tears. "Who?" he asked, confused.

"The one up there."

"Go-?"

"Shh," Morrigu said sharply. "Wait until I'm gone. Then you can pray all you like. Probably won't hurt you to do so, either. Go on then, take a look at that leg. It's not half bad."

Michael opened his eyes and glanced down, where the sharp burning pain was quickly fading into a dull ache. The flesh was sealed, the wound gone. All that remained was the bloody tear in his trousers and a faint white scar on his skin in the shape of a crow's head.

"Rather a nice job, I'd say," Morrigu cackled, her hands balled on her hips. "So you'll not forget out of who's line you've gotten the better blood." She leaned forward and tousled his black hair. "You've your mother's look about you," she said. "But let's hope you've your father's skill as well. I'll see you again."

The rising sun shot arrows of golden light over the withered field of scorched grass. As she walked away from him, Michael saw the shadow of Morrigu's long slender figure contract into the compact body of a crow, wings outstretched to catch the wind. He squinted, a hand held to shield his eyes from the bright sunlight, as he watched her rising higher and higher until she was no more than a tiny black speck in the wide blue sky. He lowered his eyes to the Night Hatchet, waiting silently for his command. The hands rustled in the wind, the old cloak of moss lifting at the dried, curled edges. The shelves of gleaming orange fungus had dulled into a dirty brown.

Mo Neart huffed into Michael's neck and raked a hoof through the grass.

"All right," Michael replied. "We're going."

He mounted up again and turned to look sadly at the ruins of Annie Mae's cabin. More than anywhere else, it had been his home. Her love and companionship had made it so. Michael turned his face toward the high peaks, the sunlight glancing off the wind-polished stones of mountain slopes. He would free Annie Mae from Red Cap's grasp, he told himself. And then he would free himself and his parents from the cold silence that had imprisoned them all. He nudged Mo Neart forward to the trail, and the Night Hatchet shuddered to life, its roots quivering out of the earth as it followed Michael.

Riding Mo Neart, it only took Michael the day to reach the high peaks. He had traveled as quickly as he could, wanting to be there well before the sun rose again. Ice-crusted blankets of snow lay in the low rocky reaches, and the bitter cold wind howled over the stones. Michael spent the night squeezed between two huge boulders, trying to shelter himself from the worst of the wind. The cold dank air smelled of coming snow. Up in the high reaches the dawn arrived long before the night had fully relinquished its authority. When Michael awoke, the wind digging icy fingers under the hem of his coat, the sky was still spangled with stars, defiantly burning in the first blushing rays of sunlight. The full moon clung to the sharp edge of the night, dusty shadows carving wistful features on its cold face. Shivering, Michael slipped his hand into his pocket and felt the warmth of the Night Hatchet's heart throbbing in his grasp.

Michael sat up and peered down the slope at the Night Hatchet, hunkered between two long slabs of polished rock, fringed at the base with pale pink blossoms. The Night Hatchet had bowed its sheered crown into the driving wind, and the tangle of roots snaked out over the rocks, lashing it securely. Twice in the night Michael had thought to release the Night Hatchet. Seeing the creature loping behind him through the rocky valleys, Michael had felt a twinge of shame. He needed the Night Hatchet. But not like this, its heart a hostage in Michael's pocket, forced to follow his demands.

Suddenly Michael stood up and scrambled down the rocks to where the Night Hatchet waited, its branches bowed down before the harsh-driving wind.

"Night Hatchet," he called, and the creature straightened its scraggly limbs with a shiver. The wind whistled through the knothole, piping a cold, joyless tune.

"I aaam heere," it said with a sigh.

Michael put his hand into his pocket, holding the heart. "I am going to give you back your heart," he announced over the keening whistle. The heart leapt in his grasp and the quickened pulse blazed with heat like a small fire. "I still need your help. But if something should happen to me, it were best you had your heart for your own keeping. Red Cap would make you his slave if he could."

The barked hands reached out blindly, the fingers grasping eagerly at the air. Michael slid the warm white heart out of his pocket and placed it carefully into one of the hands. The piping whistle changed at once into a fast and reckless tune. The Night Hatchet folded another hand over the throbbing heart and pressed down on it gently. When the hands opened again, Michael was shocked to see the white oval heart transformed into a small brown acorn. Instead of returning the heart into its chest, the Night Hatchet placed the acorn heart amid a cluster of similar dried nuts concealed in its leafy branches.

"You haave honoor after all," it said, and Michael thought he could hear the gladness in its scratching voice. "I will heelp you aaas I proomised. Bring him into meee and I will hoold him foorever."

"Are you that powerful?" Michael asked uncertainly.

"Had you noot given meee back my heart, I could never have aided you. But with it, I am without peer in theese mountains. Look where they come." The Night Hatchet's barked hands turned silvery palms upward, and Michael raised his head to stare into the cloudless reaches of the morning sky.

They appeared at first as no more than streams of thin clouds, trailing between the last sparkled light of the evening stars. But the clouds thickened into the rainbowed bodies of swimming trout, their sides shimmering with scales of faint green, gold, and red. As they approached the stony peaks, the clouds burst into a fine veil of mist, and out of the mist, the dew-spangled figures of the Sidhe took on solid form, their horses touching blackened hooves to the gray stones. They came with their retinues, some on foot wearing silver chest plates and carrying pike-headed spears across their shoulders. Others wore jerkins of leather tooled in red and green, carrying quivers of arrows at their hips and the curves of long bows slung across their backs.

As Michael watched them assembling across the terraces of weathered stones, he noted that the gathered host separated itself into two distinct sides. He knew them all, remembered their different histories from his mother's stories and recognized their faces from his own recent memories as a crow in the starlit courts of the Sidhe. To Michael's right, mounted on a silvery gray horse, was Ruan Luimneah, king of the Isle of the Living. And beside him Aebinn, the queen of Munster, her flaming red hair a competing fire to the newly risen sun. Wearing a mantle of white swan's feathers was the fair-browed Angus Og, the god of love; and beside him rode the soft, curved body and gentle face of Aine, the goddess of fertility.

It saddened Michael to see that his mother was not waiting among this lighted host. Instead she was standing, pale as a willow leaf, on a barely perceptible border between the brilliant morning light and the dark edge of a wintery shadow. Beside her was Morrigu, her face split by the light, one half white and full at the rounded edges, but dark and near shapeless where it was cast into the shadows on the other side. She smiled, and her stark white teeth gleamed from the shadows. Finvarra stood among them as well. The yellow curls were brightened by the light into gold on one side of his handsome face and tarnished by the shadows on the other.

Michael turned to his left, seeing now that he stood enclosed within the dark arch of the shadow's penumbra. Jake Talking Boy had been right, Michael realized, staring at the wintry faces of the Sidhe that claimed him in the shadow. He had indeed been walking among death's realm, for these were the kings of the Land of the Dead. Spreading out over all of them and casting the shadow was the gray-misted cloak of the King Trom Ceo

Draochta. He was chief among the kings of the dead, and in the shelter of his fog-ladened cloak awaited his cohorts. The black-haired Donn Ceiv Fionn from Magh Hi sat astride a swayback, piebald nag, surrounded by manservants with snarling wolf faces. Next to him on a smoke-colored horse was Donn Binne Eachla Labhra, his long angular face ending in a square blunted jaw, the lower teeth jutting up between the closed lips. And last, Michael saw Donn Ferine O'Conail of Knocfierna—or Red Cap, as some had chosen to call him—sitting on his soot-black horse, his cap of oiled red hair smoothed down over his narrow skull.

"Never let the mark know what the real stakes are," Poker Alice had advised Michael long before. "Keep your face dead. If you let on too early, you'll give away the best part of your game. Give them nothing and take everything. Got it?" Michael heard those words and he steeled his features into an empty mask to hide the pounding rage in his breast.

Standing in attendance on Red Cap's horse were four ghostly wraiths, their human souls claimed in bondage. One pushed back a black-brimmed hat, and Jim Delaney's haggard gray face stared back out of hollowed sockets. Beside him, the Strayhorn brothers, Ludie and Barney, gazed listlessly at the ground, their shoulders hunched and their ankles crippled by shackles of briars. And last, Michael saw Ned, his child's face withered into features of gray dust.

Red Cap eased himself from the golden saddle of the black horse, and Michael felt a second jolt of rage. He swallowed it, felt it stabbing like a thorn ripping the sides of his throat. Annie Mae was sitting on the black horse behind Red Cap. Her empty face was whiter than snow, her lips a faint purple smudge. Her yellow hair had lost it color, hanging limp over her shoulders like ice-burned flax. The spark was gone from her coal-gray eyes. Her arms were trussed behind her, her white hands bound at the wrists. Her shoulder blades arched cruelly back like the broken wings of a captured swan. Smiling coldly at Michael, Red Cap jerked Annie Mae's stiff form by the torn sleeve, and she toppled over the side of the horse. She made no cry of pain as she fell onto the rocks, lifeless as an old doll. Blood bloomed on her forehead like a splash of holly berries against the white of her frostbitten skin.

Michael willed himself not to look at her but kept his eyes trained on Red Cap's arrogant face. Whether a king's game of chess or a beggar's game of cards, it was all the same: Give away nothing.

"So, crow's shit, have you come to be beaten, then?" Red Cap sneered.

"I've come to play chess," Michael answered calmly.

"Then you've come to lose."

"My father before me didn't."

The sneer on Red Cap's face tightened and his eyes flared red with barely concealed anger. "Get out the board and we'll see then who's master here."

Wordlessly, Ludie Strayhorn shuffled forward. He laid out a gaming board on the face of a flat gray boulder. And then he hobbled back to wait beside his brother. Ned came forward, his bare feet drifting over the rocks, and from the deep pockets of his ragged vest he pulled out the chess pieces. He set up the game and, when he was done, lifted a sorrowing child's face to stare at Michael. Jim Delaney and Barney Strayhorn each brought forth a stool, the seats covered with gold-stitched tapestries.

"Will you be crows or swans?" Red Cap asked mockingly.

"It doesn't matter. Both may win with skill," Michael answered as he sat down. He looked over the field of chess figures and drew in a steadying breath. It was no different than at home. How many times had he sat like this, his face tense and expectant, as the pieces were readied for battle?

Red Cap moved a white pawn to knight-four and began the first game. Automatically Michael responded, moving his black pawn to knight-four. The clicking pieces were moved quickly and with skill, setting up for the intricate confrontation. Michael felt a dizzying sensation come over him. The board wavered, as though submerged just beneath the surface of a clear pool of water.

As he made his next move, Michael knew with a startled shock that he was moving his pieces from memory. James McBride had often schooled him from the written games of well-known masters, handed down as part of the canon of chess lore. Looking over the board, Michael found himself anticipating every move of Red Cap's white pieces and was compelled to make the correct replies with the black. He knew too that the game would end with white being victorious, and that there was no way he could change the outcome. Then Red Cap hesitated, his hand paused over the battle, before he moved his bishop. It was the wrong move, Michael thought. The wavering haze over the gaming board cleared abruptly, and as Michael stared at the unexpected configuration, he tried not to let the surprise show on his features.

Red Cap had made a deliberate error. He wanted Michael to win.

Michael thought quickly as he slammed his pieces into an impromptu attack. There was a reason Red Cap was letting him win, but what? Though uncertain, Michael didn't hesitate to press his advantage. He needed to win if he was to free Annie Mae. Two moves later and he had routed the white king into a corner between a waiting bishop and an aggressive knight.

"Mate," he announced softly.

"So it is," Red Cap answered, leaning back and looking unperturbed by this loss. "Claim your prize."

"Free the woman," Michael ordered.

Red Cap shrugged his shoulders and gave a dry chuckle. "Fool. You would have done better to look after your own skin, me boyo." But he reached into his pocket and handed Michael an ivory-handled dagger. "Cut the ropes and free her yourself."

Michael went to where Annie Mae lay bundled like a frozen sheaf of wheat on the rocks. He sliced the dagger into the ropes and yanked them from her wrists. At once Annie Mae groaned, curled up her knees, and began to shiver violently.

Michael took off his coat and wrapped it around her quaking shoulders. "Are you all right?" he asked, stroking her white cheek.

"Cold, so cold," she murmured, and her eyelids fluttered. "Ain't never felt such a coldness. Like the Devil hisself gripping me with a hand o' icy hatred." A faint blue glimmered in her eyes like the slow, unfurling bud of an iris.

"I'm sorry, Annie Mae. It's my fault."

"T'ain't completely, neither," she said with a tight shake of her head. "My own, for not being smarter. I done opened the door to him thinking h'it was you." And then she gave a vague smile, the purple tint of her lips warming to a rosy blush. "Course, I did manage to give 'em hell for a bit. Only got off one good shot, but I bit someone deep and would've drawn blood if'n they'd a had any."

"Can you walk?" Michael asked.

"I can try."

"Good, then come and sit with me while I beat this bastard at his own game," Michael whispered.

She nodded, and Michael lifted her up from the rocks. He put his arms around her waist, helping her when she stumbled on numb feet over the rocks. He set her down again beside him, leaning her chilled body against his thighs. Morrigu tossed him a woolen cloak stinking of smoke and burned leather. He put it around his shoulders, grateful for its warmth.

"To the second game," Michael said. "I'll play the crows again."

The gameboard was reset, the chess pieces returned to their starting squares. Michael could feel Annie Mae's leaning body warming his thigh and he thought of how empty his life would be without her. His expression faltered for a moment, a look of stricken panic that tugged the corners of his mouth. He glanced up and saw that Red Cap was watching him with cool amusement. Michael swore, realizing that he had betrayed himself. He reclaimed his calm expression and told himself not to falter like that again. His life and Annie Mae's would depend upon it.

They played the second game, and for a second time Michael saw the gaming board waver beneath the power of a spell. For a second time, he was struck by the familiar pattern of the game. He knew it, knew in advance every move that Red Cap would make and every move that he would be compelled to use to counter the attack. Compelled until the moment when Red Cap unexpectedly broke the pattern. Once more he played the wrong move, and the sudden open road to an unexpected victory spurred Michael to a win.

"You've won a second time, crow's shit," Red Cap said with a thin-lipped smile. "What prize do you claim?"

Michael looked up, hiding his troubled feelings. Something was going on here. Red Cap had fixed the games. Michael had no control over the games as long as they were played according to the original game. But Red Cap should have won twice already. So why had he changed it at the last moment? Why had he made it possible for Michael to win not once but twice?

"Your prize?" Red Cap said gruffly. "Name your prize or forfeit."

"Release the souls of my friends that you murdered," Michael answered sharply.

Red Cap gave a dark laugh and a snigger rippled

through the shadowed kings. "See where he cares more for the dead than his own skin? Do I not take care of your dead properly? Do I not give them work?"

"Let them go," Michael repeated.

Red Cap shrugged. "Suit yourself." He raised his long white hand in the air and a brisk wind circled through his fingers. It spiraled higher into a narrow funnel of twisting smoke. The funnel lifted from his fingertips and spun toward the wraiths. It touched Jim Delaney first, and the dusty body separated at once with a sigh into a soft green mist. It passed over the twin wraiths of Barney and Ludie Strayhorn, and the shackles fell away from their ankles as they were lifted into the twisting column. And last it touched Ned, and a brief smile parted the gray lips just as his ghostly form disintegrated. The twisting column of green mist hovered over Michael's head, and then it was carried away by the gusting winds.

"To the third game, crow's shit," Red Cap snarled.

Michael studied the sky, watching the last threads of the green mist fade beyond the horizon. Why had Red Cap let him win? He lowered his glance at the sound of Red Cap's cold insult and saw Red Cap's eyes stray to Eileen's pale, drawn face. And then Michael knew. It was to hurt her. To let her hope that he might win, only to have her watch him lose this last time. He would punish her by crushing that hope, making her witness her only child's defeat.

"It doesn't matter half so much which games you win or lose, as long as you're the one making the decision," Poker Alice had told him. So far Red Cap had made the decisions. Michael knew that whatever glamour had been laid against the chessboard to let him win the first two games would now let him lose. But he had prepared for such an event. He would lose this game because he had intended to lose all along.

"I'll take crows for a third time," Michael announced. As the pieces were set up, Michael stared out at the Night

Hatchet, waiting hunched down among the rocks nearby. Nothing in the wrecked and blasted body drew the Sidhe's attention to it. It was a dying tree, weatherbeaten by the wind and clinging with its gnarled roots against the rock face. The kings of the dead and even Red Cap himself had not given it a second glance. As if it sensed the crackle of Michael's thoughts, the Night Hatchet slowly straightened its stunted limbs. The chest doors parted without a sound. It was ready.

Michael returned his gaze to the chessboard. He inhaled, trying to calm the surge of impatience in his pulse. Soon, he warned himself. Soon this would be over.

They began the third match and Michael watched another familiar game unfold beneath his eyes. The pieces moved as they were forced to, duplicating the brilliance of their original players. But this time Michael knew as the familiar game took shape that there would be no wrong move, no sudden opportunity to win. Still cheating, Red Cap would force this unfair victory over Michael. Michael glanced sidelong at Red Cap and saw that he was grown overly confident in his playing. Red Cap was certain of himself, certain the cruel victory would come as he had planned. Good, Michael decided, allowing his hand to move the black pieces in a losing game.

"Check!" Red Cap snapped.

Michael feigned anger, tried to recover, and knew that he would be forced to make a fatal mistake.

"And mate," Red Cap shouted as he played the last move, knocking Michael's black queen out of the game and exposing the lost king.

Next to him Annie Mae cried out angrily, clutching at the hem of the woolen cloak. He pulled her hands away from him and moved his stool a little to one side so as to be clear of her body. She mustn't hold him now! And as if silently understanding him, she let go at once, but she remained crouched at his side.

"Claim your prize," Michael said.

"You, crow's shit. I claim that you must serve me in the place of those you freed."

"No, no," Eileen shrieked. "You can't do that!"

"Oh, but I can," Red Cap snarled. "Oh, but I will. I'll dye my cloak in your spilt blood, me boyo, and I'll make you run before the tearing jaws of the hounds, over and over, until you'll wish it were true death you could have."

Michael bolted up from the stool, flinging the chessboard into Red Cap's malevolent face. And without stopping he ran, scrambling down across the rocks, hearing the outraged shouts of the onlooking kings. Behind him, he heard Annie Mae screaming defiantly and knew she had thrown herself in Red Cap's way. Michael could hear Red Cap bellowing as he fought to get away from her, but he didn't dare stop and turn. Instead he made straight for the opening trunk of the Night Hatchet.

The wolf-faced servants bayed. Stealing a quick glance over his shoulder, Michael saw them loping over the rocks alongside Red Cap, their claws striking the granite rocks and firing sparks into the air. A spurt of strength forced itself into Michael's legs, and this time, without a fight, he flung himself inside the opened rib cage of the Night Hatchet's trunk.

The stench was the same as before, but the dark rust-colored walls coated with slime were not there to entrap him. A seam in the bark split open in the far wall of the trunk, and Michael leaned against it, waiting until Red Cap had tucked his head and then his arm into the Night Hatchet's chest. Facing Red Cap, Michael pressed his back deeper into the fleshy walls behind him. The seam parted under the strain with a wet sucking noise, drawing him away from Red Cap's reach. Red Cap lunged farther in, a dagger striking out to slash at Michael's chest. Then Red Cap roared with surprise as the tangled roots lifted without warning and tumbled his body forward into the hollow chest cavity. The spiked ribs closed down on Red Cap, pinning him to the floor of the trunk.

At the same time that Red Cap was falling headlong into the Night Hatchet, Michael was being pushed out the splitting seam on the far side of the trunk. He freed one arm from the wet spongy wood and waved it in the cold air. Michael shoved against the splitting wood, and then his shoulder and head emerged, covered with a thick film of slimy muck. Annie Mae was there, shouting and calling his name. She grabbed his waving free hand and, bracing her foot against the roots, yanked him the rest of the way out of the Night Hatchet's trunk. He sprouted from the trunk like a huge wet limb from the base of the tree. When his feet were freed, Michael kicked and rolled away from the Night Hatchet and into Annie Mae's arms. Behind him the torn, woody flesh sealed itself closed again. Sitting back on her haunches, Annie Mae held him across her lap in her arms and her warm tears washed over his face.

"Oh, my heavens above!" Annie Mae exclaimed in a breathless gasp. "Look, Mike, looky there!"

Michael raised his head from between her arms to look behind him. The Night Hatchet was groaning, struggling to contain its thrashing bounty. The branching arms were clutching at its sides, holding shut the doors to its chest. Red Cap's voice boomed and echoed in the hollow trunk. The pitted black bark bubbled and swelled, a pair of hands trapped beneath the surface pushing out against its hull. And then a wooden mask of Red Cap's face jutted between the Night Hatchet's shoulder blades, eyes shut, mouth open and screaming. Thin slabs of bark peeled away from the cheeks, but the spongy wooden flesh held firm. The Night Hatchet would not relinquish its prisoner, no matter how hard he struggled. Red Cap's anguished face submerged again, disappearing as the bark closed over it.

The trunk shuddered quiet for a moment. But in one final burst of rage Red Cap slammed his body against the walls of the Night Hatchet's trunk. Michael saw the raised outline of his form, his shoulder straining hard against the Night Hatchet's rotting hull. The Night Hatchet gave a long howl and the hands clapped at its sides wildly. A wave of blue-green lichen sprouted along the raised edges of Red Cap's emerging form. It covered the straining form like a brittle cloth, thin scales of dried leaves spreading out over the peeling bark to form a net. A wail of defeat sounded through the hollow throat and the knothole piped a shrill, hard tune. All across the blue-green lichen there erupted the brightly jeweled blooms of a bleeding red fruit. The wail faded, but the red-blooming lichen continued to sprout and bleed over the rotted trunk of the Night Hatchet. And then it was quiet.

Michael stood up and touched the bark-covered death mask of Red Cap's face. The closed eyelids were scaled with the blue-green lichen and dotted with the tiny red fruit. The fruit gathered along the lines of his frowning mouth and clustered in the shallow holes of his nostrils.

"It isss done," the Night Hatchet said. "No mooore. He isss mine now." The Night Hatchet tugged its roots free from the rocky soil and then it made its slow and cumbersome way down the mountainside.

Behind him, the Sidhe broke into a loud and angry argument.

"I say it's wrong. Red Cap had a right to claim his prize!" shouted the horse-faced king.

"He cheated," Michael said sharply, turning to face them. "He had a right to nothing."

"The boy is right," Morrigu declared. "We all saw it happen. So Michael was fair and smart in his cunning. Besides, it's best this were done and done forever."

"Let him go," Angus Og spoke up, and though the dark kings continued to grumble, they made no further protest. Angus Og looked up into the brightening sky and nodded. "It is time we were away."

Almost as quickly as they had come, the Sidhe lifted into the thin mountain air and dispersed in the showering light of the morning sun. The fog-heavy cloak of Trom Ceo Draochta formed a dark cloud, and into it the kings of the dead returned, leaving behind the wind-polished rocks glistening with frost. Farther down on the mountain slopes, white fleecy clouds had marched in, covering the sight of the green pine trees below. It seemed to Michael that he floated among the clouds on this small gray island alone with Annie Mae and Eileen.

Michael held his hands out for his mother's foot as she mounted again on her gray mare.

"I too must go, my son. And this time I'll not return to you, until you are at your death," she said. She leaned down to touch him on the hair, his cheek, and his shoulder. "All the words I could not say . . . When I fled with your father, Red Cap threw a curse after us. We might love each other, and our child, but we would never be able to speak of it aloud. It pained me to see you look so unhappy as a child."

"I'm all right now," Michael said. "I know who I am."

"And well you do," she answered with a laugh, and her green eyes gleamed bright as emeralds. "But go to your father and soon, for I may not. Tell him that you are free. That he is free. And ask him to forgive me."

"I will," Michael answered. "I promise."

Eileen turned to Annie Mae. "You've a good and stout heart," she said. "You'll keep him well. Take this as a wedding present from me." She gave Annie Mae a purse.

"What's in it?"

"Gold. Real gold." Eileen chuckled. "Not fairies' gold that will turn to mud. There's a valley down below, on the ocean's side, where the grass is sweet and green all year. The stallion will take you. Buy the land there and you'll never want for anything."

"Thank you, ma'am," Annie Mae said in a hushed voice.

Eileen looked up to where the last star was fading into brightening sky. She smiled eagerly and inhaled the cold air. Michael felt the pull at his breast, saw again drifting over the far horizon the misted blue line of her home. The gray mare leapt into the air and galloped upward, carried over the sky by an arching road of mist. Michael watched his mother go, not with sorrow this time but with a quiet joy. Released at last, she was going home to live again among the Sidhe.

Michael put his arms around Annie Mae and kissed her hard on the lips.

"Gawd, but you taste powerful awful. Like stewed toadstools." She laughed when he finally released her.

"Sorry," Michael apologized, wiping from his face with the corner of his coat the remaining slime from the Night Hatchet's flesh.

"I don't much care, I'm just so darned glad to see you again," Annie Mae said, putting her arms around his neck. "Let's go down to that there green valley. We done deserve it."

"Annie Mae," Michael said softly, holding her around the waist. "Can you go ahead without me? I have to go home first. To Gramercy Park in New York. I have to see my father once more. I'll be back as soon as I can."

Her smile crumpled, and her blue eyes darkened. "Aw hell. Always leaving."

"The last time, I promise," Michael said. "It's something I have to do. Take Mo Neart, and I swear I'll be back as quick as I can."

"But how will you git to New York?"

"As the crow flies," he answered simply.

She tilted her head to one side, the blond hair streaking across her face. Then she smiled, understanding lighting in her eyes.

"As the crow flies, huh? Well, I guess it's what I got to expect, lovin' a conjuring man. Though it is a mite strange, even for me to figure."

"I'll be all right," Michael reassured her. "And I'll be back next year before the summer is over."

"Promise."

"I promise."

Michael helped her up onto Mo Neart's back. He clasped his hands over hers as she took uneasy handfuls of the stallion's mane. "Mo Neart will get you there, quick and easily. Don't be afraid."

"I ain't skeerd," she protested. "It's just a long way up here is all. I hate the way my feet dangle." She leaned down and kissed his upturned face once more. "Well, no point hanging round here." She gave the stallion a kick, and Michael watched them leave, the stallion lightly picking his way among the rounded backs of the boulders and Annie Mae twisting around to wave goodbye.

"Where'd you say home was again?" she asked.

"Gramercy Park. New York."

"I'll write you when I find that land!" she shouted back.

When they were out of sight at last, Michael turned his face into the wind and closed his eyes. Morrigu had told him he had only to will it and the change would come over him. He thought of himself as a crow; the black wings sprouting from his shoulder blades, the sharp beak in the front of his face. He remembered the feel of the wind driving beneath his chest, snapping the pinion feathers and lifting him higher in the air. He thought not of the fear but of the exalted freedom of flight.

Michael stretched out his arms, feeling buffeted by the driving winds. He shivered as his clothing slipped away from his body. He opened his mouth to cry out as he felt the sheath of feathers ease over his naked skin. The sound of his cry was a harsh-throated caw, and when he snapped his eyes open he saw the land falling away below him and disappearing beneath a veil of clouds.

Thirteen

T here were very few who came to attend James McBride's wake on the first two days and none at all willing to stand the heat of the third and final day. Michael didn't blame them. In July the house at Gramercy Park was hot and stuffy, and even though Mary had kept the shades drawn and the windows open, there was no disguising the odor of death. The smell didn't bother him. It had been familiar enough to him when he traveled as a crow. Michael sat alone in the parlor beside his father's casket and thought of the events that had changed them all since the last time he'd sat a wake in this room.

He had flown as a crow throughout the winter and arrived home to New York in the late March. The snow was melting into cold slushing rivers that flooded the city's gutters and pooled in the old fountain of the park. Michael had spent a week flying through the city searching for the tattered remains of clothing cast into garbage heaps, or frozen and forgotten on narrow back porches. It had been difficult, dragging the sodden garments into a hiding place in the alley. But when he had at last found a pair of trousers, a coat missing its sleeve, and the torn remnants of a shirt, he deemed himself ready. Late one night, in the shadows of a dark alley, Michael had transformed himself from a crow into a naked man again. He'd shivered, quickly donning the clothes that his crow's eyes could only guess might fit him as a man. The trousers were much too short, exposing most of his calves and bare feet. The shirt was huge, his skinny neck sticking out of a wide collar that was missing its buttons. The coat didn't close, and the one sleeve pinched around his shoulder.

In the still room, Michael laid a hand on the edge of the casket and laughed out loud. He must have a looked a fright, remembering the horrified expression on Mary's face when she opened the door to him. Standing there barefoot in the melting snow, his tangled black hair down to his shoulders, and the tatters of ill-fitting clothing flapping. She had nearly slammed the door on him until he called her by name.

"Jesus, Mary, and Joseph!" she had cried out, falling on her knees and tears spurting from her eyes.

"It's me, Mary, Michael," he had said, trying to talk quickly while she continued to cry and pray at the same time. "I'm sorry—I look awful, I know."

And then she had grabbed him firmly by the arm, yanked him into the house and shut the door loudly behind him.

Once the fear and relief had been wept out of her, she'd yelled at him, excoriating him with her lashing tongue even as she drew the water for a bath and dragged the stinking rags from his body.

"Stop," he had commanded as she went for his trousers. She'd hesitated. "I said, stop. It's enough. I'm a man now, Mary. I can handle my own washing up."

She had tucked her arms beneath her bosom and scowled at him. "If it's a man you are, Michael McBride, then you wouldn't have run and left that man up there on his own, worried half sick to death about where you were and were you dead or were you living."

"I know I left," Michael had said wearily. "I'd no choice back then. But I've returned. Now go and let me make myself presentable."

It had pained Michael to see his father that first time. James McBride had withered in his absence. The wide shoulders had sagged, and the barrel chest had grown feeble. A rim of gray had clouded the edges of the dark eyes and the hair had grown white at the temples. He had been sitting before the chessboard, the pieces ready for battle but seemingly frozen and unable to move in that quiet room.

Michael had sat down opposite his father as he had always done. But the man wouldn't look up from the gaming board, nor did his hands lift from his blanketed lap to take the chess pieces.

"So you beat the bastard, did you?" James McBride had asked in a gruff voice.

"I didn't lose," Michael had replied softly.

And then James McBride had looked up, a smile taking the corners of his dry mouth. The eyes had stared at Michael hungrily, as if seeing him for the first time.

"She give you that eye when she left us," James had said. "That's how I knew she still loved me and you." The older man had leaned back in his chair and coughed heavily. When the spasm stopped, he took a sip from a whiskey glass. "Had she let you stay blind to her world in both eyes, you'd have gone on in life never knowing about her and me. And most likely you'd have hated me for all my coldness to you. And had she given you both eyes of fairy, you'd have forgotten me entirely and gone away into her realm. But she gave you the sight to see us both, so I knew that time had not changed her heart toward me."

"She asked that you forgive her," Michael had said.

James McBride had shook his head. "No need. I never blamed her once. The pair of you were my heart's joy, though there was little enough way to show it." He had begun coughing again, the spasms deep and wracking in his chest. "I'm tired, Son. Help me to lay down."

Michael had helped his father into the bed and there James McBride had remained throughout the spring and into the summer, never once leaving it again until he died.

The problems of the house had fallen into Michael's hands. There was no money left, for they had built their fortunes on reserves of fairy gold, and with Eileen's departure it had vanished from the banks. Throughout the spring Michael sold off the furnishings, the paintings, the silver, and the crystal until the house was stripped bare of almost everything that had once given it grandeur. He was able to put away enough for a decent funeral and to buy a plot next to his mother's grave at Greenwood. Bridget had left for a sister in Philadelphia and Mary had agreed to stay until after James McBride's funeral. Then she was leaving for a brother and his wife living in Boston.

The clocks had been stopped for the wake, but still it seemed to Michael that time ticked away noisily in the room. He realized it was the rapping of his own heart, anxious to be done with the dreary task of burying his father. He missed him as much as he missed his mother. And though there had not been much joy in any of their lives, they had found it at the end and it had been all the sweeter for fear of never having it at all.

"It's time. They've come for the body," Mary said softly, the black rosary beads clicking through her fingers.

"Good." Michael sighed and stood up as strangers entered the room. They sealed the coffin and, with Michael at the head, carried the body of James McBride out of the house and into the hearse waiting in the street below.

Michael blinked at the bright sunlight, his face lifted to the call of starlings in the park. The sun was warm, and in spite of his grief, he felt a peace settle over him. From the branches of an elm tree, small figures of bundled twigs bowed low to him, their hats pulled off to show their respect. And as the hearse made its way through the city, Michael saw more of them, peeping out from the shadowed doorways, looking down from the ragged nests of pigeons, standing unseen on street corners and riding on the manes of city horses. The denizens of the fairy world paying a final respect to the passing corpse of James McBride.

"Michael, I'm away now," Mary said, tying the black ribbons of her hat under her chin.

"Take care," Michael said, giving her a brief hug.

"Will you be all right then?" she asked, her face puckered with worry.

"Yes. They come to get the keys of the house this morning. They'll pay me, and then I'm away too."

"Oh, I almost forgot," Mary said, her nose growing red as she held back tears. She put her hand into her skirt pocket and pulled out a tattered white envelope. "This came for you late yesterday while you were out."

Michael took the envelope and his heart leapt at the sight of the scrawled return address. California. Annie Mae.

"Good news, I hope?" Mary asked.

"I'm thinking it is," he answered, eager to rip open the letter but wanting to wait until he was alone. He walked Mary to the transom cab and kissed her once more on the cheek.

"I'll be fine. And I'll write."

"Good boy," she said, sniffing back tears as she got into the cab. "Goodbye. God bless."

He caught the last train out of Union Depot Station. He knew the route by heart: first north to Niagara and then straight across the face of the continental United States. He had enough money to buy a decent ticket, a suitcase, and some extra clothing. He could have traveled more easily had he traveled as a crow. But he wished to bring with him the only two things of value remaining in the house at Gramercy Park; James McBride's chess set and his mother's jar of fairy ointment. And one other thing. Michael patted the letter in his pocket, the words memorized. But he couldn't resist taking it out and, holding it up to the oil lamp, read it again.

She couldn't spell. Or maybe she spelled the way she spoke. In either case it had taken Michael a few hours to decipher all the news she had sent to him. But it was one paragraph that had stopped him, made him rush to read it over and over again until he was certain of its meaning.

"I done laid in this spring and momma and boy are doin well. Looks ta be greened eyed and tow haided. The grass is coming on and the stallion done got hisself a prty mare to."

Annie Mae had a son, green-eyed and towheaded. His son and hers. Michael leaned forward in his seat, willing the train to go faster as it pulled away from the station, the racket pounding in his pulse. "Come on," he whispered fiercely to the clacking wheels. "Faster!" Michael smiled broadly as the land suddenly surged past his window. Overhead, the trailing moonlight, thin and white as a woman's handkerchief, waved farewell to the speeding train.